Women in Their Beds

Also by Gina Berriault

THE DESCENT

THE MISTRESS

CONFERENCE OF VICTIMS

THE SON

THE INFINITE PASSION OF EXPECTATION

THE LIGHTS OF EARTH

Women in Their Beds

New *and* Selected Stories

Gina Berriault

COUNTERPOINT
WASHINGTON, D.C.

The author gratefully acknowledges financial assistance from the Ingram
Merrill Foundation, the John Simon Guggenheim Foundation, and the
National Endowment for the Arts.

Many of the stories in this selection were published originally by *American
Short Fiction, Contact, Esquire, Genesis West, Harper's Bazaar, The Kenyon
Review, Mademoiselle, Paris Review, Ploughshares, Redbook, San Francisco
Review, The Saturday Evening Post, The Sound of Writing, The Threepenny
Review, ZYZZYVA*, E. P. Dutton, and Charles Scribner's Sons. The
author gratefully acknowledges their permission to reprint.

Library of Congress Cataloging-in-Publication Data

Berriault, Gina.
    Women in their beds: new and selected stories / Gina Berriault.
    1. Manners and customs—Fiction.   I. Title.
PS3552.E738W66   1996
813'.54—dc20   95-51079
ISBN 1-887178-10-4 (ALK. PAPER)

FIRST PRINTING

Book design by David Bullen
Composition by Wilsted & Taylor

Printed in the United States of America on acid-free paper that meets the
American National Standards Institute z39-48 Standard.

COUNTERPOINT
P.O. Box 65793
Washington, D.C. 20035-5793

Distributed by Publishers Group West

Again for Julie Elena

Contents

3   Women in Their Beds

17   Who Is It Can Tell Me Who I Am?

34   A Dream of Fair Women

42   Soul and Money

58   The Island of Ven

67   Lives of the Saints

78   Stolen Pleasures

94   The Overcoat

102   Zenobia

109   The Woman in the Rose-Colored Dress

113   The Infinite Passion of Expectation

121   Nights in the Gardens of Spain

131 Bastille Day

141 God and the Article Writer

147 Wilderness Fire

153 The Bystander

161 Death of a Lesser Man

169 The Search for J. Kruper

185 The Birthday Party

194 The Cove

201 Sublime Child

212 Around the Dear Ruin

222 The Diary of K. W.

238 The Stone Boy

250 Anna Lisa's Nose

264 Works of the Imagination

271 The Mistress

278 Lonesome Road

283 Myra

291 The Houses of the City

298 Nocturne

306 Like a Motherless Child

316 The Science of Life

320 Felis Catus

337 The Light at Birth

Women in Their Beds

Women in
Their Beds

*D*r. Zhivago . . .

Over the hospital's paging system the three pranksters sent their solemnly urgent voices along the corridors and into the wards, imbuing each name with a reverential depth.

Dr. Jekyll . . .

They were actors and playwrights, these three, Angela and Dan and Lew, social workers only temporary, offering their wit as a lightening agent to the dread air in this formidable row of faded-brick buildings, grime the mortar. Out of place, this row—it belonged in another part of the country, more north, more east, under slanting rain in Seattle or slashed by cold winds in Chicago or on that penal island off New York, someplace where the weathers punish the inmates even more.

Yet here it was, in San Francisco's warmest neighborhood and only a short walk from the broad grassy slopes and flourishing trees of Dolores Park where, on Sundays in summer, their troupe, their quick-change dozen actors, set up their shaky stage and satirized the times with their outrageous comedies, their own Commedia dell'Arte, come alive again now in the Sixties. Their high-flung voices, along with the noises they made that thumped and banged on the neighborhood doors, might even have reached the hospital's murky windows, sounding within like the mutterings inside the head of the patient in the next bed.

Dan held a master's in political science and Lew a bachelor of arts in drama, but Angela, a small-time, odd-job actress, bold on stage but not as herself, had no degree whatsoever.

"Say you do," Dan insisted. "Give yourself an M.S. in sociology and a B.A. in psychology. Imagine you're speaking the truth. You do it all the time on stage."

"I don't know how long I'll last," she said.

"Nobody knows that," said Lew. "They're all wondering the same thing in there."

"I mean I may not last more than a couple of days."

Angela Anson, her name in a plastic badge on her blouse, confidante without credentials, passed up and down the women's ward, telling those on her list where they'd be going, what haven with its ominously pretty name or the bed that was waiting at home, whether longed for or not.

Unlike the men's ward where, she was told, men cursed and struck the air and straggled out into the halls on their thwarted way home, this women's ward was a quiet one. Three long rows of beds, one row along each long wall and one row along the back and, on overcrowded days, another row down the center. Narrow beds with rails that went up and down, white sheets sliding on rods for each woman's very own curtains when the doctors came by. Earthquake-prone, each morning the women's ward appeared to have undergone a quake in the night. The row of beds down the center gone, or the back row gone, and the shocked atmosphere like that after a quake. *What's happening here?* The question on each face upon a pillow. A quake of the mind, a quake of the heart.

Dr. Curie . . . Dan's good morning to Angela.

"Bad dreams at night," she'd told him. "My mother berating me for what? It must be because I never knew enough about her. She may have wanted to unfold herself for me and never could. Their lives must be unfolding before their eyes, in there, and they're unfolding mine. They're unfolding me. Do you know what I mean?"

Dan said he sort of knew. So she was . . . *Dr. Curie* . . . discoverer of so much that was undetectable and that might not even exist.

Her step, always a light step, was even lighter here, a step for museums and churches, sanctified places that always made her feel unworthy. *The county hospital is not a holy place, Dan said, and you were not hired for the role of St. Teresa of Avila. She kissed the lepers' lesions and that's not in your line of duty.* Her step was light for another reason. She wished to disappear from this unfolding scene as the women did, overnight, two, three, or an entire row at a time, gone to places called home or gone for reasons unknown to her, and as the interns also disappeared and were replaced by lookalikes.

The illustrious doctors, long dead or never alive, whom Dan and Lew were calling for, seemed more solidly in person than these young interns who stepped from bed to narrow bed, graceless, at a loss, not yet adept in the presence of women in their beds, maybe any woman in any bed, anywhere. Dan called these interns by their first names, drank coffee with them, gave them his dissident view of Vietnam, and, more often than not, he was the one calling for the imaginary doctors, convinced they'd be around long after the real ones, the sleep-deprived, baffled fledglings, were gone a thousand times over.

An Audience of One who never blinked. They had to imagine that God was watching, or that's what Angela had to imagine for them, these women in this pale ward, so they'd not be overlooked. So many persons in rows—it was a common enough sight across the world in Vietnam, on the television screens that seemed invented for just that repetition of wars and disasters that laid people out in rows. Over the other scenes there was always a terrible struggle in the air, but in this women's ward there was a yielding to whoever was watching over them and to the medication that must seem like a persuasive stranger entering their most intimate being for their own good. What an unbearably rude intrusion, then—Angela appearing at bedside to tell them where they'd be going next.

"Where?"

This one, this woman, fifty, pink-champagne hair, must have run away from home at nine and kept on running away. The nights of her life on a barstool till 2:00 A.M. and the last hours of the morning with a new-found friend, down in the dubious comfort of his bed. A chic hat and a string of pearls and a job, all that to begin, and then the nylons bagging at the knees and ankles and the high heels bending inward.

"Where?"

"Laguna Honda." And Angela saw this woman's face draw up from her frightened heart a small girl's look of daring to flee.

Laguna Honda. Like a monastery, like a huge echoing nunnery on a hill, it belonged in Spain in the Middle Ages. With a tower, and within the tower a dimlit archway, the only light above the thick black trees whenever Angela drove past at night. She drove fast around the curve to escape her imagining of pale faces floating on deep black waters.

"You can't do that. My daughter won't let you."

Every day this mother promised the appearance of the daughter, but the daughter wasn't showing up yet. Wasn't it glib to say that the daughter was abandoning the mother because the mother had abandoned the child? A child belongs to the world—that was Angela's explanation. But if this woman was *her* mother she'd come and stand at this bedside just as she was doing now and just as she'd appeared by her mother's bed in another ward in another city. *Your heart sinks down with your mother's, Angela said to the daughter who wasn't there. Your heart sinks down and leaves your breast and may never come back. But when you're out in the street again it comes racing back, bursting with grief.*

Angela said, "My supervisor is still hoping a bed will turn up somewhere else." Oh, God, did she say *turn up*? There was no way of saying it to ease the fear of the next bed. "More where you'd like."

"No bed in this goddamn world is where I'd like."

Later that day Angela caught sight of her in a curtained-off section, her face shocked by what her limbs were doing without her consent, trying to run away with her as she'd run away before, over and over. *Withdrawal from alcohol, Lew explained. It never leaves the body without a terrible lovers' quarrel.*

Dr. Faustus . . . Dr. Faustus . . .

At her back now, the woman to whom she listened evasively sideways, head bowed, unable to come face to face.

"I beg you."

Nod, Angela, nod, and listen with one ear.

"I beg you, please ask the doctor to let me go home."

That voice, a trembling thread trying to get itself through the eye of a needle. Angela had heard it before, years ago.

"I'll ask again."

That arrogant doctor, that one with the impatiently jiggling knee, the disposing gaze—he was the one Angela had asked. Why had she picked him? To humanize him, when she ought to turn her full gaze upon this pleading woman and humanize herself.

She did. She looked into the woman's eyes and came face to face with her own Aunt Ida. That's who this woman was, after twenty years, up from that bed in the Home for those who were never to leave. Way back on the stage of her childhood, there was Aunt Ida in bed, white hair boy's cut, the thinnest wrists, the scarcest voice, the largest, darkest eyes, and there was Angela's mother in the visitor's chair, smartly clad even though the cloche hat and Cuban heels were already ten years worn, and there was Angela, five years old, plaid skirt, black patent-leather pumps, born entertainer, reciting the tale of that terrible battle between Ivan Skvinsky Skzar and Abdul Abulbul Amir, the threats, the oaths, the blows. There was little Angela at bedside, unable to believe what her mother had told her, that Ida had been the most beautiful of the five sisters, and here was Angela now, unable to believe that this woman at her elbow had ever been other than who she was now, had ever been young, a girl, twelve, sixteen, eighteen, in that flowering time.

From her very first hours in the ward she had tried to picture them when they were young, wanting to come to their rescue by reviving them as girls again. *Oh, such lovely girls!* Wanting to do for them what she hadn't done for her Aunt Ida.

"I try to imagine them when they were girls, but I can't," she told the head nurse, Nancy, and the nurse, already verging into that same anonymity of aging, turned her head for Angela to see her deliberately uncomprehending face. "Why would you ever think to do that anyway?"

Dr. Mabuse . . . Dan's voice.

Dr. Mabuse, that decadent doctor, dispenser of opium, was calling her to join him for a coffee break in the cafeteria.

"Were you ever in Père Lachaise cemetery?" she asked him.

"You mean have I risen?"

Dan, so healthy, his cheeks childishly rosy, his hair darkly shiny, the kindest heart, the hardest head, wrote a crackling political column for an underground weekly.

"My year in Paris, my Marceau mime time, I wandered around in there," she said.

"Gravely there?"

"Colette's monument resembles a bed."

"Nights, does she romp around on it?"

"Afternoons, too," she said. "Maybe beds are where women belong. Half the women in the world are right now in bed, theirs or somebody else's, whether it's night or day, whether they want to be or not. That's where the blame lies for some infamous messes. Take that bed of Hamlet's mother, for example, or Desdemona's, because that's where Iago saw her in his fired-up imagination, a high-born slut, sleeping with a blackamoor. I could go on and on. You persuaded me to ask for a job in this place and now you can listen to the consequences. Now I see women as inseparable from their beds."

"Bedded down in eternity?"

"Could you see that goes on my tombstone? On second thought, I don't want a stone over me. I never want to be confined. So just wrap me in my cloth coat, forget the ermine, and leave me out on some high mountain."

Dr. Freud . . . please . . .

Overnight, a girl lying in the narrow bed made narrower just by youth's full size and restlessness. Dark, tumbled curls, a broad face, paled and alarmed by the pumping out of that handful of pills from where they'd settled in for a long night. Off to the psych ward at the end of the day, she was no concern of Angela's.

"Please, Miss," as Angela walked by. "I'm not allowed to go to the lavatory and the nurse won't come."

Angela handed up the bedpan, defying whatever rule there might be that forbade a social worker this act of mercy. Struggling out from under the covers, the girl sat awkwardly down on the pan, atop the bed, large, long legs bared and bent.

"Lie down, lie down," Angela urged. "You do it lying down. Under the covers." And the girl went awkwardly under, probably awkward at all of life's necessary acts, suicide among them.

Angela put the bedpan under the bed and stayed on, wanting to ask outright: *Why did you want to die?* Knowing there was no answer that could be brought to the surface by a stranger at bedside or even by a social worker with honest credentials who'd ask the same question in cleverly curative ways. Angela Anson had had no simple answer, either, and wasn't asked, because nobody knew about her attempt. A skinny sixteen, awkward at everything and even at how to hope, she was saved by that very awkwardness, and she wanted to say to this girl: *After that bungled act I left my awkwardness behind, and now I remember it sort of fondly, like I would a crazy childhood girlfriend.*

Dr. Freud . . . Lew telling Angela that the hour was near for a visit to the psychiatric ward. She'd asked him about it. Could she peek in for a minute to see where that girl was going?

Somewhere in another of the grim buildings she slipped into the entry of that ward. The very small entry, the only place allowed her, had space enough for the Judge, a large, high-chested fellow in a finely tailored suit, the three men in gray-drab, depleted by fear of their own minds' doings and trying not to slump, and barely enough for herself.

The Judge's voice was cleaving its way through the soiled air, asking legalese questions and informing each of his destination, which asylum, what refuge. Like a scene in any number of plays, where an assassin or a priest comes to tell the prisoner what his future looks like, this was a scene in a debtors' prison for those who couldn't pay back all that civilizing invested in them. She'd been in even closer proximity to this Judge. A wedding reception at the Stanford Court Hotel atop Nob Hill, where she'd carried trays loaded with prawns and oysters up to that buttoned-up belly.

Over in a few minutes, this orderly dispersal of the deranged. The Judge left and she followed at a discreet distance, noting his brisk sort of shuffle, a slight uncertainty of step that came from sitting in judgment for so many years. If she were ever to play a high-court judge on the stage in the park, she'd stuff a bed pillow vertically down her front and take those small steps, the uncertainty in the head repressed all the way down to the feet.

Dr. Caligari . . .

Only an illusion, that this woman was a dwarf. Recovered now, she was going home this hour, and all Angela had to do was walk along beside her in that enforced wheelchair ride to the exit and beside the slouchy orderly doing the pushing. Angela thought *dwarf* because of her theatrical tendency to recognize types from bygone centuries, and dwarfs seemed of a time of mass deprivation. This woman in the wheelchair, her gray hair stubble-cut, was deprived. A cleaning woman, she'd fainted on the job—pneumonia—and they'd had to bring her son along since there was no one else to take care of him while his mother was away. So many hiding places in the city, you never could know what went on in them until someone was brought out and then maybe went back in again.

Hop-skipping down the corridor toward them, impeding their progress, a young doctor, an intense one, hair askew.

"Let me see your hands."

Angela's hands began to rise, palms forward. Was there some new scan that doctors had, a scientific palmistry for detecting liars and impostors and actors?

The young hyperactive doctor was bending toward the woman in the wheelchair, whose hands lay humbly in her lap, blunt hands, curved to the shape of mop handles, vacuum cleaner handles. She uncurled them under his scrutiny.

"Can you tell me," he asked, "why your son has six fingers?"

The woman's eyes were shifting along at floor level.

"My mother cursed us."

"Who?" Wobbling off his track.

"They cursed us."

Dazedly stepping aside, the young doctor allowed them to proceed down the corridor, the orderly pushing, Angela guiding.

At the side portal they waited for the son to be brought from the adjacent building and for another social worker who was to convey mother and son back to their rooms. Out from the other building and down the path, the son was being swiftly borne toward his mother, the orderly mockingly happy to be pushing the wheelchair of this mute density of a man with two fingers too many. A rough spot on the pavement and off he flies, this son, onto the lawn where he lies docile, waiting to be lifted.

Dr. Caligari . . . please . . .

Lew, responding to her call, showed up in the women's ward and escorted her out into the air, around a corner where she'd never been. Lew, whose long face knew everything before it was told him, listened to her anyway.

"Doctors don't know what they're getting into when they get to be doctors," she told him. "How could *she* know why her son's got that extra little finger alongside his proper one? One finger too many, or two too many, it's just a clue to what goes on in the dark where your life gets twisted into the weirdest shape before you're even born. Suppose he came into the women's ward and asked them why they're in there. They'd say, like, Oh, sure, Doctor, my old man beat me up, or my lung collapsed, or I was hit by a trolley. They'd see he was simpleminded and they'd answer him like that, because how can you say to a doctor, My karma hurts me?"

"Lower your voice."

"I don't care who hears."

"Never take a deep breath in there," he cautioned. "Take it every morning before you go in. You've lasted how many days? Six already? But be warned."

Lower your voice, take no deep breaths, step softly, and you'll be fine. When she caught the old Gypsy woman watching her, Angela flashed an impersonal smile as proof that she knew what she was doing in that ward. The Gypsy woman was sitting up in bed after three days under covers and her own matriarchal bed was awaiting her return. A Gypsy queen, ninety-six years old. Over her bony face a blending of gold leaf and copper, her sea-green eyes sunken under mole-brown lids. Around her head a kerchief, blue and red. No resemblance to the Gypsies who went up and down the train in Spain, the tiny mother and her daughter who might have been sixteen or six, begging their way. This one must have eaten very well, this one must have wrung the necks of hundreds of fat chickens and pulled out big handfuls of feathers. Fear wasn't her bedmate here, Faith was and probably had always been, keeping her heart beating for so long.

Shrewdly, she was gazing at Angela as at someone who could be ensnared by flattery. After a while she beckoned.

"Give me your hand."

On your way back into life, do you fit yourself into who you were always expected to be, for a safe return? The very thin, limp hand, covered with brown patches like islands on an old sepia chart, turned over Angela's hand, and Angela's palm lay open to the future like a part of herself that hadn't been attended to as it ought to have been, considering its potential.

"A long life."

That index finger, its knuckle like an ancient tarnished coin, traced a line so slowly it seemed a very long way, pausing where that high road was joined or crossed by low roads, by roads not taken, and by roads down which hitchhikers came to thumb a ride. Not until she'd stepped into this ward had she begun to trouble herself over the span of her life, and now she was being told what she didn't want to know after all.

"You are a wayward girl?"

Wayward? That word wasn't around anymore. It belonged to old-time bawdy music hall skits. If she was wayward, it must be evident enough without her palm revealing it. Unlike the nurses, so trim, so starched and white, combed and capped, Angela was artfully indifferent, her dark hair untamable, her fingernails clean but their polish chipped, her blouse clean and ironed but with one button sewn back on with an unmatching thread, black kohl all around her eyes, a cheap ring from Chinatown on one finger and an even cheaper ring from a street fair on a little finger. Anyone could spot her for a working hippie, a counterculture actress, a wayward girl.

"I'm an actress," smiling like one.

Mockery now in the glintless eyes. Was mockery, too, a life-renewing pleasure? "Actresses like jewels? Yes? Yes, I know, yes. Tomorrow my children will bring my jewels for you." The mockery grasping back that gift of a long life, the giving and the taking away all in one breath.

Under the covers again the next morning, the Gypsy woman was identified only by the colored kerchief. Out of the corner of her eye Angela saw this flattening down and felt some shameful relief from that gaze. Kept most of the day at her desk in the row of social workers' cubicles, she did not come up to the ward until late afternoon.

Oh, God, what a handsome lot they were, that woman's children. Or grandchildren. Seven of them, gathered at the bed. Visitors—friends, pastors, relatives, nuns—came around in the evening hours, but here was this Gypsy family in the afternoon. Unreal, their garments biblically splendid as that coat of many colors, and all with golden skin. They were her children of whatever generation, and all to live as long as the mother.

The bed was empty.

"Candles. Can you bring candles?" a daughter asked, and a son said, "Please. Candles," a singer's sorrowing voice.

Candles? She went in search. None in the nurses' station. No candles in the desk of the social worker on vacation, now known as Angela's desk. Drawers she hadn't opened before held only a coffee mug, a quicky-glance mirror, breath sweeteners, postcards, and in the larger, bottom drawer, a pair of high-heeled pumps to wear on dinner dates. Only two of the bona fide social workers were still at their desks, and they shook their heads. No candles, and they asked no reason for candles. Maybe the lights had gone out in the lavatory.

A cubbyhole grocery store was near, a few minutes' walk away. No candles there. Sold out. Candles were a necessity in every friend's apartment. Round as oranges, long as tapers, and ordinary ones, the soft light of the flame intensifying the marijuana mood.

When she returned, empty-handed, the archangelic children were gone.

Night in her own bed, the bed she was sure to remember as the one in this period of her life, lying beside her lover whose bed it was, too, she wondered if those women ever wondered about her, about where her bed was and whether she shared it and with whom. If wonder and curiosity were signs of life, she'd give them a boost back into life by telling them some things about herself while waiting for sleep.

Listen, my dear alones, over there across the city. Do you remember how each time you lay yourself down in a bed you wondered, if even for a moment, what you were doing there? And what about the beds you thought you'd chosen yourself? Do they now seem chosen for you? Destiny's hand patting them down. *Lie here, lie here.* God must surely have created beds for sharing, for most of mine were shared and see the ways you've shared yours, given your children to hold dearly close and given your mates and your lovers. And maybe that's why a bed of solitude is so sweet, so sweet, if it's only for a while and not forever. And even if it's forever, I don't know that yet. Tonight I'm lying beside a man, a friend, who is as much in need as myself of a friend to lie down with, make love with, share the rent with, share soup with, break bread with, and lie down with again. Over against the wall, his side, is a large orange acrylic nude, because he's an art student and large nudes promise largeness of future and fortune, as always. This bed, if you want to know, is sprinkled with those tiny pellets of lint that never get to form in your beds, and it's in a very small concrete apartment, a basement apartment that's next to the boiler room, if a boiler is that monster hot water tank that supplies steamy hot water to the tenants on the six floors above, and through the night that tank heats up all of a sudden, over and over, with a rush and a roar, scaring me out from under my camouflage of sleep and unheard by my bedmate. I remember that first bed ever where I lay beside a lover. It was a bed I didn't know was there, it was just a wall in a darkened apartment, and out it came and down, like a meaning unfolding in that time when so many meanings were unfolding and I was just fourteen. Oh, then there was the bed in that home for unwed mothers, the Crittenden it was called, a name like a chastising ruler, but really a kind place, a big brick building as ancient as Laguna Honda and the place where you are tonight. A man comes to sit by his mother's bed every afternoon. Have you noticed him? Fifty, but resembles a fawn, wears a suit, a tie, places his hat on his knees. A gentle man, a fine son, and the head nurse Nancy is in love with him. I won't be mortally wounded when the son I gave life to sits someday by the bed of a mother who's not me. Old mothers in their beds all look the same. Some night, some day, there'll be Angela Anson herself in your row, and what will I say to soften the heart of the social worker who I'll dislike at first sight? Why, I'll say I was an actress with a flair for comedy, even called delightful in the theater section of the Sunday papers, even called delectable, and I'll know as I tell her, if I tell her, that she won't believe a word of it. I'll say I'd thought an actress had a special kind of destiny, a beneficent role to play, bringing to life a lot of other women. Maybe, to amuse her, I'll tell her about the pranks we played, Dan and Lew and myself, calling for those doctors who were so real for us and unreal for everybody else. And if she's not amused, I'll tell her, whether it's true or not, that Dan became a high-class political columnist, syndicated, and Lew a drama professor at a prestigious university, but I won't tell her that all my stages were small ones, if that's true for me. I'll say all that, hoping in my heart, my frightened heart, that I've persuaded her not to drop me off into that black lagoon. Oh, my dears, have you ever heard these lines? *I in my bed of thistles, you in your bed of roses and feathers.* I thought it meant the other woman's bed, *her* bed of roses and feathers, where the lover I'd loved so much was lying, but now I know it means so much more and I'll tell you why. Just remember the beds where you wished you weren't and the beds where you wished you were, and then name any spot on this earth that's a bed for some woman this very hour. A bed of stones and a bed of earth trampled by soldiers and a bed of ashes, and where you're lying now, where you never wanted to imagine yourselves. If I'd wished for a bed of roses and feathers, and *I did, I did,* now I don't want it so much anymore.

A candle. The candle she'd been looking for was on the table in plain sight, an average one, white, flickering away as candles do, showing her the plates and glasses and paint tubes around it, the clothes on the chair, his orange nude against the wall, Molière's plays on the bed, the covers over the sleeping man beside her and over herself, not alone and yet alone. If she were to take that candle up to the ward, a light for any woman leaving at any time, even when she herself wouldn't be there anymore, would that be going too far? An actress, carried away by her role?

Dr. Curie . . .

Once again, Dan was bidding her a good morning. She heard his voice along the ceiling of the ward as she went up one aisle and down another, carrying the white candle in its wooden holder. In the ward's daylight its tip of flame was probably not discernible by the women at a distance, but surely they knew the candle was lit and the women who were closest to it knew.

At her back now, Nurse Nancy. "What's this all about?"

"The Gypsy woman," said Angela. "Her children asked me to bring a candle."

"That was yesterday," said Nurse Nancy, the only nurse with gray hair and whose step was flat, wearier than the other nurses' steps. "They've got their own to-do, whatever they do. They've got their own candles." Searching Angela's eyes to see if this act confirmed a strangeness within.

"I thought the women might appreciate it," said Angela.

"The other ladies don't know she's gone. They've got their own problems."

And Nurse Nancy blew out the flame, with a breath that failed to be strong and unwavering but did the job anyway.

Lightly, then, a touch at Angela's elbow and a touch at her back, touches to assist her to stay on her feet and to point her in the right direction. Or were they touches of complicity?

Who Is It Can Tell Me Who I Am?

*A*lberto Perera, librarian, granted no credibility to police profiles of dangerous persons. Writers, down through the centuries, had that look of being up to no good and were often mistaken for assassins, smugglers, fugitives from justice—criminals of all sorts. But the young man invading his sanctum, hands hidden in the pockets of his badly soiled green parka, could possibly be another lunatic out to kill another librarian. Up in Sacramento, two librarians were shot dead while on duty, and, down in Los Angeles, the main library was sent up in flames by an arsonist. Perera loved life and wished to participate in it further.

"You got a minute?"

"I do not."

"Can I read you something?"

"Please don't." Recalling some emergency advice as to how to dissuade a man from a violent deed—*Engage him in conversation*—he said, "Go ahead," regretting his permission even as he gave it. Was he to hear, as the last words he'd ever hear, a denunciation of all librarians for their heinous liberalism, a damnation for all the lies, the deceptions, the swindles, the sins preserved within the thousands of books they so zealously guarded, even with their lives?

With bafflement in his grainy voice, the fellow read from a scrap of paper.

> *Greet the sun, spider. Show no rancor.*
> *Give God your thanks, O toad, that you exist.*
> *The crab has such thorns as the rose.*
> *In the mollusc are reminiscences of women.*
> *Know what you are, enigmas in forms.*
> *Leave the responsibility to the norms,*
> *Which they in turn leave to the Almighty's care.*
> *Chirp on, cricket, to the moonlight. Dance on, bear.*

The fellow granted his listener a moment to think about what he'd just heard. Then, "What do you make of it?"

"What do I make of it?"

"What I make of it," said the intruder, "is you're supposed to feel great if you're an animal. Like if you're talking about a spider or a toad. Am I supposed to do that?"

"Do what?"

"Like thank God because I'm me?"

"That's for you to decide. Take your time with it." Shuffling papers on his desk. "Take your time but not in here."

Watch your step with anybody playing dumb, Perera cautioned himself. They sneak up on you from behind. This fellow knew just what he was doing, pulling out a poem by Rubén Darío, reading it aloud to a librarian so proud of his Spanish ancestry he kept the name his dear mother had called him, Alberto, and there it was, his foreign name in a narrow frame on his desk for all who passed his open door to see. Maybe this fellow had been stabbed in prison by a Chicano with the name Perera, and now Perera, the librarian, a man of goodwill, a humanitarian, was singled out among his fellow librarians.

"What do you figure this guy's saying? Wake up every day feeling great you're you?"

"If that's what you figure he's saying, that's what he's saying. That's the best you can do with a poem."

Out in fistfuls from his parka pockets, more scraps of paper. So many, some fluttered to the floor. Cigarette packets inside out, gum wrappers, scavenged street papers of many colors that are slipped along underfoot by the winds of traffic, scraps become transcendentally unfamiliar by the use they'd been put to: Lines of poetry in a fixatedly careful, cramped handwriting.

"That spider, you take that spider." Entranced by a spider that only he could see, swinging between himself and Perera. "That spider is in its web where it belongs. Made it himself, swinging away. Sun comes out, strands all shiny, spider feels the warm sun on his back. Okay, glad he's a spider. I can see that. Same with the cricket. Makes chirpity-chirp to the moon. I can accept that. That toad, too. I can see he likes the mud, they're born in mud. It's the bear I can't figure out. Would you know if bears dance in their natural state?"

"Would I know if bears dance?"

"When they're on their own?" A cough, probably incited by some highly pleasurable secret excitement from tormenting a librarian. "What I know about bears," answering himself before his cough was over, "is bears do not dance. It is not in their genetic code. I'll tell you when they dance. They dance when they got a rope around their neck. That poet slipped up there. A bear with a rope around his neck, do you see him waking up happy, hallooing the sun? Same thing."

"Same thing as what?"

No answer, only another cough, probably called up to cover his amusement over an obtuse librarian with a silk tie around his stiff neck.

"You know anything about the guy who wrote it? The bear didn't write it, that I know."

"No, the bear did not write it. Darío wrote it. A modernist, brought Spanish poetry into the modern age. Born in Chile. No, Nicaragua. Myself, I like Lorca. Lorca, you know, was assassinated by Franco's Guardia Civil." Why that note? Because, if it happened to him, Alberto Perera, here and now, his death might possess a similar meaning. An enlightened heart snuffed out.

"When he says like, Spider, greet the sun, where do you figure he was lying?" Slyly, the fellow waited.

"Was he lying?" Always the assumption that poets lie. Why else do they deliberately twist things around?

"What I mean is," grudgingly patient, "where was he lying when the sun came up?"

"The spider, you mean?" asked Perera. "Lying in wait?"

"The poet."

"The spider was in its web. I don't know where the poet was."

"I'll tell you. The poet was lying in his own bed."

"That's a thought."

"That's not a thought. That's the truth."

"A poem can come to you wherever you are," Perera explained. "Whatever you're doing. Sleeping, eating, even looking in the fridge, or when you think you're dying. I imagine that in his case he wakes up one morning after a bad night, takes a look at the sun, and accepts who he is. He accepts the enigma of himself."

"Are you?"

"Am I what? An enigma?"

"Are you glad you wake up who you are?"

"I can say yes to that."

"You give thanks to God?"

"More or less."

"Great. I bet you wake up in your own bed. That's what I'm saying. What's-his-name wouldn't've thought up that poem if he woke up where he was lying on the sidewalk."

"Darío," said Perera, "could very well have waked up on a sidewalk. He pursued that sort of life. Opium, absinthe. Quite possibly he was visited by that poem while lying on the sidewalk."

"Then he went back to his own bed and slept it off."

With trembling fingers the fellow gathered up his scraps from the desk. Trembling with what? With timidity, if this was a confrontation with a guardian of the virtues of every book in the place? As he bent to the floor to pick up his scraps, the crown of his head was revealed, the hair sprinkled with a scintilla of the stuff of the streets and the culture. How old was he, this fellow? Not more than thirty, maybe younger. Young, with no staying power.

By the door a coughing spell took hold of him. With his back to Perera he drew out from yet another pocket in the murky interior of the parka one of those large Palestinian scarves that Arafat wore around his head and were to be seen in the windows of used-clothing stores, and brought up into it whatever he had tried to keep down. Voiceless, he left, his bare ankles slapped by the grimy cuffs of his pants.

Perera imagined him shuffling down the hall, then down the wide white marble stairs, the grandiose interior stairs, centerpiece of this eternal granite edifice. As for Darío's admonition to the spider to show no rancor, that fellow's rancor was showing all over him. Yet his voice was scratchily respectful and his fingers trembled. Anybody who inquires so relentlessly into the meaning of a poem, and presses the words of poets into the ephemerae of the streets, would surely return, borne up the marble stairs by all those uplifting thoughts in his pockets.

Alberto Perera, a librarian if for just a few months more, shortly to be retired, went out into the cold and misty evening. A rarity, in this time when librarians' ranks were shrinking down as his own head had shrunk while bent for so many years over the invaluable minutiae of his responsibilities, including the selection of belles lettres, of poetry, of literary fiction. The cranium shrinks no matter how much knowledge is crammed inside it. A rarity for another reason—a librarian who did not look like one, who wore a Borsalino fedora, his a classic of thirty years, a Bogart raincoat, English boots John Major would covet, a black silk shirt, a vintage tie.

Never as dashing as he wished to appear, however. Slight, short, and for several years now the bronze-color curls gone gray and the romantically drooping eyelids of his youth now faded flags at half-mast. Dashing, though, in the literary realm, numbering among his pen pals, most dead now: Hemingway, a letter to Perera, the youth, on the Spanish Civil War; Samuel Beckett, on critics mired up to their necks in his plays; Neruda, handwritten lines in green ink of two of his poems. What a prize! Also a note from the lovely British actress Vanessa Redgrave, with whom he'd spent an hour in London when he'd delivered to her an obscure little book of letters by Isadora Duncan, whom she'd portrayed in a film. And more, so much more. Everything kept in a bank vault and to be carried away in their black leather attaché case with double locks when he left this city for warmer climes. It was time to donate it all to an auction of literary memorabilia, on condition that the proceeds be used to establish a fund for down-and-out librarians, himself among them soon enough.

Further, he was a rarity for choosing to reside in what he called the broken heart of the city, or the spleen of it, the Tenderloin, and choosing not to move when the scene worsened. Born into a family of refugees from Franco's Spain, Brooklyn their alien soil, he felt a kinship with the dispossessed everywhere in the world, this kinship deepening with the novels he'd read in his youth. Dostoevski's insulted and injured, Dickens' downtrodden. Eighteen years ago he'd found a fourth-floor apartment, the top, in a tentatively respectable building, a walking distance to the main library in the civic center and to the affordable restaurants on Geary Street. Soon after he moved in, the sidewalks and entrances on every block began to fill up with a surge of outcasts of all kinds. The shaven heads, the never-shaven faces, the battle-maimed, the dope-possessed, the jobless, the homeless, the immigrants, and not far from his own corner six-foot-tall transvestite prostitutes and shorter ones, too, all colors. A wave, gathering momentum, swept around him now as he made his way, mornings and evenings, to and from the library. There was no city in the world that was not inundated in its time, or would be in time to come, by refugees from upheavals of all sorts.

On gray days, as this day was, he was reminded of the poor lunatics, madmen, nuisances, all who were herded out of the towns and onto the ships that carried them up and down the rivers of the Rhineland. An idea! The mayor, having deprived the homeless of their carts and their tents, would welcome an idea to rid the city of the homeless themselves. Herd them aboard one of those World War II battleships, rusting away in drydock or muck, and send them out to sea. The thousands—whole families, loners, runaway kids, all to be dropped off in Galveston or New Orleans, under cover of a medieval night.

He ate his supper at Lefty O'Doul's, at a long table in company of other men his age and a woman who looked even older. Retired souls, he called them, come in from their residence hotels, their winter smells of naphthalene and menthol hovering over the aroma of his roast turkey with dressing. One should not be ashamed of eating a substantial meal while the hungry roamed the streets. He told himself this as he'd told himself so many times before, lifelong. He knew from saintly experiments of his youth that when he fasted in sympathy, punishing himself for what he thought was plenitude, his conscience began to starve, unable to survive for very long without a body.

A brandy at the long bar, and the bartender slapping down the napkin, asking the usual. "When you going to sell me that Borsalino?" Then, "This man's a librarian," to the bulky young man in a broadly striped sweater on the stool to the left of Perera. "He's read every book in the public library. Ever been in there?"

"Never was."

"You can ask him anything," said the bartender, and the man to Perera's right did. "Do you know right off the number of dead both sides in the Civil War?"

"Whose civil war?"

Taken for a tricky intellectual, he was left alone.

A theater critic, that's what he wished to be mistaken for, passing the theaters at the right time as the ticket holders were drifting in and the lines forming at the box office. Women's skirts and coats swinging out, swishing against him, and a woman turning to apologize, granting a close glimpse of her face to this man who appeared deserving of it. A critic, that's who he was, of the musical up there on the stage and of the audience so delightedly acceptive of the banal, lustily sung.

Past the lofty Hilton at the Tenderloin's edge, whose ultra-plush interior he had strolled through a time or two, finding gold beyond an interior decorator's wildest dreams. Its penthouse window the highest light in the Tenderloin sky, a shining blind eye. Around a corner of the hotel, and, lying up against the cyclone fence, the bundled and the unbundled to whom he gave a wide berth as he would to the dead, in fear and respect. Over the sidewalks, those slips of refuse paper he'd always noticed but not so closely as now. Alert to approaching figures, to whatever plans they had in mind for him, and warily friendly with the fraternal clusters, exchanging with them joking curses on the weather, he made his way. Until at last he stood before the mesh gate to his apartment building. A gate from sidewalk to the entrance's upper reaches, requiring a swift turn of the key before an assault. The gate, the lock, the fear—none of which had been there when he moved in.

The only man in the Western world to wear a nightcap, he drew his on. Cashmere, dove color, knitted twelve years ago by his dear friend and lover, Barbara, a librarian herself, a beautiful one. Syracuse, New York. Every year, off they'd go. Archaeological tours, walking tours. Three winters ago he was at her bedside, close by in her last hours. She, too, had corresponded with writers. Hers were women—poets, memoirists—and these letters, too, were in his care. Into his plaid flannel robe, also a gift from her, the seat and the elbows worn away. He always read in this robe in his ample chair or at the kitchen table or in bed. Three books lay on the floor by his bed, among the last he'd ever consider ordering for any library. One had seduced and deceived him, the second was unbearably vain, and he was put to sleep by the third, already asleep itself, face down on the carpet.

When he lay down the inevitable happened. At once he wondered where the poetry stalker might be, the librarian stalker with the excitable cough. Could Darío have imagined that his earnest little attempt to accept God's ways would wind up in the parka pocket of a sidewalk sleeper, trying to accept the same a hundred years later?

At his desk he was always attuned to the life of this library, as he'd been to every library where he'd spent his years, even the vaster ones with more locked doors, tonnages of archives. This morning his mind's eye was a benign sensor, following the patrons to their chosen areas. He saw them rising in the slow, creaky elevator, he saw the meandering ones and the fast ones climbing the broad marble stairs, those stairs like a solid promise to the climber of an ennobling of the self on the higher levels. The largest concentration of patrons was in the newspaper and periodical section, always and forever a refuge for men from lonely rooms and also now for those without a room, all observing the proper silence, except the man asleep, head down on the table, his glottal breathing quivering the newspaper before his face. In the past, empty chairs were always available; now every chair was occupied. And where was the young man whose pockets were filled with scraps of poetry? In the poetry section, of course, copying down what the world saw fit to honor with the printed page. *Anything in books represents the godlike and anything in myself represents the vile.* Who said that? A writer, born into grim poverty, whose name he'd recall later. If you felt vile in the midst of all these godlike volumes, what restless rage!

"Am I butting in here?"

Same parka, grimier perhaps. But look! His hair rose higher and had a reddish cast, an almost washed look from the rain. His eyes not clearer, not calmer, and in his arms four books, which he let fall onto the desk.

"This is not a checkout desk," said Perera.

"That I know. Never check out anything. No address. If you try to sneak something out you get the guillotine. You get it in the neck."

To touch or not to touch the books. Since there was no real reason not to touch, Perera set the four books upright, his hands as bookends.

"Who've we got here? Ah, Rilke, the *Elegies.* Good choice. And here we've got Whitman. You know how to pick them. Bishop, she's up there. And who's this? Pound? Sublime, all of them. But don't let yourself be intimidated. Nothing sacred in this place, just a lot of people whose thoughts were driving them crazy, euphoria crazy or doom crazy, and they had to get it out, see what *you* think about what they're thinking. That's all there is to it. Librarians in here are just to give it a semblance of order. I'm not a high priest."

"Never thought you were."

"Ah," said Perera, and the books between his hands resumed their frayed existence, their common humanity. One, he saw, had a bit of green mildew at the spine's bottom edge. It must have been left out in a misty rain or someone had read it while in the tub.

"Can I get you some coffee?" inquired the visitor.

"Strange that you should ask," said Perera. "Got my thermos here. A thirst for coffee comes over me at this hour." How closely he'd been watched! And now forced to take the plunge into familiarity, a plunge he would not have taken without further consideration if this man were the sole homeless man around. They were empowered by their numbers.

From the bottom drawer he brought up his thermos and his porcelain cup. The plastic thermos cup held no pleasure and he never used it. He'd use it now and not bother to guess why, and bring up also the paper bag of macaroons.

"Suppose I sit down?"

Perera nodded, and the guest sat down in the only other chair, a hard chair with an unwelcoming look, a chair used until now only by Alexa Okula, head librarian, and Amy Peck, chief guard, who often described for him the assaults she had suffered that day and where in the library they had occurred.

With both hands around the cup, the guest had no trouble holding it. "This is like dessert," he said. "This is great. Got sugar and cream in it." He was shy around the macaroons. Crumbs were tripping down the parka and when they reached the floor he covered them with his beat-up jogging shoes.

At that moment Perera recalled the very recent tragedy at the Sacramento library. When did the shooting occur? Right after a little party celebrating the library's expanded hours. And what did the assassin do then? Fled to the rooftop, where he was gunned down by the police. It was simple enough to imagine himself dead on the floor, but not so easy to imagine this fellow fleeing anywhere, hampered by the bone-cold ankles, the flappy shoes, the body's tremble at the core.

"You remember that poem?" his guest asked.

"Not verbatim," said Perera. "I did not memorize it."

"You can remember the bear, can't you, and the spider and the toad, anyway? How they're supposed to greet the sun because they are what they are?"

"That I remember," said Perera.

"What I'd like to know is, what am I?"

"You can figure you're a human being," said Perera.

"That's what I thought you'd say. What else you were going to say is, you're a human being by the sweat of your brow. Beavers, that don't take into account beavers. Beavers are dam builders. Then you take those birds who get stuff together to make a nest for the female of their choice. Other birds, too, I've seen them. Can't stop pulling up weeds or whatever stuff is around for a hundred miles, pull this out, pull that out, and off they go and back in a second. Then there's animals who dig a burrow, one hell of a long tunnel in the ground. They can't sweat but they work. It's work, but that don't make them human."

"Work does not get to the essence, I see your point," said Perera. At a moment's notice he could not get to the essence himself and he wished he had not used that word. It could only mean further trouble.

"Okay, take you," said the visitor. "Would you say you were human?"

"I've been led to believe that I am," said Perera.

"What you base that on," said his guest, "is you get to keep guard over this library and you got every book where it's supposed to be and in addition you got it up on a computer, what is its title, what is its number, who wrote it, and maybe you got in your head the reason why the guy wrote it. So in that way you can say you're human and maybe you're glad about it even if you don't look it. Okay, now let's say you're through work for the day and you walk home. Or you go on and have yourself a turkey or whatever they got there, roast beef, chicken and dumplings. Then you go along by that theater, maybe even drop in yourself at fifty bucks a seat in the balcony. After that you go on to your apartment, which is in a bad, I mean *baaad* neighborhood, and you unlock that gate. And then what?"

"I can't imagine."

"You don't have to imagine. You're in your own bed. Got a mattress that's just right for the shape you're in. Maybe you even got an electric blanket. Got pillows with real feathers inside, maybe even that down stuff from the hind end of a couple hundred ducks. Nighty-night."

"So now I'm sure I'm human?"

"So then the sun comes up and what do you say? You say what that spider says. Halloo, old sun up there, had me a good sleep in my own web and now I get to eat some more fat flies. Halloo, says the toad, now I get to spend the day in this hot mud some more. Halloo, says the bear, now I get to dance some more with this rope around my neck. Halloo, says this guy, Alberto Perera, now I get to go to the library again and talk to this guy who can't figure out why he can't halloo the sun with the rest of them."

A flush had spread over the fellow's face, over the pallor and over the pits, over all that was more appallingly obvious today. From his parka he brought out the Arafat headpiece and hid his face in it, coughing up in there something tormentingly intimate.

Alexa Okula, head librarian, passing by and hearing the commotion, paused a moment to look in and Perera held up his hand to calm her fears for his safety. Nothing escaped her, only all the years of her life in the protective custody of tons of books and tons of granite. Soon to be released, just as he was to be, all she'd have was her stringy emeritus professor of a husband and her poodles. Unlike himself, who'd have the world.

The fellow sat staring at the floor, striving to recover from the losing battle with his cough.

"You suppose I could spend the night in here?"

With *unthinkable* on the tip of his tongue, Perera said nothing. Accommodations ought to be available for queries of every sort at any time in your life.

"Looks like it ought to be safer in here."

"Unsafe in here, too," said Perera. "This fortress is in a state of abject deterioration. The last earthquake did some damage, along with the damage done by the budget cuts, along with the damage by vandals. Time's been creeping around in here, too. The whole place could collapse on you while you slept."

"I can handle it," said the supplicant. "Nobody's going to throw lighter fuel on me and set me on fire in here. Nobody's going to knife me in here, at night anyway. Lost my bedroll. I left my stuff with this woman who's my friend, she got room in her cart. I had a change of shirt in there, I had important papers, had a letter from a guy I worked for up the coast. I was good at hauling in those sea urchins they ship over to Japan, tons of them. They love those things over there, then there wasn't any more. Where the sea urchins were, something else is taking over, messing up the water. I'm telling you this because I don't drink, don't do dope, don't smoke, so I sure would not set this place on fire if I was allowed to sleep in here." He was talking fast, outrunning his cough. "The cops took her stuff, took my stuff, dumped it all into the truck. Ordered by the mayor. She lost family pictures, lost the cat she had tied to the cart that sat on top. She was crying. I was in here talking to you."

"It must be damn cold in here at night," Perera said.

"Maybe, maybe not, and if it's raining maybe the roof don't leak."

"Dark, I imagine," said Perera. "I've never thought about it. I suspect they used to leave a few lights on but now it's dark. Saves money. Let's say that once the lights go out you can't see a thing. Your sense of direction is totally lost, you're blind as a bat, and I'm nowhere around to guide you to the lavatory and I wouldn't know where it was myself. You might be pissing on some of the noblest minds that ever put their thoughts on paper."

"I wouldn't do that."

"They do get pissed on, one time and another, but not by you or me. So let's say you're feeling your way around, looking for a comfortable place. Okula has a rug in her office and it's usually warm in there. She exudes a warmth that might stay the night. But how to get there?"

"I know my way around."

"You do seem to," said Perera.

"What you could do when you take off, like your day is done, see? You just leave me in here and close the door. I wouldn't care if you locked it."

"I can lock it," said Perera, "but not with you inside."

"Is there some of that coffee left?"

Perera, pouring, was planning to wash that porcelain cup thoroughly. If it was pneumonia gripping this young man, it would get a more merciless grip on him, twice as old. Or if it was tuberculosis, it would bring on his end with rapacious haste and just as he was about to embark on his most rewarding years.

This time the guest took longer to drink it down, the hot coffee apparently feeling its way past the throat's lacerations.

"Let's say it's like that darkness upon the face of the deep," Perera said. "That same darkness the Creationists are wanting to take us back to. Dark, dark, and you need to find yourself a comfortable place. Now let's say you're at the top of our marble stairs and you don't know it. You take a step and down you go. Come morning, they open up and find you there."

"You think so?"

"You'll be on the front pages in New York, Paris, Tokyo. A homeless man, seeking shelter in San Francisco's main library, fell down in there and died. A library, imagine it, that monument to mankind's exalted IQ.

I'll say you dropped by to chat about poetry. I'll say we spent many pleasant hours discussing Darío's *Filosofía*."

Contempt in the eyes meeting Perera's. "What're you telling me? You're telling me to lie down and die?"

"Not at all. All I'm saying is you cannot spend the night in this library."

Scornfully careful, the fellow placed the porcelain cup on the desk and stood up. "You want me to tell you what that poem is saying? Same thing you're saying. If you can't halloo the sun, if you can't go chirpity-chirp to the moon, what're you doing around here anyway?"

"That is not what it is saying," said Perera.

"To hell with you is what I'm saying."

Gone, leaving his curse behind. A curse so popular, so spread around, it carried little weight.

Closing time, the staff and lingering patrons all forced out through one side entrance and into the early dark, into the rain. Perera hoisted his umbrella, one slightly larger than the ordinary, bought in London the day he met the actress, years ago. It will never turn inside out, the clerk promised, not even in Conrad's typhoon. And it hadn't yet. Lives were being turned inside out, but this snob of an umbrella stayed up there. A stance of superiority, that was his problem. A problem he always knew he had and yet that always took him by surprise. And how did he figure he was so smart, this Alberto Perera? Well, he could engage in the jesting the smart ones enjoy when they're in the presence of those they figure are not so smart. He could engage in that jovial thievery, that light-fingered, light-headed trivializing of another person's tragic truth, a practice he abhorred wherever he came upon it.

Onward through this neon-colored rain, this headlight-glittering rain, every light no match for the dark, only a constant contesting. *There is a certainty in degradation.* You can puzzle over lines all your life and never be satisfied with the meanings you get. Until, slushing onward, you've got at last one meaning for sure, because now its time had come, bringing proof by the thousands wherever they were this night in their concrete burrows and dens. There was no certainty in anything else, no matter what you're storing up, say tons of gold, say ten billion library books, and if you think you can elude that certainty it sneaks up on you, it sneaks up the marble stairs and into your sanctum and you're degraded right along with the rest.

For several days at noontime Perera looked for him in the long line at St. Anthony's, men and women moving slowly in for their free meal. After work he climbed the stairs to Hospitality House and looked around at the men in the collection of discarded chairs, each day different men and each man confounded by being among the unwanted many. Here, too, he knew he would not find him. The fellow was a loner, hiding out, probably afraid his cough was reason to arrest him.

A rolled-up wool blanket, a large thermos filled with hot coffee, a dozen packaged handkerchiefs, a thick turtleneck sweater, a package of athletic socks. Perera carried all this into his office, piecemeal, as the days came and went, and these offerings had the same aspect of futility that he saw in the primitive practice of laying out clothing and nourishment for the departed.

He braved the Albatross used-book store not far from the library, trying not to breathe the invisible dust from the high stacks of disintegrating books, and in the dim poetry section came upon some unexpected finds. Ah, hah! Michaux, *My life, you take off without me*, and Trakl, sad, suicidal soul, *Beneath the stars a man alone*, and Anna Akhmatova, *Before this grief the mountains stoop*, and Ah! Machado, *He was seen walking between rifles*. Comments in the margins, someone's own poem on a title page, bus schedules, indecipherable odds and ends of penciled thoughts intermingling with the printed ones. He wanted to keep these thin volumes for himself and instead he did as planned. He bought a green nylon parka in a discount place on Market Street, slid the books into the deep pockets, and folded the parka on top of the pile.

On the morning of the twelfth day, before the hour when the public was admitted, Perera entered by the side door, bringing a pair of black plastic shoes, oxford style, made in China, recommended for their comfort by a street friend wearing a pair. The door guard silently led him to the foot of the marble stairs, where Okula, cops and paramedics and librarians were gathered around a man lying on the lowest step.

Perera had never fainted and was not going to faint now, even though all the strength of his intelligence was leaving the abode of his head to darkness.

"Mr. Perera," Okula was saying but not to him, "was an acquaintance of this man. Wasn't he?"

Nobody was answering, though Perera gave them time.

"Occasionally," he said, "he stepped into my office. My door is usually open." Sweat was rising from his scalp. "Did he fall?"

"More like he lay down and died." The paramedic's voice was inappropriately young. "T.B. Take a look at that rag."

"You say you knew him?" A cop's voice. "Do you know his name? He's got nothing in his pockets."

"No," said Perera.

"Any idea where he concealed himself in here?"

"Hundreds of places." Okula, responding. "We check carefully. However, anyone wishing to stay in can also check carefully."

"What you might be needing is a couple of dogs. German shepherds are good at it. Dobermans, too. A couple of good dogs could cover this whole place in half an hour."

Kneeling by the body, Perera took a closer look at the face, closer than when they sat in the office, discoursing on the animal kingdom. The young man was now no one, as he'd feared he already was when alive. The absolute unwanted, that's who the dead become.

"Did this man bother you?"

It would take many months, he knew, before he'd be able to speak without holding back. Humans speaking were unbearable to hear and abominable to see, himself among the rest. Worse, was all that was written down instead, the never-ending outpouring, given print and given covers, given shelves up and down and everywhere in this warehouse of fathomless darkness.

"He did not bother me," he said.

The door to his office was closed but unlocked, just as he'd left it. Scattered over his desk were what appeared to be the contents of his wastebasket. But unfamiliar, not his. So many kinds of paper scraps, they were the bits and pieces his visitor had brought forth from that green parka. Throwaway ads, envelopes, a discount drugstore's paper bag, business cards tossed away. On each, the cramped handwriting. By copying down all these stirringly strange ideas, had the fellow hoped to impress upon himself his likeness to these other humans? A break-in of a different sort. A young man breaking into a home of his own.

Perera sat down at his desk, slipped his glasses on, and spread the scraps out before him as heedfully as his shaking hands allowed.

A Dream of Fair Women

*L*ike a night sentry on the border between India and dream country, Singh, the restaurateur, watched her from the little lamplit bar, his post. Over six feet tall, he was made even taller by his emerald green turban, and his Nehru jacket was as white as Himalayan snow. Alma was the last waitress to arrive, and even though she was on time the near-miss must seem to him a portent of ruin. The most famous of roving gourmets was to be his guest this night, a man who would either place the restaurant on the map of the world or obliterate it with a few cruelly chosen words or no words at all.

The tiled cubicle restroom was still fragrant with the colognes of the other waitresses who, by arriving early and lighting the candles on all the tables, were like angels promising a celestial ending to this night. She slipped her costume on, drawing up the long cotton underskirt, smoothing the snug silk vest over her breasts, draping the red silk sari around her waist and over one shoulder, her hands weak with fear over her own night apart from the restaurant's night. While she was at work this night, her lover would take away his possessions—a simple task, there were so few. They had agreed that the most bearable time for both was when she was not there. All afternoon she had raged against the woman he was going to, and now she could not even clear her ravaged throat to see if she still had a voice. And he had held her, he had caressed her, his face confounded. He was like someone dispatched to the ends of the earth, with no idea of what was to happen to him there.

The sitar music began its nightlong spiraling from the stereo in the alcove next to the restroom. She folded her clothes into her canvas bag, carried her coat and bag to the employees' closet, and emerged into the opulent dark of the dining area.

Early diners waited at the bar, and over their heads he signaled her to escort them to their tables. His wife, Lila, the hostess, was in the kitchen, overseeing the preparation of the dishes to be set before the honored guest. A feast was in the making, created by the three silent Indian cooks, women of the same birdlike smallness, the same dark skin, their dark gray hair drawn back into a knot at the nape of their thin necks, their heads always bowed over their tasks.

The restaurant this night was more than ever like a stage, and, to Alma's eyes, unforgivably deceptive. Light from the candles within the faceted glass globes on the tables glided up and down the waitresses' saris and shimmered along their necklaces, turned ivory the waiters' white turbans, and glinted off the engraved brass trays, large as giants' shields, hanging on the walls. The candles set aglow the faces of the women at the tables, and she saw—more sharply than ever—how, tables apart, a room apart, women glanced at one another as if by mistake, as if indifferently, to see who was most beautiful of all.

At the bar, Singh appeared more Indian than ever, drawn up to his full height by the advent of the famous gourmet. But only Singh and the two waiters and just one of the three waitresses were authentic. None of the patrons—she was sure—suspected that he was born on a dirt farm in the San Joaquin Valley and had never set foot in India, nor that both waiters, flawless as a maharaja's servants, were students enrolled in business administration classes, nor that the one Indian waitress—Kamala, aloof, remote—spoke street language in the kitchen, ridiculing the diners, and was a fervent belly dancer. The rest were impostors. She was one herself, her parents Chilean. Lila was from the Detroit ghetto, but Indian ancestry could easily be imagined for her large eyes, her prematurely white hair and dark skin, her thin little hands. Marlie was ghetto-born, too, but her silky, gold-flecked, flitting presence so mesmerized the patrons that two or three or four men dining together would loudly declare, for all to hear, that Indian women were the most beautiful in the world.

When Alma came to the bar with her little brass tray to order drinks, Singh was gazing out over the tables, losing his way by candlelight, his soft, dark face plump with desire.

"That woman at the corner table," he said. "What a face! Right out of those old movies where they come down those long, curving stairs to breakfast. Who is she? She looks familiar."

Every beautiful woman is always someone waited for and always recognized as someone seen before. Alma had never told him this notion of hers. For one reason, he wouldn't know what she was talking about, and, for another reason, she'd be confessing a bewilderment of her own.

"Remind me," he said, pouring drinks. "Remind me to tell you about a woman I knew in Texas. She looked like that. She almost died when I left. Why I ran out on her I don't know. I was just a dumb kid, knocking around. I thought I had my destiny to look after. She would've left her husband for me. A filthy rich oilman, but she would've left him. In my life nothing synchronizes."

On quiet nights, when his wife wasn't there, and when all the diners had left, then how many intimate things he told her about the women of his past, about what pleased them in bed, what subtle artistry of his. On busy nights when his wife was there, and after the restaurant doors were closed, then the departing waiters and waitresses would pretend not to see what was going on at the bar. Lila, on a stool, was bent low over the counter, fiercely accusing him of present affairs, past ones, and those to come, while he ranged within his small space like a tiger tormented by its keeper.

At the top of the stairs, Lila was welcoming the celebrated columnist, her face endowed by that guest with a brief flare of tender, pleading beauty. Alma, waiting at the bar for a glass to be filled, saw closely how affected Singh was by the famous gourmet—a man unexpectedly brisk, trim and gray, like an executive with no time or talent for savoring—and by his companion, another familiar beauty. Their presence stole away Singh's natural suavity, his air of reserve. He stepped out from behind the bar and, towering over the couple, shook hands with the man and bowed his head quickly to the woman, then gave them back to his wife, who led them to their table, her head high, her silk garments floating.

"What's her name?" he asked Alma. "She's an actress. I've seen her, but I can't remember which movie." With unusually hasty hands he concocted the third Pimm's Cup for her tray, fumbling the long slice of cucumber.

It was in those moments of their arrival that he first appeared to have lost his wits. Alma blamed the loss on the woman of shocking beauty and on the man who could either make or break the restaurant, but, as the evening wore on, the reason for his odd behavior began to seem not so simple. On other evenings he would wander among the diners, shaking hands with steadfast patrons and with celebrities he recognized—a violinist, a comedian, an opera singer—his eyes darkening to a degree in accord with the patron's significance out in the world, and he would chat for only the graceful length of time, longer for the lesser ones, shorter for the greater ones. But this night he remained behind the bar, gazing out to the couple at their table apart.

Hovering over the couple, Lila confided to them the ingredients of each dish as it was set down by their waiter, and the number of seconds, the number of minutes required for two and more ingredients to fuse perfectly.

"He won't talk to them," she complained to Alma in the kitchen, appealingly, as though Alma could persuade him, and resignedly, because the pain of this frustration was hers alone, and out she went through the swinging doors, followed by the waiter, bearing on his tray the evening's most elaborate offering, roast pheasant glazed with gold leaf, a bird of molten gold.

This hours-long homage to the famous guest recalled to Alma the Shah of Iran's great feast for select hundreds of the world's celebrities and dignitaries. The magazine had shown luxurious tents where they slept, and the banquet like no other, and the long parade of waiters bearing peacocks on trays, their fantastic plumage adorning again their roasted bodies. She felt scorn for this guest who was mesmerized by the food set before him and who seemed unaware of time and how it steals away every morsel, like a cunning beggar.

Eventually, Singh gave in. It was at the very end of the meal, which had become a celebration of the lives of the two guests, with gifts from the sea, from earth's black loam, from vine, from tree, from the perfumed air. He stood above them, gazing at the face of the gourmet, a face soothed by the many gifts but tantalizingly withholding gratitude, patches of lacy capillaries like a clown's rouge on cheeks and nose; and gazing, in turn, at the woman's lifted face and at her throat, that lovely channel down which all the bites had slipped, and at her body, languidly sloping under the weight of so much adoration. To Alma, glancing by, all the gifts seemed given to the woman in exchange for just the sight of her. Singh leaned toward them to catch their words of praise, but his face was mournful, as though he had come to confess the failure of his own attempts at a plenteous life.

At his nod, Alma brought out the woman's fur coat from the employees' closet where diners' priceless coats were hung. The woman had come prepared for San Francisco's cold, whipping fogs that often swept in on summer nights. It was customary, when diners were leaving, for Singh or Lila, or both, to signal Alma, if she were free, and she would come to help them put on their coats. The departing guests would stand with their backs to her, and if they were unfamiliar with the courtesy, their shoulders would stiffen; others would slip into their coats with affected ease as if their wraps were held up for them by someone invisible or by the world's esteem. But this extravagant night roused her resistance to this act that humbled her, and her arms refused to hold up the woman's coat. When Singh saw that she was in trouble, he took the coat from her and lifted it to the woman's bare shoulders. The woman turned her head toward him, knowing—Alma was sure—how pristine a profile of beauty appears, like a very brief and partial view granted to mortals. So close was that profile, he seemed to tire instantly.

They were the last to leave. Alma watched them go as she went among her tables, blowing out the candles. On his way out, the gourmet was introduced to the three Indian gentlemen, the restaurant's financial backers, all in dark suits. They stood up at their table, and, unsmiling, shook his hand, afraid perhaps that if they were to smile he might deceive them later. At the bar he was introduced to the restaurant's publicist, Patricia, who had induced him to come, but when she stood up from her stool she began to sway. She had drunk too much, celebrating his presence, and from a distance she appeared to be swaying with religious awe. Then they were gone.

A jostling wave of relief rose up in their wake, doing away with everyone's roles and with all glittering. The only light left was from the brass carriage lamps at the bar and the candles on the table where the three backers sat over their vegetarian delicacies. In this intimate dimness they gathered together for a little party.

Lila poured drinks and carried them to whoever wanted one, while Singh wandered among them, empty-handed, uncritical, uncommending, voiceless. Kamala unwound her green sari, pushed the elastic band of the long underskirt down below her belly, and began her dance. From the stereo rose her delirious music. She danced barefoot, her hands, her arms gliding desirously, her belly moving with many little leaps and undulations. Her husband, who often accompanied her home, came up the stairs and paused at the top, watching her, pleased and uncomfortable. The two waiters, now in their leather jackets, heads bare, feigned indifference. Marlie, a faux fur jacket over her sari, sat at the low cocktail table, restlessly peeling her nail polish, lifting her eyes only to see if her lover had arrived—a young doctor who would take her to his apartment. Alma, her costume again in the canvas bag, stood close to the stairs. When the dance was over she would leave, and no one would know that she had left and that she had left alone.

"Where is your friend tonight?"

There was so much that was intimidating about Kamala's husband, a high school mathematics teacher—his precise words, his eyes demanding correct answers. He and Alma's lover had often sat together at the bar, waiting to escort their women home. If he were able to understand the garbled language of loss, she might be able to say to him, *I don't know*

*where he is, he's with someone else but I don't know who she is and I don't
know who he is anymore and I don't know who I am anymore, either, if I
ever knew.*

"A sculpture class at the art school. They stay late," she said.

The three thin women from the kitchen slipped by, passing close to
her, their work done, cheap sweaters, old coats over their faded saris.
They said good night to no one and were noticed by no one as they went
down the stairs and into the night.

Then Singh, among the few who were gazing at the dancer, toppled
to the floor, striking against his wife, who fell with him. At once the waiters lifted her, and Marlie ran to the alcove to turn off the music. The
three financial backers bent over the man on the floor, and one, still
clutching his large white napkin, shouted Singh's name warningly, hoping to alarm him back to life and his responsibilities. When they stepped
away, the waiters then knelt by him, softly calling to him, and one laid an
ear to his chest and felt for a pulse at his wrist. Nothing. A napkin wet
with ice water was passed from hand to hand and spread over his brow, a
jigger of brandy was touched to his lips, and when it was seen that he was
far, far beyond these clumsy persuasions, they stepped away from him.

He lay on his side, his turban tipped, his white jacket twisted. Someone had removed his shoes, thinking that would relax him. His trouser
legs had slipped up, and narrow shins were exposed above his black silk
socks. On some nights after the restaurant closed, he had worn his turban, his Nehru jacket, out into the nightlife, a short walk away, visiting
the bars and the amateur strip show, a presence so startling and impres-
sive that people made way for him.

Wailing, Lila roamed among the tables, flinging her arms out and
crossing them against her breasts, over and over, a ritual of grief and disbelief. The publicist was sobbing, head down on a table. Alma, along
with Marlie and Kamala, wept quietly in the kitchen. They had been
fond of him, they had exchanged little jokes about him and he hadn't
known why they were laughing.

No one left until he had been taken away, and then they left together,
down the steps carpeted in persimmon. The cold of early morning broke
the group apart. They went off to their cars, Lila to be driven home in her
car by one of the Indian backers, the other two to follow in their car.

Alma watched her walk away, a very slender woman in a long pale coat, her sari stirring around her ankles, losing its color to distance.

Alma was driven home by the waiter who had served the famous gourmet. At the restaurant he seldom spoke. Now in the car he said, "Terrible, terrible. I think he was only forty." The rest of the way he was silent.

When she entered the dark apartment she did not switch on a light, seeing well enough that her lover's possessions were gone and the apartment empty despite her own things solidly there. She lay down in her clothes, calling on sleep to postpone her confrontation with her own unsolvable loss. An hour later or a minute later she was wide awake, already sitting up. It was not loss lifting her from sleep, it was gratefulness that her lover, no longer there, was taken from her only by the dream, only by that.

Soul and Money

Often, as he went about the task of living a useful life, he wished for a weekend in that desert town where everything was out in the open, where all the tricks were there at hand to out-trick money's own. Once again, then, he was on his way, this time a long way round, wanting to see his only brother again, but without any reason why.

He spent the flight hour to Los Angeles trying to plumb the unfathomable persons of his life, among them Bianca, his wife. After twenty-three years of loving fidelity, sudden change. That blazingly beautiful, upper-middle-class, university radicalized young woman, who, at twenty-four, had married him, twenty years older, because he was a man of words, a working-class savant, quoting Marx, Frantz Fanon, Bertrand Russell, that wife had now, at last and yet too soon, taken a lover. A professor of sociology, she had fallen in love with a young, prematurely honored physicist, crossing over in erotic haste into another dimension, wherever that fellow was to be found. Such a highly intelligent couple, you could just imagine the ecstasy they achieved in bed with their combined IQs. And he, her husband, who had imagined himself young forever because he wasn't ailing in any part and had sired two marvels, a boy and a girl, ten, twelve, was beginning to suspect that he might have overestimated the value of his presence among them.

He did not speak to the man in the next seat. Served coffee, he kept his gaze on his cup. The young radical he'd been, that witty, proselytizing youth who had loved to hear himself speak to strangers, surprising them with his adroit combining of charm and a left-wing view, would never recognize the man he'd become. A recent letter from a former comrade, cheaply retired in Mexico, had spelled it out in a simple sentence: *My age appalls me.* What they saw in their mirrors was not just themselves grown considerably older but an ideal world nowhere near accomplished in their lifetime.

The faces he glanced into on his way out of the airport reminded him of what his grandmother used to say. *A cada loco con su tema.* Each lunatic with his own theme. And what was his? When a lifelong theme is lost there must be another to take its place.

The taxi went out over monstrous freeways. Monsters rise up overnight while you sleep. You wake up in the morning and find yourself riding on their backs. By the light of tall candles in silver holders he dined on thick ham and baked potato, the sour cream dollop one of the finer things of life. The wine was poured into gold-rimmed auction glasses, fatigued ware whose lights had gone out. This fare every night had plumped out his brother's face, confining the spirit in a padded cell. His only brother, Fred, called Frederico by their grandmother, subscribed to the way things were in the world, like their German immigrant father, cabinetmaker and restorer of antiques, whose shop he'd taken over. And his brother's likeness now to their father was unsettling: the spectacles, the pale skin, the limp, colorless hair, the young and combative square jaw gone under. This brother of his, younger by two years, was looking older than himself, who took after their Spanish mother, his hair dark, silver only at the temples, eyes jet-black like Picasso's, as Bianca used to say. Maybe his young wife had kept him young, lean, easy in the hips, and maybe his hopes for that egalitarian world had kept him lively in the head. Of both those elixirs of youth he was now deprived. Glancing up, he caught his brother's wife glancing away. A psychotherapist, she slid like a ferret into anything hidden or latent.

Out in the living room, she lay down on the sofa, a way of telling him, their guest, that whatever he had to say wasn't important enough for her to sit up to receive, and his brother slung himself out in his reclining chair, eyes on the soundless TV. Newscasters without voices seemed to be speaking from beyond the grave. The silent news could be a courtesy shown their guest or it could be an insinuation: if their guest could hear what was going on in the world he'd come up with a smartass refutation.

"You bound for somewhere else?" his brother asked.

They knew nothing about his gambling. If that therapist over there knew, she'd have herself a fun time stripping away his excuses. The excitement of it wouldn't be enough of an excuse.

"Never ask him where he's going." Laughing, she turned on her side, facing him. "That radical rag you used to write for, didn't they send you on secret missions? Moscow? Managua?"

"All in my head," he said.

"Were you ever paid a cent for that column?"

"Never was," he said. "They had me tied to the chair. Black bread and water. A fifth of vodka on Saturdays."

"I liked that byline you picked." She must store up that mocking laughter all day, listening so seriously to her clients.

"Glad you liked it," he said. "You never told me. Joseph T. McGettigan. I chose it for its sound of muscular intellect." None of his readers, if he'd had any, had known of his other self, himself, Walter Stenstauffer, union piecard, longshoreman, who everybody knew was long-winded but who nobody suspected could write tightly within a column inch.

"I liked that paper's name, too. *Arise.* So much more exciting than a name like the *Times* or the *Herald.* What did we do with our copies, Freddy?"

"Glad you liked that name, too," he said. "I wish you'd told me these things. I'd have hit you up for a donation." He knew *she* knew that *Arise* had leaped from that rousing song to the world's proletariat and down onto the title page of that thin and thinner weekly, a paper probably not read or even glanced at outside Berkeley's city limits. And he also knew what she did with those few copies he'd brought with him, one visit long ago. They'd got them out of sight fast, probably twisted them up to kindle a blaze in their fireplace. Were there any copies left anywhere? He had none himself. Fifteen years of *Arise*, every copy overloaded with world-shaking crises, with alarms, analyses, denunciations, with prophecies of victory for the oppressed and defeat for the oppressors, until the paper itself and not capitalism went belly-up.

She crossed the room to give him a good-night kiss. Body language! Something everybody knew about long before the psychologists named it. Like the swaggle of her hips, like the rolling lift of her breasts, as if she wished to seduce him while she disdained him. She kissed the top of his head and tiptoed out. Bare feet, too! Like counseling him to let it all hang out.

Alone with his brother, he was surprisingly overcome by affection for him and for the crazy family they'd come out of. Little Grandma gone, his mother's mother, squat, raucous, a volatile mixture of Basque and Spanish. He heard her threatening to never again cook another meal and never to lend a cent and never again to allow him and his brother, bleeding street fighters, into the house. Their mother gone, early on, their young mother gone from that porch where, dying, she sat in her rocker. One time, at the end, he'd come home from school and found her lying on the steps, and he and his grandmother had helped her get up, and her long hair came loose from the clip and swung across his face, and he'd never forget the sick feel of it, nor the wasted arms, nor the blood on her dress, and that night he'd worked out God's defense to keep his fists from shaking at the ceiling: God gave the tuberculosis bugs their own turf, out of the kindness of his enormous heart. Gone, too, Uncle Ricardo, their mother's brother, arrogantly handsome as a bullfighter, picking quarrels with his two little motherless nephews, stealing their coins, vying with them for the love of their grandmother who loved Ricardo above all others anyway, always serving him the largest portion of the leg of lamb.

"You remember when we thought Ricardo was the one who killed that woman?" Why, now, was he bringing up that long-gone enemy of theirs?

"It could've been any one of her studs, but we knew it was him," his brother said. "Grandma put him to bed with a hot water bottle, said he was contagious. But the cops didn't really care who killed a black whore, and Ricardo got out of bed and ate three pounds of sweetbreads." His brother gave a short, enjoyable laugh.

"What're you laughing at?" he asked amiably.

"What the hell," his brother said. "You think he should've got the gas chamber? You ought to have seen him on his last birthday, a skeleton, jaundice, wearing that same black fedora, same striped suit, same black-and-white wing-tip shoes."

At the time, Frederico, the kid, had threatened to turn in his Uncle Ricardo, and their grandmother had threatened to chase the boy out of the house and never let him in again. Was he nine then? And now this brother, Fred, Freddy, lay before his TV in his lounge chair, accepting violence all around. And he remembered himself, daring her to throw them both out. As for what had become of *him*, Little Walter, feisty kid, he'd grown up to become such a threat to the pillars of civilization that the FBI kept a bulging dossier on him, now no doubt in the archives, no longer among the alive and kicking dossiers. If his grandmother had sensed what was to become of him, she would have clasped him to her bosom and begged him never to open his mouth again.

"What the hell, right," he agreed. But his compliance alerted his brother. He could see his brother thinking: *Lefty Walter, here, always pretends to agree and then he tricks you.* Obligingly, he tricked him. "If some people—and I'll spare you their names—get away with murdering thousands, why can't Uncle Ricardo get away with just one?"

A wary silence from both of them. As always, there was only so far he could go, only part way into any topic, no matter how innocuous, before the conversation was ambushed by unforeseen meanings.

"Grandma's nuns," he said. "They sat around the table, trilling like birds, eating her cold sliced lamb and potato salad and that flan pudding of hers. She always laid out that big crocheted tablecloth for them. That day she shoved Ricardo into bed, she told them her son was sick as a dog." He laughed, his own derisive kind of laugh. "She didn't know how true it was. The nuns told her to pray to Jesus and he'd make her son well again, Jesus being a son himself. Did you save any of her Jesus pictures, hanging up everywhere?"

"Saved the frames," his brother said. "The ones she brought from Europe. I was cleaning them up, chipped the black paint off one. Guess what was under the paint? Gold, filigree gold. She brought it across that way so nobody'd steal it, and I guess she kept it from Ricardo, that way." A pause. "You still got something against religion?"

"I'm reconciled to it," he said. "It's like making peace with the inevitable." And he waited for the next query he knew was following right along.

"Do you still belong to the Party?"

"Left it years ago," he said. "I thought I told you. You think it's a brand on my hide for the rest of my life? I left to avoid jeopardizing Bianca's career. She could've got blacklisted, the underhanded way, for what her husband was up to, if anything. I had some other reasons, like my natural animosity for officials of any persuasion. Hackles rise."

"You kept on talking the same way," his brother said.

"It sounded that way to you," he said, "because you're a squarehead, like our father. You had no room in your head for what got into mine. I had a world of room in my head and the world got in."

"Everything in your head was political," his brother said. "That's all I knew about you. You told me who to vote for, and when the guy got elected and did something you didn't like, you called him a son of a bitch. You told me who the sons of bitches were in France or Africa."

"What got into my head," he said, "I call it an Elation. Nobody else I know calls it that and I never tell them what I call it. I'm telling you because it came into my head when we were brothers together and I know you won't tell anybody. You couldn't, because you don't know how."

"When you were a kid," his brother said, "you never stopped talking. Is that it?"

"I got elated," he said, "over the prospect of a whole other world. Not a Utopia, a real world where everybody's looking out for the good of everybody else. Share and share alike. Like you told me they said in the navy, He who has none, take one, he who has two, turn one in. A world without all the miseries I won't bore you with."

"If that's what you gambled your life on," his brother said, "you should've known you'd lose."

"You figure I lost?" he said.

"If you're having trouble sleeping," his brother said, rising up from his recliner, "I'll tell you how to fall asleep. What you do is forgive yourself.

Francie tells her patients this thing she thought up. She tells them, For-giveness means giving up all hope for a better past. It stumps them for a minute and then they laugh and then they fall asleep."

He didn't try it. He slept how he wanted to sleep, restlessly and recriminatively.

Out in the overcast morning sun, his brother waited with him for the taxi. "Where you going?" Carrying on the mocking humor of the night before. "Around the world?"

"May do that," he said. "May stay over on the other side."

"What's over there? China?"

"I don't know what's over there. Could be some other dimension no-body's thought up yet."

They shook hands, his brother's eyes tired of him, of the dim enigma of who he was.

Swinging forward, halting, trying again, the train began the journey. He sat by the window, nobody beside him, his canvas bag tossed up on the rack, his leather aviator jacket on top of the bag, his wallet buttoned down in his trouser pocket, and gave himself over to the ride. Nothing like it. His kind were accused of wanting to take over everything, the rail-roads, the oil refineries, the banks, the movies, and all the ships at sea. He'd be happy with one train. He dozed lightly, he read a Noam Chom-sky lecture. The red sun at the horizon bathed the desert in oxblood, and every person coming down the aisle was tinged with it. Then in the deep portentous blue of the coming night, he thought of his first wife, Rachel. They'd taken the train to New York on their honeymoon, and she'd told him about the desert prophets, and the handwriting on the wall, and where King Nebuchadnezzar wound up, eating grass like a beast in the field. Nineteen, he'd been a tabula rasa for her, that Jewish girl who thought the earth and all its creatures were sacred. Lying beside her, gaz-ing out through the berth's small window, he saw the night and its dis-tant, fleeting lights as she saw it. So many years later he felt again his grief over her death. They had gone up to Canada, convinced McCarthy was taking over the country. A winter evening, Rachel and their little son crossing the icy street, a skidding car, and Rachel leaping to push the boy out of the way. Their son, growing up, wandered the world on his own, barefoot among the hordes of India and the hashish squatters of Morocco, then, regaining himself or an altered self, he'd put himself through law school. A public defender, wearing decent shoes.

At the call to dinner he put on his jacket, spruced up in the lavatory, and, swaying with the train's sway, agile, with conforming grace, he went down the aisle. A young woman, coming toward him, lit up at his approach. One of those sweetly stirring exchanges, one of those affinities. Lightly, swayingly, they brushed past each other, smiling. Was it this sort of brief reflection in a young woman's eyes that was to keep him up with the world from now on?

Riding backwards, across the table from a very elderly couple, he felt young again by comparison, a youth of sixty-seven. The husband, staringly, speechlessly old, was pressing his spoon edge down hard on a chocolate mousse, expecting resistance. The wife was curious, the wife was alive, her dark eyes appraising him. His tie puzzled her. She wasn't acquainted with arty stuff. Bianca, my wife, picked it out, he could say. If you could only meet Bianca you'd like my tie.

"Where you going?" she asked, and, before he could answer, she told him they'd visited their eldest daughter and family in Pasadena and were on their way home to Chicago. Practiced in the intricate art of conversation with the majority, he told her he had two children, a girl and a boy, both exceptionally bright. His boy, he said, might very well grow up to be another Albert Einstein. If he said he had a grown son by a first marriage, that might damage the lovable image of an older father with two adorable, affordable youngsters.

"On your way home to them?"

"I just left them behind," he said. "I'm on my way to Las Vegas."

She blew on her coffee, smiling a worldly smile. "You're a gambler."

"A lifer," he said.

"We've never gambled," she said.

"Try it," he urged. "Get off with me." They'd never risked a penny. Their pennies and their lives were risked for them. If that youth he used to be were sitting at this table, you could count on him to belabor that point.

They were leaving, the husband rising tall in a baggy suit, the wife pausing by the table to bend down toward him with a tamed flirtatiousness, wishing him luck, shaking her beads at him.

Every arrival before this one, he had felt not yet born, on his way to being born. This time an encumbrance of loss had come along like a down-and-out friend. He always chose a motel, the transients' ambiance, instead of the casino hotels' thousand cells, where the urge for escape was muffled by carpets and cushioned chairs. He shaved, took a fresh shirt from his bag, left his leather jacket in the closet, and stepped out into the glittering night.

He seldom wandered from the casinos inhabited by the low-income crowds and the immigrants, whose numbers were always increasing. Under surveillance for most of his life, here he merged with these crowds, of no interest to anyone, under no suspicion of wrongdoing. His habitual gesture to begin was to glance up at the windows in the ceiling, the eyes in the sky through which somebody concealed watched everybody below, but not especially him. He set his sight ahead again and saw before him—Disaster! A comrade out of the past.

The fellow, gray now, skinny as ever, harried as ever, camouflaged by a Hawaiian shirt, was standing behind the players at a crap table, hands in his pockets. If all the years of hope for change in the world had come to nothing, if you were jinxed by the failure of the future, then the worst thing that could happen to you here was to run into somebody jinxed right along with yourself. They were losers of epic proportions.

The fellow turned his head, and, a yard apart, they were locked in a doomsday embrace.

"Been here long?" he asked, smiling dryly.

"Just got here."

"Just got here myself. Care for a drink?" Why was he asking this when his only wish was to escape?

Every time, before, when he'd sighted a comrade in this town, he'd put a distance between himself and the other. Now here they were in the casino's cocktail lounge, so close at a very small table they must look like a couple of comic conspirators.

"You ever see Mel?" the fellow asked.

"*Arise*, right? Last editor, right? Saw him eight, nine years ago. I thought I heard he died."

"That was Hank."

"That's right, it was Hank." Hank he could not remember at all. "You know who else died?"

"Who?"

He ventured a mix of his own name with his *Arise* byline. "Walt McGettigan."

"I guess I heard."

"Maybe it was Arnie Walters," he said, saving himself in the nick of time. He'd never known nor heard of an Arnie Walters.

"You mean Walters, sure," said the other. "Disease with a screwy name. Must've been ninety-nine. Said he knew Steinbeck."

It was coming: what in the past had particularized this man. The Paper Saver, saving every issue of *Arise*, piling them up in his garage, in his closets, in his basement if he had any. Not one issue unaccounted for. Star salesman, selling copies, one, two, three, or none, at factory gates, leaving them in depots, on cafe tables, on bus seats. Petitions, too. After his eight-hour job, and on weekends, too, he'd gone door-to-door with petitions in hand to save a black prisoner on death row in Georgia, Alabama, California. No one so trustworthy, so trusting. His eyes were still the eyes of the believer, and his name was what?

"Momentous times, right?" he said. "So how do you guys feel, now that everything fell apart?"

"Everything did not what you call fall apart." The fellow was already adamant. "It was forced apart. It was conspired against and bashed apart. It did not fall apart of itself."

"I won't argue that point with you," he said, wanting never to argue any point, anywhere, anytime. "I won't argue how much of one reason and how much of the other. The fact remains it's kaput."

"What is kaput? Define your terms."

"The Soviet Union is kaput."

"Lower your voice."

"There is no reason to lower your voice when you say the Soviet

Union. Everybody says it now. Why can't we talk so you can hear me? You ought to be a little deaf by now. You're my age, I'm a little deaf. You guys were always deaf to my input, anyway. I always liked to joke around, bring you some relief from the weight of the world on your heads. What I'm saying is, that's life. Everything goes kaput, whether it's pushed or of its own nature. Your role models, your marriage, your prostate."

"You must've been expelled."

"Expelled hell," he said. "I quit. Got out before the shit hit the fan. Don't ask me what shit, what fan."

"I'm wasting my time here."

"Wait," he said. "I haven't talked with anyone for years, so you can see how much I appreciate talking here with you. I meant to ask, do you still hoard all those copies of *Arise?*"

"I do."

"You ever think about renting a dumpster?"

"Why would I want to do that?"

"You got them in chronological order?"

"What do you think?"

"You ever refer?"

"Refer? The other day I was referring to the Cuban Missile Crisis. Sure I refer."

The man's faith was unbelievable. If faith was a curative of bodily ills, then all those copies of *Arise* might cure humanity. That's how he must have viewed that paper: a prescription nobody went and got filled.

"Fifty-two weeks a year," he said, taking his gambling tablet from his shirt pocket and writing down his calculations. "Multiply that by fifteen years and you've got yourself a Mount Everest of papers. Pick any day, any year, refer to anything, any event, even one that turned out all right, a triumph of justice. I'm saying you couldn't stand it. Seven hundred and eighty issues, whatever, informing you that your life was like a fart in the wind."

"What you're forgetting," the fellow said, "is the dialectics. When you take two steps forward, you got to take one step back."

"You got it wrong," he said. "It was one step forward and sixteen steps back, and your last step backwards lands you flat on your back in your grave."

His table companion was getting up. "I only got a couple days here, this trip. Got to get around." And the man was gone, ducking around the waitress coming to see if they desired more.

Alone again, he left the casino and entered the one across the street, putting that delayed distance between himself and the other. Caught up in the crowds, he wished for the crowds to absorb him completely and the fellow completely, so that neither would ever again glimpse the other, each lost among the many, pasts unknown.

At the nearest blackjack table he sat down and began the evening in earnest. His stratagems worn out by overuse, he lost and kept on losing. Unable to extricate himself from this engulfing wave of loss, he played on until rescued at last by a steadfast sanity that always hung around like a guard in charge of a lunatic let out for recreation. Rising abruptly, he sat down again at the next blackjack table. Here he connected with a wave of luck and, grimly surprised, remained in his chair until the wave left him for somebody else.

At 4:00 A.M. he stood up, eyes out of focus, and walked away, hearing the din again, full blast. The amount he'd lost at blackjack was nowhere near enough to drag him down into this eternal dimension, but here he was, in the midst of masses and masses of lost souls, each one plugging away at getting God's attention. *God, it's me here, it's me, now let me see what you've got for me, God.* He'd found himself in this dimension before, but not so fatally as this time.

Jostled along, unsteady on his feet, he looked forward to an early breakfast to restore his balance. Betting that the Paper Saver, avoiding him, had gone on to the farthest casino, he entered again the one where they'd met, sought out the most obscure booth in the restaurant, and lost his bet. The fellow sat way inside the bulging booth, eating fried eggs and hash browns.

With no greeting, he sat down opposite.

"I've got something to tell you," he said.

Suspicion in the fellow's eyes, like the membrane that comes up over a bird's eyes.

"Something's on my conscience," he said. "Neither you nor I want me to talk loud, but I'd be competing here with the general din. What I've got to tell you calls for some privacy. You got a room around here where we can talk?"

With a sideways nod the fellow got up, and together they made their way through the crowds to the elevators. In the ascending elevator the name of his companion came to him. Bertrand. The same name as that high-class, high-minded British philosopher. If that wasn't it, he'd think it was, anyway. It gave the fellow a breadth and a height beyond appearances.

The drapes were open. Only the vacant night sky out there, aglow and not from the stars. Bertrand locked the door, lit the lamps, and closed the drapes.

"We're ten stories up," he said. "You think J. Edgar Hoover is out there, looking in? The man died before we did, I assure you."

"I do things my way," said Bertrand. "Let's hear it."

"Sit down," he said. "I can't make it short." Someone, enraged by some loss, of a bet, of a woman, of his mind, had slashed the seat of the only chair, a desecration overlooked so far by the cleaning women. He swung the chair around for Bertrand.

Bertrand sat down. "Don't tell me, I know. You infiltrated. Named names for the FBI. So now your conscience hurts, except you guys got no conscience."

"That's too ordinary," he said. "Those guys chaired the meetings. I couldn't remember your name even if I wanted to. I used to see you around, that's all. I heard about your dedication, some friendly jokes about how you used to leave the paper in laundromats, like those evangelical pamphlets that tell you how one guy called on God and was rescued out of one hundred and twenty who perished. Then God set him up in a small business."

"*Arise*," said Bertrand, "was no God-help-me thing."

"What I'm saying is, you've got my respect. I need to talk and you're the one I want to hear me."

Bertrand waited, the blue wings at the sides of his jogger's shoes eager to bear him away.

"Name's Joe McGettigan," he said, "just to remind you that you must've read every word in my column. You've got some thoughts in your head that came right out of mine. So what I'm going to tell you now, you'll know is sane and reasonable."

"Get on with it."

"You've heard about what's called a state of denial," he said. "Most everybody's in it, some all the time, others part of the time. It comes over me when I come here. What I say to myself is that I'm here for the pleasure of it. It's a recreational addiction, one of those. Tonight I acknowledged what it's all about. We come into this desert to find God."

Bertrand was already highly annoyed. "My father was a raving preacher, used to whip me with his razor strop, bare ass. I read about a minister's son going on a murder spree, six people across two states. So I left home at an early age to save my moral sense. I buried that strop in a little cemetery in Kansas, just outside Topeka. Left a note under a rock. Went, Here lies God. Slain by my own hand. Try and find me."

"Calm down," he said. "We always thought we knew what everybody was thinking. This time you don't know yet. This God I'm telling you about is not the one you buried back in Kansas. My son, he's ten, very bright kid, keeps me up on the latest thinking in that direction. He tells me a lot of physicists are into God now. I'm a working stiff myself, what do I know, but I got a sense of what he's talking about. Just the other day he told me about a professor he heard about, a physicist, who discovered what electricity is. We think electricity is electricity and that's all we need to know. But one day this fellow found out just what it *is*, and he runs out onto the campus, sobbing. Sobbing. My son was impressed by that story, of course. I never inquire into his religious beliefs, I know he's got some, but that discovery was such a tremendous one he said to me, 'Joe,' he calls me Joe. 'Do you think maybe the answer has something to do with God? Do you think maybe it's God's breath?'"

"*Whose* breath? *God's* breath?"

Bertrand was up.

Nimble of foot as he was nimble of mind, he barred Bertrand's way to the door. "Give it some thought. When you think about these forces we're talking about, like electricity, like magnetism, like what is gravity, you have to start thinking that money is also a force. Same sort. You don't see *them*, you just see their effects. Take the stock market. You feel its force in there, moving through space, knocking people around, but do you see *it*? When you think about the billions the defense industry scored on the Cold War, did you see it? What you saw was all the smashing it can do if you were watching that Persian Gulf business. Yesterday, if my son had asked me, 'What's money, Joe?' I'd have said, 'Money's money. Study the *Wall Street Journal*.' You know what I'd tell him now? I'd tell him that tonight I made this tremendous discovery. I'd tell him that money is God's circulatory system."

"Out of my way."

"Wait," he said. "Wait. What I'm getting at is this confession and I'm confessing for both of us. You and I come to this place with a purpose in mind we both deny. We come here to undermine ourselves, we come here to subvert our hopes for the human race. We come here to see what we're up against. Same thing Jesus was up against. The greatest gambler who ever lived, staked his life on a whole different kind of world. Went around telling everybody how much his father loved him. Gambled on that and lost."

"You went crazy," said Bertrand. "I should've said I didn't know you."

Opening the door, he stepped aside for Bertrand. "You go East and I'll go West, or I'll go East and you go West. The choice is yours."

Without another word they went out into the corridor. Three, four couples, the kind who enjoy themselves despite their age, or because of it, and more so in like company, were crowding into the elevator. Loudly, generously, paunches and bosoms jostling similar ones, they made room for the two thin, somberly silent men who must seem to belong to a whole other species.

Out in the street again, alone again, he was assaulted by real time, by the dawn. Finding his way to his motel through the throngs arriving and departing under the brightening sky, he apologized to Bertrand for his performance that made the man seem a child. It was the way he entertained his kids, caricaturing theorists of all kinds, so they'd not grow up to be idolators. When he got home he'd tell his son about his mind-blowing discovery, what money really was, and his boy would be rolling on the floor, laughing and howling.

Lying on his bed in his underwear, he passed into the only dark available within the unmercifully vast light of a desert morning, and just as desperately came awake, knocking the flimsy bedside lamp to the floor, wanting up from this bed lain in by fifty thousand strangers, some dead now, fallen down dead in the casinos or here where he lay or after they got home, everything too much of a shock, the winning and the losing. All their lives, the winning and the losing.

Struggling with his clothes and with sleep, he got dressed in dumb haste, not glancing at his watch to see what time it was, whether still dawn or night again, wanting to catch the next plane out, wanting out forever from this place where all was lost.

The Island
of Ven

"*E*leanor, listen to this: *In the evening after sunset, when according to my habit I was contemplating the stars in a clear sky, I noticed that a new and unusual star, surpassing all others in brilliancy, was shining almost directly above my head, and since I had, from boyhood, known all the stars in the heavens perfectly, it was quite evident to me that there had never before been any star in that place in the sky. A miracle indeed!* Eleanor, you know what it was? A colossal stellar explosion, a supernova. But back then they thought the heavens were changeless, and so there's young Tycho Brahe gazing up at the new star one calm evening and he figures it's a miracle. No telescopes yet and he didn't need one. Even when the sun came up he could see it."

Noel read quietly, a lodger respectful of the hour of midnight in this foreign city and of the little family who had rented out a room on this night of the tourist season when all hotels were filled, and who were asleep somewhere in the dark apartment. Like a tour guide whose memory wasn't equal to the task, he was sitting up in bed, reading over salient points from his colorful book on European astronomers. A tour guide, but hers alone.

The beds were single, and he had pushed them together so he could take her in his arms and comfort her in the night, though she never asked for comforting. She lay with her hands under her cheek, palms together, watching his profile as he read, and loving him almost reverently, yet at a distance from him, as though she loved him only in memory; and at a distance from their son beyond the actual miles, wherever he was on his own journey; and at the farthest distance from their daughter, Nana, a distance never to be comprehended, even as the child's sixteen years of life had become a mystification of the mother.

"Listen, sounds like he went 'round the bend: *The star was at first like Venus, giving pleasing effects, but as it then became like Mars there will come a period of wars, captivity and death of princes, together with fiery meteors in the air, pestilence and venomous snakes. Lastly, the star became like Saturn, and there will finally come a time of want, death, imprisonment, and all sorts of sad things.* Sounds like he freaked out. Imagine Einstein writing all that in his journal?"

She saw him as he must have been when he was a boy, six, seven, adjusting the telescope an uncle had given him, bringing a star down close to his backyard for the first time, convinced then, he had told her, that the sound of crickets all around in the summer night was really the music the stars were making. On so many nights of their years together, when he sat late over his work and she heard him go out into the garden to gaze at the stars, she wondered if he were seeing all things again as indivisible, or trying to or not trying anymore. The measuring of vast distances, incredible velocities—it was this that enthralled him. At parties, when the guests wandered out into a patio, a garden, lifting their faces to a placid moon, he would gently remind them of something they may have neglected to remember, that those far lights and all the galaxies were racing away from the earth and from one another. *The farther the distance from us, the faster they're leaving us behind. Imagine four hundred million miles an hour?* And they would smile complyingly as over a joke on them all.

His face was softened by the lamplight, and she saw again how Nana had resembled him, and felt again the same mute alarm that, back home, drew her up from the bed in the middle of the night, alone as if she had no husband nor ever had children nor even parents to begin. This journey was his offering of love, a healing quest. By visiting together the places where the early astronomers had lived, the narrow Golden Street in Prague, a castle in Italy from where one had viewed the heavens, he hoped to humanize them for her. They, too, had suffered afflictions of the soul, yet despite their earthly trials they had never turned their eyes away from that marvelous beckoning up there.

The lamp was switched off. Darkness now in this room in a stranger's house, this night and one more night when they returned from their day's trip to the island. Noel bent over her and kissed her face, imperceptibly, as you kiss a sleeping person lost in the self. She said, "I'm awake," and he took her in his arms. Branches stirred close to the small, high window, and distant sounds from the Tivoli Gardens—fireworks and music— trembled against the glass. She lay very still, keeping down her alarm. Any movement, no matter how small, might wake the little family, like a cry from out of her sleep.

By boat from Copenhagen to the town of Landskrona, on the Swedish coast. Old brick buildings, factories blowing out sulphurous smoke. And now by a tough little boat, its yellow smokestack the only touch of color on the heavily gray Baltic Sea, or a slender finger of that sea, but so wide both shores were lost to view. A sea she had never thought about or ever wished to cross. They had climbed up from the hold to stand on deck. She had felt confined down there, under false protection from the wind-driven swells the boat was striking against. The other passengers, Swedes, Danes, seemed content down there on hard benches, in company of their bicycles and crates of beer and fruit. Like a willing patient wanting to believe in a cure, she kept her gaze straight ahead to see the island the moment it came in sight.

She must have blinked, she must have glanced away. The island had risen suddenly. The stark look of it from afar gave her an imagined view of tremendous rocks under the water, close below the boat. An island precariously small, leveled down eons ago by fierce winds and sweeping torrents and monstrous waves, until water and wind calmed down and lay back. The inhabitants now, how did they feel about it? *Stay calm*, they must tell themselves to stay calm, and if the waters began to rise again and the winds to stir again, some exquisite instrument, designed by a mind like Noel's, would detect the slightest threat in the depths of the sea and in the atmosphere, and everyone would be warned to jump on their bicycles and pedal away to the nearest church, which, since it was already four, five hundred years old, was to last forever.

A harbor town for the trusting. Their houses, gardens, fences, trees, all on the very edge of deep gray waters, their little sailboats pleasantly rocking as if upon a transparent azure sea. The boat was moored, the passengers walked their bicycles up the rise and rode off past an approaching wagon drawn by two tawny horses and followed by two men walking leisurely. The horses stopped, the passengers climbed down. Except a little boy and his mother, the boy asleep on the blue wooden bench, his head in his mother's lap, tiny purple flowers clinging to the edge of his jacket pocket. The visor of his cap was tipped back, baring his face to the sky. He opened his eyes and, surprised by the sky, closed them again, and Eleanor, watching, pictured his face growing older each day to come, each night to come, less and less surprised by the sky. Carefully, mother and child climbed down.

"Tycho Brahe's museum?" Noel's voice always sharply friendly in a foreign land.

The driver, up on his high seat, appeared to nod.

The wagon joggled along the road that must be in the very center of the island, like a spine, and Noel sat very erect. The pale sun was turning his light hair to silver, a swift aging he didn't know about. Some of the gray of the sea was taken up and spread in a high, flat film over the sky, and the shadow of it crept over the land, over the fields the same tawny color of the horses, and over green meadows and their few black cattle, and over the thatched roofs of cottages and barns. Roofs like that in a picture she had painted, years ago. Nana, in her small chair by her mother's chair, had watched the picture come to life, sooner for her than for all the other children who were to see it later in an opened book: under an indigo sky dotted with white stars, a small cottage, and a cricket in the nightgreen stalks of grass. Unlike that painting years ago, these roofs could be overrun with rivers of fire.

The horses were halted. The driver waited for someone to climb down. Nobody did. "Tycho Brahe," he said to the air.

Noel leaped down and helped her down, and the horses clopped on.

No bicycle, no wagon appeared along the road from either horizon. The silence must be the presence of the sea, unseen but all around, a silence not to be trusted. Across the road, a deserted Turistgarden, white slat tables and chairs under trees, and, farther back, a yellow-brick hotel strung with colored lightbulbs. On their side of the empty road, a red-brick church with a slate roof, with pink roses in the yard, and, back along the road a few steps, the Tycho Brahe Museet. Closed, so small it must contain only a few precious books, a few drawings.

Giant mulberry trees towered over the little museum, and there, under the trees, a tall stone statue. The Astronomer.

"It's him!" Noel hurried toward it, as though the statue was the man himself, about to flee.

She found him roaming around the statue, gazing up with scholarly respect and peering down at the indecipherable inscription carved along the base. Almost twice as tall as any man, the Astronomer wore a ruff around his neck, a cloak that hung way down to the soles of his boots, knickers of many stony folds, and down at his side he held a quadrant. His head thrown back, he was scanning the heavens, his goatee pointing at the large shallow bowl of earth where his observatory had been. Out in the fields behind the Astronomer, a farmer was burning chaff, and the long, long ribbon of smoke stayed close to the ground. A tractor started up, and a frightened rabbit bounded along before it.

Noel took her hand and led her down the slope of the wide grassy bowl, and they stood within the lost observatory, within the Castle of the Heavens, as fancifully, as airily beautiful as castles that are only imagined. Every stone gone, carried away by the peasants, nothing left, and, where the foundation had been, now filled with five centuries of earth. A toad at her feet stayed where it was, unafraid of large, slow animals. Up there at the top of the castle in the night, how did the Astronomer look to a boy on the highest branch, straining his neck to see? Was he plotting an invasion of the heavens? Was he a predator on the trail of one of those heavenly creatures formed of stars? Night after night, did the peasants lie awake, expecting avenging angels to come swooping down?

"Eleanor, are you hungry? Are you thirsty?"

They sat down by the toad, and Noel brought up from his knapsack a bottle of mineral water, cheese, bread, sweet crackers, raisins, and chocolates.

"If you eat this raisin, all my wishes will come true." He kissed her temple.

She took the raisin on her lip and swallowed it. All his wishes, she knew, were for her recovery and hers were not. With jokes, with conundrums, he hoped to take her back to that spirited time at the beginning of their future together. A young couple again, picnicking on the spot from where a universe had flowered.

Along the road, in search of the Astronomer's underground observatory, Noel's light boots stirring up puffs of dust, her sandals stirring up none. She had got so thin, her bare legs, so thin, were a warning to her. The winds, Noel was saying, had buffeted the castle, interfering with the precision of observations, and so the Astronomer had taken his instruments underground. And what did the people think of *that*, she wondered. What did they think when they saw him walking along this very road at night, wrapped in his long cloak, his gleamy, gloomy eyes always upward, at his side a servant with a lantern, cautioning him about his step. Did they think he was hiding from the wrath of God? That all would perish but not him? That when he poked his nose out of his underground refuge, that silver nose that replaced his own lost in a duel, it would not melt, it would only turn gold, reflecting the unearthly, revenging fire?

Off to the side of the road, children were running about within a fantasy circle no larger than their own yard, a playground of copper objects in the geometrical shapes of a dome, a tent, a cone, upon a carpet of short, dry grass.

"Come look," Noel said, and she stepped into the circle.

Skylights, these copper forms were the Astronomer's skylights that he had opened to the night's panorama, segment by segment. Scales of green-blue patina covered them, and hinges hung loose. The little girl slid down the slanting copper lid over the entrance door, and the two boys followed after, all shouting dares, their voices ringing far on the still air. Then on they went, circling the skylights.

Noel opened a section of the dome, and the children came up beside them, the little girl pressing close to her. Seven feet or so down to the earth floor, to rocks and bottles and rainwater. While Noel and the children looked down, while the children shuffled their black leather sabots, and a rooster crowed nearby, she gazed at the girl's blond hair, how silky, how shiningly new under the sky. The little girl was the first to laugh, a mocking titter, and the boys took it up, roughly. They already knew there was nothing down there.

Out on the sea again, the waters darker, films of rain in the distance, the island sliding under. Through heavy dusk, the boat approached Landskrona, and, from far, she mistook the trees of the town for black piles of iron ore.

They sat in a dimly lit waiting station, on a bench against the wall. She was thinking that there was an everywhere that Noel and the others could never measure, even with their perfect and indisputable instruments, even with the finest device of all which was their minds, and this everywhere, always beyond them, was grief and was what inconsolable meant. She was thinking that someone, somewhere in the world, goes out into that everywhere and never comes back. Noel touched her knee, bringing her back.

Yellow lights, white lights were moving toward them through the murky night, along with the hushing presence of a large boat bound for Copenhagen. She wanted to stay up on the deck, in a sheltered place, watching for shore lights. Noel said it was too cold up there, but he wouldn't go down into the salon unless she came with him. She went down, then, into the rousing noise of drinkers at every table and the portable organ's music, pounded out by a young man in suit and tie. Glasses were everywhere on red tablecloths, gliding on spilled beer. A woman was dancing alone among the dancing couples, her eyes closed, the flesh of her lifted arms swaying.

Noel found places for them at a long table near the entrance. She sat down next to a handsome old man in a dark suit, and a dancing restlessness in his legs brought his heavy shoe against her sandaled foot. Unaware of her presence until then, he looked at her and apologized. Then he looked at her longer, trying to see if he knew her, if she had left her place for a while and now had come back and was beside him again.

Noel, leaning across her, asked him where the boat was from.

An excursion boat, he said, leaving Copenhagen in the morning and returning at night, and the whole day's pleasure was evident on his rosy face, a look that was perfectly at home and that might have been there the first day of his life.

"American?" he asked Noel.

Noel nodded.

"Did you come by flying machine?"

She nodded, looking into his face and imagining him as a boy, out in the night, his eyes lifted to a moving light lower than the stars, an amazing machine that flew through the air and filled the dome of the sky with an echoing roar. An event as much of a miracle as the Astronomer's star.

"We went to Tycho Brahe's island," she said.

"Ah, yes," he said. "A tourist garden is there. My sister was there for the honeymoon."

"One night," she told him, "he saw an immense star that wasn't there before. He said it meant the death of princes, all sorts of sad things. He believed, you see, that our destiny is in the stars."

He was amused by her, she could see. He must hear this kind of talk from strangers in taverns, fellow passengers aboard excursion boats, their need to be intimately serious rising fast like the foam on their beers.

"Yourself," she said, "do you believe that?"

"Ah, yes. Yes."

They held each other's gaze, the way she'd seen strangers do in a public place like this, people caught up in a surprising kinship sparked by the closeness of bodies. Strongly old, this man. How many beloved faces had he gazed into just as he was gazing into hers? The other faces gone, each one, while he lived on and on. A time to be born and a time to die. Wasn't that the only way to accept their going? Wasn't that the portent in every star in the sky and in every sky that ever was? He must know this, and know it by heart.

An uproar, louder shouts, louder music, everyone cheering on a young man who had leaped to a tabletop and was dancing up there.

In the taxi to their tranquil street of trees, Noel was silent, wondering, she knew, if she had gone over the edge, if she had given over her mind to the Astronomer's superstitious one.

A lamp was on in the hall, for them. The little family was asleep. When he lay down in his separate bed, he leaned over her and brushed the wisps of hair from her forehead, hoping to clear her mind by clearing her brow. She lifted her arms, and, holding him, a picture of the Astronomer composed itself for her eyes and for her hand someday: up in his observatory, the young Brahe, his face lifted to that brilliancy, to that inescapable portent, its reflection floating in his eyes, and in the gems on his plump fingers, and in the waters of a fountain, and on every leaf turned toward the heavens.

Lives of
the Saints

*W*hen Milo Jukovich was nineteen he introduced himself to his father. The encounter took place at the unveiling of his father's *Three Angels* on the steps of the loftiest cathedral in Los Angeles, before the archbishop, film celebrities, the mayor, and a back row of priests. Spectators, massed on the sidewalk and street, were also witness to the sculptor's alarm at the approach of this finely handsome youth in a dark suit, esthetically tieless, a slender young man who evoked the sculptor himself as he may have been at that age, climbing the stone steps to his present self. The ceremony was over, the television cameras departing, the participants chatting in the shadow of the *Angels*, when Milo confronted his father.

Bowing his head in awe and fear, smiling with trembling lips, he said, "I wonder if you recognize me. I'm Milo, your son."

Juri Jukovich leaped away. He leaped backwards, bumping into the archbishop, and that esteemed person's vestments, lifted on the wind, partially concealed the artist as he paused there behind the heavier man to take a long, piercing look at the stranger who was claiming a relationship not less sacredly binding than that of mother and child. Then he fled into the dim and glowing interior of the cathedral.

Alicia, Milo's mother, had been Juri's one and only wife, and when their brief union ended—while their child was still in the womb—the sculptor declared publicly that he had never lain with a woman, that at the age of twelve he had vowed to remain celibate and was still so at forty-four. The several women who always claimed loudly, in cafés and in other artists' beds, to have been his mistresses were all invalidated. Shortly before his son's birth, his chisel struck the first block of marble from which a saint was to emerge, the *Santa Clara*, and his ardent devotion to his Saints Series was cited by one prominent critic as proof of the artist's chastity.

Alicia herself blamed Juri's extreme jealousy for the end of the marriage and disavowal of his only son. A beautiful girl, her long dark hair bound up with narrow satin ribbons, she was eighteen when they met at a welcome party for Jukovich, who, already famous, had come out from New York and with his own hands was building himself an adobe studio on the highest accessible mountain in Santa Barbara. All evening he kept his distance from her, never spoke to her and never let her out of his sight, as if her very presence threatened him with irreparable harm. But the next day he knocked at her door, his arms and his pockets filled with wild lupines, poppies, and rattler grass.

They were married soon after.

When Alicia told him she was pregnant, Juri begged her not to allow a child to disturb their sublime union. She refused to consider the ways and means of denying birth to the child within her and fled to Yugoslavia, Jukovich's birthplace, where Milo, too, was born, in Dubrovnik. On her return to America she settled in San Diego, her own birthplace, and wrote to Juri, inviting him to come meet his son. Juri wrote back only to deny his paternity, and she sued for divorce. All this Milo was told at a very early age, and, though he could not understand it yet, he sensed the implications of it for him just by the way she held his gaze.

Unlike Jukovich, the man his mother married when Milo was four loved generously. An impresario, he was the bosom friend of singers, acrobats, musicians. Milo, wakened in the night by a man's voice tenderly singing, soft-footed his way to the study door and from there watched his mother's husband wandering the room alone, a glass of wine in one hand, a slice of panettone in the other, singing between sips and bites. At times, Milo felt that he would like to love this man.

Alicia and Milo clipped pictures of Jukovich from magazines and newspapers, most of them of the artist beside a saint sculpture larger by far than the man himself. So Milo observed with growing fear the change in his mother's contours after she explained to him that his stepfather and herself had created another person. He suffered nightmares about a monster boy far larger than other boys' brothers, and the fact that the boy was to be a half-brother caused him more trouble, not less. After that first half-brother was born, another half-brother came along, and then a half-sister, and Milo withdrew further and further at each birth, despite favors and kisses showered upon him by the mother and father of the other children.

At twelve Milo began violin lessons. He rode the bus once a week to his teacher's studio and often, on the way back, got off the bus partway to transfer to another bus that took him to a park where his father's *San Diego* stood within a circle of treasured trees. Hidden behind a tree like a spy, he watched closely for holy vibrations, saw none and felt none. His father had created an ugly chunk of brownish stone with purple blotches, its face ridiculously small for the rest of it, but would never admit he'd created a living and breathing son, better looking by far than this thing called a saint. If your father was just an ordinary father and told everybody he had no son, people would call him a liar. But if your father was famous for all the saints he was making and said he had no son, then he had no son, period. Milo, distressed, wandered the park until dark and, returning home late every time, was always gratified to see his mother looking worried.

At the university he chose to major in art history, enrolling in the summer session. Since he was not a participant in human time—his birth unacknowledged by his father—he felt his own time was lost time and he studied relentlessly, hoping to catch up with everyone else. Girls hung around, for he was mature, eloquent, and scholarly, but his time was spent poring over art books in libraries and examining every sculpture and painting in museums and galleries.

Curious about his name, the students sent one among them to approach the subject. "You've heard the scuttlebutt about Jukovich?" the fellow asked, falling into step with Milo. "They say he had a son who died at birth, and he got this fixation he was being punished for making out with a woman. Worse, a married woman. So he decided he was finished with that part of himself. Tragic."

"It's true he had a son," Milo said, "but I never died."

Not breaking his stride, Milo turned his head to see the effect of this. Awe. The student was in awe of him, as though Milo had just appeared on earth at that moment, fully formed.

It was then that Milo approached his father, having seen in the eyes of the prying student the terrific effect of his own presence on the world. But Jukovich's denial of his son, so publicly at the unveiling ceremony, was ruinous.

Milo writhed in his bed all night, burning with humiliation. For days he lay wrapped in blankets. The only food he could stomach was warm milk with bread pieces in a bowl, and this his mother brought him, always with a kiss for his brow. When he was able to sit up, he began a critique of the art of Juri Jukovich. Late into the night he wrote, examining with excruciating insight the artist's Saints Series. He pointed out the absence of faith and fervency in the figures, comparing them with sculptures of other renowned contemporaries, as, for example, the work of Henry Moore. The figures of that artist communicated with the universe, as did the Easter Island faces, as did Giacometti's minuscule and elongated figures, drawn out on the rack of cosmic anxiety, distillations of that artist's staring need to believe in something more than nothing. As for Jukovich's saints, they were born good children who never cried and who grew up unafflicted by doubts, their huge size a reward for obeying their parents and eating everything on their plate. They were unrelated to the emaciated saints on Byzantine frescoes in the monasteries of Cappadocia and Greece, their faces tormented by temptations, their hair years long, hanging to the ground. Often, in the still of the night, Milo laughed out loud at his own pedantry and presumptions, and more than the critique itself his laughter helped to heal him.

Signing the critique with a pseudonym, he mailed it to the university periodical. When a suspicious fellow student, periodical in hand, sat down at Milo's table in the café and asked him if he'd written the essay, Milo raised his eyes, so purely honest they left no doubt about the eyes as windows of the soul. "I figure it's the work of some shithead, some ignoramus, somebody holier than thou. One of those," he said. "A nobody."

Alicia was a woman of boundless compassion, always ready to grant understanding to the misunderstood, and when Milo gave her a copy of the periodical, without comment, the author of the Jukovich critique was kindly counted in among the benighted. She said he was probably a sadly envious young man, an iconoclast, a misfit. Then Milo wished he had never even learned the alphabet. With this attempt to bring down his father he had only revealed his own evil nature.

The next day in anatomy lab, leafing through the catalogue of a cat supplier, he was dismayed by photos of the warehouse interior with shelf upon shelf of cat cadavers. His mother was very fond of cats, and two or three were always asleep on his bed. Any day now a dead cat would be set before him. Then he felt that he himself would someday be as anonymously dead as these cats, each one's unique personality eventually forgotten by those who had named them and perhaps had loved them. Alone in the lab he bowed his head to the black counter, vowing never to betray again his kinship with all abandoned creatures.

On foot, with bedroll and pack on his back, Milo set out on his pilgrimage, wanting to find in each of Jukovich's saints that same love for all creatures of the earth who were abandoned or thought they were. If he were to gaze long enough at each saint, he might find himself bathed in emanations of love and his existence prized beyond measure. Tucked in his breast pocket was the little book *Guide to the Jukovich Saints*, a publication of the California Tourist Bureau. His mother, as usual up earlier than the others, kissed him and adjusted his backpack, and he walked out into a summer that was to become the hottest on record for the entire state.

After trudging Highway 5 north for two hours, he was picked up by a couple his own age. He sat in the back seat with a huge dog whose gagging odor mingled with the heady fragrance of the joint the couple was smoking and of every joint they had ever smoked in that rattling car. They offered to share with Milo but he told them he hoped to alter his view of existence by other means. He told them he was the son of Juri Jukovich and on a pilgrimage to every one of his father's saints, and they told him that the *San Francisco* was located in the rose garden in Golden Gate Park, and if he ever made it up there he could crash at their house. He knew that the sculpture overlooked the Bridge, at a great height, but he did not correct them, for courtesy's sake. The girl turned around often to gaze into his eyes, a gaze he took for seductive longing, until he began to wonder if her face was reflecting a spiritual longing on his own face, an expression he was pleased to learn about. They left him off in San Clemente. No ride after that one was to be so pleasant.

The *San Clemente—aluminum, 8 ft.* stood on the beach, affixed to a concrete base, unshakable by whatever storms might come sweeping in off the Pacific. Milo, reluctant to remove the beach towels drying over its head, sat down to wait. A girl in the scarcest bikini he had ever seen sat down beside him. She asked him why he was sitting there with all his clothes on, and he told her he had come there not to hang out and enjoy the beach but to admire his father's sculpture, above them. She said he was wrong, that it was not a sculpture but a state-of-the-art sewage disposal plant and that's all it was. She wandered off and toward evening the owners of the towels took them away. Then the face of the saint reflected the sunset clouds ablaze over the entire sky, and figuring this reflection was evidence of the spirit inherent in the sculpture, Milo lay down to sleep at its feet. Lovers around him in the warm dark kept him awake, but at last the sand cooled, the lovers left, and he slept. When he awoke he found himself within a vast, dense fog, and now he saw that the saint was desecrated by obscenities scratched over its surface. Cold and saddened, he gathered up his belongings and made his way out from the fog.

The *San Pedro—lindenwood, 7 ft.* graced the roof of the harbormaster's office. Painted, it resembled the figures at the prows of old sailing ships. Gazing at it from the pilings among the private yachts, he saw Jukovich's intentions. With face set serenely forward, with hand over its thrusting heart, this saint could be counted on to guide you through the chaotic, dark night of the soul, just as the old carven figureheads had carried voyagers over tumultuous seas to shore. Closer, he saw that the paint, once deeply luminous, gemlike, was scaling off, fading, so that the face resembled that of a blind leper. He wondered then if the artist had intended this disintegration in order to affirm the spirit of universal love in beings considered loathsome, or who were pariahs, or who ought never to have been born. Seagulls had left a redemptive white mantle over the figure.

The *Santa Catalina—buff marble, 9 ft.* was situated, he read, atop that island's Blackjack Mountain. Yachtsmen, engrossed in polishing and varnishing, failed to hear him ask if they were bound for the island. Others, hoisting sail, seemed anxious to leave him behind—a space case, unshaven, his clothes evidently slept in. At last one lean and aristocratic yachtsman—white pants, white deck shoes, white polo shirt—told him to hop aboard, and where did he wish to go?

The wind died down as they were making their way out of the harbor, and Milo's benefactor discovered that the engine would not work without fuel. While frighteningly large container ships loomed past the becalmed sloop, the man became abusively drunk. After several staggering attempts on Milo's life with an iron spike and a galley knife, the man fell down on the deck, beyond reviving. Wind filled the sails at that point, and Milo piloted the boat safely across the channel.

Dawn was already breaking when he touched the island, and so he set out to climb the mountain before the day got too hot. He climbed to the top and then beat the bushes all day under the merciless sun. The *Santa Catalina* must have been stolen. Exhausted from the previous night's ordeal and the day's futile search, Milo lay down to sleep on the base of the missing saint. So far, whatever Jukovich had hoped to reveal in his hulks of marble and wood and metal wasn't evident yet to his son's eyes and heart. All that he knew for certain was that his bones ached, his jaw moaned where the iron spike had skidded by, his eyes burned, and the soles of his feet were molten lead. Then the moon rose.

The moon rose, a full moon so unexpected, so filled with its own intentions, it was the most alarming thing he'd ever seen. Unable to take his eyes away, he watched every inch of its slow and unimpeded glide. Until he saw that while he was watching the moon itself, it had immersed the mountain in a sea of moonlight, slipping into the weave of his thin blan-ket and bringing forth little silver threads to rise and sway en masse, as it did the silver hairs on his arms and hands. Small white spiders sprayed over him and a silver raccoon drifted by, while a nightbird went on and on with its long, involved story, almost desperately, because the same moon might never come by again and the bird had a lot pent up in its breast. The spirit of everything alive was amove in the moonlight, of everything that had ever been born and of everything coming up alive in the future. At the peak of it all Milo wondered if he were feeling what the buff mar-ble saint would have felt if she weren't missing.

Some of the Jukovich saints were commissioned by the cities that bore their names, others by public utilities and oil corporations and banks, and still others by philanthropists. Controversy erupted over one, the *San Bernardino,* when a reigning philanthropist there donated it to the city, suggesting the steps of the city hall. A referendum was called for by op-ponents, and the majority of residents voted against the emplacement of a sectarian object on civic property. Art Lovers, a group of artists, interior decorators, actors, and architects, trucked the sculpture out to a site in the San Bernardino mountain range, visible from Highway 15. *Gray granite, 12 ft.,* it blended so well with the boulders that Milo, on foot, passed it by.

Almost felled by the heat of those desert mountains, dazed, Milo wandered into the Cucamonga Wilderness area. A helicopter on surveil-lance from the Marine Corps Training Center dropped down and hauled him aboard. Since he was so darkened by the sun, and his hair, unwashed for so long, had turned black, he was mistaken for a terrorist. They searched his backpack and his person, and relayed his description to Ed-wards Air Force Base, the Naval Weapons Center Mojave Range, and Fort Irwin Military Reservation, all within that inhospitable region.

As the helicopter hovered above what appeared to be a stone curiously shaped like a man, Milo recognized the saint.

"That's my father's *San Bernardino!*" he cried, pointing.

The sergeant assured the crew that Jukovich was not a name from the Middle East, though he didn't know where it was from. He released Milo, setting him down on Highway 15 again. The crew waved good-bye and Milo waved back until the helicopter disappeared into the devastating waves of desert heat.

On the road again he was picked up by a black car resembling a huge shark with sinister fins. From a seat in the commodious interior which was filled with several electric guitars and sound equipment, he thanked the two men by praising them.

"What's this car?"

"Where you been? This here's a 'fifty-nine Eldorado hearse."

Slumped down in repose, neither man turned around. The hair of the musician at the wheel was a burning bush, so massive it obscured Milo's view of the road ahead. Leaping from stereo speakers underfoot and overhead, hard rock struck at all parts of Milo's body before escaping through the open windows. Despite this assault, Milo fell asleep.

At San Luis Obispo he woke in a panic, afraid he had missed some saints. The musicians got out with him to stretch their legs, and he saw that their legs, in black leather pants, were extremely thin and so were their bodies. Coke heads. Seeing, then, that his own legs and body were even thinner than theirs, he wondered how to explain, as facilely, his own condition.

The *San Luis Obispo—black granite + stainless steel, 7 ft.* stood in an industrial park in company of a few straggly trees, erected there by a chemical corporation whose trucks roared around it. Milo sat on the employees' bench before the sculpture. The chemicals in the air had pocked the granite and stained the steel. Furthermore, it was only a block with a round steel head bent way down between its chunks of feet. All day he sat on the bench in staring search of the spirit of love somewhere within that figure, whose deterioration was certainly not the artist's fault. This saint lacked any and all redeeming qualities, rousing in Milo a desire to dissociate himself from the artist.

At nightfall Milo tore up his identification—his driver's license, his university card, his credit cards. As he was depositing the handful of scraps in the brimming trash can, he was arrested for vagrancy. At the police station, when it was made clear to him that by obstinately refusing to tell them his name and residence he could be charged with any number of crimes, from misdemeanors to felonies, he gave in. The police called his mother and she verified him. After that, they proved to themselves that there was no crime committed anywhere in the whole country for which a Milo Jukovich was wanted by the law, and only then was he released from the longest night of his life.

One morning, as he was making his way down from the Santa Cruz Mountains to the city of the same name and the sculpture there, which he hoped was to make up for all the others found wanting, he paused at an extinct one-pump gas station to fill his canteen and douse his hair and face. When he stepped onto the porch of the very small grocery to thank the proprietor for the water, his attention was caught by the morning newspapers in their rack. Not the headlines. Something else was signaling him: JUKOVICH DIES IN EGYPT.

Struck in the eyes by the rising sun, he had a difficult time reading the particulars. Jukovich, he read, was dead from a heart attack while exploring caves in the Egyptian desert where the early Christian saints dwelled. The artist, he read, was on the last lap of a pilgrimage to the world's sacred places, among them Kyoto, Mecca, and the highest Buddhist monasteries in Tibet. Jukovich had devoted his life to his Saints Series, hailed by critics as the most uncompromisingly religious art since the twelfth century. An ascetic, he often fasted. His only marriage was brief, childless, and ended in divorce. The last photo of Jukovich, taken shortly before his departure, accompanied the front-page item. Milo leaned away from it, avoiding his father's eyes though Jukovich was not facing the camera. The artist was standing beside his most recent sculpture, a rose marble *Santa Rosa*. He wore only a loincloth and sandals. The muscles were bunched up on his bony legs, and his brow, also bony, was crossed by a rolled bandanna.

The girl in charge of the grocery was studying a physics textbook at the counter, eating an apple and combing her hair, obviously about ready to go down to her classes at the university.

"My father just died," he said, smiling over his whole sun-blackened face, his tears mingling with water already there from the dousing. Shocked by his smile, he saw that she was not.

"Did he leave you a fortune?" she asked.

"He left *me*," he said.

Out in the sun again, he climbed a low hill to the oak at the top and walked around the trunk a few times, under a restless, shadowy flock of vultures up in the branches. Juri Jukovich was gone, leaving his son incontrovertibly alive, ecstatically alive, born for the first time in his life. Jukovich had taken the gift of life meant for his son and given it to his outsize saints, instead, and on whom it hadn't worked. Contrary to that old saw about art being long and life short, it was the other way around. He lay facedown under the tree and bit off some grass near the roots, chewing to distract his smile, but it would not give in, and so he lay there the entire day, smiling into the earth.

Stolen Pleasures

*E*very house had a palm tree and a lawn, and some had a piano inside, a dark, sternly upright object in its own realm called the living room. Delia and her family had no piano and therefore no living room. Living, their kind, went on everywhere in their house, smaller than the other houses and closer to the alley. It was the piano that made a room into a living room, because the piano, she figured, promised the children of the family happy lives to come if only they'd learn to play it.

The piano, a huge, flat, forbidding face, until her best friend, Ellsworth, across the alley, sat down before it, lifted the long upper lip, baring the long rows of black and yellow teeth clamped together in an unsightly grin, and with nervous fingers picked out cajoling sounds that meant *Please, piano, piano, open up a happy future for me, for me, piano, please, for me, for me.*

Inside, where you couldn't see what was going on, a lot of little hammers were beating on strings. A hidden cruelty in there, it seemed to Delia, slumped down on the floor in a corner, chewing on the untied strings at the neck of her soiled dress. Without a piano, were her parents doubtful of her and her sister's future? Would they die while children? That very year, while Delia was seven, she was struck by a car, and her hair had to be cut short and away from the wound that became a scar the size of a silver dollar behind her ear, and that very year, her sister, Fleur, fourteen, came down with scarlet fever, and Delia spent gentle hours in bed with her, peeling away the shedding skin. Could they both have died that very year because they had no piano? While Ellsworth's small fingers begged the piano for a future happier than hers, she picked grass off her bare, dirty feet and tauntingly wished for his mother to come home and find her there, his undesirable best friend.

When she grew up, Delia still saw herself as outside the realm of music. And if you were a man interested enough to take her out on a date and talk to her about a famous pianist or sax player or a concert you'd been to, you'd wonder why she couldn't look you in the eyes at that point and why she got clumsy, knocking a fork to the floor or tipping over her wineglass.

For a time there was a violin in the house that had no piano. Fleur never really asked for the violin, she never asked for anything, and so the granting of the violin seemed only to comply with the high school principal's decree that every student learn a musical instrument. The only thing Fleur ever asked for was a pair of glasses so she could read the blackboard at school. She was lagging far behind the other students and ridiculed by them and even by the teachers. She asked their father each semester, and he said neither yes nor no, and when she was already fifteen she told him she'd drown herself in the ocean, it was only a mile away, and then she was granted glasses. Delia, too small then to know the depths of frustration in her sister's breast and in her father's head, learned only later from Fleur when she was old enough to know. But the night their father brought the violin home and Fleur opened the case and lifted it from the green velvet lining, for that moment Fleur, too, was assured a happy future.

Virginia, Ellsworth's sister and Fleur's best friend, came across the alley to take a look at the violin. Since her father, she said, played the organ in church and her mother sang in the choir, and she herself played the violin and the piano both, Fleur could never hope to catch up, though there was no harm in trying. Was it winter and early dark, that evening?

Once Delia followed Fleur to her violin lesson down the street and stood outside to see how Mrs. Chase opened the door and let her sister in. Without a smile, Mrs. Chase stepped back and in went Fleur, head bowed, careful not to bang the violin case against anything, especially not against a woman so plumply elegant, her dress of large flowers and gathers, her blond hair drawn smoothly back to reveal her whole pale, prettified face.

Fleur practiced at night after she'd done her homework, though their father turned the lights out at half-past nine. Not just a time called a Depression, called Dark Times, not just the War and the blackouts (if a light showed through a tear in your window shade you'd be guilty of the deaths of thousands), not just a father denies you the light to learn something by. Fleur began to deny it to herself.

Fleur carried notes from their mother to Mrs. Chase, promising to pay, notes she had to write herself because their mother couldn't write as well as Fleur, whose handwriting was perfect penmanship, slanting always in the right direction like a constant catching up. Fleur didn't cry when the lessons came to an end. Delia saw Fleur cry only once and that one time was in the years to come. That one time was when Delia was fourteen and in high school and Fleur was already twenty-one, and they were living in an even barer house somewhere else, and their father was dead. Fleur's wish to go to the School for Nurses, far from home, where she was accepted and where she could live and where Virginia already was, that wish was drowned that day in the flood of tears and Fleur was carried away with it. She was to spend all the years of her young life tending their mother and doing the tasks a mother does. Fleur sat in a room by herself, crying for hours, and nobody went in to her though the door was open. Delia didn't go in, she was afraid to go in.

When Delia was very little, three, four years old, and Fleur went off to school on a day of high winds, then Delia would stand by the window and pray that her sister not be swept away. Even then, Delia sensed a waiting emptiness in Fleur that might never be filled with experiences other girls were to have. It set her apart from the girls she walked to school with. She'd be the one the winds would carry off.

When Delia was seven, with a voice of her own, she became her sister's protector, chastising grocery clerks and strange men, whoever happened to notice how one of Fleur's eyes slid upward whenever it felt like it. "Do you know your eye's crooked?" they said, and "Can't you look straight at me?" and the shock of their demands did bring it down. Holding Fleur's hand, she shouted, "You don't ask that question!" She told them to leave her sister alone, she told them to mind their own business.

When their mother went for strolls in the evening, Delia went with her, and, passing Ellsworth's house, they heard the piano and the violin at the same time, and even Mrs. Walshman singing. Fleur always stayed home, figuring out her homework and cutting pictures out of magazines and pasting them in a scrapbook, and when the stroll was over and they came into their little house, there was Fleur at their only table, pasting things without ripples, writing under the picture what it was: A Castle in Spain, A Movie Star, A Bouquet. Under the lamplight she was beautiful in Delia's eyes, a girl with auburn curls and large brown eyes, a girl who'd come quietly there when they were away.

Delia was afraid to wonder if Fleur was not loved by their parents as much as she was. That imbalance was like a burden on Delia. It wasn't enough that their parents had named Fleur after a heroine in a romantic novel that their father read to their mother, evenings, while she was carrying Fleur inside her. Something more was needed. She asked Fleur if she loved their parents, afraid that if she did not she'd be punished by God. Fleur, whose faint frowns always seemed over something else, said that she did.

Once Delia took the violin from the closet and carefully looked it over to see why it had failed to bring to Fleur the same kind of future as Virginia's. The very shape of it, and the glossy wood, and the curlicues, and the tiny wooden bridge that held up the strings—how untouchably perfect it must seem to Fleur who was so cast down by her shortcomings and mistakes. That night at the table cleared of supper things, Delia sat across from Fleur and drew the violin on a piece of her sister's lined tablet paper, and drew her sister playing it, bow in hand.

"Is that me?" said Fleur. "It looks like a little ant I saw playing Mrs. Chase's violin. She said it had no future and crushed it dead."

Fleur's hesitant jokes surprised people, but they never took Delia by surprise because Delia knew what Fleur had inside herself to say when the chance came.

A hint of a bountiful future touched Fleur once more as the violin had seemed to do. When Fleur took Delia to a movie matinee, Fleur's ticket won a complete set of sherbet goblets. Delia would hold one up to the light and imagine that someday they'd live in a very nice house where the amber goblets would really belong. Only tapioca pudding was eaten from them. Years later, when their mother died and Fleur came to live with Delia in her apartment in San Francisco, she brought along the three that were left of the goblets, and for the very first time in their lives they ate sherbet.

"Sherbet is what the very rich eat between courses," Delia said. "It cools their mouths, it sort of cleanses their taste for the next thing. I read that somewhere." It wasn't something she'd read, it was told her by a lover who knew a lot about what the rich did, but there was no point in telling her sister that small truth. Fleur was like truth itself and other truths were negligible.

A Black Sheep. Their mother said their father was a Black Sheep, and so did his two brothers, who came once to visit. They wore suits that had no wrinkles, and Delia guessed that their shirts were not washed and ironed by a wife or a daughter, as her father's shirts were, but by someone not part of the family. They must have grown older faster than her father. Their faces were creased, their hair already gray, while her father's hair was dark and curly all around his bald spot. One brother was a furrier, the other a jeweler, but they brought neither furs nor jewels. They brought only their Black Sheep tag for this youngest brother, who put his head to the side and smiled, too, over what they called him. So a Black Sheep was not so bad a thing to be, if he could smile over it.

The brothers looked around in a way that seemed not looking, not interested, that saw emptiness where there was no overstuffed couch and no rugs and no piano and no real living room. They did not look at Delia, but they looked at Fleur, who did not look even once at them, and they saw more than Delia had seen before and opened to her eyes her sister's long shapely legs and high breasts and what appeared to be Fleur's desire to conceal herself. A desire that was modesty, her father explained to his brothers, which made them smile once more.

Silent critics of their brother, they diminished everything down to what they'd expected of a Black Sheep. If Delia's father had wanted something from them, it wasn't given. The brothers had come from Denver, where their old mother, who was in her nineties, and their father, who was even older and who went to a synagogue every day to praise God, lived in a large house of three stories. Once in a while Delia heard her parents mention her father's sister, Sophie, but she seemed to be dead.

Their father said he was born "at the turn of the century," and his family in Denver, he said, didn't know that when one century comes to an end, another century begins, and times change, and people's thinking changes. His family, he said, was stuck in the Past. His brothers were married to very rich and homely women, sisters, who didn't invite him into their homes when he was visiting his family.

Delia's mother was always charmingly lively around people, even those she didn't know. She was born in a very small country over in Europe, whose name neither Fleur nor Delia could remember when teachers asked where their parents were born. When Delia did remember, she was ashamed to say it because nobody had ever heard of it. Aunt Goldie, their mother's sister, and her daughter, Cousin Jean, came once in a while when their father wasn't home. They drove up in a big Packard, bringing chocolates and cookies, Jean in furs and diamonds given her by a generous man who was in the movies, in exchange, their mother said, for Jean's own kind of generosity, her plumpness and her kisses and high spirits. Jean tried to teach Fleur the fox-trot, but Fleur kept looking down at her feet to make them mind, and they wouldn't, and Delia, trying, too, wasn't much better at it because she was watching Fleur to help her out. Delia tried to listen to the song Jean was humming, but it was a song just for people who knew how to dance to it.

Their father told their mother about intelligent men he had interesting talks with, and so Delia hoped he had friends away from home, probably at the company where he was a printer, friends who simply never had time to come to visit. Together with their mother he had one friend at home, but since Mr. Bonner was their mother's friend, too, and called her Eva, and came by to see her when their father was away, he could not be confirmed as more their father's than their mother's friend. He and their father talked together in the yard and shook hands whenever they met, and he called their father by his first name, Maurice, though their father called him only Mr. Bonner.

Mr. Bonner honored them by coming to their house, while other bankers were to be seen only at their desks. He always wore a suit the color of cream, a Stetson hat the same color, and his shoes were always polished, and not, Delia was sure, by his wife, as her father's were, every night. Taller than her father, who was stocky and whose chest was broad and who had a bushy mustache and wore a cap and a wrinkled brown suit from a department store basement, Mr. Bonner stood stolidly high, his face smooth as a woman's, his eyes so palely blue Delia wondered if her father's brown eyes could see more.

Mr. Bonner sang whispery songs just for himself to hear. Some times, when Mr. Bonner came to see their mother, she would leave what she was doing and go off with him, telling Fleur she was coming back very soon. She wore just her housedress and her legs were bare, a tall slender woman with dark, bobbed hair. One dress that Delia was to remember had little orange flowers in the print of it.

On one of those afternoons when their mother was gone, Delia persuaded Fleur to come with her into the front house where the oil workers lived and who were away at work on Signal Hill. They always left their back door open, the screen door banging away in a warm wind all day. Delia's mother, who was their landlady, called the oil workers by their first names and cleaned their house and made their beds for them. On Sunday afternoons when their girlfriends were visiting, Delia went in and accepted oranges and Oreo cookies and pretended she wasn't watching the way their girlfriends smoked, how they held their cigarettes and how they crossed their legs.

Fleur came reluctantly, that day, to the oil workers' house. Like her housekeeping mother, Delia picked up coins from the bedroom rug and set them in an honest row on the dresser top. That seemed a good deed to Fleur, who picked up a round, golden compact and set it alongside the coins.

Delia said "Open it up," and Fleur would not, so Delia did. The cake of rouge was a rose petal larger than any real one.

Delia swept the kitchen floor. Then she went on into the living room, directly to the phonograph, and lifted the lid.

"You shouldn't do that," said Fleur.

Wanting to hear for herself the music the pretty women danced to,

Delia set the needle down at the edge of the record. The music blared out without a beginning and didn't go back to start over. It came faster than other music and was made by many people who all seemed to know that what they wanted from life was just what they'd get, and much more, and soon, even right that instant. Her mother had said it was Jazz. The music invited her in and pushed her out. The music was the property of the pretty women who kicked off their high heels and swished their skirts around their hips and threw themselves down on the oil workers' laps. She lifted the arm to make the music stop, but the arm got away from her small sneaky hand and cut a long willful scratch across the record.

Years later, when she came to live with Delia, Fleur, bothered by memories imposed on her just as their life back then had been imposed on her, asked Delia, out of the blue, "Do you remember Mr. Bonner?"

Delia said that she did. She remembered that Mr. Bonner had visited one time after they'd moved, when their mother was already blind, and that a few years later a letter had come from his son, telling them that his father had died.

"Do you remember that quarrel Mama and Papa had?"

Fleur, asking that question, opened up for Delia the realization that the quarrel between their mother and father, their only quarrel she'd ever heard, was not really about politics, as she'd always thought. Their father had just come home, he was sitting in a chair, taking off his shoes, and he was saying that Mr. Bonner called union organizers wild-eyed Reds, that Mr. Bonner was a leech, that it wasn't the meek who were going to inherit the earth. Fleur and Delia, trembling on the other side of the half-open door, were told to go away.

"What makes you remember that quarrel now?" Delia asked.

"I don't know," said Fleur.

But Delia knew. By bringing up that scene, Fleur was divulging at last her long-ago wondering about their mother's stolen pleasures. Within a year or so after that quarrel, they lost their little house and the house where the oil workers lived, and moved to a lying-low kind of house that wasn't theirs, that was next door to a squab farm, from where the feathers off the poor caged birds drifted over and down onto their beds and bare floors. That's where they were when their father died, and that's where they were when darkness closed in around their mother, and she sat before her little radio, listening to the serial romances and waving her hand before her eyes, hoping to see it take shape again out of the dark, and when she couldn't bear the dark anymore she tore at her face, and they struggled with her to hold down her arms, Fleur on one side, Delia on the other. That's where they were, still, when their mother's hands began to twist up, her hair turn stiff and gray, her body become hard peaks and hollows under the blankets, and that's where they were when Fleur must have given up wondering, almost forever but not forever, what stolen pleasures were all about.

One night when they were undressing in Delia's apartment, by their two single beds, Fleur, her back turned, modest even in the presence of her own sister, said, "I want to tell you something," and waited until they were both under their covers and Delia had switched off the lamp between them.

"When you began to stay out all night, do you remember?"

"I remember," said Delia.

"Do you remember how Mama used to say you were like Sophie?"

Their mother had said it from her bed, aware in her darkness that Delia was slipping on her coat. Who knew when Delia would come back and who knew what she did when she was away? *Sophie had terrible moods, like you. Sophie made trouble for everybody, like you. You just came home this morning, why can't you stay and rest?* And what had Delia answered, shocking herself with that answer? "I'll rest in my grave," she had said, and saw how it shocked their mother, too, this gripping sense of mortality in a girl so young.

"You never thought how hard it was on me," said Fleur.

Delia had lost touch with Fleur in those years of her desire for the love of men, those years of humiliating herself for men in the hope of proving unforgettably precious to them.

"When you stayed out all night, Mama said terrible things were going to happen to you. She never slept. Nights were like nightmares for me. I told you but you didn't care. Then you left me alone with her forever when you came here."

Then Fleur turned away. She had so much to say it could be said only a little at a time.

At certain times in the night, Fleur's breathing took on the sound of sorrow kept down in her breast. Of sorrow that her young life had been taken from her while she'd hoped it was yet to come. And Delia said to her sleeping sister: I had to leave, I had to find my own life, but it was never and may not ever be the life you thought I was enjoying. Mean things happened to me I never told you about. Not terrible things like Mama said were going to happen, just mean things that make life itself seem mean and you wonder why you're living it. I took a job where I did the dishes and polished the silver, and for that I got a room near the kitchen, and so I didn't have to pay rent anywhere and I could send money to you to add a little to what Papa's relatives sent. I'd come home there from my other jobs, and one night when I was drying the dishes, the family kids, a boy and a girl, twelve, thirteen, kids with cold hearts, used the dish towels like whips and slapped me in the face with them. I put my hands over my face, that's all. I used to be your defender when I was a kid, I used to fight back for you, but I couldn't do it for myself.

Delia took Fleur to the museums. Culture meant that you could fill the emptiness of your life with marvelous things that were out there for everyone to share in. They wandered over the marble floors, attempting interest in the paintings and the sculpture and the rooms of historical furniture, Fleur soon wearied by her incomprehension of so many objects of value. There was always one woman in the museum throngs, or a child, who kept glancing at Fleur to figure her out: her refugee look, her sacrificial look, her look of displacement. No one could ever even hope to know where Fleur came from.

She took Fleur to a bookstore a friend had told her about, where you could look at handmade books that were works of art, the words of famous writers exquisitely printed on the finest papers you would ever see. Collectors paid a lot for them, her friend said. Distant, delicate guitar music seemed to be inviting into the store even those not about to buy anything. A woman came out of her office, suspicious of these two who must look abashed by their own selves, like thieves who had just stolen something from somewhere else. Delia sensed Fleur moving back in fear from Mrs. Chase, who had never been paid for those last violin lessons.

Taking Fleur's hand, such a small hand for an older sister, Delia urged her on to the array of open books along the shelves.

Fleur took her glasses from her purse and put them on, using them as an invitation to touch a page.

"It's a poem," said Fleur.

"There are gloves for that," said the watching woman, and so there were. A basketful of white cotton gloves. "If you don't put them on you'll have to leave. I'd rather you leave."

Shakily, Fleur put her glasses away.

"My sister's hands are clean," said Delia. "You're the one who shouldn't touch."

They left, Fleur's head bent, Delia's high.

"People always looked down on us," Fleur said that night.

"Not everybody," said Delia.

"Everybody."

"That's an awful way to think."

"Papa's family did," said Fleur. "They looked down on us. Papa said they were so strict, how they had separate plates for milk things and separate plates for meat. I used to think they looked down on us because we didn't have separate plates."

Delia waited.

"That wasn't why," said Fleur.

"It was because he was a Black Sheep, that's why," said Delia.

"You remember the night they took Papa away to that charity hospital?" said Fleur. "I went with him because Mama couldn't and I was the oldest and you stayed with her, and in the ambulance they said he'd better sit up, that was best if you had a heart attack. I held his hand. He was cold but he was sweating, and I thought he was sweating because he was afraid he was going to die. When we got there they wouldn't take him up to the ward until he answered questions. I wished the nurse would stop asking so they could take him up and take care of him. He was sitting up like they told him to and his chest was bare, it was glistening. The nurse was asking him what his mother's maiden name was, and he said it was Taubes, and she said No, that's your name, that's not your mother's maiden name, and he said it again, and finally she took down that name. I thought he gave her his own name because he was so afraid he was going to die he couldn't think of the name she wanted."

Delia tried to recall how old Fleur was, that night their father died.

Eighteen? That night, years ago, Fleur had found her way home from that distant hospital, showing up at dawn. Delia, afraid that Fleur was lost, was gone forever along with their father, stood away from her when she appeared at last. Stood away in grief for Fleur and for their father, both. Pale Fleur, saddened by life and by death.

"I went up to where he was," said Fleur. "He told me he wanted a drink of water, and I told the nurse but she said he wasn't allowed any water, and she told me to go home. I didn't go. I stayed out in the hall and I looked at him from far and he could see me. I think I saw when he died."

Fleur turned to face the wall.

They did not go to concerts, not even to the free concerts in the public groves. Nor did they go into the churches where you could sit in a pew and watch the choirs sing or listen to the organ. Music in churches was for those who saw God differently than the way Delia saw Him. They had a radio but seldom turned it on. Once, in a store, Delia caught sight of an entire orchestra on a large television screen, and she paused to watch. The pianist, under the grand piano's slanting wing, was grimacing as if in pain, and so were some of the other musicians, as if they were striving to keep up, as if the performance was an ordeal. She did not hear the music, she was put off by the faces. Some musicians Delia passed on the street, carrying their black instrument cases, seemed troubled by a problem she'd never know anything about, unless it was about making a living, and that one she knew very well.

A friend, a man who had been her lover, gave Delia two tickets to a concert at the Opera House, tickets that had been handed on to him, and she took Fleur with her into that marble palace where neither had been before. They sat in the grand tier among hundreds of strangers in rustling clothes appropriate for the occasion. Everyone must have known beforehand what the music was to mean to them or they would not have packed themselves in so tightly, on so many levels, all the way up to the ornate ceiling. While everyone else basked in the tumultuous river of sound, Fleur seemed drowned by it, so much more defeated by the uncountable number of instruments than she'd ever been by the one violin in her own timid hands. The music was so meaningful yet without any clues, except for a single clue once in a while, one instrument alone trying to tell them something that everyone else already knew.

"We'll go soon as we can," Delia whispered, close to Fleur's ear.

When they lay down that night, Fleur asked, "The man who gave you those tickets, who is he?"

How do you say to a woman who has never had a lover, *He was my lover?* How do you say, *He's my friend* to a woman who had no friends?

Delia waited to answer until she had switched off the lamp. Then she said, "Do you remember Virginia, the day she brought her boyfriend for you to see? She came all the way to where we'd moved, and you put on your coat and walked out on them. You didn't come back until they were gone."

Over there in the dark, Fleur's reflective voice of remorse. "Did I do that? Did I really do that? I'm sorry if I hurt her feelings." The mortal pain of envy lay buried under the years.

After a while Fleur said, "You remember that job I had? That one in the dime store?"

"I used to go in after school," Delia said, "and you'd slip me a chocolate. I was so proud I had a sister who worked there."

"A man used to pick me out," said Fleur. "There were three girls but he'd always ask me to wait on him. When I think about him now, he must've been what I am now, near forty, and I thought he was old. I mean I was frightened, he was so handsome. One day he wanted to walk partway home with me. I couldn't say he couldn't do that, so I walked in the wrong direction, a long way, with you and Mama waiting for me to come home. You know what I told him? I told him our mother was beautiful and our father was dead, and I said she liked to go out. Why did I say that about poor Mama?"

Fleur, who seldom spoke, whose thoughts were so concealed that people figured she had none, told her lie about their mother to entice that stranger away from herself, down a wrong path away from Fleur, crazily struggling with desire, one evening years ago.

"After you left," said Fleur, "she never wanted me to even go to the store, but I had to go and I tried to be back as soon as I could. Once a man in a car drove up alongside me as I was coming home. He asked me to go for a ride with him. It was summer, I had on a little sleeveless blouse, and I wanted to go. I wanted to know. Mama was afraid of what could happen to me and she'd be left alone. When you were with us, when we both had jobs and took care of her when we got home, and locked the door at night and put a chair up against the knob, she wasn't so afraid. But when you left, she said we just had each other. She said you'd forsaken us."

"I didn't forsake you," said Delia. "I came back when I was between jobs and that was often because all I could find were temporary jobs. When I came up here I was sure I was going to be punished for leaving you and Mama. I was afraid there was going to be an earthquake just to punish me, and buildings would fall on me, and you wouldn't have anybody to rescue you when Mama died. I wanted to stay alive to rescue you."

Fleur had already turned toward the wall. If she forgave anyone in her life, she was so quiet about it you never knew.

Fleur came to the city in old clothes. Some things were patched in many places. She had spent her evenings over meticulous little stitches, years of stitching that women didn't do anymore but that Fleur did, living in a remote place in time, kept back in the century before she was born.

With new clothes on, with a haircut, with lipstick on, Fleur went out to look for work. She never criticized the persons who turned her away. She accepted their indifference to her, their effacing of her, their edict that there was no place in the world where she was needed. She ate hardly anything, because, she explained, she wasn't earning anything. Delia offered delicacies she had never bought for herself.

"Mama told me something," Fleur said one night, a voice from out of those isolating, effacing years. "I don't know why she didn't tell you. Unless because you went away. She said Sophie had a baby."

Delia sat up to hear. The world was opening wider than it had ever opened before, and closer than ever in that widening world was her sister Fleur and Fleur's voice.

"She said that baby was Papa. She said the man who was his father was a married man, she said he was a doctor. She said when he was dying he begged to see Sophie again, but they wouldn't let her go to him. That's all I know and I don't want to talk about it anymore."

Nothing more was needed to fuel Delia's imagination. At the turn of the century, a doctor's waiting room in a prospering city, atop silver mines, must have had a long leather divan, rugs, heavy curtains that he closed across the windows, shutting out the late afternoon light. Sophie never came to him at night. He'd be home with his wife, and she, chaste young woman, home with her parents and her brothers. Delia, entranced in her bed, slipped Sophie again and again into her lover's embrace. No brief embrace, no cruel embrace, and not just one embrace. Long embraces, while the century turned them over and over together.

Out on familiar streets, Delia saw strangers of every age who could be related to her, no matter how distantly, because anyone might be related some way to the unknown man. She knew she was exaggerating that possibility, but the world was wider, and she could imagine whatever she wished.

One night Delia asked just one question, saying she wouldn't ask any more. "Did Mama tell you what became of Sophie?"

"I guess she died," said Fleur.

Delia could imagine Sophie, if Fleur could not and did not want to. A captive Sophie, raging along the dim hallways of that three-story house, deprived of her son though he was there, at table with her, or anywhere in the house. Did she never go out into the street with him, holding his hand, setting his cap aright, pointing out this and that, her voice light and lyrical with the pleasure of his company? Was she carried away to an asylum or did she take her own young life?

Delia took a closer look at furtive old women, alone in cafés, their gaze kept down on their pastries. Clothes like Fleur wore when she came to live with Delia, faded and mended. Sophie might have become one of those old women. Nobody knew what pleasures life had stolen from them or what pleasures they'd stolen from life, if any. Delia was afraid that Fleur and herself would grow old that way, each alone in a little café, or alone together at a table in a corner, Fleur more alone than herself because Fleur was the loneliest person in the world.

One evening on her way home, passing under an open window close above her head, Delia heard a woman singing. The music was from a radio, and the woman's soaring, silvery voice brought back her mother's laughter when their father swept her off her feet and carried her around in his strong, muscular arms. Then she felt a wave of love for them that she had not felt so overwhelmingly when they were alive. She listened until the song came to an end, not caring if the person inside the house were to look out and find her there, under the window, like a beggar or a thief.

"I heard a woman singing," said Delia that night. "It was so beautiful it made me cry."

"That last night I was alone with Mama," Fleur said, "I was sitting by her bed, waiting for them to come and take her to the hospital, and I was singing. She asked me, 'Why are you singing?'"

"What did you tell her?"

"I said I didn't know I was singing."

Never had Delia heard Fleur sing. Nobody else had ever heard Fleur sing. Only their mother had heard Fleur sing.

The Overcoat

*T*he overcoat was black and hung down to his ankles, the sleeves came down to his fingertips, and the weight of it was as much as two overcoats. It was given him by an old girlfriend who wasn't his lover anymore but stayed around just to be his friend. She had chosen it out of a line of Goodwill coats because, since it had already lasted almost a century, it was the most durable and so the right one for his trip to Seattle, a city she imagined as always flooded by cataclysmic rains and cold as an execution dawn. His watch cap came down to his eyebrows.

On the Trailways bus the coat overlapped onto the next seat, and only when all other seats were occupied did a passenger dare to lift it and sit down, women apologetically, men bristling at the coat's invasion of their territory. The coat was formidable. Inside it he was frail. His friend had filled a paper bag with delicatessen items, hoping to spare him the spectacle of himself at depot counters, hands shaking, coffee spilling, a sight for passengers hungrier for objects of ridicule than for their hamburgers and French fries. So he sat alone in the bus while it cooled under the low ceilings of concrete depots and out in lots under the winter sky, around it piles of wet lumber, cars without tires, shacks, a chained dog, and the café's neon sign trembling in the mist.

On the last night, the bus plowed through roaring rain. Eli sat behind the driver. Panic might take hold of him any moment and he had to be near a door, even the door of this bus crawling along the ocean floor. No one sat beside him, and the voices of the passengers in the dark bus were like the faint chirps of birds about to be swept from their nest. In the glittering tumult of water beyond the swift arc of the windshield wiper, he was on his way to see his mother and his father, and panic over his sight of them and over their sight of him might wrench him out of his seat and lay him down in the aisle. He pressed his head against the cold glass and imagined escaping from the bus and from his parents, revived or destroyed out there in the icy deluge.

For three days he lay in a hotel room, unable to face the two he had come so far to see and whom he hadn't seen in sixteen years, the age he'd been when he'd seen them last. They were already old when he was a kid, at least in his eyes, and now they seemed beyond age. The room was cold and clammy, but he could have sworn a steam radiator was on, hissing and sputtering. Then he figured an old man was sitting in a corner, watching over him, sniffling and sadly whistling. Until he took the noise by surprise and caught it coming from his own mouth, an attempt from sleep to give an account of himself.

Lying under the hotel's army blanket and his overcoat, he wished he had waited until summer. But all waiting time was dangerous. The worst you could imagine always happened to you while you were waiting for better times. Winter was the best time for him, anyway. The overcoat was an impenetrable cover for his wasted body, for his arms lacerated by needles, scar on scar, like worms coming out, with the tattoos like road maps to show them the way. Even if it were summer he'd wear the overcoat. The sun would have to get even fiercer than in that story he'd read when he was a kid, about the sun and the wind betting each other which of them could take off the man's coat, and the sun won. Then he'd take off his coat, he'd even take off his shirt, and his parents would see who'd been inside. They'd see Eli under the sun.

With his face bundled up in a yellow plaid muffler he'd found on the floor of the bus, he went by ferry and by more buses way out to the edge of this watery state, avoiding his mother by first visiting his father.

Clumping in his navy surplus shoes down to the fishing boats riding the glacial gray sea, he was thrown off course by panic, by the presence of his father in one of those boats, and he zigzagged around the little town like an immense black beetle, blown across the ocean from its own region.

On the deck of his father's boat he was instantly dizzied by the lift and fall and the jolting against the wharf, and he held to the rail of the steep steps down to the cabin, afraid he was going to be thrown onto his father, entangling them in another awful mishap.

"Eli. Eli here," he said.

"Eli?"

"That's me," he said.

Granite, his father had turned to granite. The man sitting on the bunk was gray, face gray, skimpy hair gray, the red net of broken capillaries become black flecks, and he didn't move. The years had chiseled him down to nowhere near the size he'd been.

"Got arthritis," his father said. The throat, could it catch arthritis, too? His voice was the high-pitched whisper of a woman struggling with a man, it was Eli's mother's voice, changed places. "Got it from the damn wet, took too many falls. Got it since you been gone."

The Indian woman beside him shook tobacco from a pouch, rolled the cigarette, licked it closed, and never looked up. "You got it before he went," she said, and to Eli, "How long you been gone? A couple weeks?"

"Sixteen years, more or less."

"Eli's my son," his father said.

The Indian woman laughed. "I thought you were Louie. Got a boat next to ours. We been expecting him. Got to tell him his shortwave radio was stolen. Storm did some damage, too. You Harry's son? He never told me. You a fisherman like your dad?"

"Nope."

"He's smart," his father said.

"Never got a kick out of seeing all those fishes flopping around in the net, fighting for their lives."

"Eli always saw stuff that wasn't going on," his father said. "That kid never saw what was real. Did you?"

"Never did," said Eli.

"You want to sit?" his father asked.

Eli sat on the bunk opposite them.

"That's a big overcoat you got there," his father said. "You prosperous?"

"I'm so prosperous I got a lot of parasites living off me."

"They relatives of yours?" she asked.

"Anything living off you is a relative," he said.

"I'm never going to live off you and you're never going to live off me," his father said.

"Right," said Eli.

"You visit your mom?" the woman asked.

"Not yet. I don't know where she is."

"Nobody," said his father, "could ever figure that out. A rest home for the time being. She lived too fast and hard, got to rest for a while. What a woman. A redhead. They burn up themselves."

"What color's *your* hair?" the woman asked.

Eli took off his watch cap.

"What happened to your hair? You're kind of bald for a guy young as you."

"Fell out."

"That's the way them punks wear their hair," his father said.

"I've been sick, that's why," he said.

"Are you hungry?" she asked.

"Can't say."

"I got some beans left in the pan, would you like that?"

"Thanks. Can't say," he said.

The woman pushed herself up in stages, her weight giving her a hard time, like a penalty. She wore a mackinaw and men's trousers and two pairs of thick socks, the holes in the top pair showing the socks underneath. Her breasts hung to her waist though she had no waist, but when she lifted her arms to light a hanging kerosene lamp he saw how gracefully she did it, her hands acting like a pretty girl's. He could have fallen for her himself when he was sixteen.

On the narrow table between the bunks she set down a battered pan and a large spoon. He scooped up a few beans, found them too much to deal with, and put the spoon back in the pan.

"Guess I'm not hungry, thanks," he said. "What I need is a place to sleep. Just for tonight. I used to sleep on this bunk when I was a kid."

"It's nice you remember," she said.

"Go ahead and lie down. See if you still fit," his father said.

"I'll wait 'til everybody's in bed."

"The army ever get you?" his father asked.

"Never got me, didn't want me."

"That's good they didn't want you," she said.

"What's wrong with the army?" his father said. "What the hell else did you do with your life?"

"You talk like his life is over," the woman said. "He's young. He's just a little older than my boy Nate."

"I wrecked it," Eli said. "You detected the secret of my life."

"Well now you see you got sick," his father said. "Could be you're being punished for wrecking your life."

"Could be," Eli said.

"Go ahead and lie down," his father said. "You look like you're about to drop dead. What do the doctors say?"

"Just what you said."

Eli lay down, wrapping his overcoat more closely around himself.

"You want me to take your shoes off?" she asked. "I got some extra socks, they'll keep your feet warm."

"No thanks, I'll be fine," he said, pulling his watch cap down over his ears and his eyes.

"We sleep aft," she said. "If you need anything, just call. My name's Myrna."

Outside his cap things went dark. She must have snuffed out the lamp. He lay in his overcoat, drawing his legs up close against his hollow stomach. Then he imagined he was a boy again, home again in the house in Seattle, under covers in his own bed while his parents drank the night away, unprotected from them but protected by them from the dreadful world they said was out there. Then he thought about the strangers he'd met, out in that world. The ones who said *Tell me about your parents, Eli*, the ones who said they were there to help him. Smirky parole officers and smug-faced boy psychologists in leather jackets, jiving with him like a cellmate, and that female social worker in her short skirt, whose thighs he'd hope to open with the shining need for love in his eyes. *In the morning of your life*. That was the way she'd put it. It made him go weak in the head, he'd say anything she wanted him to say, and he'd blamed this old man on this rotting boat and he'd blamed his mother, wherever she was, for what had become of Eli. They had pried out his heart, those prying strangers, and the empty place left behind was where death got in. He knew this for a fact.

At dawn he was wakened by his shivering body. Out on the pier, the cold salt wind stiffened him, almost blinding him, so that he wound up a few times at the pier's edges. When you look back, he'd heard, you're turned into salt, and that's what was happening to him. If he fell into the sea he'd disappear faster than he was bound to already.

For two days he wandered Seattle. Now that he was near to his mother he wanted to go on by. He had betrayed her, he had blamed her for Eli. Somebody was to blame and he didn't know who. If his father was right, then Eli was to blame for what he'd done to himself, and proof was in the punishment. Once and for all, Eli was to blame.

They told him at the desk that his mother was ambulatory and could be anywhere. The old women in the rows of narrow beds, and the women in their chairs between the beds, hadn't much left of womanness in them, but their power over him was intact. He went along before their pale faces staring out at the last puzzling details of the world, himself a detail, a cowering man in a long black overcoat, who might be their long-lost father, come to visit.

There she was, far down a corridor and out, and he followed her into a paved yard, walled in by brick and concrete. She put her hand to the wall to aid herself in open space, reached the bench and sat down, and her profile assured him he wasn't mistaken.

"Mother, it's Eli," he said, taking off his watch cap.

She raised her eyes, and one eye was shrewdly narrowed and the other as purely open as a child's, the blue almost as blue as ever.

"Eli," he said. "Can I sit down?"

"Room enough for everybody."

He sat, and she paid him no attention.

The day was cold, but she had come out wearing only a sagging sweater, a skirt, pink socks, and sluffy shoes. From a pocket of her sweater she took a scrap of comb and began to comb her hair. The comb went cautiously through the tangle of flame-red and gray curls.

"Mother, I'm Eli," he said. "Eli, your only child."

"You're right about that," she said. "Had one and that was it. Well, no. Had another but lost it in the womb. Fell down or was pushed. Things come and go. I figure they go more often than they come. Not much came my way but I lost more than I had. If you see what I mean."

"Mother, I wish I'd stayed around," he said. "I wouldn't let him hurt you anymore."

"Who hurt me?"

"Dad did."

"Oh, him? Once in a blue moon I get a postcard. One time he visited but I was ashamed of him. He walks like an old dog with something wrong in his hind end."

"Mother, don't be afraid to look at me."

"I don't see as good as I used to," she explained. "In the past I used to read the teeniest print. When I was a girl, believe me, I was the smartest in my class. The best looking, too. It wasn't just my red hair, it was more. I was wild to begin. That and my hair drove everybody wild. It's contagious."

"Look at me," he begged. "Come across."

She drew the sweater over her breasts and kept her arms crossed there. "We had ourselves an earthquake today. Did you feel it? Bricks fell down. We thought the whole damn place was coming down."

"I wasn't here."

"Were you scared?"

"I wasn't here."

"Go on. I bet you were scared."

"I died in it," he said. If she wanted his company in her earthquake it was no trouble to oblige. It made no difference, afterwards, when or where you died, and it was easier to tell her he was already dead than tell her he was going to be soon, maybe even before he could get up from this bench.

Slowly she turned her head to take a close look at him, this man who had sat down beside her to belittle her with his lie. "You never died," she said. "You're alive as me. I saw to it. Nothing got by me. Awful things happen to boys out there. I'd wake up in the middle of the night, sure somebody was out to harm you that exact second. I'd yell, 'Run, Eli, run! I'll take care of this fiend!' And that's how I rescued you, every time."

"You did. Every time," he said.

Off in a corner, facing the wall, he covered his head with the overcoat and in that dark tent wept, baffled by them, by the woman over there on the bench, combing her hair again, and by the old man on the rocking boat. They were baffled by what had gone on in their lives and by what was going on now and by whatever was to go on, and this was all they had to offer him, Eli, come back to them, baffled enough by his own life.

Zenobia

*. . . and in the innermost room, the holy of holies,
the soul sits alone.*

EDITH WHARTON

*S*o high and mighty, like God who gave life to Adam and Eve and set their names down in the Bible, you gave life to me and set my name down in a book. One can't outlive God but I have outlived you, and I say this to you where you lie in your tomb, far across the ocean in a foreign land: Edith, you shall never forgive yourself for wronging me.

Silence, the wind's gone on. No whistlings, no growlings, no loose boards banging. My heart's flapping against my ribs where I could not always hear it before. Pitiful bird, it wants out from where you caged it for me. When the wind sweeps down again, I pray it breaks this house into a thousand pieces and throws onto the snow the mildewed beds nobody's slept in for years and years, where mice make their nests, and the black-crusted pots and the cracked dishes and this splintery rocker where I sit in my gray wrapper that's ages-thin, ages-old like a dead bird's feathers, and this greasy table where you sat us down together, the three of us, your beloved Ethan and your darling Mattie and your dread Zenobia.

Such a kind name you gave to him, a name like his heart beating, muffled deep in his chest . . . Eee . . . thun . . . Eee . . . thun, and such a sweet name you gave to her, a name like a crisp of maple sugar melting in his mouth, like the whirr of a dove's wings . . . Matteee . . . Matteee . . . and such a twisted stick of a name you gave to me. Z is the letter at the end of the alphabet, there's no place after Z. It's a crisscross gate that nobody can get past if they want to see what's there. Once I saw a dried-up skin from a big lizard that was brought from the underside of this earth. Zenobia ought to be the name of that creature.

Milliners' hats laden with flowers, gowns of silk and velvet, the stitches invisibly tiny, shoes of Spanish leather with fancy heels and jeweled buckles, everything upon you handmade by other persons always bent over their tasks, and pearls, endless strands of pearls, and furs, and ribbons, and billowy lace over your bosom. So proud you were of your bosom, any woman with less than yours you mocked, you pointed out as a failure of a woman, as you did me. Oh, and the many mansions where you dwelled, your Persian carpets, and marble fireplaces, and your pure white bed with tasseled canopy, and high windows that opened onto fragrant gardens. And how many times did you cross the ocean as if it were a lake and belonged to you? How could you be expected to know what my deprivations were, so immensely more than all your possessions, which I did not covet in the least.

Where I'll begin is where you began, though now the truth will be told. Winter, yes, it was winter, ice hard under the snow and the trees encased in ice, when I was brought into his house to tend his mother. And I did tend her, hand and foot, as I had done for so many others, and when she was buried out there under the snow, why then he asked me to marry him and stay on. Yes, it was winter and you were right, a young man of twenty-one would not have asked me if it were spring, seven years older than him, and come into his life in that winter of his mother dying. I did not belong in the spring, I was condemned to remain in that winter of his memory, and the aches of winter got into me. Oh, hear me! all parts of me cried. How they begged for love and tending like little children weakly crying, and often I had to lie down, and take my spoon of medicine, and wrap myself warm.

Oh, Lord, why did you bring her into my life? Oh, Lord, is she my fate? That's how he looked at me. Night after night he turned his back on me. Year after year we lay side by side, untouching. I was not born mean, meanness set in, took its time like a disease. Meanness came and filled up the spaces where his love was not. But how shamelessly, Edith, you made the most of my meanness! You made my hair sparse and tangled and gray, and my body thin as a rake, and my eyes lashless, and my neck scraggy, and you took away my teeth, every one, so poor Ethan had to see his wife's false teeth in a glass every day, and asthma, you gave me asthma, and that was further proof of my bad nature, like God's punishment of me.

But, Edith, I was only around thirty-five when you described me so and not like I am now in my old, old age. Recollect, Edith, how I was in the time when I was still a very young woman, before I ever met him, how my own eyes saw myself. Tall, and how gracefully erect I stood, and how I looked directly at everyone and at children, too, so they'd feel grown up. My face some thought austere but kindly so, and my hair was black and shone in lamplight and firelight, and my hands were long and gentle. I was the young woman who tended the sick and whose presence was welcomed by them when they opened their eyes and found her sitting at their bedside, knitting or reading.

You likened this house to a gray gravestone and that's how it was for me, still in my youth. I did my chores as he did his, every season of the year, and at night we lay down together in that room at the top of the steep, narrow stairs that I've not climbed in years and years, not since he died. And after a while, as we lay apart, with his back to me always, I became as empty of love for him as he was empty of love for me. But my heart was hurting over its emptiness, and even in the day I'd slip up to that bed and lie alone to soothe it. Once, when he was out at the mill, I wept, but very quietly so he wouldn't hear if he came into the house. I wept over who I had become, dislikable as he saw me, someone I was not before. It was a grievous thing that had come about.

Before I ever knew Ethan Frome, before I ever knew he was on this earth, there was good in me. A nurse in that doctor's office over in Betts-bridge, that's who I wanted to be, back when I was twenty. A white smock and a white cap on my smooth black hair, and both of us, the doctor and myself, doing good, and there might come a time when he would want me to never part from his side. So I heard he was wanting a nurse and I went, but there was the chosen girl already, her eyes bright for being the chosen one. They knew already she was to be at his side forever. He said to me he'd heard about my gift for caring for the sick and I knew he said *gift* because that word was to make up for not choosing me. Never would I go back to him, that's what I vowed, but when I was ailing I went to him. I put myself through the humiliation of her dark, bright eyes so sympathetic because she knew why I'd come back.

My feeling for that good doctor helped me get through the years. That secret feeling, all to myself, helped me to look up into his face and wait for his hands to be placed upon me. It got me up into the train and up the stairs to his office, and he grew older along with me, and that helped. And though he had not chosen me he must have come to cherish me for all the longing in my body. A kind man, he was kind to me, his hands were kind upon my body when my body was young and when it was old, and one day when I was surely old he took my hands in his—we were sitting and facing—and bowed his head, and when he lifted his head his eyes held tears. He'd known all along what my ailment was but he couldn't tell me, he had no words. It wasn't a name in his *Disease and Medicine Manual*.

The way Ethan complained about my trips to the doctor, about his errands to the post office to pick up the medicines I'd ordered, that way of his was like the way squirrels pack their acorns inside their cheeks. He'd be silent, but the complaints dragged down his face, and, if the tonic made me feel kind of light in the head, I'd want to laugh at how he looked. I had to go up to bed and hide the laughing in my pillow, where it changed itself into grief. Edith, you who had every reason to laugh aloud, how could you know how a laugh that's hid turns itself into grief.

When I asked Mattie Silver to come into this house and help me with the chores, it was not just for my sake, it was for her sake, too. She had no mother or father and was in poor health. Recollect, Edith, that she blossomed while she was here, and recollect I urged her to go down to the dancing in the church basement where she could meet a young man who'd fall in love with her and make her his wife, and recollect I urged her to go to picnics in the summer with other young people round about. I knew it was Ethan who scrubbed the kitchen floor and churned the butter when he thought I slept, doing those chores to spare her, though I pretended not to know this.

Was there a hidden intention in my heart when I asked her to come into this house? Was I wanting a girl who'd be like a ray of sun, who'd stir up some life in that pillar of stone, that Ethan, who'd got old while he was young, while both of us were young? If that was my intention it was not a shameful one. But when I saw that what I longed for from him was given to her, was given to Mattie, why then I banished her. I could not bear how she joined with him to render me so hateful. Tell me, Edith, if you know, what Sarah felt when she banished Hagar, when she sent her out into the wilderness. Mattie carried no child with her as Hagar did. She carried Ethan's love, and I thought his love was as much a treasure as a child. I do not think so now.

Yes, it was cruel of me to banish Mattie. But when they rode that sled down the hill and into the elm and were split asunder forever, that was not my deed, that was not my doing. It was Mattie who was Death's handmaiden, not I, and the night I banished her, and Ethan took her down to the train, that was the night she did Death's bidding. Death left that sled waiting there for them, and together they rode down that hill and into the elm, and Ethan sat in front to protect her, wanting to be the one to die if one was to go on living, and she sat behind him, clasping him, and Death sat behind her, clasping them both. Old trickster Death, Life tricked him back.

It hurts my shrunken heart to call him a coward, but he was that. Ethan was a coward. He could have run away with her, he could have borrowed a small sum from a friend in town, enough for train tickets to get them to someplace where work was to be had for the asking. He would have paid it back, he was an honest man and everybody knew that. But wasn't there a nettle of dishonesty in his heart? You said his conscience told him not to forsake me, not to leave me with nothing but a poor farm and mill beyond my health to manage. But didn't he forsake me when he chose to die? A forsaking most awful!

Edith, I'll tell you what I would have done if they had died that night.

I would have taken the blame on myself. What else could I do but live out my wretched life, guilty of their deaths? But when they returned into this house, broken in body and spirit, Mattie to spend the rest of her years wracked by pain, whining for me to tend her, which I did, and Ethan grown stonier, a stone man lamely striving to attend to his tasks, why then I saw that I was not to blame. I saw it was their fate and I saw it was my fate to care for them.

Often I mused on what I would have done if they had run away together. Often I used to remember one day in the spring of the year, one day when Ethan was away in town and Mattie had not come to us yet. I saw a young man out by the mill, his easel set up, painting a picture. It was in that time when I began to see how Ethan never cared to look into my face and, whenever he did look, a puzzlement came into his eyes as though he felt a pain somewhere. So I got my courage up and walked out to where the young man sat on a rock, and I stood behind him to see how a painting appears in the very making of it. I stood behind him to keep him from taking notice of me, afraid he would look up into my face the way Ethan looked at me, like I ought not to be there. He turned his head, he looked up at me, and what did he do? He smiled, he said, "Can I take the liberty and make a painting of your mill?" Oh, take the liberty and ask afterwards! I liked that, it amused me. He was a stranger, someone I'd never seen in town or passing by on the road. He said he'd come down from the state of Maine and was bound West. He said he wished to be an artist. High mountains and dense, tall forests and rushing rivers, that's what he'd paint, and he looked into my face while he told me, and I saw that my face gave him pleasure.

Oh, take the liberty! That's what I would have done if Ethan and Mattie had run off together and left me on this forsaken farm. I would have packed my satchel and my portmanteau and climbed aboard a train bound West, and gazed out the window at what there was to see across this vast country. City spires in the midst of wheatfields, and miles of orchards with fruit on the bough, and high bridges over broad rivers, and mountains of clouds the likes of which I'd never seen, and birds of a kind I'd never seen before. And there'd be a city where I'd stay, and there'd be an old couple in a fine house of many rooms, and I'd tend them and see they kept neat, and on my days off I'd wind my black hair in a fashionable way with tortoiseshell combs, and hold my head high, and go out to see what that city had to offer.

Edith, you never looked into my face the way that young painter did. You saw Ethan, you saw the twist of his body and his suffering face, and your heart was moved by what had befallen him. But your heart was un-moved by what befell me that day I came to tend his mother, that winter day I stepped down from the train, and he took my satchel from my hand and said my name, Zenobia, and my own heart was moved by him for the rest of my days.

The Woman in the Rose-Colored Dress

*M*y mother took me along to that party because my thirteenth birthday fell only one day after, and she said we could imagine it as a party for me, a birthday party that only we two knew about. Wandering away from my mother and the friends embracing her, I went out alone into the rooms where the strangers were. Whenever I glanced up I met a glance, and nobody spoke jokingly to me the way they do to a child, and when men came up to me they treated me with a kind of knowingness, as if I were already steeped in the experiences I had only imagined.

I can see myself in memory as if I were observing another girl from a corner of a room: how she looked in a pale green dress that clung to the small breasts and the rounding hips, not in gathered stuff nor pleats anymore, not in autonomous material, but in the kind that conformed to the young body that was just beginning to make itself known, or its willingness known, or its own will known. And I can see how she turned to tantalize in profile, her fair hair cut short to her shoulders, no braids, no barrettes anymore, and I can hear a fragment of her voice, a voice that was changing like a boy's voice changes, but hers changed by anticipation, not high and uncertain like a child's.

My mother and I remained apart. I remember seeing her in a group way off in another room, and I remember wanting to be with her, because, as when I was a child, she'd serve to protect me from persons who were overwhelming, and I remember being glad about the distance between us. With her bracelets clinking on her wrists, she gestured her flattery at the hostess and at the women's figures and at the men's wit and wisdom, hypnotizing everyone into harmlessness.

My father came late to the party. We held hands and wandered around, popping canapés into our mouths and drinking whatever was presented to us in so many tinkling glasses, and when we had our fill, not just of food and drinks but of shrill voices and bursts of laughter, we found a room where nobody was. We sat down on an antique couch that I thought was too precious to sit on, a deeply blue, velvet couch, curved like a crescent moon, but there we sat and patted our stomachs and sighed long sighs from a surfeit of pleasure.

The young woman came in timidly, as if she needed to ask a favor from persons who had never seen her before. She seemed unsteady on her feet, and I guessed it was because of the drinks she must have had. She sat down at the other end of the couch, on the other side of my father, and then I knew she had followed us.

"This is Mary, my daughter," he said to her, but it was more like a warning and not an introduction, and he didn't tell me her name.

"How are you?" he asked her.

"You know how I am," she said.

"Mary, will you go?" he asked me, only it was a command. "Where's your mother?"

But he wasn't much of a figure to command. There was a roughness in his throat like a cough held back, and his eyes were afraid. If he lost the authority of the father for that moment, he gained another kind, and it was the authority of the man experienced beyond his family's ever knowing. What he knew about his own life that his family didn't know seemed to grant to me my own untellable experiences to come. It was as if he gave me carte blanche to the world.

I couldn't get up and leave them. I thought I might, but I couldn't.

She didn't wait for me to go. She said to him in a low voice, her sidelong gaze on her hand smoothing the velvet of the couch, "I want to ask you if you ever came over to see me. I moved away so that when you came by you'd see I wasn't waiting for you, but after I moved I wished I'd stayed in the same place and gone on waiting."

She was no longer the fearful young woman in awe of my father. She was a voluptuous woman, with heavy thighs under her rose-colored silky dress. And when my father realized that I saw her as he had seen her in the past and must still see her in the present, then he got up and strode away from us both.

For a few minutes I sat with her, not saying anything, as I would with a friend who had confided in me. She was stroking the couch, her hand moving in little circles toward the empty place where my father had been.

When I left her, I did not go trailing after my father. I wanted to find my mother, instead, and put my arm around her as a way of asking forgiveness. I felt that I could not look my mother in the eyes for a long time to come, and it wasn't because I knew she was betrayed and couldn't tell her. With my discovery of my father and the woman, I hadn't thought about her.

Guests were moving in a crowd toward the grand piano, where the entertainer was seating himself to play. I joined them and was pushed up close to him, a young man with slick, silvery curls and a smile that showed baby-small teeth. I'd heard he was a cousin of the hostess, a singer who was making a name for himself in nightclubs and at big parties. A black bow tie wobbled as he chatted with the guests gathering around the piano.

The song he sang—his voice as changeable as his face, one moment quivery and the next moment smooth—was about a couple of lovers whose ineptness increased with their desire. Something went wrong for the lovers at the end of each stanza, after which he banged on the keys to emphasize each of their ridiculous disasters.

They were all packed elbow to elbow, three deep in a ring around the piano, and all were laughing on cue at each defeat of the lovers. Their eyes were closed up tight with their laughter or swam sideways, and one man kept his cigarette clamped between his lips just so the smoke drew his lids together. They were averting their eyes from everyone else's eyes.

My mother was in the crowd. I saw her across the piano, her face closed in between two other faces. She was sliding her eyes and clicking her tongue and laughing, like all the others around her, and I felt an uprush of love and concern for her. She had support in numbers, but no matter how many joined together at that piano and everywhere else to belittle lovers, I knew that all attempts would end in failure.

The Infinite Passion of Expectation

*T*he girl and the elderly man descended the steep stairs to the channel's narrow beach and walked along by the water's edge. Several small fishing boats were moving out to sea, passing a freighter entering the bay, booms raised, a foreign name at her bow. His sturdy hiking boots came down flatly on the firm sand, the same way they came down on the trails of the mountain that he climbed, staff in hand, every Sunday. Up in his elegant neighborhood, on the cliff above the channel, he stamped along the sidewalks in the same way, his long, stiff legs attempting ease and flair. He appeared to feel no differences in terrain. The day was cold, and every time the little transparent fans of water swept in and drew back, the wet sand mirrored a clear sky and the sun on its way down. He wore an overcoat, a cap, and a thick muffler, and, with his head high, his large, arched nose set into the currents of air from off the ocean, he described for her his fantasy of their honeymoon in Mexico.

He was jovial, he laughed his English laugh that was like a bird's hooting, like a very sincere imitation of a laugh. If she married him, he said, she, so many years younger, could take a young lover and he would not protest. The psychologist was seventy-nine, but he allowed himself great expectations of love and other pleasures, and advised her to do the same. She always mocked herself for dreams, because to dream was to delude herself. She was a waitress and lived in a neighborhood of littered streets, where rusting cars stood unmoved for months. She brought him ten dollars each visit, sometimes more, sometimes less; he asked of her only a fee she could afford. Since she always looked downward in her own surroundings, avoiding the scene that might be all there was to her future, she could not look upward in his surroundings, resisting its dazzling diminishment of her. But out on these walks with him she tried looking up. It was what she had come to see him for—that he might reveal to her how to look up and around.

On their other walks and now, he told her about his life. She had only to ask, and he was off into memory, and memory took on a prophetic sound. His life seemed like a life expected and not yet lived, and it sounded that way because, within the overcoat, was a youth, someone always looking forward. The girl wondered if he were outstripping time, with his long stride and emphatic soles, and if his expectation of love and other pleasures served the same purpose. He was born in Pontefract, in England, a Roman name, meaning broken bridge. He had been a sick child, suffering from rheumatic fever. In his twenties he was a rector, and he and his first wife, emancipated from their time, each had a lover, and some very modern nights went on in the rectory. They traveled to Vienna to see what psychoanalysis was all about. Freud was ill and referred them to Rank, and as soon as introductions were over, his wife and Rank were lovers. "She divorced me," he said, "and had a child by that fellow. But since he wasn't the marrying kind, I gave his son my family name, and they came with me to America. She hallucinates her Otto," he told her. "Otto guides her to wise decisions."

The wife of his youth lived in a small town across the bay, and he often went over to work in her garden. Once, the girl passed her on the path, and the woman, going hastily to her car, stepped shyly aside like a country schoolteacher afraid of a student; and the girl, too, stepped sideways shyly, knowing, without ever having seen her, who she was, even though the woman—tall, broad-hipped, freckled, a gray braid fuzzed with amber wound around her head—failed to answer the description in the girl's imagination. Some days after, the girl encountered her again, in a dream, as she was years ago: a very slender young woman in a long white skirt, her amber hair to her waist, her eyes coal black with ardor.

On the way home through his neighborhood, he took her hand and tucked it into the crook of his arm, and this gesture, by drawing her up against him, hindered her step and his and slowed them down. His house was Spanish style, common to that seaward section of San Francisco. Inside, everything was heavily antique—carven furniture and cloisonné vases and thin and dusty Oriental carpets. With him lived the family that was to inherit his estate—friends who had moved in with him when his second wife died; but the atmosphere the family provided seemed, to the girl, a turnabout one, as if he were an adventurous uncle, long away and now come home to them at last, cheerily grateful, bearing a fortune. He had no children, he had no brother, and his only sister, older than he and unmarried, lived in a village in England and was in no need of an inheritance. For several months after the family moved in, the husband, who was an organist at the Episcopal church, gave piano lessons at home, and the innocent banality of repeated notes sounded from a far room while the psychologist sat in the study with his clients. A month ago the husband left, and everything grew quiet. Occasionally, the son was seen about the house—a high school track star, small and blond like his mother, impassive like his father, his legs usually bare.

The psychologist took off his overcoat and cap, left on his muffler, and went into his study. The girl was offered tea by the woman, and they sat down in a tête-à-tête position at a corner of the table. Now that the girl was a companion on his walks, the woman expected a womanly intimacy with her. They were going away for a week, she and her son, and would the girl please stay with the old man and take care of him? He couldn't even boil an egg or make a pot of tea, and two months ago he'd had a spell, he had fainted as he was climbing the stairs to bed. They were going to visit her sister in Kansas. She had composed a song about the loss of her husband's love, and she was taking the song to her sister. Her sister, she said, had a beautiful voice.

The sun over the woman's shoulder was like an accomplice's face, striking down the girl's resistance. And she heard herself confiding— "He asked me to marry him"—knowing that she would not and knowing why she had told the woman. Because to speculate about the possibility was to accept his esteem of her. At times it was necessary to grant the name of love to something less than love.

On the day the woman and her son left, the girl came half an hour before their departure. The woman, already wearing a coat and hat, led the way upstairs and opened, first, the door to the psychologist's bedroom. It seemed a trespass, entering that very small room, its space taken up by a mirrorless bureau and a bed of bird's-eye maple that appeared higher than most and was covered by a faded red quilt. On the bureau was a doily, a tin box of watercolors, a nautilus shell, and a shallow drawer from a cabinet, in which lay, under glass, several tiny bird's eggs of delicate tints. And pinned to the wallpaper were pages cut from magazines of another decade—the faces of young and wholesome beauties, girls with short, marcelled hair, cherry-red lips, plump cheeks, and little white collars. She had expected the faces of the mentors of his spirit, of Thoreau, of Gandhi, of the other great men whose words he quoted for her like passwords into the realm of wisdom.

The woman led the way across the hall and into the master bedroom. It was the woman's room and would be the girl's. A large, almost empty room, with a double bed no longer shared by her husband, a spindly dresser, a fireplace never used. It was as if a servant, or someone awaiting a more prosperous time, had moved into a room whose call for elegance she could not yet answer. The woman stood with her back to the narrow glass doors that led onto a balcony, her eyes the same cold blue of the winter sky in the row of panes.

"This house is ours," the woman said. "What's his is ours."

There was a cringe in the woman's body, so slight a cringe it would have gone unnoticed by the girl, but the open coat seemed hung upon a sudden emptiness. The girl was being told that the old man's fantasies were shaking the foundation of the house, of the son's future, and of the woman's own fantasies of an affluent old age. It was an accusation, and she chose not to answer it and not to ease the woman's fears. If she were to assure the woman that her desires had no bearing on anyone living in that house, her denial would seem untrue and go unheard, because the woman saw her now as the man saw her, a figure fortified by her youth and by her appeal and by her future, a time when all that she would want of life might come about.

Alone, she set her suitcase on a chair, refusing the drawer the woman had emptied and left open. The woman and her son were gone, after a flurry of banging doors and good-byes. Faintly, up through the floor, came the murmur of the two men in the study. A burst of emotion—the client's voice raised in anger or anguish and the psychologist's voice rising in order to calm. Silence again, the silence of the substantiality of the house and of the triumph of reason.

"We're both so thin," he said when he embraced her and they were alone, by the table set for supper. The remark was a jocular hint of intimacy to come. He poured a sweet blackberry wine, and was sipping the last of his second glass when she began to sip her first glass. "She offered herself to me," he said. "She came into my room not long after her husband left her. She had only her kimono on and it was open to her navel. She said she just wanted to say good night, but I knew what was on her mind. But she doesn't attract me. No." How lightly he told it. She felt shame, hearing about the woman's secret dismissal.

After supper he went into his study with a client, and she left a note on the table, telling him she had gone to pick up something she had forgotten to bring. Roaming out into the night to avoid as long as possible the confrontation with the unknown person within his familiar person, she rode a streetcar that went toward the ocean and, at the end of the line, remained in her seat while the motorman drank coffee from a thermos and read a newspaper. From over the sand dunes came the sound of heavy breakers. She gazed out into the dark, avoiding the reflection of her face in the glass, but after a time she turned toward it, because, half-dark and obscure, her face seemed to be enticing into itself a future of love and wisdom, like a future beauty.

By the time she returned to his neighborhood the lights were out in most of the houses. The leaves of the birch in his yard shone like gold in the light from his living room window; either he had left the lamps on for her and was upstairs, asleep, or he was in the living room, waiting for the turn of her key. He was lying on the sofa.

He sat up, very erect, curving his long, bony, graceful hands one upon the other on his crossed knees. "Now I know you," he said. "You are cold. You may never be able to love anyone and so you will never be loved."

In terror, trembling, she sat down in a chair distant from him. She believed that he had perceived a fatal flaw, at last. The present moment seemed a lifetime later, and all that she had wanted of herself, of life, had never come about, because of that fatal flaw.

"You can change, however," he said. "There's time enough to change. That's why I prefer to work with the young."

She went up the stairs and into her room, closing the door. She sat on the bed, unable to stop the trembling that became even more severe in the large, humble bedroom, unable to believe that he would resort to trickery, this man who had spent so many years revealing to others the trickery of their minds. She heard him in the hallway and in his room, fussing sounds, discordant with his familiar presence. He knocked, waited a moment, and opened the door.

He had removed his shirt, and the lamp shone on the smooth flesh of his long chest, on flesh made slack by the downward pull of age. He stood in the doorway, silent, awkward, as if preoccupied with more important matters than this muddled seduction.

"We ought at least to say good night," he said, and when she complied he remained where he was, and she knew that he wanted her to glance up again at his naked chest to see how young it appeared and how yearning. "My door remains open," he said, and left hers open.

She closed the door, undressed, and lay down, and in the dark the call within herself to respond to him flared up. She imagined herself leaving her bed and lying down beside him. But, lying alone, observing through the narrow panes the clusters of lights atop the dark mountains across the channel, she knew that the longing was not for him but for a life of love and wisdom. There was another way to prove that she was a loving woman, that there was no fatal flaw, and the other way was to give herself over to expectation, as to a passion.

Rising early, she found a note under her door. His handwriting was of many peaks, the aspiring style of a century ago. He likened her behavior to that of his first wife, way back before they were married, when she had tantalized him so frequently and always fled. It was a humorous, forgiving note, changing her into that other girl of sixty years ago. The weather was fair, he wrote, and he was off by early bus to his mountain across the bay, there to climb his trails, staff in hand and knapsack on his back. *And I still love you.*

That evening he was jovial again. He drank his blackberry wine at supper; sat with her on the sofa and read aloud from his collected essays, *Religion and Science in the Light of Psychoanalysis*, often closing the small, red leather book to repudiate the theories of his youth; gave her, as gifts, Kierkegaard's *Purity of Heart* and three novels of Conrad in leather bindings; and appeared again, briefly, at her door, his chest bare.

She went out again, a few nights later, to visit a friend, and he escorted her graciously to the door. "Come back any time you need to see me," he called after her. Puzzled, she turned on the path. The light from within the house shone around his dark figure in the rectangle of the open door. "But I live here for now," she called back, flapping her coat out on both sides to make herself more evident to him. "Of course! Of course! I forgot!" he laughed, stamping his foot, dismayed with himself. And she knew that her presence was not so intense a presence as they thought. It would not matter to him as the days went by, as the years left to him went by, that she had not come into his bed.

On the last night, before they went upstairs and after switching off the lamps, he stood at a distance from her, gazing down. "I am senile now, I think," he said. "I see signs of it. Landslides go on in there." The declaration in the dark, the shifting feet, the gazing down, all were disclosures of his fear that she might, on this last night, come to him at last.

The girl left the house early, before the woman and her son appeared.

She looked for him through the house and found him at a window downstairs, almost obscured at first sight by the swath of morning light in which he stood. With shaving brush in hand and a white linen hand towel around his neck, he was watching a flock of birds in branches close to the pane, birds so tiny she mistook them for fluttering leaves. He told her their name, speaking in a whisper toward the birds, his profile entranced as if by his whole life.

The girl never entered the house again, and she did not see him for a year. In that year she got along by remembering his words of wisdom, lifting her head again and again above deep waters to hear his voice. When she could not hear him anymore, she phoned him and they arranged to meet on the beach below his house. The only difference she could see, watching him from below, was that he descended the long stairs with more care, as if time were now underfoot. Other than that, he seemed the same. But as they talked, seated side by side on a rock, she saw that he had drawn back unto himself his life's expectations. They were way inside, and they required, now, no other person for their fulfillment.

Nights in
the Gardens
of Spain

*T*he boy beside him was full of gin and beer and wine and the pleasant memory of himself at the party, the great guitarist at seventeen, and he had no idea where he was until he was told to get out. His profile with that heavy chin that he liked to remind everybody was Hapsburg hung openmouthed against the blowing fog and the cold jet-black ocean of night.

Berger had no intention of forcing him out, but to command him to get out was the next best way of impressing his disgust on his passenger. "I asked you when you got in, friend, if you had money for the bridge toll and you haven't answered me yet. You want to get over this bridge tonight and into your little trundle bed you look for that two bits because I'm sick of paying your way wherever we go and getting kicked in the face for a thank-you. What the hell did I hear you say to Van Grundy? That you got bored by musicians because all they could talk about was music?" His breath smelled of cheese and garlic from all the mounds of crackers and spread he had eaten, not the kind of breath to accuse anybody with. "And that meant me, of course, because I'm what's known as your constant companion, that meant old ignoramus Berger. For a guy who's got all the famous relatives you're always bragging about—big dam builders, big mummy diggers, big marine commandants—you ought to be able to come up with a miserable nickel once in a while." He held out his hand for the coins that David was searching for and found.

"What the hell." David gripped his guitar between his knees again, settling back uncomfortably. "You sore because they wanted *me* to play?"

He shifted into low to start the car again. "You don't know what anybody wants, you're too busy playing all night."

The boy waited a minute, then sprang the big psychological question with a rare timidity in his voice: "You sore because it's me that's going to play for Torres tomorrow?"

"Jaysus Christ, I'm sittin' next to Freud here!" he cried, disgusted.

They went on in silence over the long bridge. The deputy at the toll gate reached out his hand to take the coins that Berger pressed into it with his gray-gloved fingers, suede driving gloves to keep his hands warm so that he could commence to play soon after entering a room, but David wore no gloves, came with cold, thin hands into a room and played slickly, charmingly, his first number and afterward blew on his fingers to impress upon the audience how cold they were still and how much they had accomplished even so.

Along under the neons of the motels, assured by the rainbow lights and the traffic signals that the time had passed for his abandonment on the bridge, the boy spoke again, "Listen, nobody's destroying you but yourself," his voice empty of experience.

Berger gave a whooping laugh. "Listen yourself, I'm not the one who's destroying himself, you worry about yourself. Some day you're going to explode, a hundred different colors and a sonic boom. Big little David, folks will say for miles around, got too big for himself. God, you slaughtered that Purcell. If you play that for old Torres he'll ask for a change of rooms after you're gone." He unloaded now all the complaints accumulated against the boy—criticism of his teacher-companion that David made to friends: "*Berger could be the best, good as Tomas Torres, but he doesn't look the part, hasn't got the urbanity, short you know, big shoulders, like a wrestler's that don't fit him, big face, and the way he telegraphs his mistakes to you before he makes them, like 'this hurts me worse than you, dear audience.' But the best, really the best, could have been the best, but came to it too late, a jazz musician until he was thirty, still got the mannerisms of a jazzman in a nightclub, smiling at the audience, smiling at himself. You can't do that with a classic guitar. He's good all right but he should have come to it at eighteen, twenty, then he would have been great.*" "Things come back to me!" Berger was shouting. "For a man of few friends, like you say I am, they come back to me!"

He drew the car to the curb, leaned across the boy to open the door. "Get out here, man. From here it's just a mile to your mother's place. I'd take you there but it's a mile out of my way."

Under the green-blue motel neon, David stepped out to the sidewalk, knocking his guitar case against door and curb and hydrant.

"You're doing it to yourself," said David again, warningly.

"You keep knocking that guitar around like a dumb bastard with a normal IQ!" he bellowed, slamming the door.

He went through the amber lights of intersections as if they were red and he was drunk. Somebody else on the verge of fame, somebody else awaiting the encircling arm of the already great, sent him, Berger, over the edge, down into the abyss of his own life. It was not fame he wanted for himself, he would never have it now, anyway, at thirty-seven, with all the faults that David had so meticulously listed for everybody. Not that, but what? The mastery, the mastery, play without telegraphing the errors, play without the errors, play with the mastery of the great yet indifferent to fame if it came. Palermo was nothing, that mecca of all the world's guitar students where Torres, old Torres of the worldly jowls, laid his arm across the jaggedy, humped young shoulders of the most promising. The photos of the students in the guitar magazines made him laugh. They came from everywhere to study under Torres at the *accademia*, they stood around the silk-jacketed Tommy like fool disciples: a middle-aged woman with a Russian name; a young curly-locks guy from Brazil, making hot amorous eyes at the camera; a stiff-elbowed kid from England who looked as if he stuttered; and the girls with their big naïve eyes and their skirts full to make it easier to part their legs for the correct position of the guitar. He saw them gathering in the hallways of some musty building in Palermo after school, saw them descend the street into the town with the stiff-swinging walk of youth attempting youth, and he had no desire to be among them, to be twenty again and among them. The older he got the less he wished for a new beginning and the more he wished for a happy ending. But sometimes, as in these last few weeks, the wish for that beginning laid him low again like a childhood disease.

Before his apartment house he let the car door swing heavily open and lifted his guitar case from the back seat. The slam of the door reminded him that there was something else in the car that ought to be brought in, but unable to recall what it was he concluded that it was nothing stealable and went up the stairs in his neat, black, Italian-style moccasins, wishing that he were lurching and banging against walls. Not since he fell down somebody's stairs six years ago, cracking a vertebra and breaking his guitar in its case, had he taken a drink, not even wine, and he had taken none tonight though everybody was awash around him, but he felt now that drunkenness again, that old exaltation of misery. Sick of black coffee after a dozen cups through the night, he found a cupful in a saucepan, heated it to boiling, poured it into a mug, and willfully drank, scalding the roof of his mouth. He opened his mouth over the sink and let the black coffee trickle from the corners, too shocked to expel it with force, bleating inside: *To hell with all the Great, the Near Great, the Would-be Great, to hell with all the Failures.*

From the windowsill he took his bottle of sleeping pills, put two on his tongue, drank down half a glass of water. He dropped his tie on the kitchen table, his jacket on the sofa, stepped out of his moccasins in the middle of the living room. He put on his tan silk pajamas (Who you fooling with this show of opulence?) and crawled into his unmade bed. At noon he was wakened by a street noise and drew the covers over his ear to sleep until evening, until the boy's interview with the Great Tommy was over.

At four, moving through the apartment in his bare feet, in his wrinkled pajamas, he tore up the memory of himself that early morning as he had once, alone again, torn up a snapshot of himself that someone had thrust upon him—a man with a heavy face in the sun, hair too long and slick, a short body and feet small as a dandy's. For with no reminders he was the person he fancied himself. But, dumping coffee grounds into the sink, he realized suddenly that the jawing he had given the boy had been given as a memento of himself, something for the boy to carry around with him in Palermo, something to make him feel closer to Berger than to anybody else, because Berger was the man who had told him off, a jawing to make him love and hate Berger and never forget him, because it is impossible to forget a person who is wise to you. If the boy never got to first base as a guitarist, then the jawing lost its significance, the triumph was denied to Berger. It was on David's fame that he, Berger, wanted to weigh himself. *Jaysus*, he wailed, *what kind of celebrity chasing is that?* He smelled of cheese and bed and failure, sitting at the table with his head in his hands. The interview was over an hour ago and now he would hear from friends the words of praise, the quotations from Torres, as if these friends of David had been there themselves to hear the words drop like jewels from his lips, all of them closer to God because they were friends of him who sat up there in God's hotel room, playing music to enchant God's ears.

So he stayed away from his friends, who were also David's friends. For almost two weeks he eluded any knowledge of that interview. He gave lessons to his students in his own apartment or in their homes, and in this time it was as if he were seventeen again, living again that period of himself. He felt as if he were instructing them without having learned anything himself first, and he hated his students for exacting more of him than he was capable of giving. Again he was in that age of self-derision and yet of great expectations. A celebrated musician would recognize him and prove to everybody, once and for all, Berger's genius. After every lesson his armpits were sticky and he would have trouble in civilly saying good-bye.

On the evening of the twelfth day he drove across the bridge to visit the Van Grundys. They were still at supper, Van and his wife and the two kids, eating a kind of crusty lemon dessert, and they made a place for him to pull up a chair. He had coffee and dessert with them, and joked with the boy and the girl, finding a lift in the children's slapstick humor, the upside-down, inside-out humor, and in the midst of it he turned his face to Van Grundy at his left, the smile of his repartee with the children still on his lips, the hot coffee wet on his lips, his spoon, full of lemon dessert, waiting on the rim of his bowl—all these small things granting him the semblance of a man at ease with himself—and asked, "Well, did Torres flip out over our Davy?"

"You don't know?" Van Grundy replied. "He told everybody as fast as if it were good news," raising his voice above his children's voices demanding the guest's attention again. "Torres kept interrupting. Every damn piece Davy played, Torres didn't like the way he played it. What's the matter you haven't heard? Something like that happens to a person he's got to spread it around, along with his excuses, as fast as he can."

The coffee he sipped had no taste, the dessert no taste. "Is he going to Palermo anyway?"

"Oh," said Van Grundy, stretching back, finding his cigarettes in his shirt pocket, offering one to his wife by reaching around behind the guest's chair, "he won't go to Palermo now. He can if he wants to, he's okayed as a pupil, but since Torres isn't throwing down the red carpet for him he won't go as less than a spectacular. You know David."

"Even if he doesn't like old Tommy anymore he can learn a thing or two from him, if he went," Berger said, sounding reasonable, sounding as if all his problems were solved by bringing reason to bear.

"He's already taken off for Mexico City. A week ago. He's going to study under Salinas down there if he can get that cat to stay sober long enough. Says he's always said that Salinas was better than Torres. He's stopping off in Los Angeles to ask a rich uncle to subsidize him. He was going to do it anyway to get to Palermo on, so now he'll need less and maybe get it easier. Hasn't seen his uncle since he was twelve. Got a lot of nerve, our Davy."

"What did you think of that Rivas woman?" Van Grundy's wife was asking, and he turned his face to hear, regretting, for a moment, that he heard her, usually, only with his ears and not his consciousness. He had known her for ten years now, she had been the vocalist with a combo he'd played string bass in and it was he who had introduced her to Van

Grundy. A pretty woman with short, singed-blond hair and an affectation of toughness. "Rivas?" he asked.

"Rivas, Maruja Rivas. The album we lent you. Last time you were here." The smoke hissed out from between her lips, aimed into her empty coffee cup. "Don't tell me she didn't mean anything to you."

"Did you play the record?" Van Grundy asked.

"I can't remember borrowing it," he said.

The last student was gone. He had come home from the Van Grundys' to find the first student waiting on the apartment steps, and he had put aside the record on a pile of sheet music and there she had waited in the silence of the confident artist. He had noticed that proud patience of hers when, in the streetlight that shone into his car parked before the Van Grundys' gate, he had looked for the album and found it on the floor, under the seat, where David had slipped it so he could sit down. After she had waited for so many days, she had waited again until the last student was gone, and when he picked up the album cover, the racy cover with orange letters on purple background and the woman in the simple black dress, there was that unsmiling serenity again.

He turned his back to the record going around, half-sitting on the cabinet, chin dipping into his fingers, elbow propped in his stomach. He cautioned himself to listen with his own ear, not Van Grundy's, but with the first emerging of the guitar from the orchestra, the first attack on the strings, he found himself deprived of caution. His head remained bowed through all the first movement, and at the start of the second he began to weep. The music was a gathering of all the desires of his life for all the beautiful things of the earth, the music was his own desire to possess that same fire, to play so well that all the doors of the world would spring open for him. Wiping his nose with his shirtsleeve, he sat down on the sofa.

With the cover in his hands he watched her as she played, though he knew that the photo was taken while her hands were still, the left-hand fingers spread in a chord. He watched her, the pale face and arms against a Spanish wall of huge blocks of stone and a gate of wrought-iron whorls. Her hair was olive-black, smoothed back from the brow, the face delicately angular, the black eyebrows painted on, the nose short, straight, high-bridged, and the lips thin and soft and attuned to the fingers that plucked the strings. He knew the sensation in the lips, the mouth wanting to move over the music as if it were palpable. *Concierto de Aranjuez*, and the fine print on the back of the cover told him that Aranjuez had been the ancient residence of the Spanish kings. *I believed myself in some enchanted palace. The morning was fresh, birds singing on all sides, the water murmuring sweetly, the espaliers loaded with delectable fruit.* Why did they quote some Frenchwoman back in 1679? He knew the place without any help. The memory of another Aranjuez came to him, the party he'd played for last summer down the Peninsula, the sun hot on the pears and the plums even at six in the evening, and the shade waiting along with everything else for the cooling night. He had played all night under the paper lanterns of the brick patio, and tiny bells were tied to the trees and tinkled in the night's warm winds, and, early in the morning when all the guests were gone, that party-thrower, that divorcée with a dress the color of her tan, had told him her checkbook was in her purse and her purse in her bedroom, and he had awakened at noon in a sweat from the heat of the day and the fiery closeness of her body. He had phoned her in the evening from the city, but she had spoken to him as to an entertainer who has already been paid and who says he hasn't. Years ago it would have been a pleasure and a joke. He had known a lot of women briefly like that, but for some reason—what reason?—that time had hurt him. Was it because it had shown him the truth, that he was no more than an entertainer, not artist but entertainer, one for whom the door was closed after the woman had bathed away his odor and his touch. The music from the fingers of that woman on the album cover caused the ache of his mediocrity to flare up and then die down. For that Madrid woman went in everywhere and took him along. The great went in doorways hung across with blankets and they went in the gates of palaces, and everywhere they were welcomed like one of the family, and everywhere they took you along.

The record went around all night, except for the hours he himself played, and he had more cups of coffee and, along about five o'clock, stale toast with stringy dark apricot jam which he did not taste as he ate and yet which tasted in his memory like a rare delight that he could, paradoxically, put together again easily. His shoes were off, he was more at home than he had ever been in his rented rooms anywhere, and the woman with him was like a woman he had met early in the evening and between himself and her everything had been understood at once. The disc went around until the room was lighted from outside and the globes drew back their light into themselves, and water began to run through the pipes of the house.

He heated the last of the coffee, sat down at the kitchen table and pushed up the window, and through the clogged screen the foggy breath of morning swept in. What was morning like in Madrid? What was her room like, what was she like with her hair unbound, in what kind of bed did she sleep and in what gown?—this woman he had spent the night with.

He tipped his chair back against the wall and the thought of David Hagemeister struck him like somebody's atonal music. Now in the morning, whose silence was like the inner circle of the record, there returned to him the presence of David, but the discord was not a response anymore from his own being, the discord was in David himself.

Davy's mother must be up by now, he thought. One morning he had brought the boy home at six, after a Friday night of playing duets here and there, and she was already up in a cotton housecoat, dyed yellow hair in curlers, having tea for breakfast and not a bit worried. She was the kind who would have sent him to Europe at seven by himself because he was the kind who could have done it fine. Carrying his cup to the phone in the living room, he sat on the sofa's arm, and after he had dialed the number he pulled off his socks, for his feet were smothering from the night-long confinement.

"Edith, this is Hal Berger. Did I wake you?" his voice as thickly strange to himself as it must be to her.

"I was just putting my feet in slippers." Her voice sailed forth as if all mornings were bright ones. She always spoke on the phone as if her department manager at the Emporium picked up his phone whenever hers rang, a third party on the line listening for signs of age and apathy.

"Where's David? Somebody said he's zooming down to Mexico," massaging the arch of his pale foot.

"He's in Nogales. It's on the border."

"What's he on the border for?"

"He's waiting for some money from me."

"What about the uncle in Los Angeles?"

"He gave him supper and twenty-five dollars to come back north on and buy himself a new pair of cords. He went to Nogales, instead, wearing the same pants, and sent me a telegram from there."

"You sending him something?"

"Yes."

He began to subtract several dollars from the substance of himself, and anxiety was left like a fissure where the amount was taken away. But then why phone her at quarter to six in the morning, rushing his voice at her with its big, benevolent question? "Send him an extra fifty for me," he said, "and I'll drop you a check in the mail to cover it." Overcome by a great weariness, he hung up.

He lay down on the sofa. His shirt stung his nostrils with the night's nervous sweat and he tried not to breathe it. In the Nogales Western Union the boy would pick up the check, the total drawn from the days of his mother's captivity behind the counter, drawn from the hours of Berger's teaching, but since it had come to him, this money, then was it not his due because he was David Hagemeister? Poor Davy H! Maybe the boy would be always on borders, always on the border of acclaim, waiting for something to come through and get him there. But once in a while, as he grew older and envious of those who had got across the border, he would hear somebody great and lose all envy. It might be, he thought, that this Rivas woman wasn't as great as he thought she was, but he had needed, this night, to think that she was great.

His crossed arms weighting down his eyes, he fell asleep to the sound of someone running lightly down the carpeted interior stairs, some clean-shaven and showered clerk running down into the day.

Bastille Day

*J*ust after one o'clock Teresa came to the San Gotardo, the last bar on her round of bars this night of her fortieth birthday, July 14, 1970. The predictions overheard when she was young, about how you were going to feel when you got to be forty, had seemed false, like laughing fools' talk, and even in the last few years when that age appeared on the horizon like a sinking ship, a sailor signaling with those little flags, precisely, futilely, even then she had refused to conform to the tyranny of numbers, just as, all her life, she'd refused to conform to popular delusions. With her, the sense of mortality hadn't waited to take her by surprise at forty. It had been with her always, a seventh sense, along with the absolute preciousness of life, hers and everybody's. But who, she wondered, could possibly guess that about her, a drab woman pushing open the door to this last bar for the night, her face puffy, her no-color hair tied back with a narrow, dangling ribbon, the tail of hair hanging out over her dark, styleless coat.

The ones usually here were here now, along with a few unfamiliar ones, the dingy place as brightly lit as a café, making no attempt to hide itself in shadows, the jukebox wearily scratching up a Hawaiian song to which an old woman was dancing an impromptu hula. Teresa sat on a stool at the end of the bar. She had heard that this place and the hotel above it were in their last days, and she asked who had bought the property. The question, put to the man next to her, was like a match that set the fuse to a string of firecrackers.

"Some Chinaman!" At the top of his lungs.

"Koreans are not Chinamen!" A woman at the middle of the bar, neatly dressed in a gray suit and hat, her pumps dangling from her toes. "A filthy rich Korean bought it."

"Ho Chi Minh bought it." Away at the other end of the bar, a portly black man in a shabby suit and hat, standing. "Ho Chi Minh is taking over soon as he wins the war."

"Ho Chi Minh is dead." The caustic woman in gray, instructive again. A seat each side of her was empty.

"Japs!" The old woman, sprawled by her table after her dance. "They were snooping around upstairs. The way you tell a Jap is they all got a camera 'round their neck. That's how they tell themselves from Chinamen."

When Teresa had entered here for the first time, just twenty-one, the other patrons had been merchant seamen and cooks and stewards from the passenger vessels, and old Italians always with their hats on. Only a few of the old bars were left in this Italian neighborhood that was taken over now by the manic façades of nightclubs where nude girls danced, and whenever she came in here now she wondered if anyone present had been among the customers years ago and grown unrecognizable. On the high ceiling the paint was the same antique ivory, and behind the bar the lineup of Fun Land prizes seemed the same. The Kewpie doll, the blue plush dog, the plaster Popeye. The flowerpot, wrapped in foil, held wax flowers in an era of plastic ones, and the two little girls in the photo garlanded with a faded paper lei were women now. Over in the dark dining section, separated from the bar by a low, flimsy partition and by a flowered curtain across the doorway, the same mural of Sicilian farm country graced the dim far wall.

Half a century ago the bartender must have been a pretty young man. His dyed black hair and baby-blue eyes evoked a movie idol of her teens whose name she couldn't recall. He might *be* that one, come into his obscurity, a tinge of green on the teeth of his winning smile. Except for two young mailmen with beards, and a tall, bareheaded young black man in a long overcoat, alone at a table, no one was younger than herself. That was comforting, if only for the moment.

At the far end of the curved bar, a man sat facing Teresa. A long, thin dead-eyed man in shirtsleeves, winking at her a lewd command. "Joe Curran," he said, to nobody in particular, "got me into the Great Lakes."

"Man, don't talk to me about Joe Curran." The woman in gray spoke into her drink, contemptuously. "You want to know who was all right? I'll tell you. William Randolph Hearst was a fantastic man. You better believe it. He called me in and said I was a fantastic writer. Are you a Communist? Yes, I said. I was always cocky honest. Nothing fuzzy. Well, he said, we just won't send you out on any labor stories. A fantastic man! But his son!"

Teresa had never seen the woman before, never in the past at demonstrations nor at any of the big parties in rented halls, benefits for this and that radical cause.

"Got to New York," the woman went on. "No job. Called Hearst in San Simeon. He put me to work on his magazine in New York. Fashion. Imagine. I retired from the Newspaper Guild because I didn't want to go through the FBI. You know who my son is? My little tiny baby boy is a big rock star. Far out. I was far out in my time. If you were far out in my time you could have got the electric chair."

"Don't die that way." The man on the woman's left, a stool between them, sat in a crouch, an uneasy man in a black suit. "You don't look so good after."

"You undertakers are 86 around here," the woman said to him. And to the bartender, "You ought to prohibit him from spreading gloom."

The man in the black suit got off his stool and moved toward the jukebox, a somber stepper, smoothing back his slick hair with slow palms.

"Play Duke Ellington!" the woman called after him without turning. "If you put anything else on I'll kill you. Your boss will be surprised when you turn up dead."

"Indian Love Call" rose up faintly from an old record, and the two mailmen got up from their table and danced a parody, cupping their ears to hear the call through dense forest.

A younger woman, Teresa's age, came out of the door of the staircase that connected the bar to the hotel rooms above and sat down at the hula dancer's table. A girl out of a fairy tale after she had come alive and become a woman and lost some teeth but not yet all her beauty. Her long black hair was parted in the center and drawn back into a bun, and her downslanting emerald eyes were made to seem even larger by the compression of the almost toothless jaws. And Teresa was drawn to her. Sweetly, keenly, the woman was someone she would have wished to be a confidante for, back in the time of the other's young beauty when the future promised wonders.

Teresa carried her beer to that table and sat down with the two women. The old one in her housedress and shabby shoes, her pink barrette slipping from her short gray hair, was still undulating to the Hawaiian music that had been left behind, long before, by other songs. And at this table Teresa felt herself warming up to embrace all the benighted persons in this bar, embrace them as if she had never expected more of them, no change for the better.

"You live here?" she asked the fairy tale woman.

The fairy tale woman clasped her bare arms across her breasts. "I used to but I can't now. I always kept my room clean and I never made any noise except when I lost my mind. The owners, they'd be happy to have me back. I'm speaking of the social workers, they say I've got to live with a guarantor. He guaranteed them he'd take care of me, so they let me out of the asylum. If you look at him and then look at me you'll see he's old enough to be my father. Over and above that, he has an apartment and money in the bank and four suits and a pension. But he's filthy. They don't know that. I'll tell you what he's like."

The woman went silent. Teresa waited.

"If you come home with me," the woman said, "and poke your head in the door, he'll see you're a woman. It's only a few blocks from here. Otherwise he'll say I've been out with a man. If I come back without my coat he'll say I left it at my lover's. I left it at home because the sun was out and I was coming right back."

"I'll do that," Teresa promised.

"My lover hanged himself. He's up there moaning." She smiled a young smile. "He's German. They're romantics. They kill everybody and they kill themselves. He says he's going to do it over again as soon as he gets his strength back."

A commotion at the far end of the bar. The portly black man slapped the lewd winker from the Great Lakes, who lost his balance and fell to the floor, along with his stool. The black man stepped up onto the fallen man's back and, hesitantly, as if he were only considering that which he was already doing, he jumped around up there. Then he stepped down and kicked the man in the face. No one shouted to him to stop, no one came to restrain him. But when he lifted a stool, straining to raise it above his head, a man left his table and with charitable ease gripped the upraised arms.

"Well, that's enough," he said humoringly. "You kicked the shit out of him and that's enough."

"He was asking for it."

"He sure was asking for it," the man agreed, taking the stool away. "You better get the hell out before somebody calls the cops."

Slowly, only wandering out to another bar, the portly black man left, his hat unmoved, his face unmoved, his eyes pleased. The lewd winker got up from the floor and fell backward against the dining room partition, causing it to shake. He set up his stool and sat down. His nose was bleeding.

"I'll drop you," he said to his assailant no longer there.

The man who had intervened moved toward the street door, and Teresa saw he was someone she had known. Someone on the periphery of those familiar faces always anticipating great changes for the world. The old woman got up from her chair and almost fell against him, and he set her right by his hand at her elbow. Teresa recognized him, then. A steward aboard the passenger ships, he had brought them news for the union paper, he had sat with her and the staff at their favorite bars and cheap restaurants. He was not of the periphery, he was in the midst. Mayer. She spoke his name.

When he sat down, the fairy tale woman started to get up. "I'm in the way."

"No, no, you're not," he said, quickly, gently, and the woman leaned back in a submissive arc.

"I'm out on the town," Teresa told him. "I told Ralph I wasn't coming home till late. No, I didn't tell him. I'll tell him when I get back."

Mayer's eyes, striving to concern themselves with this woman he probably barely remembered, were no longer pure of shape and color. The flesh around them made them less revealing, made them flat and noncommittal. She wondered if she had looked at him with desire, in the past. She had felt desire toward a number of men in that time when they had all conferred over how to right the world. Once in that time she might have made love with him in a dream.

The bartender swung up the empty stools and slid them upside down onto the bar. The fairy tale woman, her arms against her breasts, stood up, Teresa and Mayer stood up, and the three went out into the night, followed by the young black man in the long overcoat, who had been alone at a table.

"You want to drink some more?" the follower asked them. "I know where we can get some whiskey. You just knock on the window. It's a liquor store. He's closed but you knock on the window and he sells it to you. He says I owe him fourteen dollars but I only owe him six. He won't sell me no more till I pay up."

The fairy tale woman was hurrying on, soberly forward into the cold mist. Teresa caught up with her, and Mayer and the other man caught up. "I don't want to be nothing but drunk," the young man was saying, behind Teresa. "I got shot three times in Vietnam. They ain't supposed to shoot at you coming down. You see that red light over there? That's how a bullet feels when it hits you. Red hot. My buddy's parachute didn't open. When we found him he was flatter than this sidewalk. You know what they do with your dog tag when you're dead? They kick it into your teeth."

Teresa's lungs began to clamor with the pain of the cold fog of summer they had to take in, so fast. The fairy tale woman had got ahead again, but at the corner she turned and stood waiting, shivering. And Teresa wondered if she, herself, was an asylum inmate, on a night out just because it was her birthday and they allowed it to her. Not somebody as sane as anybody else, a woman with a good job and a scholar-husband reading into the night with the gas heater on or lying warmly asleep in his separate bed, books fallen to the floor.

The four of them stood in a huddle on the windy corner, the fairy tale woman afraid to urge them on. Teresa saw the fear of desertion in her pinched face that, under the harsh streetlight, was the face of a woman twice as old.

The young man was reluctant to part from them. "You got some crazy city," he said. "I was working the other night where my friend works. Up the street. I was washing dishes over at Mike's when this girl walks in. I looked so hard my eyes watered. Nothing on." His shoulders raised against the cold, his hands in his overcoat pockets, he walked backward a few steps. "It's been nice talking to you."

Three abreast, Teresa and the fairy tale woman and Mayer went on, Teresa on the inside, bumping against walls, and Mayer on the outside, nimbly stepping off the curb and around hydrants.

"You want my coat?" he asked the woman.

"It smells like a man," she said. "He'd smell it on me even after it was off."

After several blocks, the woman took Teresa's hand and drew her into the marble entrance of an old apartment building. Four doors in a row faced the street. The woman pressed a button, the buzzer sounded, and she opened the door.

"My friend walked me home," she called up.

Drawn in by the woman's hand, Teresa also raised her face. Almost imperial, strong, an old man was leaning on the banister at the top of the carpeted stairs, and his very white, smooth hair and his very white shirt shone under the light. The fairy tale woman started up the stairs. Teresa closed the door.

They walked back the way they had come, unspeaking, Teresa stumbling only once, so far. She had no direction now. "I can't make it home," she said. "Over the bridge to Berkeley and another bus stop in the heart of darkness. Nothing's running this time of night. Or far between. I think I'm scared."

"You can sleep at my place," he said.

"You sleep on the bed, I'll sleep on the sofa."

"What makes you think I've got a sofa?" He told her he had a couple of rooms, a few blocks away, that he and his wife had separated a month ago, and that he was a ship's clerk now; then he was silent again.

Up three flights of stairs in an apartment building, the climbing, the key in the lock, quietly done. The bed was covered neatly with an Indian cotton spread. A clean place, a scent of toilet soap, even of apples, a Gauguin print on the wall of warm-fleshed Polynesian women. Teresa sat down in a chair and felt for cigarettes in her purse. His silence was telling her that she was a burden, unexpectedly added to some he already had, that this was a bad night for him because of her.

Mayer lit a hissing gas heater. "You can lie down."

She lay on the bed in her coat, flat on her back, shoes pointing ceilingward. And out of the blue, just like the winking man at the bar who rose up out of the Great Lakes, just like the rest with their memories that were like non sequiturs to everyone else, she said, "Some people we used to know got prosperous. Briggs is in real estate, I see his name in the papers. He wanted to change the world so he built half a million tract houses. Rupert is a restaurateur, he doesn't even have to cook anymore, he just shakes hands. Look at me, I'm a computer. Not rich yet, just upward mobility."

"How's Ralph?"

She gazed at the Gauguin print, her eyes evading the question. "Ralph's got himself a Ph.D. He's an associate professor."

"Of what?"

The long way around, tell it that way, the only way. "Well, first it was going to be Philosophy. He switched over to Economics and then he switched over to Modern European History. We felt it was all right for him to take so long. I had jobs. Anyway, I always felt he was like the favorite child of Time, if you know what I mean. I think those others, the ones who got prosperous, they're like favorites of Time, too. They just had to wait to get over their bleeding heart phase."

When it was spoken aloud it had a maudlin, abusive sound, just what was to be expected of her at the end of her night's roaming. Some other nights, too, had their maudlin endings. Not long ago, coming home late, after having found no one in the bars whom she had known, she had thrown herself down by Ralph, asleep. She had sat on the floor, crying loudly to wake him and crying long to keep him awake.

"Mayer," she said brightly, "I bet you didn't know today was Bastille Day." She slid upward to lean against the headboard, nudged her shoes off and over the side, and shook her head to clear away the complaints. Her hair came loose from the ribbon and hung in strands to her shoulders, and, possibly, she looked young again.

"Never gave it a thought," he said.

"I know because it's my birthday. Same day. When Ralph told me a long time ago that my birthday was Bastille Day I said—listen to what I said, you won't believe it—I said, So *that's* why I've got this urge to release everybody from bondage. I said, Isn't that the day the French peasants let loose the political prisoners? And he said, They released seven and they weren't politicals. They were after ammunition. And I said, Well, they made it a holiday, it must have meant a lot for the Revolution, you know, storming the Bastille. And he said, If you want that day for your very own, it's yours."

The room went dark. He had switched off the lamp. She saw him sit down in a chair and take off his shoes. "A great day for a birthday," he said. "I wish it was mine."

"You take the bed, " she said. He must be angry with himself for bringing her home. "I can sleep in the chair."

"Get under the covers," he said, wearily.

She got in under the blankets, her coat on, and he lay down on the outer edge of the bed, under the covers. She lay as close to the wall as she could get without touching it. Though she kept her face a few inches away from the wall, the cold came out of it like a ceaseless exhalation. Some nights she could scarcely breathe, and the doctor had told her that if she failed to stop drinking and failed to stop smoking, if she didn't begin to take care of herself, wear warm clothes in cold weather, then Oh! Beware! If she ever came down with pneumonia, she was a goner. And she knew she would die in her bed while Ralph read on and on in his room about great upheavals, debacles, revolutions, carnage. And when she was gone, he would simply go on as before, a slouchy, boyish, finical professor, and if his eyes were seen to be red-rimmed the cause would not be sorrow; he had always a problem with sties. She wanted to tell this to

Mayer, to believe that he was the one she had been longing to find, the one who would care about whom she had become and what was to become of her, but her talk would seem only the ragtag end of her night's roaming. She listened to his breath change as he fell asleep. She heard his breath take over for him and, in that secretive way the sleeper knows nothing about, carry on his life.

God and the
Article Writer

*O*ne night toward the end of the marriage, James G. Burley, an article writer, was wakened by someone's heavy breathing. He switched on the bedside lamp but when the scene was lit he was confused over how to respond, whether to make a joke of it or to be alarmed. His son, sixteen years old, was confronting him with a shotgun in his hands. While Burley debated with himself, his wife leaped out of bed and tore the gun from the boy's shaking grip.

After a confinement of two months in a psychiatric ward, the boy went to live with a foster family and enrolled in another school. At the end of the semester, the region's gas and electric company awarded the boy a bronze paperweight in the shape of a bolt of lightning, first prize for the most interesting scientific experiment by a high school student. The boy's marvelous recovery failed, however, to recover his parents' marriage.

Burley's wife, a nurse, moved into an apartment close to the convalescent home where she was employed. She took with her all the furniture and he did not object. He loved her and wanted not to deprive her. His dearest wish was for their reconciliation. If only that wish were granted he would be eternally grateful to Whoever took care of wishes. His wife refused to see him or to speak with him on the phone. Often, now, living alone in a residence hotel, the article writer wondered if the end of the marriage had come about not with his son's attempt on his life but way back on the wedding day. The dictum he had come across years ago in a manual on how to write for a living, that the end of the story was inherent in the beginning—did it apply as well to life?

So, alone, without wife or son, pained by his wife's absolute rejection of him and by the greater mystery of how his life had come to this stage, he went on with his writing. Always a hard worker, now he worked even harder because the meager income from his articles, an income he and his wife called chickenfeed, was enough for his son's support but barely enough, after that subtraction, for his own needs. On his hotplate he cooked rice and bony stews, and his breakfast was coffee. He ate on the same table where he typed his articles. At times the thought of suicide snaked over the page, a glittering viper. Then his nimble fingers at the keys would curl into helpless fists and his tired head go down to the typewriter's cold metal.

One day he got into his 1969 Chevrolet, bought in a used-car lot after his wife claimed their later model, and drove the sixty miles from San Francisco to Saratoga to interview the renowned physicist Ancel Wittengardt. The physicist was now a controversial figure, plunged into disrepute by some of his colleagues and apotheosized by the rest. The assignment was Burley's first from a national weekly, *Instant*, devoted to articles pertinent to the very moment. He was instructed to be brief.

At the time agreed upon he was seated in the physicist's kitchen, accepting gingersnaps from a carton and nodding his thanks for milk, poured by his host into a plastic cup. Had he been given a choice he would have chosen to conduct the interview in the study. Here in the kitchen he felt that he was treated lightly, expecting at any moment to be treated rudely. It was his experience that no matter how warmly he was greeted by celebrities, sooner or later they granted him a reason for disliking them.

When he set his pen to his tablet he saw that the pen was out of ink. Lint clung to the nib of the second pen and he wiped it away, staining his thumb and index finger. Lately, he was without protection against contempt, real or imagined. His shirts now were seldom laundered and his two suits reeked with the stale and bitter tobacco odor that permeated his hotel room and caused him to gag when he first set foot in that room. Some persons of the punk rock world whom he had interviewed were far from clean, but their failings had reflected on him as contempt.

"Sir, you are a Nobel Prize recipient. What year was that?" he began, smiling his congratulations as brightly as though the award had been announced that very day.

With the edge of his hand Wittengardt brushed crumbs from the table, catching them in the palm of the other hand, then dropping them to the floor. The physicist's smile appeared to be over something that lay farther back than the year of the award.

A news item, three weeks ago, about the death of the physicist's wife had prepared the article writer for a man in mourning. Instead, all curtains were parted, sunlight streamed into every room, a canary warbled on and on, inanely ecstatic, and the man himself wore an old sport shirt figured gaudily with tropical fruits. The sun, the physicist's smile, the song of the bird—all were puzzling. Anything contrary to Burley's expectations seemed a deliberate attempt to humiliate him.

"Well, sir," he began once more, "I understand you've come up with a whole new theory about the universe. Some big bang in the mind, eh? If you like, you can begin with the equation and go on to explain it in terms for the average Joe." A year ago he had quit smoking, but a suspect granule remained in his throat. He coughed briefly.

Wittengardt sat up very erect, like the smartest student in first grade, who is always bursting with answers. "Ah, but the equation has slipped my mind." The lapse appeared to delight him. "Something so apparent requires no equation. So I let it go. For over fifty years I worked it out by logical progression, and then—whoosh! In an instant I realized I had known it all before I began. I had known it so well it must have scared me out of my wits. And a scientist scared out of his wits, what's to become of him?"

Just below Burley's heart, anger bit. He kept his attention from it by patting his breast pocket for cigarettes no longer there, by fingering around in his larger pockets for the indigestion mints that had disappeared days ago from the twisted foil.

"Sir," he began again. "You scientists have always waged your internecine wars. If that equation of yours is heavy ammunition, our readers will want to see it with their own eyes. It's bound to become as familiar as Einstein's E=mc². So let's get on with it."

Obligingly, Wittengardt rose and paced the room, raptly attentive to what Burley hoped was his memory. Then, raising his head, tossing back from his brow a lock of gray hair, and settling one hand on his hip, he began. "There is no existence except God. He is and there is with Him no before or after, nor above nor below, nor far nor near, nor union nor division, nor how nor where nor place. He is now as He was, He is the one without oneness and the single without singleness. He is the very existence of the first and the very existence of the last, and the very existence of the outward and the very existence of the inward. So that there is no first nor last nor outward nor inward except Him, without those becoming Him or His becoming them. He whom you think to be other than God, he is not other than God."

Wittengardt clapped his hands together once, a gesture of surprise beyond all other surprises of his life. "An Arab fellow, a poet. He beat me to my theory by seven hundred years. You can say that I took the hard way and got there a bit late. Or you can say there is no late and no early. That way I won't look like a slowpoke."

The shorthand scrawled over several pages was not to be of any help to him, Burley knew. He was lagging, though every word the physicist had uttered was there in the tablet.

Wittengardt sat down again, but only to draw on a pair of black rubber overshoes, and Burley wondered if the man had received a signal from somewhere that rain was to fall the very next moment. "Come," he said, "and have a look at my garden."

With tablet and pen in hand, Burley followed him into the garden, noting for his own secret use the ravages of time on the man's head and neck. The man was so fragile that death in the guise of anything, in the guise of air, could whisk him away from his anchorage in rubber overshoes. Unspeaking, he followed, feeling more slighted with every step, dismissed by Wittengardt's agility and by his absorption in the unwinding of hoses. And the garden itself troubled Burley. The flowers were so profuse, their fragrance and colors so varied and so mingled, the entire garden so lush and so involved with its own growing and blooming, that he felt himself under attack. The beloved persons of his life who had brought him pain had assaulted him in just this way.

"Sir," he said, when at last they came around to the gate. "I must tell you the fact of the matter. We have not yet begun."

"You are so right!" the physicist agreed, grasping Burley's hand and shaking it heartily.

Under the gate's arch of jasmine Wittengardt waved good-bye, and Burley saluted with two fingers to his temple as he drove away. At the first stop sign he tore off his coat and loosened his tie, but an entanglement other than his clothes was at work upon him. As evening came on, passing motorists signaled to him by blinking their headlights, and after many miles he realized at last that he had neglected to turn on his own lights.

Weary past relief, he lay down on his bed. A day ago the presence of his dead grandfather came to reside with him. Although the room in which that old man had lived was in another hotel in another city, this room had become that other. When he was a boy in his teens, agonizingly ambitious, knowing his faults more than they who pointed out his faults to him, always in a turmoil over his desires and the premonition of their defeat, Burley had visited his grandfather almost every day. By impressing the old man with life's wonders, he developed his powers of persuasion over his own future. The old man never bathed or changed his clothes and hardly ever spoke, but the boy sat by him faithfully, attempting to engage him in conversation about politics, great discoveries in medicine, and historic battles. The old man had been an electrician, and one night he did away with himself in that hotel room. Not much knowledge of electricity was required to accomplish that deed, but, for the boy, the act was a prodigious one. Almost twenty-five years later, Burley, lying on his bed, was urged on to his own end by the suspicion that this was his last chance.

Carrying his hotplate, he went down the hall to the bathroom shared by the tenants on that floor. There he turned on the faucets in the gray, claw-foot tub, and the water rose. Then he plugged the hotplate into the wall outlet, and, by the time he removed his clothes, the round little burner was beaming away on the toilet seat. A pellet of rice, stuck to the coils, began to stir. With the hotplate in both hands he lifted his foot to the rim of the tub. At that moment he began to consider the possibility that suicide was not what it used to be. An authority figure, bearing an evanescent resemblance to Wittengardt, was denying him a way out. Without bothering to dress, carrying his clothes and his hotplate, he stepped out into the hallway that had become, easefully, surprisingly, like one in his own home, and passing down that hallway he nodded on his way to an elderly woman returning from a late-night television show down in the lobby.

The hotel manager, a young man in derelict jeans and T-shirt, his long hair in nervous strings, appeared at Burley's door the next morning. The other tenants, he said, were disturbed by Burley's unsociability, and he asked that the room be vacated.

Burley found a hotel in a neighborhood less littered. The lobby was as drab as the other lobby but considerably larger, and its mottled ruby carpet was vacuumed twice a week. The monthly rate for his room was only six dollars more, and although the room was not larger than the one from which he was evicted, it had two windows, side by side, and the other had but one. The genial woman clerk brought up from the basement, with his help, an extra table for his typewriter and papers, and he set to work again. In his letter to the editor of *Instant*, he explained his failure to turn in the Wittengardt interview by calling the physicist obstinately taciturn.

Almost every night, now, he was wakened by the night itself and whatever were its particulars. If rain was pouring down the panes of his windows, he fixed his gaze on the street lamp's shimmer between the grimy strips of the venetian blinds. And, with morning, he was always surprised by the everyday sight of his naked feet setting themselves down on the threadbare rug. He desired nothing, neither the return of his wife nor his son's love. He was in a state of astonishment but he did not yet know over what.

Wilderness Fire

A wilderness fire was raging in the mountains east of Los Angeles, and a great brown cloud of smoke, tinged copper by the sunrise, lay over the desert and the small towns she passed through on her way to her mother. The first few miles she was alarmed under the cloud. Only in a nightmare could the sky be like this. Or was it this bad only because she wanted to turn back and the smoke gave her a good enough reason? If she wasn't going to be forced over to the side of the road by the highway patrol and interrogated as to why she was driving so fast in this smoke, she just might pull over on her own, under that long row of eucalyptus up ahead, under those towering, dry, lonely, gray trees, and bend her head to the steering wheel and sleep. Sleep, to put off the moment when she would embrace her mother, bringing her news from the world outside the pink stucco bungalow on the desert's edge.

She went past the eucalyptus row and past the acres of fields planted with something she'd never remember the name for even if she were told twelve times; past shacks far away at the end of dirt roads; past a huge, dusty fig tree branching out over the highway; past a black dog ambling along in a ditch. On the seat beside her—the novel, untouchable, ominous, like an object stolen from a tomb. It slipped closer when she took a curve, and she hit it away with the side of her hand.

The folded letter slipped out from the book and fell to the floor, and it, too, slipped sideways. It was slipping close to the pedals and in another minute she could put her foot on it and grind it down. *All those who practice this profession betray. No, not all. Not the great ones. But maybe they betrayed, too. Just because everybody said "See how far they can see into the human heart," that didn't exonerate them in their own eyes. I have betrayed you, your confidences, your soul, and I will regret it for the rest of my life.*

She went faster past the entrance to a trailer park. Above the hedge the trailer homes swept by with their green awnings of rippled plastic. Oh, thank God her mother didn't live in a trailer park. She almost wept, imagining it. The heat of this desert edge was enough, and to have to live in a trailer with all its dinky built-in things, with plastic flowers planted in tanbark by the doorstep—that was the end. She had always wanted to be rich, not just for herself but for her mother, too. And she had never got rich and never would, not the so-so actress that she was, and married, not now but not long ago, to a man just as poor, though he was going to be less so, now, because his novel might elevate him into all kinds of upper brackets.

The scorched air, the dark cloud were almost left behind. The tall, tall date palms, acres of them, she was passing had always seemed from some far reaches of the earth, brought to a desert from deep swamps, and grotesquely lonely, out of place. She had told only her mother about how they looked to her. Who else would see they wanted swamps? And her mother had agreed they did look like prehistoric swamp plants, out of their element, enduring.

On the outskirts of the town where her mother lived, she slowed down past clapboard houses and stucco bungalows, low to the ground, some in weeds, some in squares of very green grass, one with the same silver porpoise-shape trailer out in back, one with the lemon tree; past the small, stucco school. And now the pink stucco house, small, too, boxlike, but showy in this place because it had two stories. Before it, a squat palm tree that never gave dates, just tiny, yellow, waxy droppings, and a midget fig tree; and, in the back, towering way above the house, one lone palm. All around the yard, a scalloped-wire fence, a foot high, protecting the house and the short dry grass and the three trees from nothing. *Oh, Mother, I had wanted an airy glass house for you by a blue, blue sea, say the Caribbean, lush plants all around with large, deep green leaves, always with drops of clear water on their surface. And birds, birds of miraculous plumage.* She parked in the gravel driveway, stuck the letter into the book and the book into her purse, and, swinging along, very erect in high heels, purse slung over her shoulder, she went up the paved walk to the front door.

For the moments of their embrace and the moments after, her mother couldn't speak, and then she went on ahead, leading the way into the kitchen, tossing her head from side to side with delight, like a child. Her mother was bare-legged and clopping along artfully on backless wedge sandals. Her flowered cotton dress had once been her daughter's in an awful movie, but it had been expensive and was kept neater now than its original owner had ever kept it. Her mother's short hair was tinted a pink-blond, like a faint reflection indoors of the exterior of the house. In the four months since the daughter's last visit, the mother seemed to have got quite a bit older. Or maybe it was the heat of the desert summer that shrinks the thin ones and expands the fat ones. And, coming along behind her mother, she said, *Mother, Mother, Mother,* just to herself. *If there was anything I did that made you get old, forgive me for that.*

"Penny, dear shiny bright Penny," her mother said, and here in the dim kitchen, the striped curtains closed against the heat swarming at the windows, here where her mother turned to clasp her again, the daughter felt again how much she was thought about in this house. Her mother's face in the shade of the room told her again how brief was the time of their knowing each other, only twenty-five years so far, and told her again of the unknowable limits of the time left.

"There's a fire in the mountains, if I smell of smoke," she said.

"You've brought me Chris's book," her mother said, hands palm to palm under her chin, like a child praying at bedtime. Bless everybody, amen.

"Oh, yes, that's right," the daughter said, tantalizingly wagging her finger under her mother's nose. "Patience, patience."

"You left so early," her mother said. "Shall I make you some break-fast?"

"Never hungry till two," she said. "Same as always. Let's just drink a toast. Some mineral water will do fine."

"Is he happy?" her mother asked. She had been an actress and had even got her name up on the screen—in much smaller letters than the leads. She had always played innocents, girls from small towns, from farms, and now, when she was called upon to express happiness, it came across like that of a girl who didn't know yet that happiness wasn't that simple. Her mother was a smart woman, but seeing her smile like that, you couldn't guess how smart she really was.

"Oh, he's happy, of course," she said, smiling at her mother the same sort of smile from the backwoods. "A novel with his name on it, what else can he be but happy? He's living with a friend of his—I guess it's a woman, he just says *friend*—at her or his apartment in New York. He's happy."

"He says that?"

"He says what?"

"That he's happy?"

"If he says so it must be so," she said, coming out smiling from behind her hands, as if she had spread them over her face only to rub away the soot or the dust or whatever that cloud of smoke had left. "He says he's going to write to you. You and he always had such wonderful discussions. Just about everything from quasars to cucumbers. He says he's going to mail you an autographed copy with something like 'Love to Melody, whom I thank for giving birth to Penelope.'"

"That's nice, but you're making it up."

The daughter was wandering around the kitchen, restlessly, as if she'd come to the wrong house and was going to have to leave at once. She came to the other end of the long kitchen, where there was a couch and a television and a sewing machine, and where, on a table, there were maga-zines and a row of African violets in little painted Mexican pots that had been hers when she was a little girl—a collection of sorts, and her mother brought over the misted glass to her, there.

"I made it up and it's not nice," she said. "He admires you for just be-ing you and he loves you. It's easy, you know, to love you. He'll just write,

'To Melody, dear friend, all my love.' Let's drink to that. If he gets to be famous, your copy will be worth a small fortune." But how little love, none at all, he had shown in his novel for her mother; she wasn't mentioned, but what he had written about the daughter was to wound the mother beyond amends.

They raised their glasses.

"Chris has a good heart," her mother said.

"Chris has a great heart," she said. "Everybody's going to know that soon, not just you and me." But she couldn't drink, because the ice cubes were making such a racket she had to set her glass down.

"Sit down now," her mother said, sharply.

"Mother, it isn't me," she said. "The girl in his novel isn't me. He got it wrong. There's no resemblance whatsoever. I never gave him all that trouble and I was never loved like the girl in there was loved. Everybody will think it's me and it isn't me."

"Where is it?" her mother asked, afraid.

"Mother, he was always fascinated by women made of words. If you want to know their names I'll try to remember. Emma Bovary and Molly Bloom and Brett, and that girl who was mad over Heathcliff. Oh, and women in the flesh, too. Of course. But when he put me into words he got me wrong. It's not me, Mother."

"Sit down," her mother said, and the daughter sat down. "It's all made up," her mother said soothingly, sitting, facing her daughter. "Everybody knows that. That's what novels are all about."

"If I gave him trouble, Mother," she said, "it was because he gave me trouble."

"That's usually the way it goes," her mother said, stroking her daughter's arms, down and down again along the long silk sleeves. "And nobody ever knows who started the trouble."

"Mother, nobody can ever know what life feels like in another person. You only think you know. I never could know him, his desires for his life, his life in here," taking her hands away from her mother's to spread them over her chest, "and he could never know me. It's unknown territory. It's unknown in here, Mother. I don't know myself. All I hear is the uproar."

"Give me your hands," her mother said, reaching for her daughter's hands again and holding them down.

The daughter had been avoiding the mother's face. She had been looking everywhere, sideways and down, anywhere but at her mother, and now she looked at her mother's face, at the slack cheeks, at the waiting fear in the eyes. And the ears through the pink curls seemed comically large, waiting.

"Once I tried to kill myself," she said, and began to sob. She pulled her hands away and held them up, palms toward her mother, and the long sleeves slipped away from the wrists, exposing on each wrist the thin, pale line of an old scar.

They stood up at the same time and came together, clasping each other. She had betrayed this woman who had given her birth, betrayed this woman's hopes for her daughter to endure, endure against all the unsolvable puzzles life comes up with. She was taller than her mother—her mother, over the past few years, was getting smaller, and the daughter was wearing high heels—and her mother's face was pressed against her breasts, her tears wetting the blouse and the nipples under the cloth. Long ago, her mother had told her that when she was newborn and began to cry, the milk seeped out at once from her mother's breasts, wetting her dress. At once, though mother and child were rooms apart.

"Mama, I didn't die," she pleaded. "You see I didn't die. I'm alive. I'm alive." But her mother would not let go and would not raise her head.

With her arm about her mother, she walked her out into the yard, because the broad desert light might force them to calm down and to endure. Even the tall palm they stood beside might force them to endure. Way far to the west, the smoke was like evening at the wrong time of day.

The Bystander

The room on Vernal Street in Los Angeles was the last room my father rented for us. In that old green three-storied house with pigeons and gables and fire escape, he went over the line and his decline wasn't anymore a matter between father and son. For he assaulted a woman in that house, the woman he had liked the most and spent some nights with. It was a Saturday twilight and I had been reading on the bed up in our room and had thought the noise nothing unusual. Outbursts of voices came at any hour from the rooms below us, and along the hallways, after two in the morning, the homing tenants bungled and cursed. But someone leaped up the stairs and threw open the door and shouted at me to grab a blanket or a coat or *something for crissakes* and wrap your old man up. He had run out of the house with nothing on but the soap from the bath he'd been taking in the woman's rooms.

Under a date palm in the yellow dirt and yellow grass of the steep front yard of another rooming house half a block away, he stood shouting threats at the woman he'd left lying on the floor; and roomers watched from porches and from windows, and across the street men and women from the bar stood under the red neon goblet, laughing. He was marble white in the twilight, and the sour bar smell of his breath mingled with the fragrance of the soap. When I tried to cover him, he struck me away with his elbow, sharp in my ribs as a crowbar, but when the police came, when he heard the siren, he allowed me to throw the blanket around him.

The ward was located in the old hospital, as it was called, a rambling place of red brick curtained by ivy, and a block west of the new many-storied structure of concrete. I brought his suitcase, as the young man social worker had told me in some huge loft of hundreds of desks and social workers in an agency building somewhere else in the city. It contained his suit of navy blue; his one white shirt and striped tie; his gray work shirt and white work socks, and his dry, bumpy, carpenter's work shoes. And over my arm I carried his raincoat and in my pocket his wallet, containing, under celluloid, a snapshot of my mother taken the year before she died—a dark-haired girl in a short, flowered dress—and a snapshot of myself at the age of five, standing high in the bowl of a drinking fountain.

The bald fellow in shirtsleeves in an office on the first floor told me, as he accepted the personal property across the counter, that my father had shown enough improvement in the past week to permit him among the more tractable patients on the second floor and that yesterday he had been moved up from the basement quarters. He told me, also, that my father had been examined by staff psychiatrists and the institution they'd chosen for him was Camarillo, in the coastal hills near Ventura. I was leaning my elbow on the counter, smoking a cigarette, demonstrating with that pose my reasonable nature. If the father was unreasonable it did not follow that the son was, also; the son might profit in wisdom from the father's breakdown in a six weeks' ordeal in hotel and housekeeping rooms. Though it did not matter to this clerk whether I approved or disapproved of their taking my father off my hands. In this old brick building of ramps and ivy and barred windows, the personal element was extraneous; it was a place run by public taxation and the public was protecting itself. The thousands of the city who had never heard of him and never would hear of him were afraid of him, and his confinement and classification was a matter between him and them.

Climbing the rubber-carpeted ramp to the second floor and crossing the hallway, I pressed the bell to the side of double doors.

"Lewis Lisle," I said to the orderly unlocking the doors.

The room I entered was long and furnished as a living room with many wicker chairs and three wicker sofas with flat and faded cretonne cushions. The patients here were males, dressed in pajama-like gray cotton trousers and shirts, and on their feet were gray canvas slippers. Some sat with relatives and some sat by themselves, and one lay on a sofa with his back outward. A group of them were conversing at the wide door to the sleeping room, and he was among them, his hands clasped behind him, his head tilted by a smug, lonely amusement with the peculiar reasoning of the others. The impact of his presence in this alien place made my throat swell, and I went up to him quickly and laid my hand on his back.

At first I thought my hand was unfelt, he responded so slowly to it, but then I saw in the slow, annoyed turn of his eyes that he mistook me for a fellow inmate, bothering him with some crazy kind of confidence. He said my name, "Arty," and the smell of oranges was on his breath. That was good, I thought; if he had eaten an orange then he was comparatively content.

"Did you have an orange?" I asked him.

"A visitor brought them to one of the boys," he said, and these were the first words exchanged between us in five days, the calmness of our voices recalling the shouting.

We sat down together on a wicker sofa, and the stun of exile was in his eyes and in his joints. He had lost more weight and his hair had grown longer and seemed grayer, an iron gray that was the heavy color of an ending; in spite of the orange, his lips were dry, rimmed by a white dust in the cracks. He sat with legs crossed, his troubled hands clasped on the upper knee.

"What you been doing with yourself, Arty?" he asked.

"Oh, I had a cold for a couple of days," I said.

"What did you do for it?"

"I did what you always said, I sweated it out."

But he was embarrassed by the absence of one front tooth, lost a few weeks before, one night he got in a brawl in a café. His tongue hissed a little in the gap.

Beyond the door to the sleeping room were two rows of cots, several of them occupied. The men lay fully clothed atop the blankets, each enwrapped in his delusions as in a mummy winding, and one turned over with a great lethargic wrench, pushing with his elbows. At a table by a window in the sleeping room two patients were playing cards, one of the players a black man, and his wife sat by him, feeding him pink ice cream from a pint carton with a little wooden spoon. In the room with us a young patient was playing the upright piano with meticulous discordancy, and among the relatives and patients and piano notes wandered an elderly man who recalled Caesar, anciently Roman, and yet would not have come to his prototype's shoulder. With warning flashes of his small black eyes he struck into being everyone he glanced at. A woman's bathrobe was tied smartly about his stocky body, a dark robe patterned with flowers.

"I want you to stay and meet my son," he said to me, laying his hand on my shoulder.

"Go on, beat it, go on," my father said to him, the jerking of his elbow establishing his brotherhood with the rest.

"He's a bastard, my son," the Caesar said.

The orderly, lounging in a wicker chair at the far end of the piano, lay his *Argosy* down upon his thigh and watched, and the old man, seeing my eyes darting to the place behind him where he knew the orderly sat, lifted his hand from me and went into the sleeping room where he stood with his back to us, watching the cardplayers.

"A son of a bitch himself," my father said, shifting position sprawlingly. "The loony tried to murder his own son. This guy is always talking about how his son and his son's wife were figuring to dig up some three thousand bucks he's got buried somewhere. What the hell he thinks three thousand bucks is? I made that much in overtime the couple years I worked at Douglas Aircraft during the war. That's what it amounts to— nothing. A down payment on a Ford, a funeral, a loan to your uncle, a week for you and me at Catalina, and it was gone. And this guy thinks it's enough to kill his son about. A loony."

The long living room was like Sunday—the inmate curled on the sofa, the visitors, the scent of oranges; the only thing missing was the comic papers. Over by a closed door to somewhere, a middle-aged woman in a black dress and a black straw hat with red cherries sat on one side of a gray-clad patient and her middle-aged sister sat on the other side of him, a middle-aged brother whom sunlight hadn't touched in a long while, a man who had probably sat all day in a screened porch. Now, out in the world, he sat watching me with fear in his pale eyes. I saw him rise and walk away, feeling more cornered by my glance than by the women who pressed him in between them. They continued to talk across him, not missing him, but I was interested in my effect on him and sought him out, glancing into the sleeping room and finding him standing sideways, ten feet away, waiting for me to meet his eyes.

"What do you think they'll do to me, Arty?" my father was asking. He slid down, resting his elbow on the arm of the sofa and, with his hands, forming an arch to hide his face from the orderly. "I'd like to get rid of this cough. My chest has been bothering me from the coughing. They had me in the basement for a while and the cold came up from the floor. Ah, Jesus, it was miserable down there, like a menagerie in the hold of a ship. The croakings and cryings."

"They do anything for your cough?"

"Nothing. The hell with them. Maybe they like you to come in with lung cancer or whatever it is I got. Maybe they want you to die as soon as you can, conditions in bughouses being as crowded as they are."

"They got these places to cure people," I said.

He laughed explosively, folding up and then unfolding so far that his legs stretched straight out and his back arched out from the sofa's back. The patient on the next sofa turned over and, his head hanging over the edge, watched my father with the unblinking eyes of a mild and curious animal.

"They give us hot chocolate before we go to bed," my father said, "and a little cookie, star-shaped. You see how far man has progressed? They never did that in Bedlam, Arty, you tell that to any cynic you meet. You tell them in the psycho ward they give your father hot chocolate and a little cookie."

We were sitting facing the double doors to the hallway, and through the screen saw an orderly come up the ramp pushing a food conveyance and wait in the hallway, ringing for admittance. He pushed the metal cart through the living room and to the closed door, and the door was left open after he had passed through and I saw that the room beyond was a dining room. Two women attendants were setting the long, dark table, and beyond that room was a kitchen with cabinets and a sink; and the sound of plate on plate from those rooms was a reassuring sound, and it seemed, though I knew it was impossible, that a wood fire had been lighted behind a screen somewhere in that room where the women set the table. The noises of the plates and silver predicted for me the meals that I would spend in company of persons whose existence I did not know of, in houses I did not know of, as I had not known of this locked living room with the gray inmates and the wicker chairs.

Over on the sofa by the dining room door the sisters wound the straps of their purses around their wrists, set their black shoes heavily on the floor, and went to the sleeping room to find their brother and say good-bye. The black woman, tall and with the composure of a civil service clerk, drew on her coat over her high shoulders.

"They make everybody leave at suppertime, I guess," I said.

"Where you going to eat?" my father asked.

"I don't know," I said, not wanting to eat anywhere.

"There's a Chinese dump around the corner from Vernal," he said. "You seen it. They got chicken giblet chop suey and they don't leave the liver out—most gyp joints save the liver for something fancy—and they got those peas cooked in the pod, you know how they do." And disgusted by his detailing of trivia, he set his palms over his eyes. Under his blindfold, his mouth asked me, "You still at that place on Vernal?"

"Yes," I said.

"You going back to your Aunt Glorie's?"

"I guess I won't," I said.

"You going back to San Diego at all?"

"No, I guess I won't." We were talking lower, for the other visitors were moving past us to the door, and the inmate lying on the next couch was awake on his back, his arms under his head.

"What you going to write to her then?"

"What you want me to write to her?"

He thought about it a minute as if he had not thought about it every day of his confinement. "Well, I'd like her to keep my tools intact," he said. "I got the key to my toolbox with me, or maybe you got it now, but that don't mean anything if she wants to sell them. I got some London spring steel saws in there I'd hate to lose. I'm afraid if you tell her where they got me, she'll sell my tools, she'll think I'm never coming back to live there anymore and hoping I won't. So you tell her not to sell my tools and that's all. Just write it in a letter and don't say anything else." He removed his hands to see if I were nodding.

"All right." I nodded.

"You could get a job in this lousy town. I was working in a laundry when I was your age."

We stood up, then, to be with the rest of the visitors gathering by the double doors, waiting for the orderly. The cardplayer, a heavyset fellow with a shaven head, came out to his wife, but the patient who was afraid of me did not come out to his sisters. Caesar, in his flowered robe, stood by the sofa we had vacated, muttering his chagrin with his son's failure to show up even at the last moment. The orderly in his white uniform strode from the dining room, jangling his keys playfully under the visitors' noses, and the visitors, stuporous from the afternoon's confinement, smiled servilely.

My father shook hands with me, it was the thing to do in public. In the corners of his eyes were white dots of weariness, and there was a sickly smell of anxiety upon him; I felt the sweat of it in the palm of his hand.

"The clerk says I can take the Greyhound bus, it'll get me there, or almost. Then I take a jitney that runs from the town to the hospital," I told him.

"They got a private bus for us patients," my father said, loudly so the orderly could hear his joking. "I hear it's a nice ride, see the ocean, see the hills, go past them mansions of the movie stars in Malibu."

The orderly, his *Argosy* folded in his hind pocket, smiled as he turned the key. There was no hanging back after that. The atmosphere of the ward became unbreathable at the final moment when the door was opened to the outer air, and I followed the three women down the ramp, out through the swinging glass doors, and down the concrete steps with the metal rail that the sisters held on to.

As I went along by the high wire fence, ivy-woven, I glanced up to the second floor, not expecting at all to locate that particular ward and was surprised to find myself looking into the windows of the sleeping room. I saw the bent heads of the cardplayers and the back of the chair that the wife had sat in. By another window in that room my father was standing in his gray garments, watching me go. And I knew then that I was guilty of something and he was accusing me of it, and it was the guilt of sight. For he was the father who breaks down under the eyes of his son, the father in his last years when all the circumstances of his life have got him trussed and dying, while the son stands and watches the end of the struggle and then walks away to catch a streetcar.

Death of a
Lesser Man

*I*n the midst of several friends drinking Danish beer from tall Mexican glasses, in an apartment of red Naugahyde furniture and black shag rugs, right at the moment when the hostess, who had been a Las Vegas show-girl, was leaning over to laugh something in his ear, right at that moment he threw himself off the couch and onto the rug. The others, his wife among them, thought that he was faking a fit to comically demonstrate the effect of the hostess's bosomy proximity or her words in his ear, although that sort of fakery was utterly foreign to his shy, gracious, reflective person. Then, because it *was* foreign, they realized it was an act beyond his control. Those who were sitting near him got out of his way and stood back with the others, who had also risen, and his wife fell to her knees at his side.

For several seconds he lay rigid, eyes up, a froth along the lower edge of his neat, blond mustache, while his wife stroked his face and fondled his hands. The others walked around in a state of shock, conversing with mourners' voices. Someone asked her if he had ever done that before, and she said, "No, never" and repeated it to the first question asked by the young doctor who, summoned by the hostess from an apartment upstairs, knelt down at the other side of the now limp man.

Claudia, the wife, stood away while the doctor with encouraging hands and *Ah ups* assisted her husband to the couch and laid him out, long and weak. She refused a chair, feeling called upon to stand in deference to unpredictable blows. The hostess embraced her waist, but she offered no yielding to this comfort and was left alone. She watched the shocked face of her husband watching abjectly the doctor's face above his, and watched the stethoscope move over the exposed broad chest. The young doctor glanced up to ask her which arm had jerked, which leg, and replying that she had been too alarmed to notice, she saw his fleeting response to her person, the same response in the eyes of men and women seeing her for the first time—a struggle to conceal from her the emotion that a woman's beauty aroused, whatever that emotion was, whether envy or desire or even fear. It lasted half a second, this consciousness of her effect, and was followed by devotion, which came over her with such force that she was again the girl she had been for him at the beginning of their nine years together.

When he stood up, shakily, joking weakly with dry lips, someone said the pickled mushrooms were hallucinatory and someone else laughed loudly and caved in. The hostess helped him on with his overcoat, and Claudia, her arm across his back, with the host on his other side, took him down the five slow flights in the elevator and along the street.

As she drove homeward she remembered with remorse their quarrel early in the evening. She hadn't wanted to go to the party. "So they don't know who the hell Camus is," he had said, tugging the words up from his throat as he tugged unnecessarily at his socks. "Why don't you get down to the human level?" They both had got down to the human level tonight, and now he was deeply asleep, his chin sunk into his muffler, his long legs falling away from each other, his hands in his overcoat pockets where, in one, he had slipped the doctor's note with the name of a neurosurgeon. The doctor had given him no sedative, but his sleep was as heavy as doped sleep.

On the bridge they were almost alone, behind them the headlights of two cars and far ahead of them, with the distance widening, the red tail-lights of one, and her fear of his sleep as a prelude to death changed the scene of the dark bay and the jeweled, misty cities ringing the bay, changed the familiar scene into the very strange, as if, were he to open his eyes, that would be his last sight of it. She felt, then, almost ashamedly, that affinity with Camus again, and although Camus was dead, the adoration that had taken her to Paris seven years ago was revived in her memory. She had gone there alone and lived there for three months, the sojourn made possible by a small inheritance from an aunt, but the money had run out before the destined meeting could take place. It was true she hadn't made much of an effort to meet people who knew him. How was she to do that? She had hoped that just by wandering the street where he might wander a chance meeting would come about and he would see at first glance how far she had come to be with him. Yet in that time she had felt her pursuit was as embarrassingly obvious as that of a friend of hers who, enamored of Koestler, had managed a front seat at a lecture, and with her transfixed gaze had caused him to stumble a time or two over his words, and, later, had accosted him in the hall and proved how deep into his work she was by criticizing some points of his lecture in which he had seemed untrue to his own self. Nothing had come of her own obsessive time in Paris, and in despair—what was her life to be?—she had returned to New York. But she had refused to board the plane to San Francisco. In the waiting lounge a terrible prophetic sense had come over her: all the persons waiting to board that plane—the chic, elderly woman in black, the young mother with her small son in his navy coat and cap, the rest, all were to die that day. She had not yet left the lounge, she was still on the bench, unable to rise, unable to return to Camus and unable to return to her husband, when the plane crashed as it was taking off. She had gone back to the hotel and cried all day in her room, shaking with fear of her prophetic sense that, if she were to heed it again, would show her in old age, all beauty gone, all curiosity for life gone, all hope for a great passion gone.

On the long curving road down through the hills and into the town, only the low white fence between the car and the dropoff into space, her sleeping husband beside her, she felt again on the verge of something more. If she had found another existence, those seven years ago, her husband would have found another wife and gone on living; now, another existence for her would be the result of his dying. The sense of crisis was followed by guilt that came on as an awful weariness, and when she roused him and was helping him from the car, she felt in her body the same weight that was in his.

She pulled off his shoes and his socks while he sat on the bed, and he was asleep on his back a moment after she had covered him to his chin. His sleep dragged on her body as she undressed and slipped her nightgown on. It forced her down beside him punitively, and she lay toward him, her hand on his bare chest, persuading him with her hand, with her heart, to stay alive. Dear Gerald, sweet Gerald, stay alive.

All Sunday Gerald slept, wakened every few hours by Claudia, who was afraid he had lapsed into a coma, and she brought him milk and toast and fruit as an excuse for waking him. After poking around a bit that Sunday evening, trying to recall the sensations, the thoughts preceding the seizure, reading the papers, showering, he returned to bed at ten o'clock and slept until noon of the next day, when she wakened him by stroking the smooth, veined underside of his arm that was bent on the pillow, a half-frame for his pale, unshaven face. She told him that the neurosurgeon could give him an appointment no sooner than Friday of that week, and this information liberated his eyes from the startled frown. If the specialist was in no hurry to see him, then nothing much could be wrong. He flung off the covers, his legs kicking and pushing out into air, and sat up. "I'll get up, I'll get up," he said.

Always he was already up and about at this hour, carving his fine wood sculptures or roaming the forest trails or the beaches, doing what he liked to do before he walked down the hill and caught the bus to the city and worked at his desk until midnight on the next day's paper. Up he got, and the moment he was on his feet again she felt again the inertia that came of her acceptance of the way her life was. The fact that he was up again, ready to return to work without having missed a day, deprived her of this crisis in her life, this crucial point of change, and, alarmed by her reaction, she embraced him from behind, pressing her face against his back, kissing him so many times over his back that he had to bend forward with the pleasure of conforming to her love.

Claudia was in the tub when he left, and she imagined how he looked going down the hill, under the arcade of trees, a bareheaded, strong-bodied man of thirty-six, going to work at the hour when most men were about to return home. At that moment, imagining him disappearing, she felt the emptiness of the house, and in that empty house felt her own potential for life. She was aware of herself as another person might become aware of her as so much more than was supposed. And, the next moment, afraid that a prowler was in the house, she climbed from the tub, shot the bolt on the bathroom door, and toweled herself in a fumbling hurry. After listening for a long minute for footsteps in the empty house, she unlocked the door and, holding her kimono closed, went barefoot through the rooms, knowing as she searched that there was no one in the house but herself.

Some nights she ate supper at home, alone, reading at the table, and some nights she went down into the town to one of the restaurants along the water's edge, went down with the ease of a resident in a tourists' mecca and was gazed at with curiosity—an attractive young woman dining alone. And some nights she went out later in the evening, tired of reading, restless, to the bookstore that stayed open until midnight, to sit at a little round table and drink coffee and read some more, the literary periodicals from England and France. The years her husband had worked days, she had held a few jobs. She had been a receptionist in a theatrical agency, a salesgirl in the high fashion section of a department store. But the artificiality, the anxiety of everyone, along with the obviousness of her own person when she was by nature seclusive, brought on desperate nights, and she had quit; yet she had chosen not to work in lackluster places. She wanted only to read. The only persons besides Gerald whom she could converse with were the celebrated writers and some obscure ones whose work she came upon unguided. It was always like a marvelous telepathy going on, both ways. While she read *their* thoughts, they seemed to be reading *hers*.

This night she took less care than usual with her clothes. Wherever she went she always took extreme care with her appearance, afraid of critical eyes. And always her head was bare, because the blondness of her hair was a loving gift from Scandinavian ancestors. The mauve silk blouse she put on was stained from wine and near the hem of the gray wool skirt was a small spot. To wear these clothes without embarrassment was, she felt, an acceptance of the stain on the soul of the woman who allowed herself to dream of another existence.

She left the old, raffish convertible by the small, dim park and walked along the sidewalk bordering the water that, a yard or so below, lapped the stone wall, and the reflection on the dark water of low-lying fog out near the channel, and the clear, faintly starred sky, and the cluster of seagulls floating where the waters were lit by the restaurant globes, all evoked the promise she had experienced in Paris. Just before she reached the restaurant that stood on pilings over the water, she heard a low whistle at her back, and a man fell into step behind her. She felt his close gaze, she felt his bumbling, beastly obstinacy, and she wanted to turn and shout at him to get away, a woman had the right to go out into the night alone, and, at the same time, she wanted to run away and escape her accusation that she had enticed him with her long, rippling, moonlit hair, her legs in black nylons, her white silk scarf with its fringed ends. On the restaurant step he spoke to her, some word to halt her or caution her about the step, and she pushed the door wildly open, banging it into a young man leaving. She chose the farthest table from the door, up close to the window over the water. The encounter with the man whose face she was afraid to see marred this night in which she had meant to be released, harmlessly, into an old dreaming of another future. She saw her hands trembling, they couldn't lift the fork without dropping food back to the plate. Able to manage only a few morsels, she waited to leave, waiting until the man must have wandered away, waiting for her heart to calm down.

But after she had gone several steps along the sidewalk, she heard his heels again. This time he did not speak, he followed as if *she* had spoken, as if they had become invitation and answer. Her heart knocking crazily, she climbed into her car, slamming the door. Her heavy skirt and coat lumped under her legs but she was afraid to take a moment to jerk them free. She swung the car around and, long before the time she intended to return, she was returning up the hill. Just before she took the first curve, her rearview mirror flashed headlights, and she took the curve too fast, almost crashing into somebody's quaint iron gate.

She stood in the unlit house, her grip on the curtains causing the brass rings to clink against the rod. If Gerald had experienced a foreboding before his seizure, this sensation must be the same. The man was standing out under the gate lamp, an obscene clod out of doorways, following a woman whom he could not believe would turn him away, a woman waiting in the dark house to open the door to him and draw him down upon her. Raising his arm to fend off the branches, he came up the path. She heard his step on the stone doorstep and heard his two raps, and heard her voice shouting, "Get away! Get away!" She clung to the curtains until she heard a car's motor start up and saw the red taillights reflected on the foliage in the yard and heard the car go down the hill.

A desolation came over her, then, as she moved through the dark house. The obscene dolt must have stolen away her dream of herself in the future, the dream that was only a memory of herself in the past, that brief time in Paris, alone, desirous of a destiny, desirous of the one with a destiny, the man who would break the hull of her guilt, guide her into the intricacies of his intellect, anoint her with the moisture of his kisses. The intruder must have stolen away the past and the future, and she was nowhere else but in this dark house where she might be forever. Her slender heel was caught by the grille of the floor heater in the hallway, and she left both shoes on the cold, trapping metal.

By the time Gerald came home all the lamps were lit and his late supper was on the stove, plates were set out on the table, and wine was cooling; and facing him across the small table she complained about the number of days they must wait before his appointment.

"Must be lots of people throwing fits," he said. And later, tossing the covers over himself, "Anyway, the serious things are nothing to worry about. By the time you've got a symptom you're usually too far gone to do much about." For a minute he lay gazing up, then he switched off the lamp to conceal his face. She heard him mutter half a word and then he was quiet. With his few words tonight he had expressed more pessimism than in all the years of their marriage. To indulge in pessimism, as to give way to anger or criticism, was to weaken the marriage, and he did not care to weaken it. He had never appeared to be dissatisfied with his life. He had not mapped out his life for a grand endeavor and been diverted. Everything about him gave evidence of his stolidity—his deliberation over small things, his way of absorbing circumstance rather than attacking it, the almost perverse unnecessity to change his existence, to strike, to wrestle, and she had clung to him for that enduring nature. But now, lying beside him, she felt in his being the invasion of futility, she felt his resentment of the specialist for his inaccessibility, and of her, his wife, for belittling him with her other life without him. The seizure and the suspense, the possibility that he might be at the mercy of physicians and of some malady and even of the end itself, all was enough of a belittlement. The husband who had always slept with a trusting face turned up toward the coming morning lay fearfully asleep, and she was afraid to touch him. She fell asleep with her hands tucked in under her heart.

Oh, God, what was going on? The obscene dolt, the faceless presence, the stranger in the night had lifted aside the hanging branches and was there, and he was cutting off her hair, crudely, with large, cold scissors. It fell in rippling, palely shining strands, moonlit, alive. It fell to the floor and the bedcovers, and her rage against that faceless presence gave way to an awful weakness as her hair was shorn. But was this really herself in a bed alone, a narrower bed? Was she really the young woman with the cropped hair, with the suffering face, the face gone beyond suffering? Was this herself? Oh, God, dear God, it was herself and she was dying years before Gerald. And how young she was, this woman, herself, who was never to know that old age she had so senselessly feared. Wailing, she struck weakly at the faceless presence cutting off her hair, but he went on cutting. In the bed someone suddenly moved, someone beside her rose up and bent over her. It was Gerald, and her terror over herself was over him instead. With both hands she gripped his wrist, calling his name into his large, gentle hand that was soothing and calming her into waking.

The Search for J. Kruper

On the plane from New York to Phoenix, where he was to stop over for a few days to enjoy the sun before going on to the Coast, the novelist Robert Klipspringer chatted with the stewardess and with the passengers nearest him, a congressman and a manufacturer of a plastic racetrack game, all of whom had recognized him. Although he knew he erred and was engaging in a grandiose comparison, he felt that the three were cognizant of the murky and turbulent weather with which the plane was contesting as his, Klipspringer's, kind of weather, for had he not, in his novel, contended with his past as the plane with the storm? He drowsed awhile, woke to find the plane swimming in the white sunlight of the desert, and, again against his will, he likened the approach of the plane toward the myriad swimming pools of celestial blue, each in the shape of its owner's desire, to his own approach toward his rewards for that scouring of his past he had chosen to undergo. A taxi carried him and his slim suitcase to one of the larger inns and, a few minutes after his arrival, he walked out, in swim trunks and zoris, across the rose terrazzo and lay down on the edge of the swimming pool.

He had flown East to confer with his agent and to sign a contract for the paperback publication of his latest novel—now and for six weeks past in a mighty lead over all others and acclaimed by the entire spectrum of the nation's critics—for such a spectacular sum that a small news item to that effect appeared on some front pages, and so he found the desert sun more enjoyable now than he remembered it from twelve years ago when he and his second wife had rested a day in Phoenix on a summer trek into Mexico. They had dared the trip on a morsel of advance royalties for his first novel and the meager savings from his salary as a philosophy instructor at a minor college in New York State. She had been taciturn and unloving in a motel room where the rattle of the air conditioner affixed to the window screen kept them awake all night, and, speaking only to quarrel, they had gone on into the Mexican desert where the heat stripped the recaps off their tires, vultures danced on burro carcasses beside the road, and for miles their headlights picked up a vast migration of toadlike creatures across the desert night. The convoluted misery of that marriage he had related in his novel, along with that of his first marriage. Was he exposing his back to the sun too long? He pushed up, dangled his legs in the water and rubbed his arms to spread the oil, and found beside him a young man who had been considerately waiting for him to sit up.

"No doubt you're exhausted after your Herculean efforts," said the young man.

Klipspringer accepted a cigarette. It was the brand that he preferred, the preference stated many times in the novel. On such a congenial basis, akin to a friendship over a decade, with his, Klipspringer's, foibles and follies and depths known, most casual encounters now began. As expected, the young man related his own past, his own life, as though over the time of their friendship he had so far failed to reveal himself to the extent that Klipspringer had done and was now in haste to attain an equality of confession. Very slender, his face fragilely handsome, his dark hair partly bleached by the resort sun, the young man revealed that he was at present employed by a socialite from the East, whom he had met in

Acapulco. Inasmuch, he said, as he spoke five languages, he was to serve as her interpreter on her trip to Europe. He told of his childhood as the son of the French ambassador to Spain, of his affair in Rome, searing and extravagant, with the wife and constant leading lady of a famous Italian director, of his sojourn up in the Sierra Maestra with the forces of Fidel Castro as correspondent for a Paris daily, and of his journey through the jungles of Mexico with the great novelist J. Kruper. While imparting this last bit, which was for Klipspringer the crowning bit that gave him, the companion of Kruper, a reflected glory as tangible as his glowing tan, the young man gazed over the pool, one leg in the water, the other bent in order that his knee serve as a rest for his elbow, smoking his cigarette from languid fingers.

Never had Klipspringer met anyone who claimed even a remote acquaintance with Kruper. It was more credible to claim, instead, an acquaintance with someone who had run across someone else, an oil driller in Tampico, a seaman in Hamburg, a prospector on a desolate mountain, who claimed to have worked side by side with a man he swore was Kruper. A claim of acquaintance with Kruper himself was not only suspect, it was an almost unforgivable undermining of the legend of that elusive man. Klipspringer, afraid that his curiosity would silence the young man, also gazed out over the pool asking at last, idly, "You say you know Kruper?"

"I'm in love with his daughter," the young man replied.

"He has a daughter?" asked Klipspringer.

"Of course. He has three."

"Which one?" asked Klipspringer, not wanting to ask that question but forced to by his confusion as to which question, among countless, to ask next.

"The youngest and, of course, the most beautiful. She has hair as black as the wings of the devil, way down to her knees."

"Does he live, as they say, in Mexico?"

"As they say."

"Born there?"

"It is his refuge."

"Ah, refuge, yes." He nodded as if he knew from what pursuit, from what tempest.

"You have heard the latest theory?"

"Which one is that?" asked Klipspringer.

"The Czechs advanced it first, after which the French translated it, then the Germans from the French, and the Mexicans from the Germans. The theory is that he killed a man. In an elevator in New York City, forty years ago. The man found in the elevator had on him the papers of a young Czech writer. But the dead man did not comply with the Czech's description. Not the age, nothing. What, then, happened to the young Czech writer? He becomes J. Kruper and flees to Mexico."

"Did he do it?" Klipspringer asked.

"He doesn't say."

"No, of course not," he agreed, in hasty apology.

"I myself don't believe that he did," said the young man. "In the first place he is not a Czech."

Klipspringer waited in silence for further revelations. Speculation was appropriate in a conversation with someone who had never met Kruper, but with a friend of the man it was like asking for betrayal.

"If you care to meet him and are someday going down to Mexico, as far as Cuernavaca, say, I will be happy to give you a letter of introduction," said the young man, still gazing out over the bobbing heads.

While the young man and his woman companion sipped cognac at the bar, after a supper as Klipspringer's guests, the writer excused himself and went up to his room to telephone his wife in Carmel. In his coat pocket was a letter to Kruper that the young man had composed at the supper table; it possessed for Klipspringer as great an urgency as a summons from Kruper. Ila, his third wife, was called to the phone by her daughter from a previous marriage. She agreed that he ought not to postpone the trip even for a day, for who knew where the man might be the day after that? She urged him to accept as true the young man's claim, for it was entirely possible that he, Klipspringer, was the one to persuade Kruper to reveal himself, he was the one to write Kruper's biography, and the young man had sensed this possibility. She could see the book jacket now: Kruper photographed at last and with Klipspringer, his reverent biographer, beside him, both men under an arcade at Kruper's villa.

After he had reserved a seat on the plane to Mexico City and replaced the phone in its cradle, he continued to lie on the bed, his shoes off, his shirt unbuttoned, the cool air from the louvered windows wafting to him the laughter and music from the night and the pool. The numbness, the faint buzz in his right ear seemed to be due not to his hourlong conversation with his wife so much as to his surprising decision to believe the young braggadocio.

From out in the pool, which he knew to be beautiful in its illumined state, green-blue and filled like a harem pool with women of various shades of brown from the desert sun, the voice of one woman came to him above the others, this one both sweet and brassy. If he strolled out from his room to the pool, all of them, each in her strategic time, would turn to gaze at him, having heard that he was at the inn and recognizing him. And if it was what he wanted, this recognition, then he ought to go and claim it, it was his. But once his clothes were off he did not reach for his swim trunks on the back of a chair. Instead, he bent to his suitcase, found his leather kit containing a miscellany of personal things that he had listed somewhere in his novel, among them Band-Aids, two extra pens, flashlight batteries, aspirins, cufflinks, eyedrops, sleeping pills, and earplugs. In the years before he overcame his fear of barbiturates, a fear he had examined in his novel, he had used earplugs on noisy nights away from home. He had not used them for years, but now he stood before the mirror of the dresser to watch himself swallow a pill with habit's ease and also slip a pink plug into each ear.

Since he did not care to go to the trouble of transferring to the bus, he proposed to the driver of the taxi carrying him from the airport in Mexico City that he continue to be carried on to Cuernavaca, and so he was— out through the city and up into the mountains above deep, immense valleys from which wisps of smoke rose high into the silent afternoon. They arrived in a rosy sunset. He took rooms in a small and exclusive hotel and ate his supper in the garden where peacocks and cranes stalked over the lawn and flew up with a clapping of wings to roost on the lower limbs of the trees whose large, fire-colored blossoms fell to the ground with the sound of a small, soft fruit. The moon rose, a warm erratic wind rose, and excited by the enchanting conditions which he interpreted as propitious he strolled out through the lobby to the taxis. The woman in the café, where he asked to be driven, was to act as his liaison with Kruper. Twelve years ago, even five years ago with three novels to his name, he could not, he mused, have approached so confident of his welcome as now. Surely a man of wide and eclectic ranging through the literature of the world, classic and current, Kruper would recognize the name of Klipspringer and think twice, think six times, before turning him away.

"*Aquí?*" he asked as the taxi swung up before the open door of a dim, hole-in-the-wall café with three tables, lopsided cloths, and four customers, three of whom were sprawled around one table.

"*Aquí,*" said the driver. On the other side of the street rose a massive stone wall, along the top of which men sat with their backs to the street, or, since they were so high, to the night sky. "*A la izquierda,*" said the driver, "*es el Palacio de Cortés.*" So it was obvious the café to the right was his destination. He had expected it to be brighter, cleaner, but might it not, just as well, be dingy and with a narrow staircase in the kitchen leading up to a room where the great man paced the floor? Or was he the heavy, elderly man alone at a table, with his gray hair shaven close and his jowls hanging over the collar of his soiled shirt and his small, pale eyes fixed in austere curiosity on Klipspringer's head poking out the taxi window?

Shaken by the conviction that the man was Kruper, Klipspringer sat down at the empty table, unable to speak, likening his abashment to that of a young novice ushered into the presence of Conrad. A number of flies flew up from the cloth, and beyond their darting bodies he saw emerge from the kitchen a girl who met the description of Kruper's youngest daughter given him by the young man in Phoenix. One thick braid hung over a shoulder and lay on her large bosom that swelled against the embroidered blouse.

He ordered a beer. Then, before she turned away, he detained her with an appealing face. If she did not recognize it, she would at least suspect that he was somebody of intelligence, somebody who intended no flippancy, no flirtation either with her or with life. "You are *amiga con Felipe?*" he asked, limited by his scanty knowledge of her language. "I am also a friend of his."

The name of the young man caused such an agitation of her plump face that he could not make out whether she was smiling or weeping.

"He told me," he said, "*su padre es* J. Kruper."

"Who is her father?" the man with the jowls demanded, his voice on guard, deep and rumbling, and, as if he had commanded it to be silent, the far-off music from the band pavilion in the plaza ceased at once on a flourish of trumpets.

"Forgive me," Klipspringer began. "I am looking for her father. You are her father?"

With the dignity, the expressionless calm of a man who has sired twenty children, and an unknown number beyond that, he nodded. Unable, any longer, to contain the emotion aroused by the name of Felipe, the girl ran into the kitchen.

"Then you are J. Kruper?" Klipspringer asked.

With his forearms on the table, the man meditatively turned his bottle of beer between his palms, taking the time that a dog takes to turn around a few times and lie down. "No, but I am his brother," he said and smiled a narrow smile of yellow teeth and gaps.

Klipspringer introduced himself, observing, as they both rose halfway from their chairs and gripped hands, that his name meant nothing to the man.

"He is here?" asked Klipspringer.

The brother shook his head as one does humorously for a child who has asked for too much.

"Where then?"

The brother shrugged. "The last letter is from Ixtilxochitchuatepec, but that means nothing. By now he may be back in Veracruz."

"Veracruz is his home?"

"Let us say," said the brother, "that the earth is his home," and smiled again his narrow smile. "I am sure you know," he said, gesturing Klipspringer to sit closer, an invitation Klipspringer accepted at once, "that many countries claim him as their own, each one claims his place of birth. But if the earth is his home, what is the difference where he first opened his mouth to bawl?"

"Yourself, you're from. . . . Let me guess," said Klipspringer as if for camaraderie's sake alone.

"Amsterdam," said the brother. "Our father was a shipwright. It was a big family, he was the third from the oldest and I was the third from the youngest, so if you want to know what kind of child he was, if he whined or if he laughed, if he did good deeds or sulked in a cupboard, I can't tell you. At the age of ten he shipped as a cabin boy and by the time I went to seek my own fortune he was already away for many years. But I met him again on a freighter to the East Indies. To make a long story short, the ship went down in the Atlantic. The captain and the rest of the crew all went down except my brother and myself."

Klipspringer sat in confounded silence. The story the man had told derived from one of the early novels of Kruper. Was the man Kruper or Kruper's brother or simply a reader of Kruper's novels?

"You are yourself a writer?" the brother asked.

Klipspringer nodded, reaching for a cigarette in his breast pocket.

"And what is it you write about?" asked the brother, offering a cigarette to Klipspringer and lighting it and his own with a finesse that was strange for the large blunt hands whose cuts were filled with black grime. Or was it ink?

At the risk of sounding melodramatic, hoping that the man would accept his words as honest and significant, he answered, "Of my life."

"Of your life," the brother mused, seriously enough, impressed enough, settling back and stretching his short, heavy legs in their baggy trousers. He gazed at Klipspringer's clean-shaven plump cheeks and, for a longer time, at his coat, at its fine cloth of subtle stripes. "Not every man has the courage to turn over his own stones," said the brother. "And because you have that courage I will give you the name of the woman who translates my brother's works. Since she does not care to be tracked down by searchers after Kruper, her name never appears on his books. She lives not far from here but you must phone to set an hour as she is a doctor and has many patients. It's possible that my brother is with her now for a few days and—who knows?—he may be acquainted with your life and rush out to embrace you."

On the paper that Klipspringer slipped across the table, and with Klipspringer's pen, the brother wrote the woman's name in a laborious script.

At four the following afternoon, the hour of his appointment, Klipspringer, in high, anticipatory spirits, pulled the rope to the side of a small, carven door and set a large bell to clanging above his head. The street on which the taxi had left him was narrow, full of stones and ruts. A manservant, an Indian, admitted him, and Klipspringer entered a tiled hallway whose opposite end opened into a small courtyard struck with sunlight. On the straight-back chairs in the hallway several Indian women waited, wrapped in brown and black rebozos, barefoot, one with a child in her lap.

He waited for the *doctora* on a bench in the courtyard and was certain that the woman whose simple and benevolent household this was would not fail to respond to his plea. He began a conversation with the manservant, and since the servant was attending to the luxuriant plants that edged the courtyard, watering them with a hose and picking off beetles, Klipspringer described for him the garden of the hotel. He knew the place, the servant said. The *doctora's* husband, the servant went amiably on, had collected many plants on long trips up into the mountains and into the jungles, accompanied by the *doctora* who took care of sick Indians. Klipspringer, at this unfolding, was struck by the conjecture that the *doctora's* husband was Kruper, whose avocation explained the man's firsthand knowledge of the Indians and the country's varied terrain. A great, unbounded desire to find Kruper was now in possession of Klipspringer. If his search had begun from curiosity alone, it had become a matter of immeasurably more than that, and at this point he was convinced that Kruper was in one of the rooms that faced the courtyard, perhaps even inspecting him from behind a curtain, and that this was the arcade, shading the windows, under which their picture was to be taken together.

Quick of step and apologetic for her delay, the *doctora* sat down beside him on the bench. She was once a comely woman; her large, dark eyes were evidence enough. He was confused by her, attracted by her remaining beauty and rebuffed by her own unconcern with it. She was untidy, her hair in a straggling knot and a spot or two of some tincture on her blouse.

"Your husband is a botanist?" he asked.

"He is dead," she said.

"Was he Kruper?" he cried.

"No, he was not Kruper, he was an English botanist," she assured him, and Klipspringer was both relieved and surprised at his error.

Over the phone the *doctora* had recognized his name; although she had read none of his novels, she subscribed, she had told him, to several periodicals from the States and had heard of him. But she did not, now, reveal anything about Kruper. Her answers were elusive of Klipspringer's questions. He saw that she regarded him as she would a patient, both respectful of his person and ruthless with his ailment, and under her influence he was convinced that an ailment had brought him here.

"Kruper visits you?" he asked.

"Never."

"So he is not here now?"

"Never," she repeated. "Even his agent in Mexico City he never sees. That gentleman deposits the royalties in the Banco de México and forwards the mail to a box in the main post office. Neither he nor I are ever visited by Kruper. The one and only time I have ever seen Kruper was in the jungle near the Guatemalan border. It was the first trip that my husband and I made into the jungle, years ago. Kruper was, then, a peddler, with burros, from one mahogany camp to another. He asked me if I would consent to be his translator, and a short while after we returned home there arrived his manuscript of that novel of the Indians in the camps. I am the one who translated it into English. I did it in the evenings, as I do now. The evenings I devote to Kruper."

"He writes in Spanish?"

"Sometimes in English. Does it matter, when eventually it is translated into twenty-seven languages?"

"Isn't there a courier who brings his manuscripts?" he demanded, pacing the courtyard that a few minutes before had seemed so exemplary, so giving in its lush beauty; now he felt unbearably deprived. "Isn't there a courier? A man whom you could follow, whom you could send someone to follow?"

The *doctora* crossed the courtyard, disappearing through a door under the arcade, leaving Klipspringer to speculate elatedly that his desperation had persuaded her to plead with Kruper to reveal himself. She reappeared with a large envelope of heavy, brown paper. "You will see," she said, "that he mails his manuscripts and that he lives in a village so small and so remote that the postmaster, if he can be called that, does not even own a rubber stamp with the name of the village. He dips his thumb in ink and smears it across the stamp."

Klipspringer held the envelope that Kruper had held, on which Kruper had written in a scrawling hand, with a thick-nibbed pen, the name of the *doctora*, the number of her post office box, the town and the state, and up in the left corner his name and nothing more, and which he had sealed and bound—there were the marks of it—with twine. It was not, he noted, the handwriting of the man in the café.

In despair he sought out his hotel on foot, climbing the hill where his hotel was situated somewhere along the endless walls of villas and of ancient churches. When at last he stood in the blue-tiled shower cubicle, his head bowed under the onslaught of tepid water, he expressed his despair with a long howl. Toward the end of his howl he was interrupted by a rapping at the door to the hall. He twisted the shower handles and in the silence, punctuated by the water dripping from his body to the floor, shouted through the wall, "You got a *problema*?"

"Señor Klipspringer, I come to solve your *problema*." It was a man's voice, low, urgent, authoritative, uneasy but not unpleasantly so, a voice familiar or perhaps not familiar. Kruper? Was it possible that Kruper, hearing that Klipspringer was searching for him so guilelessly, so earnestly, so hopefully, had decided to spare him further torment and appear in person at his door? With his towel grasped around his waist he flung open the door and saw that his visitor was the *doctora*'s servant, pressing his hat to his chest and solemnizing his face.

"The *manuscritos* come by mail, that is true," the servant said as he stood in Klipspringer's room. "But it is not true, also. Do you yourself believe that *manuscritos* so valuable he would give to the *custodia* of the mailman? No. I will tell you what happens. Kruper gives the *manuscritos* to a man who brings them in his hands to the post office in this town. The man gives them, with a few pesos, to the clerk who puts the *manuscritos* into the box of the *doctora*. Kruper has much *confidencia* for the *doctora* but he is afraid, also, that the *doctora*, who, you understand, is in love with him, will ask a few questions of the man. She will tell him to sit down and bring him coffee and *pan dulce* and ask him if something hurts, his foot or his heart, and soon she will know everything and arrive at the house of Kruper with her black medicine bag and her nightgown."

"Go on," Klipspringer urged as he dressed.

"Once I sat down to drink pulque with him," the servant said. "He is *norteamericano*, like yourself. He was born in El Paso and has white hair and a scar on his face. But I waste time to tell you these things when you can meet him yourself. We can go now to the man that brings his *manuscritos*. The sister of this man was the wife of Kruper. She died in childbirth and the child also."

Since the servant had come on foot, Klipspringer and he went by taxi into the heart of town, to the edge of the labyrinth that was the marketplace. With the servant leading the way with rapid steps and a skilled serpentining through the throngs in the narrow streets, Klipspringer followed over ruts, some filled with black water, and under canopies of grayish cotton squares, ducking his head to avoid the low ones. The evening sky was still light above the canopies but everything under them was suffused with a blue dusk: the piles of fruit, the trays of yellow and purple and red beans, the pots and shoes and hanging blankets, and the peddlers, men and women, some of whom were packing their wares away. The turnings they took were innumerable but at last his guide came to a halt before a row of medicinal herbs in great variety, filling baskets and in mounds on the ground, each kind with its sign claiming its specific cure. The young man who emerged from among these herbs possessed, at least in the twilight, as innocent a face as Klipspringer had ever seen, as though a daily imbibing of brews from all his herbs barred from his system all diseases of the body and the spirit.

With his mouth to the ear of the herbalist, the servant explained the purpose of Klipspringer's presence. The herbalist smiled and nodded and, in turn, spoke a few words into the servant's ear. "He says," the servant informed Klipspringer, beckoning him to come closer, "that he will do it for you because I ask him to do it. I have told him that you are the man that Kruper will be happy to see." Again he spoke into the herbalist's ear and again the herbalist spoke into his. "Kruper," said the servant, translating, "lives in a house between the house of this man's mother and the house of his uncle in Iguala. If you will give him paper he will make a map so you do not become lost."

On a slip of notepaper, the herbalist drew a map consisting of a line with one small square at the end of it and, across from the one square, three more small squares, with an X in the middle square. So now it was Iguala, Klipspringer mused; it sounded like a lizard in the middle of a desert. Only God—and, he hoped, some bus depot clerk—knew where it was. The herbalist gave over the map with a smile whose respect made it difficult for Klipspringer to dispute, to himself, the belief of these two that he was the man whom Kruper would welcome. For this respect and for their guidance Klipspringer laid several twenty-peso notes across the palm of the servant and as many across the palm of the herbalist, and was led out from the labyrinth and into the plaza, where he shook hands with the servant and was left to himself. The lamps were now lit and hundreds of black birds were streaking in from all over the sky to shriek and squabble in the trees of the plaza.

On the bus to Iguala that he caught early the next morning, or barely caught, as he had permitted the crowd of people in the cavernous, fume-filled depot to rush up into the bus before him, he stood at the rear, forced there by latecomers filling the aisle, his face at a level with the shelf that was laden with baskets and rope-bound suitcases and, close to his eyes, a sack that moved. When the bus, grinding and roaring down the street, was stopped short by traffic crossing its path and he was thrown onto the lap of an Indian woman in the last seat and, rising, was thrown again to her lap, another seated passenger unfolded a spare seat into the aisle and Klipspringer sat down, facing front. When he gazed ahead his eyes were confounded by the close and far legs of the many men in the aisle. When he glanced to the right, his face was six inches away from the back of the head of the passenger in the aisle seat who was gazing out the window; it was the same to the left, and both obstructed his view of the countryside. Occasionally, a passenger got off at a village or along the highway; more often, someone else climbed aboard. Some passengers struggled with stuck windows and failed. The sun beating on the roof of the bus made the interior even more malodorous until, after a time, it seemed to Klipspringer that the bus was panting a mixed odor of poultry droppings, ripe squash, exhaust fumes, and odors he could not identify, and that this exhalation was inhaled by the passengers in lieu of air.

He sat with his suit coat on his lap, his shirt wet across his back, unable either to lean back against the woman's knees or to stretch his legs forward, and growing more alarmed each mile with his gullibility. It was incredible, he thought, that he had allowed himself to be duped into the belief he could find Kruper and to be machinated onto this bus to Iguala with these strangers all oblivious of the task he had set for himself, four years ago, of baring his life, and oblivious of how he had accomplished the task, neglecting nothing and withholding nothing, baring all: verbatim revelations to his psychiatrist; the scenes with his wives, the spoken and the unspoken and the unspeakable parts, and with his father, mother, mistresses, friends, and enemies; the journals where the dregs were, the journals without deletions, without change. Not one of them knew that in his own country hundreds of thousands held in their hands at that moment the chronicle of his life, eight hundred pages encased in a jacket bearing seven poses of the author, a large one on the front and six smaller ones on the back, and with his name three times larger than the title.

A sensation of suffocation set up before his eyes the item to appear on the front pages of his country's daily papers: died in Mexico on a second-class bus to Iguala. But only he, the expiring man, knew it was in the midst of fears and fumes and in search of J. Kruper, and that he searched for Kruper because he, Klipspringer, as his fame had grown, had found his own life more fascinating material than any other man's and now was confined way down at the very bottom of that life, and that he searched for Kruper because to find him was to find the means by which Kruper forgot the self that bore a name and became all others, became nobody and everybody. At that moment he was suddenly intolerant of his own name. If he threw his wallet under the seat of the man to the left or the right, he would, he reasoned slyly, die without a name, unidentified, a man in an expensive suit and shoes, whose body nobody would know what to do with. For dead and without papers he could be either a Canadian, a German, a *norteamericano*, or an affluent Mexican who had hopped aboard the wrong bus.

Iguala's dust rose in a cloud as the bus rattled into the depot lot, denying him further time to throw away his wallet and to die. His coat over his arm, his handkerchief to his eyes to wipe away the attacking dust, and gripping his suitcase, he staggered down, knocking over a pail of hot water in which several ears of corn were floating. Down on hands and knees, the Indian woman, whose produce it was, picked up the corn from under the passengers' trampling feet. He paused to make amends, then went on, observing how, on the instant, a thick dust coated his wet shoes.

Out in the street, which was like an adobe passageway, he turned to the right, as directed by the map. The sun was incredibly hot. He was hungry and thirsty and wished that he had bought a tangerine or two from a peddler in the depot lot, but a superstitious hope that some repast would be offered him by Kruper, a repast for a pilgrim who has at last arrived, had dissuaded him. The herbalist's map was simple: at the end of the street and across from a *tienda* stood three houses, the middle one the house of J. Kruper. Yes, far away was the *tienda*, its soft-drink sign and cigarette sign bright spots of color on the side wall facing the town. By its door two dogs lay on their sides, unmoving. An impatience even stronger than he had known before the other doors where Kruper was to be found, an impatience so strong it was an exultation, gave him the eccentric energy to run a few yards between every few yards of trudging. Yes, there was the row of adobe houses, small, yardless, undecorated, but not until he stood in the street with his back to the *tienda* and the dogs did he accept the fact that the house in the middle was not there.

He set his suitcase in the center of the empty lot, sat down on it, and for a long time gazed out on the endless earth, across tremendous, barren valleys to a far rim of craggy mountains and to the milky-blue sky, rippled with the heat, that swept back over all. The absence of the house and of Kruper was, he thought, all, all as it should be. A yellow dog with one ear slunk around him, its lip lifted, its eyes sidelong, touched its nose to his shoe and returned to the street.

At the airport in Mexico City, after he had wearily fumbled his papers before two of the battery of immigration clerks, he entered the waiting room and, since it was crowded, sat down on a bench near two women already sitting there. As he gazed out through the glass at the field and the plane with its attendant figures, he was aware that the women near him were now silent. Then, as he expected, he heard his name and felt his arm touched, and turned toward them an exhausted yet benign and grateful face.

They were attired in pastel suits; their hair, also, was pastel, and clusters of gold and glass baubles hung from their slim wrists. One, he learned, was the wife of a dentist; the other, her sister, the wife of a storage company president. Since a few minutes were left before departure time, he ordered a round of drinks from a white-jacketed young man, and as he drank, now with a sister on each side, he laughed with them over their jaunt, enjoying their obligingly pliable voices, happy when called for and thoughtful when called for, enjoying their appreciation of his presence. At the loudspeaker's bilingual call he went out with them, still with a sister at each side, along the covered passageway and into the sunlight and, after them, up the steps and into the plane.

The Birthday Party

$\mathcal{T}$he boy, wakened by the sound of his mother's heels as she went past his door, ran out into the hallway. She turned when he called to her. She had her coat on; her face was without makeup, and pale.

"Where you going?" he cried.

"Get back in bed," she called back. "You're old enough to be left alone."

"*You* get back!" he shouted.

She went on through the living room, her head down.

"It's very late," he pleaded. "I'm already in bed."

"When you wake up I'll be back already," she said. "Call Grandma if I'm not. If I'm not, then I'm never."

When the room was empty he heard, from where he stood in the hallway, the faint music from the radio. In the past few weeks, she went out often during the day or was not home when he returned from school, but she always came back before it was time for supper; she left him often in the evening, but the girl from the apartment downstairs always came in and did her homework at the desk and stayed with him; she wept often and brooded often, but she had never left him late at night and had never threatened not to come back. Though she had wandered the apartment all evening, saying no word to him, her jaws holding back the furor so forcibly she could not open them to eat or speak, he had not expected her to go out in the middle of the night.

He ran into her bedroom. It was untidy; a dresser drawer was out, her white negligee was on the floor, and the big, black marble ashtray on the bed table was filled with cigarette butts. The bed's silk spread was wrinkled and there were small depressions where her fists had pounded. He crawled under the covers and lay down in the center of the bed, and the return of sleep was like her return.

The sun, and the lamp still lit, shocked him awake. Afraid that she had not returned, he leaped from the bed and ran out into the hallway, calling. She answered from his room and sat up in his bed when he went in. She was in her slip, her coat and dress on the chair.

"You said you weren't coming back!" he shouted. It sounded like an accusation that she had not kept her promise.

"That's all right," she said. "If I hadn't, you're seven years old, you're old enough to do without me. That's a sign of maturity, to do without a person."

"You said you weren't coming back!" he shouted again. He stood in his pajamas in the doorway, terrorized by her troubles that had driven her out at midnight and detached her so from him that her return seemed imagined. The man she was going to marry—who was going to be a more fatherly father, she had said, than his own had ever been—had not come by to see her for many weeks, and it was to see him that she had gone out in the evening so many times, and it was probably to see him that she had gone out last night.

"I always come back," she said. "Like the cat the man was always trying to get rid of in the song. He tied her to the railroad tracks and he threw her into the ocean with a rock, but she always came back the very next day." She reached to the chair, her fingers digging into her coat pockets. "Well, no more cigarettes." She shrugged. "All I did was drink coffee at the places that stay open all night. You would have enjoyed it. Saw two motorcycle cops eating hot apple pie. They had their helmets off and they looked human. And I slept in the car a little while, but my legs got cramped. You should see the stars out there at four in the morning."

She tossed off the blankets, hung her clothes over her arm, and walked past him in her bare feet to her own bedroom. He followed her, unwilling, now that she had returned, to let her go from his sight.

"Who's going to take me to Molly's party?"

"I'll take you," she said. "Grandma's going early, and it's out of her way to pick you up, anyway. But, my God, it's not until two."

"We've got to buy a present," he said, afraid that nothing would be attended to from now on, that everything would be neglected; using the party to urge her to look after him again, to distract him again, and engage him again.

She picked up her negligee from the floor and clasped it around her and roamed the room, looking for cigarettes. She gazed into the oval mirror above her dressing table, while her fingertips felt among the jars and bottles for cigarettes. "Oh, don't you fret, don't you cry," she said to him mockingly, gazing at herself as if trying to accept as herself the woman with the swollen eyelids. "We'll be there on time and we'll bring a present, too. You're an anxiety hound," she said. "Oh, the champion anxiety hound."

He began to prepare himself for the party, searching for his shoe polish kit and finding it in his closet under a stack of games. He sat down on the floor and polished his best shoes. He was not fond of Molly, who would be nine, and he saw her seldom, but he prepared himself now as if he and Molly were the best of friends. In his pajamas he went into the bathroom and combed his hair, wetting it until it was black and drops ran down his face, and combing it over and over. He slipped on a shirt, put on his suit and turned the shirt collar down over the collar of the jacket, the way his mother always did. At noon he called to her from her doorway, waking her.

In the jewelry store, where he had gone with her a few times to buy presents, they looked at a tray of bracelets. Around the walls were large, colored pictures of coats of arms; on the counter tops were silver trays and bowls and candlesticks. When she asked him if he preferred a silver chain with charms or a silver chain with one small pearl dangling from a silver claw, he did not balk at a choice, as he had done in the past when he had not cared and had known that even if he cared she would have made her own choice. He put his finger on the one with the pearl. Like himself in the past, she did not care, or else he had persuaded her with his decisiveness, for she nodded at the salesman, who smiled as if it were the most appropriate choice anyone would ever make and caught it up with graceful fingers.

He followed his mother down the few stone steps to the terrace above which strings of red and blue triangular flags crossed from the upper windows of the gray stucco house to the balustrade. Under the flags, a throng of children wandered in twos and threes and clustered together over games, their voices rising high on the warm, still air. His mother had a little swing to her walk that implied that parties for children were what she liked best in life, and, walking this way, went into the midst of so many children that he lost her. At the moment he saw her again, his grandmother clapped him over the ears, lifting his face to hers and kissing him on both cheeks. Above her head, as she bent to him, the flags burned their colors into the clear sky.

With her hand on his shoulder, his grandmother led him away to a corner of the terrace, where Molly's mother was trailing her bare arm above the long table, dropping colored candy, tiny as seeds, into the red crepe-paper basket at each place. He could hear the small sound of the seeds falling because the commotion of the children was far enough away.

"We filled them all last night," she said. "Tons. But today they look half-filled. Up to the brim, that's the way," she said, motioning him to cup his hands and pouring candies into them. He began to help her, awkwardly, following her to drop a few more into baskets she had already filled. "Where's your mother?" she asked.

"She just stayed a minute, to kiss Molly," his grandmother said. "She's coming back later to pick him up."

"Is that you, Elsie?" somebody called to his grandmother from the kitchen. Because his hands were empty and Molly's mother seemed to have lost all sense of his presence, he followed his grandmother. She was small and quick in her coral dress, and her large, yellow beads made a faint jangling. In the white, sunlit kitchen, Molly's grandmother, in a smock stitched with a large, red rose whose stem was as long as the smock, was sticking tiny pink candles into the high, pink cake. Her hand, small and bony, covered with brown spots like freckles melted together, was trembling. She was his grandmother's best friend; they were so close they were like sisters.

"Tell me if I ought to use the white candles, if you think I ought to use the white candles," she begged.

"You can alternate," his grandmother suggested.

"Oh, that's strange, don't you think? Who does that?" the old lady demanded crossly. One pink candle fell into the thick frosting. "Oh, pick it out!" she cried to him. "Your fingers are littler!" But while he thought about the possibility of his clumsiness, she darted her hand in among the upright candles and picked it out herself. "All the same color!" she cried decisively. "Little girls like pink." But in a moment she was undecided again. "Elsie," she wailed, "is pink all right?"

The old woman's wailing over the candles alarmed him. He wondered if his mother was gone already, and he went out the back door of the kitchen, down a narrow passage overhung with vines, and out onto the terrace again. She was not there among the children; he leaned over the balustrade, and she was not with two other mothers standing and chatting in the small garden below, and again he felt the terror of the night before. He was afraid that she would not return for him, that her threat of the night would be carried out that day, and he wished that he had not gone off with his grandmother and that he had not reminded his mother of the party, and he imagined himself fighting her, if she had remembered the party herself—clinging to the bedpost and to the railing on the front steps and to her.

A little girl passed by, ringing a bell, and he was jostled along by the other children toward the birthday table. In the throng roving around the table he looked for his name on the triangular paper flag above each crepe-paper basket. There were so many names that, after a time, he got confused and found himself going around behind the same chairs, now with children seated in them. Then he read only at empty chairs and found his place. Under a high, red paper canopy affixed to her chair back, Molly sat at the head of the table. At her elbow, the many presents were piled in a red paper cart with blue wheels. The cake was carried in by Molly's mother, followed by his grandmother bearing a great, cut-glass bowl of pink ice cream. Molly's grandmother went along behind the children, pouring pink juice from a large, white china pitcher into paper cups; another pitcher, of glass, frosted from the cold liquid, waited on a corner of the table.

Molly braced her hands against the edge of the table and blew at the candles. Seven stayed out, two flared up again.

"You're too excited," her mother cried. "You're gasping." Although her voice was amused and loud, he heard an edge of annoyance. Molly, after a calm, deep breath, blew again, and the two little flames became rising wisps of smoke.

Molly's grandmother sat down beside her to eat a bit of cake. He was next to her, around the corner of the table, and her bony knee knocked his. "Oh, I think this is the nicest party I've ever been to!" she cried, beating the edge of the table with her fingers as if rapping time to a tune. Her voice seemed to him deliberately quavery, appealing to the children. "Isn't it, dear? Isn't it?" she begged him, patting him on the knee with rapping fingers.

Molly, under her canopy, lifted the presents one by one up from the ribbons and rustling papers. Each time she swung to the side to take a present from the cart, or clapped her hands, her long hair bounced against her back. The children nearest her, himself among them, fingered the gifts piling up before her—a long bow and a leather quiver of arrows; a small doll with a bald head and three wigs, dyed red and yellow and black, each like a puff of cocoon silk; a lifelike poodle dog of dark gray wool; a white petticoat with blue ribbons entwined in it, for which she kissed her grandmother, whose restless hands rested for that moment on the wrapping papers she was folding. The transistor radio she turned on at once, and the tiny, crackling voices of the singers went on and on under the tissue paper and other presents. She held up the bracelet, shaking it high above her head, as if it were something musical, and dropped her hands to open another present. There was a gift from each one at the table and from other people who were not there—uncles and aunts who lived in other cities. There was such a profusion of gifts that it seemed to him the reason for the party was more than that the day was her birthday. The party, he felt, was to take care of any crying to come.

On the terrace a puppet tent had been set up, a rickety frame draped with red cloth. Up high in it, like a small window, was the stage. The children sat on the ground, and behind them sat the women in bamboo chairs. From the corner of his eye he saw his grandmother in her chair; he saw the coral dress and heard the beads jangle whenever she shifted her body or clapped. Last night his mother had told him to call his grandmother in the morning, and her presence now, a few feet away, at this time when the party was tapering off and some mothers were already returning and watching the puppet show, was like proof that his mother would not re- turn. Up on the little stage the jerky puppets with cawing voices, the In- dian chief with a feather headdress, an eagle, a bluebird, and a pioneer boy with a coonskin cap, shook their arms and wings and heads at one an- other and sometimes collapsed over the edge of the stage. The laughter around him startled him each time, because he was watching the steps from the street and each mother coming down.

When the curtains jerkily closed, a young man with a beard, wearing a tunic of coarse cotton embroidered in red, and a woman, with long hair that hung down her back like a little girl's, came out from behind the stage. The man bowed; the woman picked up the sides of her wide, flowered skirt and curtsied like a good and proper child. Some of the mothers slipped sweaters over their children's shoulders and guided them across the terrace and up the steps, and some gathered in a cluster with Molly's mother while their children gathered around the puppeteers to see the puppets put away in the tapestry satchel, each one waving as it went down. From a chair he watched the women and children climb the steps, until only one mother was left, chatting with the three other women while her two daughters wandered the terrace with Molly. He was watching the red tent carried up by the couple, swaying between them, when he saw his mother coming down, nimbly sidestepping. He saw her change the expression of her face, smiling at the couple and ex- pecting to smile at whomever she saw next. She waved to him, the only child among the empty chairs, a wave that implied she knew the party had been wonderful, and crossed before him to the women. She had a sweater on now, as did the other women whose circle she joined. He saw his grandmother kiss her on the cheek, grasping and shaking her elbow, and his relief was expressed for him a little by his grandmother's emphatic claiming of her.

"So, Molly?" his mother called to the girl. "How does it feel to be nine?"

"What?" called Molly.

"To be nine? How does it feel?"

"Oh, I feel the same, I guess," Molly called back, a slight wonder and vexation in her voice. She went on wandering with the other girls—some purpose to their wandering that only they knew—their heads bent over something in her hands. The light wind picked up the ends of their hair and the ends of their sashes.

Molly's mother laughed. "In a few years she'll begin to feel the difference," she said.

"When she begins to feel it," her grandmother said, "you won't need to throw any more parties. She won't let you. Isn't that so, Molly?" she called, but her voice was too frail to be heard far.

"She can't know if it's so," said her mother, again with that loud voice that was both amused and annoyed.

His mother motioned to him and began to move away from the others, and his grandmother joined her. He got up from the chair and was a step ahead of them. All over the terrace the seedlike candies lay scattered, and a few ribbons, here and there, were blown along an inch at a time.

"You act like you want to get away," his mother said behind him, raising her voice a little to make sure he heard, but keeping it too low to be heard by the women they were leaving. "I came down and saw him in that chair as if he were suffering punishment," she said to her mother. "This morning he couldn't wait to go. He was ready at six."

"It wasn't that early," he said, hurt by her ridicule.

"No, he wasn't ready at six. I was out till six," she said, and the sound of the anguish remaining in her throat from the night silenced the three of them.

"Is it over? Is it all over?" his grandmother asked her as they climbed.

He turned, because he no longer heard their heels on the stone steps, and saw that his mother was covering her face with her hand, and with the other hand was clutching her purse to her breasts. The way her chest bowed in and the way her fingers spread, trembling, over her face made her appear as frail as her mother.

"Ah, not here, Lovely. Not here," his grandmother pleaded, touching his mother's fingers. So much love went out to her daughter that her old body seemed depleted suddenly. "The children, they can see you," she warned. "They can see you and they've had such a nice day. Ah, not here." With her arm around his mother's waist, she made her continue up the steps. Before he turned away, he saw the three girls gazing up at them curiously from under the strings of red and blue flags fluttering in the wind.

The Cove

Sometimes the realtor's listings book will fall open to the photographs of homes not within the means of the couple on the other side of the desk, and the wife will put out her hand, almost instinctively, to see what is beyond them. Of the several properties, the couple will pause longest over a particular house on the leeward side of the island. The woman will wish aloud that they could afford it, laughing, sighing, drooping, indecorous in a time that calls for reserve, while the husband will nod and agree robustly, even goddamning. They select, after the usual excursions with the realtor to several houses within the city and on its expanding edge, a house not much different from the one back home. The property that they coveted is shown only to those fortunate families for whom every hour is opportune. Persons who sometimes roam through houses they cannot afford in order to impress the realtor, or—though they have not met him before—vindictively waste his time, never venture onto the verdant grounds and across the threshold of that property. It is much too ideal to violate with one's lack of promise or even with that vindictiveness against the realtor that asks no reason for itself. Whoever might have in mind to dare an excursion is deterred by what might be suspicion on the part of the realtor: although everything is amiable and potential as they sit around his desk, elbows almost touching, knees almost touching, hands touching over maps and matches, a gulf suddenly divides him and them.

The realtor unlocked the wrought-iron gate, swung it open and stepped aside, waiting until all the members of the family had passed into the garden. Following at a discreet distance in order not to interfere with their breathtaking entry into a domain certain to be theirs and free of intruders such as himself, he bowed his head to choose the next key from the green leather case in the palm of his hand—both case and keys given him by the owner. The father went first along the path, his index finger held by the youngest of the four children, a girl of two who was walking clumsily on her toes. They were followed by the two boys, one twelve, the other nine, both lean, both wearing tan knee shorts and white pullovers edged thinly with red. The eldest, a girl of sixteen, strolled behind the boys, the wide pleats of her short white skirt parting and closing. The mother, young in spite of the number of her children, was the last of the procession except for the realtor who was, respectfully, not a part of it, following the mother by a yard, observing as if against his will how the flowers in the cloth of her dress vibrated with the movements of her body and with their own disputing colors. In the center of the emerald dusk of fern and bamboo and flowering shrubs, the father paused and so the rest paused. The garden was filled with a humming that seemed to emanate from its own exuberance until it became apparent that the sound was the sea's constant humming rising up through the density of mountain stone. Two myna birds flew up from a lichee tree in the garden, flapping over the road and settling in a breadfruit tree high on the upper slope.

The realtor unlocked the heavy teak door, found that it stuck, and pushed, his brow against it. The members of the family fanned out across the large room toward the wall of sliding glass that gave them an immense view of the sea. The realtor slid open one segment of the glass and they walked out across the terrace and over to the stone wall, and all, leaning there, gazed out on the masses of land to each side, tremendous green shoulders of earth that seemed to recede and swell in the hot light; gazed down on the vertical, winding stone stairs and, at its foot, far down, the cove. Black, volcanic rocks edged the cove, molding it into the shape of a three-quarter moon. The sea broke on the barricading reef and, after heaving and swelling on the inward side of the reef, swept almost languidly across the cove, breaking again.

The realtor took the liberty of leaning his elbows on the wall, along with the rest of them. The soft, ascending wind pressed his shirt—so white it shone in the sun—against his chest. For a few moments the shirt beat against his chest as if stirred by the beat of his heart, then the wind continued up and his shirt hung loosely again, unstirring. He was neither tall nor short, neither fat nor lean, but this averageness was like a happy medium he had attained by his own efforts. The surface of his face was receptive of all reasonable requests; under the surface, as if it were a matter of modesty, lay a look of gratification for pleasures granted to past clients. In the eyes of the father, who was a shrewd man and who considered shrewdness a virtue, the realtor was a simple man, lacking shrewdness. The realtor was silent while they gazed down, musing and exclaiming, as if even one word might be an intrusion as intolerable as an uninvited guest down with them in that pricelessly private cove.

When they began to enter back into the house to inspect the rooms, the realtor walked by the side of the father, pointing out the stoutness of beams, the solidity of the teak floors, the lavish use of marble. Servants were no problem, he told them, although he would advise them not to inquire at the village. They might find someone there, but someone unreliable who would prefer to reside in the village and come to work in the morning, if that someone felt so inclined. In his office was a list of servants with references, and one couple—Japanese—he heartily recommended. The realtor did not accompany the father and older children down to the cove. He remained in the house, strolling from room to room with the mother and the little girl, and waiting with them in the garden for the others to climb up.

The father returned carrying the coat of his dark mainland suit over his shoulder. His tie hung over the other shoulder, blown back by the warm wind down in the cove. The two boys refused to sit down, though they were panting from the climb. They stood shifting weight from one foot to the other, excited, tossing their hair from their brows. Their tennis shoes and white socks were wet and sand laced their bare legs. Although, with other clients, the realtor, by habit, strained to hear low conversations going on across a room from him or in the back of his station wagon, in order, later, to contradict spontaneously as if he had not heard the criticism or adverse speculating, and although he often used a contemptuous indifference to jolt the obsequious into action and the hostile into a recognition of the value of his time, with this family he was almost deaf, almost mute. While they were gathered again in the garden, the realtor thumbed through a black leather notebook, inquiring if they might care to see another house, closer to the city, with pool and an acre of garden, or a large apartment, a condominium, with a spectacular view. The father, still exhilarated from the descent and his exploration of the cove, suspected that this reminding of other places was a strategy to rouse the family to a desperate desire for this one. He smiled tolerantly, clapped his elder son around the shoulders, and moved toward the gate. The realtor followed the family, swinging the gate closed and locking it while they stood by the road, gazing up at the rest of the land above or gazing out to sea, familiarizing themselves with the spot.

By early June the family had moved in. Canvas chairs and chaise longues colored the terrace and in the cove a small rowboat rigged with a yellow sail resembled a floating flower. Children called to one another up and down the stairs, their voices always on the verge of echoing, and sometimes a brightly colored garment or towel lay for a night and part of the next day on the steps or on the sand and, seen from above, the fallen cloth claimed that region for the family. The fragrance of plumeria and flowering ginger drifted down to the cove and the scent of the sea rose, permeating the rooms of the house. At certain times of the day, early morning and late evening, the water in the cove was like a giant, dark, narcissist's mirror overhung by the mingled scents. Four cousins, ranging in age from seven to eleven, came over by plane from the mainland in July. They came all together, although from two families, the older ones in charge of the two younger. They were met at the island airport by the entire family. It was already early evening by the time the children got down into the cove. The sons and elder daughter of the host family ventured out farther toward the reef than their cousins who, adrift for the first time in the sea, were awed by the gradual loss of the others to the dusk and distance and by the eeriness of their containment in that large stone bowl that seemed to shrink when they dropped their heads back and gazed up at the great shoulders of earth and, far up yet only halfway up, the lighted house that hung in the green, darkening mass.

The realtor passed the house once, with him in his station wagon an executive of a hotel chain who was interested in acreage on the island. The client was talking incessantly, and the realtor did not glance out to find the foliage and the gate that marked the property until they had passed it by a mile.

On days that were oppressively warm, the damp heat, the metallic, lifeless shining of the waters, the steaming garden, and the land mass on which the house was perched, all seemed to comprise an initiation. They were more conscious than ever that they dwelled on an island. On more pleasant days it had begun to be as habitually under their feet as the continent they had been born to. Now the heat loosed the moorings of the island and of the memory, and the continent itself seemed to have been no more solidly in place than the island. The children swam in the morning and again in the afternoon, played cards and other games under the three large umbrellas on the sand, and indolently amused themselves in the house. The mother took her dips in the morning before anyone was up. The air was already warm and the sun bright, but a diffident presence was with her: a coolness that she was certain she would not have found had her family accompanied her. The father swam in the afternoon with the children. Each parent had a time that favored him.

After his swim, the father lay prone on the sand, his feet toward the land, his head toward the sea. He closed his eyes, hearing the water, the barking of the small black poodle running back and forth in the shallows, and the voices of the smaller children under the umbrellas. He lifted his head from his arms to face the other way, glancing out to the figures borne high on the serene, incoming swell. Three were more or less in a row, the fourth, his elder son, was at a farther distance, treading water. He laid his head down again and did not see the boy tossed into the air. One of the younger boys on the sand saw and laughed at what he thought was his cousin's amazing antic. His son's scream came to the father in two ways: it came over the water and it came through the sand, reverberating against his body. The boy was in the same spot, his arms raised. A few yards from the boy a dark fin detached itself from the dark, swarming spots that plagued the father's vision in the intense light, circled the boy, and disappeared. The boy disappeared with it, lost like the fin in the glittering air and water.

Their excitement in the water deafened the rest of the children to the terror in the cry. The father running into the water was a common sight to them, and their abiding in the water for so many more hours of the day gave them, as usual, a secret sense of their superior adaptability. The great, dark body gliding past them and around and beneath them sent them to shore as clumsily and eccentrically as if they had never learned to swim. The children under the umbrellas huddled down on their haunches, facing the sea or facing the cliffs, screaming the name of the creature. The father felt the shark pass under him and glimpsed it, and his own body seemed to dissolve, as if that languidly, monstrously gliding creature destroyed him without touching him. Way above the cove a child was climbing the steps, screaming up to the house the same word as the children below, and stumbling on the dog that ran up before him and stopped and ran up farther, barking all the way.

The daughter, with the help of the older boys, pushed the small dinghy across the sand and out into the water. Alone, to leave room in the boat for her father and brother, she rowed out to the place where her father was diving and waited there, the boat rocking and tugging away from her oars. She watched for the fin and for the large, dark body again, sighting neither within the great bowl of water, luminous, clear, except for the spreading and separating patch of blood a yard from the boat. The father rose and dove again, rose and clung to the side of the boat, and the sound of his breath was the sound of their terror as they drifted, rocked by the water and by the boat's own rocking. When he had rested for a few minutes he dove again and when he rose he lifted up to her the body of the boy. Her thin arms straining, she held to the body against the tug and drag of the water while her father swung himself up into the boat. Then together they drew the body up.

The realtor unlocked the gate and stepped aside to permit the family to precede him. The family crossed the garden, the children, a small boy and a girl, maneuvering around and between their parents in order to lead the way. Not all of the family were present. Two of the older children were in boarding school and a third child was in college. Rain had fallen only a few minutes before; steam was rising along the roof and a glittering was going on in the shade of the garden. A few doves were stirring in the trees. When the realtor moved toward the house the parents followed without lingering. The realtor spoke very little as he led the way out onto the terrace and back through the rooms, as if words were unnecessary since it was obvious that the property was to belong to this family. The mother was confused by the certainty. Before marriage she had been a hungry actress, and the years of her marriage—only the two younger children were hers—had not overcome her mistrust of certainty. She felt the need to catch the eye of the realtor and, even if her glance appeared to be flirtatious, convey to him her desire to comply. He did not meet her eyes but, his head bowed as if in solemn understanding, he moved away to lead the family farther.

Sublime Child

*J*oseph Carmody was conspicuously absent from the funeral of his dear friend and mistress of five years, Alice Lawson. The ladies in black, climbing into their cars in the misty cemetery, liked him less and with a definite sense of relief, for they had admired him only for her sake. But when, on the long drive back to the city, Alice's daughter, Ruth, asked querulously, "Where was Joe? I wanted to hold his hand," those in the car with her glimpsed reluctantly all that he had meant to the girl and her mother.

He came that evening to visit Ruth, said his good evening to the other visitors—Alice's sister and cousin, two small, wealthy women—somberly settled his hefty body at the other end of the sofa from Ruth, who was lying under a comforter, and with weary grace accepted his coffee. While he was stirring his sugar in, more visitors came—the two tall, gray-haired women from the next apartment, who smoked cigarettes and wept, recalling their maternal love for Alice and hers for them, and then, to change the subject for Ruth's sake, told of the ups and downs of their dress shop to the cannily curious relatives. But the neighbors left soon enough, realizing that it was a family gathering, and after a moment the cousin went into the kitchen to rinse out the cups, and the tap water ran on and on in a forlorn pitch.

Vera, the sister, piled her big tweedy coat over her black jersey dress and sat on a chair arm, swinging her foot and chatting with Joe. "She talks about living in a guest house. I agree it's good experience living with strangers, but it's only good if you've got a family to come home to. If you've got nobody then it's lonely, it's a substitute and you know it. You think so?" She strongly resembled Alice—the light curly hair, the angular face, the tiny, almost skinny body—but her mannerisms were of a different nature; she talked fast, she fussed. "I told her to come and live with Gordon and me. The girls adore her, they think she's so grown-up, being seventeen and all. Then in another year if she wants to move, that's fine. It'll be a healthier thing to do then because she'll have a family, she'll have us."

Joe looked down at his coffee cup, gazed over at Ruth, saying appealingly with his large brown eyes that he was in no condition to give an opinion now.

"She doesn't know enough about life, don't leave it up to her," Vera protested. "God knows she's been through enough this year, but at her age you don't learn from your experiences, you repudiate them. She'll think it's tragic and interesting living among strangers, but all the time she'll belong to nobody and pretty soon she'll take up with some kid who'll be mama and papa to her. She'll think he knows all the answers because he recites Eliot, when he won't even know how to blow his nose."

The cousin returned from the kitchen, picked up her furs, and threw the strap of her alligator purse over her shoulder. The two women bent to Ruth, kissing her on the mouth, sadly, emphatically.

The carpet in the hallway silenced them the instant they left the apartment. That sudden silence always aroused in Ruth the suspicion that visitors stood for a few minutes listening to what was being said about them. Was Aunt Vera laying an anxious ear against the door, afraid that her niece actually would accept the invitation? In that carpeted after-quiet, Ruth recalled her mother's complaints about Vera's lack of sisterly love, recalled the whisperings of the two little girls on their one and only visit to their Aunt Alice, a few weeks ago.

"Shall I heat that cocoa?" Joe asked. "Don't you want it? What did you have for supper?"

"Some toast and an orange."

"What do you want to do, starve?" He stood up, took the cup from her. "It must be an old superstition still in our blood. We've got to atone for all our sins against the departed one, so we fast. Well, you're going to eat something. You think she wants you to starve yourself?"

While whatever he had found in the kitchen was heating on the stove, he returned to her and penitently squatted down on his heels beside the sofa. "You want to know why I didn't show up today?" he asked. "Because I didn't want to remember it. I didn't want to superimpose it on the things I wanted to remember." He covered his eyes with his hand. "Sometimes I wonder at myself," he said. "In order to make her sufferings bearable— to myself, I mean—I likened her to Camille. Not that the illnesses were the same. Your mother's was much harder to bear and less adaptable to any romantic story. But that was the only way I could bear the human, the ugly part of things, by likening her to a romantic figure."

She was frightened, called upon to listen with her mother's alertness and comprehension, called upon to reply with Alice's sweet, analytical voice. Why wasn't her mother here, somewhere in the empty apartment, to consider his apology and reply to it? She, the daughter, had no ability to ease him. As long ago as she could recall, she had been honored by her mother with listening privileges; she had been allowed to listen to conversations. Now she was expected to act as an adult and all she could do was complain for herself. "Joe, I don't feel well."

"It's no wonder," he said. "No food."

He tucked in her feet, felt her forehead and discovered a slight fever. He brought her a cup of hot bouillon, a rye and ham sandwich, and a heart of celery, and sat on the sofa by her feet, smiling over the paradox of her eating well and dropping tears into her food. And she felt that she had clumsily, yet deftly, helped him.

"If you don't want to live with your Aunt Vera, don't then," he told her. "What's her husband, a wholesale auto dealer? Sounds stimulating."

"I don't want to leave yet," she said.

"No, I imagine not," he agreed. "Anyway, a guest house might turn out to be rather disappointing. Sometimes, you know, the test of maturity isn't how well we mingle but how we handle solitude. If you get lonesome here, you can ask a friend to come and stay with you."

"And will you keep an eye on us, Joe?"

"Honey, honey," he said, squeezing her blanketed foot. "Do you need to ask me that?"

A month went by before she asked a friend to stay with her. She preferred in that time to return alone to the still air of the little apartment, to live alone among the articles made by her mother's nimble fingers—the needlepoint cushions, the hooked rugs. On Friday evenings Joe took her to supper and to a concert or an exhibit, and he was all the company she could handle, for her attempt to be the comforting companion that her mother would have urged her to be proved exhausting; and ineffectual. He had sunk into a bitter mood, recalling in detail the times that he might have been more considerate of Alice. When, early in the fifth week, he came by to tell her he could not keep their appointment, she invited Carol to supper for that Friday and during the evening, listening to records, it was always on the tip of her tongue to ask this neat, this dark-eyed girl to live with her; but to invite her was to betray Alice and Joe. The following Monday, sitting by Carol in their French class, she extended the invitation out of the clear sky, and on Saturday Carol moved her things in a taxi from the small room she rented in a family house, and Ruth transferred her belongings to her mother's small, sacred bedroom, giving the larger, airier room to her friend.

That evening Joe brought up a delicatessen spread to honor the girl he was to meet, and he complimented Ruth on her choice of a roommate. Carol was reciprocally impressed with him. Her curiosity camouflaged by her wit, she learned that he was an attorney and a scholar, and she engaged him in an evaluation of some of the modern American poets.

Everything—the conversation, the spiced meats and black pumpernickel, the bottle of *vin rosé,* and the two girls yearning toward him—reminded Ruth of the time when her mother had been well. Yet somewhere in the midst of it Carol grew quiet and began to watch her. The girl had leaned her elbows on the kitchen table and cupped her flushed face in her hands in order to watch her better, and Ruth was caught as by a camera in an attitude of feverish animation, her thin arms widespread in a fancy gesture.

"Is he a relative?" Carol asked when he was gone.

"Of a sort," Ruth said.

"Oh?" said Carol, clearing away the plates and glasses.

"He wanted to marry my mother."

"Why didn't he?"

"He's already married." She felt pressured by Carol's silence. "His wife and he, they grew apart. I mean, she's a shallow sort of person, likes clothes, likes to compete. But she's dependent upon him, she says she loves him more than life and that she'll kill herself if he leaves her." But she had never met Joe's wife, and conjuring up an image of her from Joe's complaints made her feel unfair. She had not felt unfair just listening and accepting.

"Was your mother a scholar?"

"A scholar? Well, in a way. But she was sweet!" She had never delineated, never evaluated her mother. Not only had the task never been necessary, even the thought of it, now at this prompting, seemed sacrilegious. She had nothing to begin the task with, nothing but her love. "When she used to get dressed up, there wasn't anybody who had more class. She liked nice things. . . ."

"But so does his wife!" Carol said, sparing of no one's feelings in her pursuit of logic.

"But my mother didn't *care* about things like that."

The elation was gone, it had departed with Joe. They tidied the kitchen, and each went to her own room. Ruth was dismayed by the girl's bright blindness. When, in bed, she opened the French grammar to recite the day's vocabulary, she could not speak aloud. Her voice was gone and it seemed to have left her that moment she had found Carol's inquiring face absorbing and rejecting her. She wondered if she had erred in asking the girl to live with her. Had she brought someone into the house who was smugly, stubbornly ignorant of life? *La vie d'amour?*

Sunday evening Joe returned, and his anticipation of the girls' attentions softened his mouth, imparted a dancer's aplomb to his heavy body.

He brought a bottle of Benedictine, and they carried their glasses to the living room and listened to him describe a day in court. Carol had lost yesterday's enamored air; she listened courteously, for, having accepted the liqueur, she owed him in return an appreciation of his wit. When he left, Ruth accompanied him down in the elevator and walked the block to his car, hanging to his arm.

At the car he said, "Well, I guess you won't be so lonesome anymore."

"Carol's nice," she said. "Except a little stuffy."

"She'll grow up," he assured her, smiling a narrow, nostalgic smile. He patted her head, resting his hand in her pale curls so that the weight of his hand was the weight of their shared sorrow. After he got into his car, she walked along the sidewalk toward the apartment while he drove slowly along beside her. She could not see him very well in the dark of the big Buick, only his hand waving, and she shivered with wisdom, hugging her arms to her breast.

It was only for a few minutes following his visits that she felt under stress with Carol. After all, why should she expect Carol to be enlivened by his presence to the same degree that she was and her mother had been? At all other times the girls got along well together, and finally, one evening, when Carol commented just after Joe had left, "You know, Ruthie, you're like a century plant? You bloom only when Joe comes by, and then so extravagantly?" the loyalty that bound the girls together, compounded of experiences in which he did not figure, allowed them to laugh together.

In June she went with Carol to spend the summer at her friend's house, on a hill below Mount Tamalpais, not quite an hour's drive from the city. They wandered into the eucalyptus grove where the warm air was saturated with the oily fragrance, and they climbed into the dense woods where they picked miner's lettuce and watched hawks soaring in the static sky. But lying on her cot at night, lying in a house her mother had never entered, under the same roof with a family her mother had never met, she had to cough into her pillow to relieve the fear of her separate existence. Not until now was the fact made clear to her that she had been left to her own devices. And sitting at the table with Carol's parents—the slight, gray-haired father who was a postal clerk and the tall, dark-haired mother who was a teacher; with the three young brothers, always fidgeting as if from a tickling to the soles of their feet; and with Carol, wearing her oldest brother's T-shirt, Ruth would remember her mother in the small apartment, and she would be confused by the number of persons around her at the table. They all had the same face, they all had the same name. If Carol had to love so many, was it possible that the girl had never loved anyone wholeheartedly? Joe and Alice and herself, they knew what love was because they had only one another.

Yearning for him, she lost weight, and she would have returned to the city if he had been there, but he and his wife had left several weeks earlier than the girls and intended to be away until September. She told no one about her eighteenth birthday coming up, but the Sunday after her birthday, Vera and her husband and the two little girls drove up to visit her, bringing gifts. They sat on the veranda with Carol's parents, and someone said that there would be no holding her now that she was eighteen, and she knew they were laughing because the wild mare implication did not fit her at all, a thin, child-size girl in shorts and bra and sneakers, sitting dutifully on a bench to receive her guests, the tan on her skin put there forcibly like a prison pallor.

When Joe came up to the apartment early in September, a few days after the girls had returned to the city, she reached out her hands to his in an attempt at that almost casual devotion with which fast friends greet each other after a separation, but before she reached him she broke into tears. He walked her over to the sofa and sat beside her, stroking her arm and laughing a little with embarrassment, commenting to Carol, standing by, that this really wasn't the way he had expected a girl of eighteen to act.

He slipped her birthday gift onto her wrist—a heavy silver and turquoise bracelet from Taos—and he unwrapped from the tissue paper two pairs of beaded white moccasins, gave a pair to Carol and placed the other pair in Ruth's lap. She quieted after a time and was able to look at him. His navy blue suit and his tanned skin made him appear thinner; he was fragrant with some spicy lotion that was the distillation of all the languid, heady pleasures of his summer; and his shirt was white as snow. But her reception of him was dispelling the healthy, end-of-summer equilibrium that he had entered with. He said that in spite of the beauties of New Mexico, in spite of the good living on his friend's ranch, something was missing from his summer, and she saw that his hands were fussing with the tissue paper in his lap. Her upset was contagious.

She glanced at Carol, who was leaning back in her chair with the moccasins on her feet, and their eyes met in spontaneous shame. This reception she was giving Joe, this deluge, was a disparagement, Ruth realized, of Carol's family, of the whole summer spent in the house among the eucalyptus trees. No one, nothing, had taken the edge off her longing to see Joe.

On Friday Joe took her to dinner, as before. Over the veal scallopini he said that his wife had bought herself a "parlor organ" and that he thought it was the silliest cure she had ever tried and entirely at odds with her character. "A piano, she could have taken up piano," he said. "But something has been nagging at her for an organ. Maybe she's getting pious in her forties, maybe she's atoning for the sin of flimsiness." He gazed at Ruth.

It seemed to Ruth an admirable thing, learning to play an instrument; she remembered that when she was nine her mother had persuaded her to take up the violin, but after a few lessons she had to give up because she couldn't remember anything, her fingers gripped the instrument with a kind of paralysis. "Isn't it all right, an organ? If she wants one?"

"Yes, of course," he said, and she saw that he was irritated by her inability to perceive his wife's motives. Any motives.

They ate in silence, his satisfaction with the food and his dissatisfaction with her answer mingling in his face.

"Carol doesn't like me, does she?" he asked.

"She likes you, Joe."

He snorted softly. Lifting his eyes, portentously large and dark, he said, "Ruthie, you're just like your mother. She was so loyal it broke your heart. If you think I'm hanging around too much, tell me to stay away. If I'm boring you girls by trying to extend the past, please don't coddle me." Then soothingly he was saying, "All right, no more. I always get self-pitying after a good meal. It keeps my weight down." And she knew that her eyes were the color of hysteria. He began to talk of the decorations in the restaurant, of the girl cashier. And the rest of the evening, spent wandering about the Museum of Modern Art, he commented on everything, persuading her with his chatter and his constant cupping of her elbow that he was entirely reassured, that he knew she was glad to be with him because he was so lively and so erudite and so dear.

He began visiting, after that, as frequently as he had visited her mother, and she felt that in this effort of his to make amends for the hurt he had dealt her that evening, he was finding release from his mocking self that even her mother had been unable to exorcise.

One evening late in October, he paused in the lobby with her as she was seeing him to his car. "All set for the holidays?" he asked.

Aunt Vera, she said, had invited her and Carol to Thanksgiving Day dinner, and at Christmas she thought she would go up to Carol's family and make her apologies for being such an unhappy guest in the summer.

"That's fine," he said. "You don't feel neglected, I bet." And they flashed smiles at each other. But he paused again out in the entrance where the slick, heavy leaves of the potted plants were bobbing in the moving mist. "Well, that's it," he said resignedly. "Sigrid's going to New York to spend Christmas with her sister, who's just returned from Europe. I'd been thinking . . . well, this is the first Christmas since Alice left and she'd probably like us to carry on in the old way just once more. We could ask her friends in the next apartment to help decorate the tree and I'd make eggnog for everybody, and then on Christmas Day I'd roast a duckling for us and bake a mince pie. You remember? The only reason I'm thinking this way is that I've made a New Year's resolution already. After the first of the year you won't be seeing so much of me anymore. It's time I snapped out of it, it's time I left. I think that you and Carol ought to move to a sorority house or a dormitory. You need to get away from the place, too."

But how could he make a cut-and-dried resolution, right in the midst of her wisdom? The thought that she had failed, after all, and he was leaving because she was obtuse was so humiliating that she overrode it by embracing his arm, begging him to please roast the duckling, to please make the eggnog.

They walked to the car with their arms about each other. "Now don't cry," he said. "Everything comes to an end." He laughed a bit when, standing by the car, she did not want to release him, and then was silent for a long minute, listening to her crying under his arm.

After Carol left, a week before Christmas, Ruth spent the days in museums, saw a play, and mingled with the shopping crowds, for the apartment with only herself in it was an expectant place. She shifted her friend's little antique alabaster clock from the mantel to the dresser in Carol's room, for it was an intruding note. Only she, Ruth, lived there. Joe came by only once; it was in the middle of the week, and he brought the tree and left for a board of trustees meeting. They spent the day before Christmas together. She met him in the lobby of his office building early in the afternoon, and they bought everything for their dinner the next day, and in an import shop where all the clerks knew him, they chose exquisite tree decorations. They carried the things up in the elevator before they went on to dinner, and the two women who owned the dress shop, hearing them laughing and complaining in the hallway, helped them to carry in some of the packages and stayed on for an hour, drinking sherry and unwrapping the decorations they all were to hang later in the evening. When finally they sat down across from each other at the restaurant table, they were weary of chatting.

Later, when they stood alone in the tiny elevator, Joe took her hand, and when she unlocked the door of the apartment he still held her hand. She entered first, raising her arms to remove her red beret, and Joe, following, clasped her shoulders. When she tried to turn toward him she did not know whether it was to cling to him or to struggle to be free, but, as though complyingly, he lifted her, and there she was, carried like her mother in his arms, and he was saying, "Sweet, sweet," his voice tangled. "Oh, God, how sweet you are!"

She closed her eyes, and was carried to his chair and down into his lap, and felt his legs trembling under her. The past year was bearing fruit, they were at last, she thought, easing Alice's concern for them both. But opening her eyes to see his face, wanting frantically to find his face familiar to her, familiar as it had been when it was more dear to Alice than to her—for only that earlier face could reassure her that everything was right—she saw only his dark head cradled on her breasts. The sight of herself lying like a babe-in-arms in the midst of his consuming figure shocked her into imagining that Carol was coming from the kitchen and saw her enfolded there, her thin legs dangling down. *No, no, don't make me be my mother*, she begged him, but it was only whimpering and, frightened by her inability to speak, she struck him with her fists.

For several minutes after her attack he wandered falteringly around the room, trying to find something to say but able only to cough from some arid place in his chest. He leaned forward on the table, knuckles on the edge, in the pose of a sagacious attorney preparing to speak, but whatever it was he intended to say he apparently decided that it was not to the point, picked up his overcoat, shrugged himself into it, and picked up his hat. And in that time, until he closed the door after him, she stood by the chair, watching.

When the hallway carpet absorbed him in silence, she went rocking about the room almost in his footsteps. "Mother, forgive me for hurting him! Mother, Mother, forgive me!" she cried and, appalled by the dryness of her eyes, she rained her fists upon her own face.

Around the
Dear Ruin

*M*y sister married Leo Brady because he was a merchant seaman and made good wages, and because he was gone most of the time. She and her five-year-old boy had been living on the sales of her cable car etchings that tourists to San Francisco picked over in the little art galleries and bookstores, and on the sporadic sales of her oil paintings. They were married a few days after he came from sea, and a week later his ship sailed again for the Orient. In the six weeks he was away, the steamship company sent her, at his request, all his wages. But the day that he returned was unrewarding for Leo.

Clara had her studio in an old building on Columbus Street. The first floor was occupied by the Garibaldi Club, whose members assembled every evening for cards; above her, on the top floor, lived two young men, a bank clerk and a window dresser. But she knew Leo's step on the bottom stair, and, lifting her head from the pillow, she said, "Why couldn't his ship have cracked in two? All the others did."

I was kneeling to help Mark, her boy, undress for bed, and I paused with my hands at his waist and lifted my head to hear her above his prattling. "Did you want anything?" She had been lying in a fever all day.

"Listen, listen!" she admonished me.

And I listened and heard the steps.

Swinging the boy lightly up, I sat him down on his bed. That day I had crew-cut his hair because he had wanted to imitate me, his Uncle Eddie, and his shorn skull sparked the tiny, blue confetti eyes that were like mine, like Clara's, and gave a malapert air to my red-striped T-shirt that I'd been wearing under my sweater and had slipped over him to sleep in; but it wasn't the moment to carry the boy out for her to admire. Wrapping him in under a couple of army blankets and a Mexican serape, I stepped out from behind the screen just as Leo set down his suitcase outside the door.

"Tell him I ate poisoned pigs' feet!" she cried in a desperate whisper. "It's called botulism. Tell him I died, Eddie," she begged. "I'll pull the sheet over my head and he'll go away."

Leo knocked shyly at the door as he opened it. When he entered, his bigness and his suitcase lent him a proprietary aura that he did not want. Up went his hand to remove his old black fedora, revealing beamingly, deferentially, his young, bald head.

"Clara's sick," I told him, when we had shaken hands.

Leo's brown eyes swelled sharply and his hands at once hung limply, unable to administer, in the artful way he felt necessary, the sympathy they held. With the contempt she had implanted in me, I thought: Why did he include himself in their marriage? If he really loved her then he would sacrificially send her his wages and never appear in person.

"She catch something?" he asked, his voice low and longing.

"The flu, I guess. She got me out of art school this morning."

"Did you call a doctor?"

"She doesn't want one."

As if walking in loose slippers, he tiptoed to her, and his throat and his eyes were full of love and of reluctant pleasure from the thought that she was helpless and he could help her. She was lying with her face toward the wall and she did not turn or move a muscle. Her long mane of coarse, unshining hair, the inert color of walnuts, lay out upon the pillow, and the very tip of this he bent twice to kiss.

"She's asleep," I said, taking my coat from the chair. "Mark's already in bed."

But he couldn't speak, so full of her presence was he, and bending again he kissed her hair for the third time.

"Eddie," she called.

The silence she ought to have kept overcame me.

"Going?" she spoke to the wall. "Okay, and always remember to contradict your teachers. It makes good biography." In spite of her dismay at his return and in spite of her weak condition, her voice took up again for Leo the thread of seduction, like a long-lost bad habit.

Leo was listening above the bed, his large body, in a leather jacket and black frisco jeans, solemn with his yearning toward the moment when she would realize, now that she was awake, that he had come home.

Imposed upon me as I ran down the two flights of stairs was the memory of all the delicacies Clara had been serving the past few weeks, the Sunday evenings I came to supper—things bought with Leo's money, like Italian pastries, lobster and crab, crème de cacao. The uneasinesss I'd felt when partaking of that food struck at me me now on the dim stairs like an accomplice Leo had left there. But I found justification for her exploiting him by recalling that all our years had been lean ones. In the town of Monterey, our father still sat in taverns, his duck pants colored by oil paint and spilled brandy. At sixteen Clara had come up the coast to San Francisco and modeled at the art schools to pay for her tuition. A plain girl, long-waisted, heavy in the legs, she had seemed, contrarily, to be burning incense to herself. Wrapped in a Japanese cotton kimono and wearing copper earrings like cymbals, she would ascend the dais, and the dropping of the kimono was always graceful and positive. Two years ago, when I graduated from high school and followed her, I arrived just in time to make the acquaintance of Mark's father, with whom she had been living for six years and who disappeared a few weeks after I met him. Small, dark-eyed, he had reminded me of a Shetland pony—any child could own him. All he left behind was a packing job in a ceramics shop and, like a guest departing, a copy of a highly literate quarterly containing two pages of his poetry. Leo Brady, a seaman with allegiance only to artists and a desire for talented women, came on the scene a year ago and had bided his time until another of her affairs had frayed and torn. The marriage, on her part, was an act of panic. The week he spent with her before his ship sailed she was drunk day and night, a half-nude, hanging-haired drunkenness that he mistook for celebration. My recall of these things, and my sympathy for her, absolved me of the guilt of complicity, leaving me free to slip out unburdened into the cool evening.

At noon when I knocked at the orange door, Leo called for me to enter. He was sitting by the window, and the glare of noon revealed strikingly the shabbiness that had accumulated since his return. Hope had ebbed from his eyes. The pinstripe shirt was partly out from his jeans and open halfway down his chest, and the black socks he'd been walking around in had fallen at the ankles and their soles were dusty. He put his finger to his lips.

"Who's there?" Clara asked.

"I thought you were asleep," he said.

"Not till I die," she said. She turned on her back, laying her arms above her head, but saying nothing more. Her face was opalescent, wedge-shaped by pain, and my heart turned over.

"Did you call a doctor?" I asked, sitting by him.

"She won't let me."

"Did she sleep all right?"

"With her eyes open."

I shrugged. "Maybe she knows what's wrong and has her own remedy." And to comfort him: "When she gets a little better, she'll realize you're home."

"She knows it," he said loudly, snipingly, in spite of himself.

"Oh, God, I know it!" There was always an unpredictability about her, and she rose onto her elbows, wildly flinging back her hair. "It wouldn't be so bad if I could just forget him when he's gone, but it didn't work." She dropped her chin toward her chest. "Eddie," she wailed, "I feel terrible. Call Dr. Larson and tell him I'm dying. Tell him to save me."

But when I stood up she stared at me with a ponderous frown, her eyes deep inside her head, like pebbles. "Where you going?" she demanded.

"You just got here. What the hell is the matter with you, you didn't have to come at all." Her strangeness poked a sharp finger into my chest, and I sat down again for a complying moment.

"You asked me to call your doctor."

"You been directing all your questions at him," she complained, "and he doesn't know a damn thing." She lay down again, staring up at the ceiling. "How simple are his wants. All he desires is to identify himself with artists. He married Clara Ruchenski because she'd had an exhibit in some dank little gallery and sold a painting once a year. How happy he was on our wedding night. I thought people didn't get that happy anymore, not since before the Flood when everybody was a brute with a big, smiling face. No, no, I'm wrong!" she wailed, tossing her head from side to side. "I take it all back. I never did think like that about Leo. I'm not a snob. Please, Eddie," she begged, "you know I'm not. You know me, don't you, Eddie?"

Leo and I stood up.

"I don't hate him, Eddie. I mean I wouldn't if I weren't married to him. He'd be a big, sweet guy with a respect for artists. That's the way I used to think, and I slept with him a few times, too."

"Be quiet, be quiet," I said.

"You shut up!" she cried, rising again on her elbows. "You're so good, aren't you? I hate to take you along to a party, always hanging in a corner like a tintype of a great artist in his youth and obscurity. If there's anything I hate it's hang-cheek people." She tossed her hair behind her and, thinking it was still falling forward, went groping for it over her breasts.

Leo was putting on his shoes and coat, his movements the sibilant, busy ones of a hurt person departing.

"Leo Brady! Don't let me hear you walking on tiptoe anymore," she cried. "I listen to your quiet and it's a terrible din."

"Lie down, Clara," I said when Leo had closed the door after him, and her hair was grimy damp to my palm.

"Eddie, Eddie!" she wept dryly, lying back and clamping my wrist in both her hands, and her bared teeth were coated with the suffering that she had concealed from us.

When I got down to the sidewalk he was standing with his hands in his pockets, squinting up at the sun, his flat, pocked face grayed by the slashing pain in his heart. "Is it time for the kid to come home?" he asked. "I could buy him a meal in a restaurant so he wouldn't have to go up."

Together we walked the few doors to the bakery, and he stared bleakly at the pastries while I called her doctor on the pay phone. Then for a few minutes I waited on the sidewalk with him for the woman who took Mark to kindergarten in her car, along with her own son, and brought him back.

"Why in hell didn't she marry Picasso, then?" he said.

Shrugs were becoming habitual with me. I was unable to tell him what I had discovered, that she had married him at the nadir of her life. She was twenty-six already and none of the dreams had come true. Leo beside me, a sailor home from the sea, a motherly young man, was unaware that he had been inflated into a grotesque figure, beyond anyone's recognition, by her fear of obscurity and anonymity.

Leo sat down on the stairs just inside the entrance, and I went up again. The door was open and inside the studio, Mark, who had returned while we were in the bakery, was leaning against the wall, crying. At first I thought that Clara was comforting him from a distance, urging him to come to her. But she was complaining about the Chinese boy who sometimes sits on a crate full of blue pigeons in front of a poultry and fish shop in Chinatown and, lifting out a fluttering bird at a time, cuts its throat while its wings stretch fanwise across his forearm. She was pleading with the boy to stop, her voice thin, bewitched, like that of a pigeon granted a human voice in the last moment of its life. Mark was crying because she did not recognize him. His back was to her and in his hands he held protectively from her his red oilcloth briefcase in which he always brought home his crayon drawings for her to see.

Leo rode a bus across the Golden Gate Bridge to Muir Woods, carrying the urn in a paper sack. Under the big redwood trees he spilled her ashes, on that spot where he had first kissed her, the day they had picnicked there and she had painted a watercolor. On his return to the city later in the day, he gave the urn to a junk dealer on McAllister Street, and there was nothing more to attend to. Mark had been taken up to Santa Rosa by his paternal grandparents, owners of a chicken ranch, responsible people who, whenever they drove down to San Francisco, had always brought money for Clara, and fresh eggs and poultry. Leo trudged down to the hiring hall, sat for a day and a half, and signed aboard a Pacific Far East Line freighter sailing for Manila, Yokohama, and Hong Kong. The night before he left he came to my room, and I served him sherry and panettone. He sipped and chewed awkwardly, ashamed in my presence, unable to formulate a reason why she had so frantically wanted to rid herself of his child that she had undergone surgery performed by nobody knew who, some man or woman in a shaded kitchen whose window we could never identify in the city's hundreds of vertical lines of windows.

With a slice of panettone balanced on his fingers, he said, "We could've afforded a kid. We could've afforded nine of them. She didn't need to worry. I got three brothers and two sisters. We didn't live on caviar, but we loved each other. My father was a skilled mason, laid the steps on a lot of those civic center buildings in Los Angeles."

A raisin from the slice he held fell to the floor, and he leaned over heavily, apologetically, picked it up and placed it delicately on the table's edge.

From Yokohama he wrote me a short letter, asking me to take good care of his record collection and the puppets he had brought from Italy, armored knights a foot high that hung on the studio walls. His letter was like a note of greeting and reminder that a connoisseur, traveling, might address to the caretaker of his apartment's treasures. On that last evening he had persuaded me to move out of my one room and into Clara's studio. "If you don't mind," Leo had said, "I could leave my things there and when I come in between runs maybe you could put me up for a couple of nights." But when his ship docked again in San Francisco he didn't call on me.

Once in a while when Clara was alive and I had an evening free from the janitor work that paid my tuition at the art school and from hand-painting silk blouses for a retailer, the labor I lived by, then I used to go down to Vesuvio's and have a glass of wine with Clara and her friends. But I never went anymore after Clara died, for mourning's sake and because of the pity that overwhelmed me whenever I remembered her lying demented and dying, and I remembered often. Since I kept away from her friends, I heard next to nothing about Leo. In January, eight months since the evening he said good-bye, I received a second letter, from Kobe, inquiring about Mark and about my studies. But he gave me no address where I could reach him, so I gathered he didn't care for an answer. Then one midnight in March I met him on the street near Vesuvio's, and a woman was with him.

Leo saw me approach and waited, blinking resignedly.

"Well, Leo," I said, shaking his hand. "Why don't you let somebody know when you get into town?" Glasses clarified his eyes now, and he wore a navy blue suit, doubly buttoned across his heaviness.

Leo introduced the woman as Evelyn, and she smiled at me nimbly, her crowded teeth curving out from under her upper lip. She was a red-haired, attractive woman, her full bosom snugly wrapped by her green silk dress. Leo asked me to accompany them to Vesuvio's, and the woman walked ahead of us, a quick ballet walk in low heels, her long coat swinging smartly. A day or so later I heard from someone at school that she was the estranged wife of the psychiatrist Irving Eidel, and that she was having an affair, in imitation of her husband.

Over the first pouring of wine, Leo clasped my shoulder. "Saw a painting of yours at the museum," he said. "You're doing all right, kid. . . . And he's only twenty-one," he said to Evelyn. The fear of ridicule took a quick sidestep across his face. "You don't paint like your sister did," he said to me. "You got human beings in yours. Her pictures all looked like broken glass. I always felt like I was walking barefoot in broken glass."

"If you'd wear shoes you wouldn't get hurt," the woman said.

"I'm not talking about art," he replied, coloring. "I'm talking about Clara. I was married to her."

"*That* I've heard before," she said, sharpening. "Is it your only claim to distinction? Haven't you even got a battle ribbon to talk about?"

Behind his glasses his eyes went small in humiliation. I put my hands against the table to move it away from him, for his anger was jamming him in between the table and the wall. But the woman slipped her arms around his neck, kissing him on his throat. "The trouble with you, Leo baby," she said pawingly, "is you don't love yourself."

"Don't give me any of that crap." Straining away from her. "You want me to kiss myself in the mirror every night?"

She began to laugh, her breasts shaking against him as she held him. He drew one arm out from her encircling arms, turned his face up and lit a cigarette. Then he gave way and laughed himself, a contrapuntal laugh, high in his nose, deep in his chest. While this was going on, four of their friends filed through the swinging doors and drew up chairs around the table. None of them had I met before.

"He's Clara Ruchenski's brother," Leo said, introducing me to one couple. "They're from New York," he explained to me. "They never met her." And he asked them, "When did you come out to the Coast?"

"Last August," the woman replied.

"She died a year ago May," he said.

Evelyn Eidel was chatting with the other couple and didn't hear. After a few minutes I left, because I had to be at the school early to help open doors, I said. But my impatience with Leo was growing unbearable and it seemed to me that I pressed my elbows to my sides not to make room for other persons but to keep myself from jolting everyone away from me.

One Sunday morning a month later, I was wakened at six o'clock by Leo knocking at my door. Defensively, he wore the preoccupied, hounded look of a fiction detective who can intrude on anyone at any hour. Sitting before my drawing board, he remarked on the changes in the studio. My untidiness prevailed. The chartreuse velvet spread that Clara had laid over the broad couch was worn away in spots; and only one painting remained of Clara's, a small abstract that I had chosen to keep. The others, big and small, had been sold at an exhibition of her work at the Contemporary Gallery. But the four Italian knights in armor hung on the wall still, and his record collection was neatly upright in its section of the record case. He didn't comment on his belongings.

"Did you hear that Evelyn and I broke up?" he asked when we sat down to breakfast. "No, you couldn't've so soon. It happened last night. Nobody's heard about it yet." He picked up his fork. "I been walking around all night. She took a liking to me at first," he went on. "Practically hog-tied me. I figured she saw me for myself, saw me with angel eyes. You know how you always wait for somebody to come along and see your heart of gold, right smack they look into your eyes for the first time?" He gave one short, great cough to clear his chest. "But she only wanted some guy to sit at her feet. No intellectual. She was roughing it." He removed his glasses and the flesh around his eyes was puffed to receive a blow.

I said, "You should have learned something from Clara. I was only an eyewitness, but I learned that you kneel too much."

His eyes jabbed at me. "Be an eyewitness to this too, Eddie," he said coldly. "You'll be an eyewitness to a lot of things before you're my age." Again he slipped his glasses on, his slow, careful hand foretelling how he would be in his old age, and, reaching into his coat pocket, he brought out a little enameled box, the kind for carrying pills. Blue roses were painted on it.

"Never showed this to anybody but you," he said. "Don't get scared, but in this box is all that remains of Clara Ruchenski. The rest of the ashes are already part of the leaf mold and people have picnicked over her. But there's a little bit of ashes in here, took it for myself when I scattered the rest. Want to see?"

With false aplomb he bounced the box in his hand in an attempt to forestall his sorrow. All at once I crossed my arms against my chest to keep down my own sorrow over Clara.

"She's in the palm of my hand," he said. "That's why I kept this. She's harmless. She's nothing. If I took the ashes between my fingers, it would powder off into air. But I'm alive, God damn it, and that means something. There's a big difference between alive and dead. This is what they come to," he said, shaking so much that he had to stand up, and he set the box down by the salt and pepper shakers. "This is what they come to. They're the stupid ones. They go crazy and eat dirt."

Jerking the chair far out with an elaborate gesture, he sat down again, pressing his forehead against the table's edge. After a while he spoke to the floor. "It's over me like a ton of water, the things I don't know." When he lifted his head to see my face, there was a red mark across his brow from the table.

The Diary
of K.W.

*F*EBRUARY 7

Often a young woman will marry an old man just because she likes his soul. But you don't see this happen vice versa. You don't often see a young fellow marry a 63-year-old woman. When this happens, which is once every 20 years, you see their pictures in the newspapers all over the country. They live in Oskeegee, Georgia, or some place like that, and he looks moronic. Nobody marries an old woman because she has a soul.

FEBRUARY 9

At noon today I was fired from my job of cafeteria substitute helper at the Eunice B. Stratton Grammar School. I was told by my supervisor to go and see a psychiatrist. But I would rather argue with God. God costs nothing and His arguments are weightier. But I confess that after I was fired, this very afternoon, I strolled into a clinic but the social worker told me it would have to be group therapy because so many people came for help and I was not a desperate case, so I strolled out again without leaving my name. I don't want to talk about my quirks to other people with quirks. It wouldn't be so embarrassing if we were all alone together, but a psychiatrist sits there listening and I've heard he doesn't say a word. You get the feeling that the ones who talk about themselves are the crazy ones and the one who sits silent is the sane one. Contrary to what I said above, God doesn't answer either. It's myself answering myself and sounding weighty, doing the job for Him. In my room I talk about my quirks to God with no embarrassment or not much. I threaten Him or disown Him, and then I answer for Him. If He'd answer, I'd die. But a man with a college education, why you expect an answer. I would rather write things down as I've decided to do in this diary and, besides, that immortalizes me, like Leonardo da Vinci. The psychiatrist takes notes, I hear, but that's not the same as keeping a journal by yourself. He can't take down the real meaning, just the cryptic stuff he swears by. He translates the quirks into a code and never knows he's forgotten something.

FEBRUARY 11

Speaking of Leonardo da Vinci (I speak of him because I can't bring myself to speak of what is closest to my heart) I was looking through his journals down in the basement of the City Lights Bookstore today and I came across one thing he says that goes I Never Grow Weary of Being Useful. That got me between the eyes. That's what I'd like to be. Useful. But nobody has any use for me so I am useful just to the two cats from upstairs and some pigeons that all look alike when I go to feed them crumbs in the park across from the Catholic Church.

FEBRUARY 16

No more delays! It's time to go back. No more sidetracks! (I began this diary with an O because it looks imposing, but no more flourishes!) It's time to go back to the day he moved in upstairs, two weeks ago, and misfortune began to fall on me like bits of plaster falling from the ceiling as the ceiling prepares to fall in from his footsteps up there which I hear like a giant's footsteps. They are quiet but of such meaning to me! The young couple upstairs who sublet the apartment and the cats told me he was Dutch and an architect and they hoped that the young man and myself would get along fabulously together. The girl uses words like that because she is jaded and must make life seem fabulous because she has only begun it and to think otherwise would be disastrous. They are a polite young couple and I know when they return they'll come down the back stairs with a little gift for me from Scandinavia or Italy, which is where interesting gifts come from that cost next to nothing. No more delays! The day he moved in I saw him from my window, I looked down at him from behind my curtains as he got out of his Fiat and lifted out some luggage, and my first thought was Now if I had a son that is how he would look, that is who he would be. How do you know? I asked myself. How do you know a son of yours wouldn't look like your father as you remember him, more like a plucked turkey than a man—Poor Father, Forgive Me!— gawky and sad, a plumber with a lower lip like a pitcher spout, same kind I've got. Or like your brother, a hulk with little hands that smelled of bay rum because his father's hands smelled of honest underground. How do you know a son of yours would look like that stranger down there? The son idea left soon enough, left me with an ache in my heart that was my recognition of him as more unmentionable than son. I have a lot of old magazines under my bed and I went through them for clippings that might interest him. I have art magazines and architecture magazines, all printed on slick paper, magazines I found two for a nickel and smelling of dampness at the Salvation Army, rummage sales, old bookstores. Well, I snipped out pictures of beautiful buildings in Brazil, in Israel, I snipped out page after page of articles that I didn't fully understand because I'm no architect and folded them neatly and put them in his mailbox which is next to mine by the front steps. Then a day later I wrote a little note, or to be precise about it, I printed it because I print nicely, almost professionally, like the print you see on architectural drawings at the museum, and I said I hoped he could make use of the articles and pictures I'd left in his mailbox, the note just an afterthought, as if I'd thought that he might be wondering who put in the clippings and it was impolite to keep him guessing. But I couldn't make myself sign my name. My name meant too much when I imagined it at the bottom of that note. It made me wonder too much who I was. I even left a painting of mine leaning up against his front door, a portrait that I did at Galileo Adult Night School, of a woman in a black lace mantilla, and it had my initials on it. My initials on that picture explain everything but he hasn't come down yet to ask me, "Are your initials KW, by any chance?" If he did come down I wouldn't tell him I lost my job as cafeteria helper. Because he would want to know Why and how can I tell him it was because of him? That would be the last thing he'd expect to hear, that an old woman he never saw before lost her job because he moved in upstairs above her. I can't even explain it to myself in this journal.

FEBRUARY 21

There is an old man I chat with whenever I meet him on the street. On a leash he's got a dog the size of a dried pea. Without a leash he wouldn't know where it was. Today I saw him coming a long way off. He walks so slowly because he went to extremes in his youth. He has pores deep as craters and a nose like a purple onion that is further evidence of extremism. Today he says, "Did you see in the paper this morning where 9 out of 10 men interviewed say they can't understand women? Women live by their emotions and men live by their minds and we shouldn't even try to figure out what you're going to do next?" "Crud!" I shout, thrusting my flubby old face in his flubby old face, and I pull up my rummage sale skirt to show him my varicose veins under the black stockings that hide the veins but not the lumps they make. "You think I got these lumps from my emotions dancing me around? I got them from mental conscientiousness," I said. "Standing-up jobs all my life, elevators, counters, cafeterias. I got a record of 63 years stability." And he laughs in a spitty way because he's got no answer he learned from a newspaper.

FEBRUARY 24

Every night he's got a woman up there. Maybe it's his sister visiting him because he's emotionally disturbed and she comes by at suppertime to bring him cheeses and chocolates and pastries to cheer him up. Or maybe it's his very wealthy mother who because she is so wealthy and swims a lot in her swimming pool and wears Helena Rubenstein cosmetics can sound so light and so young up and down the stairs. She is up there now, I can hear her heels tap-clacking around up there. Sometimes in the morning he comes down the stairs singing and I have to clap my hands over my ears, I can't bear to think he comes down happy because the woman was with him the night before. It's his sister, I'm sure of it, and he sings because he has Dutch chocolate in his pockets to eat while he sits at the drawing board. Why doesn't he investigate? Old fool, what does he care there is an old woman down below who lost her job? You could never convince him it was his fault. What I should have done is write down what happened the day it happened. Now it is confused in my memory. Besides the intervention of time, which is a bad enough intervention, I haven't eaten well. The money from the last check went on the rent and the utilities and some small items of food in addition to the chicken necks which I cooked up for the two cats although I ate the broth myself. Not only do I feed myself but I feed the two cats that he forgets to feed. He is too busy feeding the girl! the girl! whatever it is she wants to be fed. Great God, what a wonderful thing to be a girl and be fed! fed! fed! until you are plump and sleek and sassy and delirious!

MARCH 2

It's wise to get down the day I was fired at the Eunice B. Stratton Grammar School, because I need to try to remember why for my own good. When the reason gets away from me I get scared and wonder what crazy fault in me did me out of a job. Why was I fired? I refused to serve the children their hot lunches. There were all those trays, there were all those little faces moving along above the trays, gazing down into the containers of vegetable soup, mashed potatoes, cream corn. Everything was as it always is in every school where I worked as substitute cafeteria helper. But I refused to serve them. Why? Well it occurred to me that food was abominable and that if they continued to eat, the kids at the Stratton School and every school in the city, if they went on eating their hot lunches every day they would only be preparing themselves to suffer, they would only grow up to suffer. The pity for them stopped up my mouth. The pity had been in my mouth for days already and I'd given up breakfast and was feeling nauseated over that variety of foods. So there I stand in my white uniform and my gray hair all neatly tied back in a skimpy ponytail with a bit of green ribbon so my hair doesn't get in the food, my hands washed, my bony hands antisepticized by the strong amber soap that drips down from a glass ball in the lavatory, and a bit of cheery lip-stick on my thin lips, there I stand with the children piling up, piling up, and I can't lift my hand with the ladle in it. No, I can't hop and skip to the piping little voices from the little heads on the trays. "Serve! Serve! What's wrong? Serve!" I hear the voices of my co-workers, of my super-visor, who is a large, sloppish woman even in the neat uniform. She is hissing over my shoulder as she shoves me aside and grabs the ladle her-self. We make a pair, I think, she with her busty waist and me straight as a uniformed stick, she the talkative, ladling, eating kind (it always made me queasy to sit opposite her after the kids were out of the cafeteria and see her talk with watery mayonnaise on her lower lip) and me the untalk-ative, unladling, uneating kind. Why right then I thought to myself that I had no business in the food industry even if it was seeing that chil-dren got a hot nourishing lunch. So I was not surprised when I was noti-fied after all the kids were served and I was still standing there with my hands hanging down that I was dismissed. It was the pity for them that wouldn't let me use that ladle. No, it was pity for myself because the young man moved in upstairs and if he came down to ask me about my initials what difference would it make since the initials belong to an old woman? The pity for them and for me is all one pity and it's got to the point now where it won't let me talk to anybody. It's difficult for me to tell the vegetable man who's in charge of the stall outside the Buon Gusto Market what I want, ten cents of broken asparagus, a wilted lettuce for a nickel, mainly because I don't want anything but you have to eat to stay alive. Sometimes he sells me what I don't ask for because he hears noth-ing from me. It seems to me that there is not enough communication to be had over small transactions like the sale of vegetables and that all my life that was all I ever had, small transactions. But he can't hear a thing so he pops the vegetables into the bags and when I get home I find myself with cauliflower and chard, things I never eat, that the very smell of sick-ens me. So I throw it all away. I can't bear the sight of food anyway so it's all to the good that it's not what I asked for. When I pass Stella's Bakery and see the cakes and hot cross buns, when I pass the Safeway Market and see the big red letters about juicy chuck roasts, when I pass the res-taurants and see through the glass the customers eating rich soup or cutting steaks or sipping wine, or when I read in the gossip column that at the Taj of India the gossiper was served fowl covered with gold leaf as in the days of the Moguls, why I think of the part in the Russian novel where the poor student sits in the railway compartment, starving, and the fat Kulak couple who are facing him take out their bread and sausage and eat without offering him any and without any embarrassment. When I eat my toast and drink my tea I feel the eyes of the poor on me. I don't feel poor when I eat so I don't like to eat. I can't seem to think about all the hungry people in the world because there are too many to think about at one time, so the student on the train is everybody, he is the children at the school, he is myself, he is hungry of body and soul. No, I don't like to eat anymore. Even if I had a job I think I'd eat less than I used to. . . . The above reason for losing my job sounds like a reasonable reason when I write it and read it, but I'm afraid that in a little while, when I'm doing something else, the reason will sound like nothing but that crazy quirk I was afraid to admit to.

MARCH 6

The upsetness is with me again. The day I was fired I wasn't upset in this way even though it was an important job and they make you sign an oath about not being a member of an organization that seeks to tear down the government. The upsetness began when I learned there aren't any jobs around for a woman who's 63 years old. I knew this before but it didn't mean much because I had a job, but when I didn't have a job anymore then the fact there wasn't any upset me. I am in the habit of stealing old Sunday newspapers from the woman who lives upstairs across from the architect. She is a mouse-sized woman who works at a florist's. She leaves the papers outside her back door intending to throw them away later, so it's not really stealing on my part but it would be polite of me to ask for them. However, I don't like to humble myself mainly because I don't care for her. It began, my not caring for her, the day I was taking an oil painting of mine down the front stairs to see if some gallery would hang it up, and she passes me going up and asks to see it, but all she can say is "Isn't that pretty?" Does she think I'm a fool that I like my work called pretty? I concluded then that she was the fool if she thought I was fool enough to fall for a word like pretty. There are fools and fools, and some you can become fond of but she is a fool that you avoid. Anyway, they insult you to your face, the want ads. They say Girl Under 25 or Must Be Young and Attractive. I used to say Crud To You, meaning the employers, but after I got fired I read the ads and got upset. Maybe I ought to go over to file for my unemployment insurance, but since I was only a part-time worker and that not regular and making close to nothing I'm not sure if anything is coming to me. Besides, there are so many people in lines and so many spaces to fill in, so much milling around and so many faces that don't know one another. The thing to do is not be upset and the way to do it is to let pleasure set in. You can make yourself glad you've got no job and glad you're not looking forward to any. This is better than being upset. Besides, since I may decide to not eat, it doesn't matter whether I've got money coming in or not. . . . It's 9 P.M. I can hear the faraway noise that comes up from the ships and the piers down the hill when they work all night and the sound of the air conditioner that goes day and night in the Roma Macaroni Factory across the street. Upstairs I hear the woman laughing.

MARCH 9

They are quarreling across the hall, the taxi driver with the Hungarian name whose grandfather was a count and his sweet, naggy wife. They have a black poodle named Valentina. They also have an old dog shaky in the legs that some family in the neighborhood abandoned when they moved away and it's got a sad, resigned look such as I've never seen on any face before, man or beast. It lies at the foot of the front steps and you have to step over him, coming or going. I wonder if I have the same kind of face with some anxiety mixed up in it. Whenever I see sad faces on cats and dogs I wonder how I look myself. Today is the first hot day of the year, it came unexpectedly, and they are getting ready to go to the beach. It's 3 o'clock already. He's carrying out canvas chairs to the car and an armload of odds and ends and he's shouting at her to "Hurry, for God's sake, or the best part of the day will be gone!" "Please! The umbrella!" she cries. "The umbrella!" and runs back up the stairs and unlocks the door again. Great God, the day is gone already and when they get to the beach, a strong wind will be blowing, cold and gritty. . . . They're gone, thank God, with their two dogs. It's a warm day, the acacia trees are dropping their tiny, rusty yellow puffs, I see sweepings of them in the sidewalk cracks whenever I go out, and the blossoms on the few fruit trees in the neighborhood smell nice, like the white mice I used to have when I was a child. Tonight I'll go up the backstairs and knock at his door. He ought to feed those two cats himself and not leave them for me to feed because I've got nothing to feed them with and I can't bear the sad faces of all the animals around here on the front and back stairs.

NIGHT OF THE SAME DAY

Maybe I ought to have a cup of hot tea to warm me up and catch my breath. My breath nowhere around when I wanted it, I went up the backstairs. Wusto! he opened the door with his brown hair up in tufts as if he or she had been running fingers through, with a dish towel tied around his waist, with a puzzled look on his face that said, Who comes up the backstairs? Who? "You forgot to feed your cats and they beg at my door. Cats," I said, "got to eat regular, like human beings." That humbled him. It's always wise to forget the formalities if you feel yourself ill at ease and begin with the attack. "Oh my, oh my!" he cried, striking his brow with the back of his hand. "The cats! I forgot to feed them!" and he turned sideways to say to the girl, "I forgot to feed them!" and I got a fair look at her from a distance. She was sitting at the table by the window, and the paper lantern of a lamp above the table glowed off her buttersilk blouse and off her red hair. I saw her dimly because my eyes had come up the twisty dark of the backstairs. She was sipping wine from a tumbler and reading a magazine and she gazed at me, that girl, with a little bit of interest and a little bit of puzzlement and that was all. She gazed at me, that girl, with no kinship in her eyes, creature of my own sex but oh so different from me, so young and so well fed with love and the stares of strangers. Maybe she's a clerk behind a jewelry counter, maybe she types all day in a tight little office, but she's only beginning. But me, even when I was a child, with the pitcher lip that was just a quaint child's lip, even then I knew that someday I'd come knocking at a back door to have a young man open it and let me see what kind of woman was privileged to sit at his table and swing her foot and sip his wine and make herself at home, at home, at home. "When you see them next time tell them to come up," he said just as the two cats ran in, and to the cats he cried, "Forgive me! Forgive me!" and smiling and nodding, nodding and smiling, he closed the door, opened it again instantly. "Can you see? Can you see?" he cried. "Here, I'll leave it open until you get down," and he did and the light was on the stairs until I got to my own door. That was kind of him, he was somebody else's kind lover who leaves the door open for an old woman to get her light by as she retreats down the backstairs on her love-shaken legs. . . . One of the upstairs cats came down again and scratched at my door and now it's walking over my journal leaving paw prints made of something resembling licorice gum. Upstairs all is still, all is shuddering with love.

MARCH 15

Maybe I'm feeling magnanimous tonight because in last Sunday's paper which I picked up yesterday on the backstairs I read an article by an eminent psychologist in New York by the name of Reik who said in the title that Men Love Work But Women Love Men, and down in the article about how When Women Claim Equality Then They Renounce Their Superiority. That made me feel good for an hour or less. It made me feel superior. But after a while I began to suspect that statement. I wondered what it was I ought to feel superior about because I didn't seem to have what he implied I had. So I went to bed sad and lay there wondering why I've always been afraid of them if I was superior. I look the other way and always have, all my life, because even when I was young they looked right through me. I was afraid of their indifference which is a worse kind of cruelty than laughing at a woman because she's odd. At least being odd you're being something more than nothing. So I went to bed sad and slept sad, but this morning I got up and began to count my superiorities because I find it upsetting to be at loggerheads with an eminent man in the Sunday papers. So I counted 26 paperbacks, a can of evaporated milk, a loaf of bread, and 5 withery apples. These are not special superiorities belonging to women alone but they were the only superiorities I could find so I counted them.

MARCH 29

All my life I never gave Life serious thought, like the people who write books about it. Oh, they get all wound up, they write 1,000 pages or they condense it down into four lines in a poem. That's the way I used to feel when I was young, that I had a lot to say. But I couldn't say it like the others and that turned me against them, it turned me away because they had so much to say that was so complicated I felt like a simpleton. Worse, like an eavesdropper. So I read only a few things in my life. But now I feel the opposite, I'm not intimidated anymore. That's a laugh, trying to find out what I'm doing here when I've already been here 63 years. The basement of the City Lights is a good place. You can read down there, they have tables and chairs, and you don't have to buy anything, nobody bothers you. Down there I read lots of great people. Not that I read them from cover to cover. I read a page and then when I lose track of a man's thoughts I skip a page, but I manage to collect a lot of insights for myself. For instance, one poet I was reading, one of his lines hit me between the eyes, I felt as if I should have read that line when I was born. It went He Never Supposed Divine Things Might Not Look Divine. There's more before and after to support that line but that's the part I remember, that's the part that made me feel not so queer all of a sudden. "Hell!" I said to everybody who all my life had looked through me as if I wasn't there. "You don't know the Divine when you're looking right at it!" Today I read a philosopher, and maybe it's really my own idea but I've got to give credit to somebody else because it's too good an idea for me to have made up myself. But this is the picture I came up with, that made me feel complicated and calm at the same time. I got a picture of my Soul. Suppose there are three heads, and the one in the middle has two faces, like Janus. The two-facer in the middle is the Soul, and one face is looking at The Person You Are and the other face is looking at The Person You Might Have Been, and both the other faces are looking at the Soul. All these heads are contained within you, but you're not the first head and you're not the third, you're the two-facer in the middle looking at both. The Soul is me. I'm not the woman I might have been under more congenial circumstances and I'm not the woman I am, old growly-gut who can't look anybody in the eyes because she's ashamed of who she is and ashamed for them for not seeing her Soul instead of her. I was able to keep this picture of my Soul intact until I got home, but once I got here and smelled the old magazines and the cat spray and the cold rubbish smell that comes up from the basement and saw I had one last tea bag, some dried beans, and 7 prunes that I found at the bottom of a canister it was hard to remain the observing Soul. I found myself becoming the old woman again with her stiff hands and her hunger and the next minute becoming the person I might have been, a smart old lady with lots of antique rings, my place of residence the mansion across the street, up on the corner of Chestnut and Grant, that nobody lives in, that belongs to somebody in Italy. The macaroni factory is at the lower corner of the block and the mansion is at the upper corner and in between is some vacant earth that's as high as the roof of the factory, with long slicks of grass and clumps of ferny fennel and Scotch broom. One day I climbed up that mound to peer through a wrought-iron gate in the stucco wall at the back of the mansion and saw a little statue of a youth above a waterless fountain in a tiled courtyard. On top of the high walls are little arches like afterthoughts loaded on, and stuck in the walls are lions' heads that gaze out over the mound and the macaroni factory and the bay. That's where the woman I might have been would live, with her wisdom and wealth and eminence. I try to believe I am the Soul in the middle but the other two keep getting the upper hand. . . . The cats are driving me crazy. They're yowling on the backstairs of the building next door because there they can look into my kitchen window and me at the table. Maybe they think they press me more with their hunger when they stare in from outside like the poor children in Hans Christian Andersen staring in at the rich eating their feasts. They yowl at me, begging and begging, and their yowls are magnified in between the buildings like in a cavern.

APRIL 7

How pale I look whenever I catch a glimpse of myself in the mirror over the basin. Sometimes I splash warm water on my face but I purposely avoid looking into the mirror when I do that. I only catch glimpses going by. Every time I glance in I'm reminded of something I read by a French woman philosopher who was very religious and wrote about God, and she said When A Beautiful Woman Looks Into The Mirror She May Think The Image Is Herself. An Ugly Woman Knows That It Is Not. So that way I try to make myself feel better whenever I look, but I make myself feel worse again by suspecting that the girl upstairs looks in the mirror and knows the image is not herself. Yes, I grant that further advantage to her, that she is not taken in, every time, by the image. Sometimes I feel that woman philosopher by my side whispering to me how human is my face and sometimes that humanness is nothing that does me any good. No, I feel too many ways whenever I glance into the mirror, so I try to avoid it. Mirrors should never have been invented. Maybe the thing to do is hang a towel over it.

APRIL 9

If I lived in the Middle Ages they would have burned me for a witch. But they would have made a mistake. I'm the extreme opposite of a witch. That's what I'd like to be, a witch—things would be at my mercy instead of me being at their mercy.

APRIL 11

Yesterday at noon I saw her again. I heard them come down the stairs and waited behind my curtain to catch them when they reached the sidewalk. She walked from the lowest step to his car and I saw that she had her red hair done up in a pouf with a big, sharp curl on each cheek pointing to her especial face like a finger saying I'll Have That One, and I saw that she had a tiny waist with roundy hips, and pointed shoes whose heels had made a feminine click and clatter on the stairs for how many weeks now? Made them going up at suppertime and coming down late or the next morning but never at noon on a weekday. I began to think about those curls on her cheeks and for the fun of it I made myself a cardboard hand, one of those old-fashioned hands you used to see pointing, and I pinned it on my straw hat with a safety pin so that it was pointed down at me. Maybe it was God's finger pointing, maybe it was God saying Look At This Woman. She's Got A Soul Because I Gave It To Her. She's Not Dead Yet Even If Some People Look Right Through Her As If She Was. She's One Of My Living Souls. But I didn't get up enough courage to wear my hand of God until today when I went out for a minute, not any longer because my legs don't carry me. I was weak from hunger and my eyes were dazzled by the daylight on the pavement. I went around the block with my hat on, down Francisco, up Stockton, and down Pfeiffer to Grant again and into my door again, so weak that I fell onto my bed and couldn't rise again for an hour. There was one of those Matson liners blowing its horn before it sailed, a blasty, bleary blow. One of those sending-off parties was going on and the horn sounded tricky as if some-body was having fun while he was warning people to get off or get on. The blowing accompanied me around the block and I took it that God was blowing a trumpet for me on my journey, or asked Archangel Gabriel to blow it for Him, so people would look at me as I walked around the block with His hand on my hat pointing at me. But what was happening was the opposite. The Dutch architect and the girl were on that ship tak-ing off for Hawaii. I knew this because he came down last night and knocked at my door and asked me if I'd be kind enough to look after the two cats until the other couple got back from Europe, and I said that I would. Here I had dreamed, in spite of the girl, in spite of knowing he wouldn't, of him standing there kind and forward and noble and asking me if my initials were KW, at last. But all he wanted was for me to take care of the cats for another two weeks until the couple got back and he didn't even offer to give me the money for the cat food.

APRIL 12

She knocked at my door with lilacs. The mouse woman from upstairs. She said the florist got a whole big bunch, and she wanted to give me some. "You can paint a real pretty picture of them," she said, but this time I knew what she meant by pretty, and I was sorry that I'd been so uppity the first time she said it on the stairs. Maybe she's only got a few words at her disposal and maybe pretty means wonderful to her. I said "thank you" and said I'd paint a picture for her of the lilacs, but I don't have the strength even if I had enough paint in the tubes. I put the lilacs in a ma-son jar. The thing about flowers is that when you inhale them it's like put-ting your face into perfumed water.

APRIL 13

Carpenters are working on the roof of the macaroni factory. On the roof there is a small frame structure that looks like a square house with one door in it and they hammer inside the door, they draw up their lumber to the roof and into the door. If they're up there tomorrow and if one of them glances across the street and into my window he'll think I'm nap-ping, an old woman lying on her bed napping. Tonight I'll leave the cur-tains open so in case I can't get out of bed in the morning whoever is on the roof can see in. The caretaker at the mansion can see in if he wants to, and the boy with the spade who climbs the little hill after school can, and the people who take their dogs up there and look out over the bay and down at the ships between the piers fanning out into the water. I've been up there myself to pry around and I know it's a view to see while they wait for their poodles to relieve themselves. Anybody up there will be able to see the woman lying on her bed and someone may say to himself that the old woman has been lying in there for 3, 4, 5 days. . . . Or maybe nobody will think anything's wrong because that thought would disturb the even tenor of their days. Maybe it will have to wait until the young couple come downstairs with their gifts. When nobody answers they'll come back the next day and then begin to make inquiries about me from the Hungarian couple, then from the landlord to see if I moved out as they have friends who would like to move in. The landlord will come over from his house with his key and as he is turning the key in the lock the girl will get a premonition and take her husband's arm and wonder if she ought to tell their friends about the apartment or not tell, because if a person died in there they might not care to be the ones to move in right after and that would be putting them in an embarrassing position.

APRIL 14

It makes no difference, your name on a gold cup or on the Social Security records or on any records. Today I remembered that my name is on the gold cup in a glass cupboard at the Eastside High School in Los Angeles. I was surprised to remember that I was valedictorian of my class. It was nice at the time in a strained way, I think I looked like a scarecrow in a peach-color lace dress and made a lot of promises for the class about what we were going to accomplish. It makes no difference, your name. Who knows who you were?

THE NEXT DAY

On the other hand it isn't his fault. It's the years' fault. The years are too much for me, the years are full of the prevailing public opinion, and what's a few days of coming up Divine from the basement of a bookstore? He moved in upstairs at the end of the years and I blamed everything on him because an excuse was what I needed, a match to set fire to the pile of years in my chest. I hate to think that prevailing opinion wasn't as prevailing as I thought it was. Come to think of it, I remember seeing lots of homely women with children around their skirts and lots of old women laughing. But that little doubt makes me feel like asking somebody for food and how do you do that without shame?

THE LAST DAY
The ceiling can't bear the weight of his footsteps. The ceiling is about to fall in. All I feel is the fall of the ceiling about to fall.

The Stone Boy

*A*rnold drew his overalls and raveling gray sweater over his naked body. In the other narrow bed his brother Eugene went on sleeping, undisturbed by the alarm clock's rusty ring. Arnold, watching his brother sleeping, felt a peculiar dismay; he was nine, six years younger than Eugie, and in their waking hours it was he who was subordinate. To dispel emphatically his uneasy advantage over his sleeping brother, he threw himself on the hump of Eugie's body.

"Get up! Get up!"

Arnold felt his brother twist away and saw the blankets lifted in a great wing, and, all in an instant, he was lying on his back under the covers with only his face showing, like a baby, and Eugie was sprawled on top of him.

"Whasa matter with you?" asked Eugie in sleepy anger, his face hanging close.

"Get up," Arnold repeated. "You said you'd pick peas with me."

Stupidly, Eugie gazed around the room to see if morning had come into it yet. Arnold began to laugh derisively, making soft, snorting noises, and was thrown off the bed. He got up from the floor and went down the stairs, the laughter continuing, like hiccups, against his will. But when he opened the staircase door and entered the parlor, he hunched up his shoulders and was quiet because his parents slept in the bedroom downstairs.

Arnold lifted his .22-caliber rifle from the rack on the kitchen wall. It was an old lever-action that his father had given him because nobody else used it anymore. On their way down to the garden he and Eugie would go by the lake, and if there were any ducks on it he'd take a shot at them. Standing on the stool before the cupboard, he searched on the top shelf in the confusion of medicines and ointments for man and beast and found a small yellow box of .22 cartridges. Then he sat down on the stool and began to load his gun.

It was cold in the kitchen so early, but later in the day, when his mother canned the peas, the heat from the woodstove would be almost unbearable. Yesterday she had finished preserving the huckleberries that the family had picked along the mountain, and before that she had canned all the cherries his father had brought from the warehouse in Corinth.

Eugie came clomping down the stairs and into the kitchen, his head drooping with sleepiness. From his perch on the stool Arnold watched Eugie slip on his green knit cap. Eugie didn't really need a cap; he hadn't had a haircut in a long time and his brown curls grew thick and matted, close around his ears and down his neck, tapering there to a small whorl. Eugie passed his left hand through his hair before he set his cap down with his right. The very way he slipped his cap on was an announcement of his status; almost everything he did was a reminder that he was eldest —first he, then Nora, then Arnold—and called attention to how tall he was, almost as tall as his father, how long his legs were, how small he was in the hips, and what a neat dip above his buttocks his thick-soled logger's boots gave him. Arnold never tired of watching Eugie offer silent praise unto himself. He wondered, as he sat enthralled, if when he got to be Eugie's age he would still be undersized and his hair still straight.

Eugie eyed the gun. "Don't you know this ain't duck season?" he asked gruffly, as if he were the sheriff.

"No, I don't know," Arnold sniggered.

Eugie picked up the tin washtub for the peas, unbolted the door with his free hand and kicked it open. Then, lifting the tub to his head, he went clomping down the back steps. Arnold followed, closing the door behind him.

The sky was faintly gray, almost white. The mountains behind the farm made the sun climb a long way to show itself. Several miles to the south, where the range opened up, hung an orange mist, but the valley in which the farm lay was still cold and colorless.

Eugie opened the gate to the yard and they passed between the barn and the row of chicken houses, their feet stirring up the carpet of brown feathers dropped by the molting chickens. They paused before going down the slope to the lake. A fluky morning wind ran among the shocks of wheat that covered the slope. It sent a shimmer northward across the lake, gently moving the rushes that formed an island in the center. Killdeer, their white markings flashing, skimmed the water, crying their shrill, sweet cry. And there at the south end of the lake were four wild ducks, swimming out from the willows into open water.

Arnold followed Eugie down the slope, stealing, as his brother did, from one shock of wheat to another. Eugie paused before climbing through the wire fence that divided the wheat field from the marshy pasture around the lake. They were screened from the ducks by the willows along the lake's edge.

"If you hit your duck, you want me to go in after it?" Eugie said.

"If you want," Arnold said.

Eugie lowered his eyelids, leaving slits of mocking blue. "You'd drown 'fore you got to it, them legs of yours are so puny."

He shoved the tub under the fence and, pressing down the center wire, climbed through into the pasture.

Arnold pressed down the bottom wire, thrust a leg through and leaned forward to bring the other leg after. His rifle caught on the wire and he jerked at it. The air was rocked by the sound of the shot. Feeling foolish, he lifted his face, baring it to an expected shower of derision from his brother. But Eugie did not turn around. Instead, from his crouching position, he fell to his knees and then pitched forward onto his face. The ducks rose up crying from the lake, cleared the mountain background and beat away northward across the pale sky.

Arnold squatted beside his brother. Eugie seemed to be climbing the earth, as if the earth ran up and down, and when he found he couldn't scale it he lay still.

"Eugie?"

Then Arnold saw it, under the tendril of hair at the nape of the neck—a slow rising of bright blood. It had an obnoxious movement, like that of a parasite.

"Hey, Eugie," he said again. He was feeling the same discomfort he had felt when he had watched Eugie sleeping; his brother didn't know that he was lying face down in the pasture.

Again he said, "Hey, Eugie," an anxious nudge in his voice. But Eugie was as still as the morning around them.

Arnold set his rifle down on the ground and stood up. He picked up the tub and, dragging it behind him, walked along by the willows to the garden fence and climbed through. He went down on his knees among the tangled vines. The pods were cold with the night, but his hands were strange to him, and not until some time had passed did he realize that the pods were numbing his fingers. He picked from the top of the vine first, then lifted the vine to look underneath for pods, and moved on to the next.

It was a warmth on his back, like a large hand laid firmly there, that made him raise his head. Way up the slope the gray farmhouse was struck by the sun. While his head had been bent the land had grown bright around him.

When he got up his legs were so stiff that he had to go down on his knees again to ease the pain. Then, walking sideways, he dragged the tub, half full of peas, up the slope.

The kitchen was warm now; a fire was roaring in the stove with a closed-up, rushing sound. His mother was spooning eggs from a pot of boiling water and putting them into a bowl. Her short brown hair was uncombed and fell forward across her eyes as she bent her head. Nora was lifting a frying pan full of trout from the stove, holding the handle with a dish towel. His father had just come in from bringing the cows from the north pasture to the barn, and was sitting on the stool, unbuttoning his red plaid mackinaw.

"Did you boys fill the tub?" his mother asked.

"They ought've by now," his father said. "They went out of the house an hour ago. Eugie woke me up comin' downstairs. I heard you shootin' —did you get a duck?"

"No," Arnold said. They would want to know why Eugie wasn't coming in for breakfast. "Eugie's dead," he told them.

They stared at him. The pitch crackled in the stove.

"You kids playin' a joke?" his father asked.

"Where's Eugene?" his mother asked scoldingly. She wanted, Arnold knew, to see his eyes, and when he glanced at her she put the bowl and spoon down on the stove and walked past him. His father stood up and went out the door after her. Nora followed them with little skipping steps, as if afraid to be left behind.

Arnold went into the barn, down along the foddering passage past the cows waiting to be milked, and climbed into the loft. After a few minutes he heard a terrifying sound coming toward the house. His parents and Nora were returning from the willows, and sounds sharp as knives were rising from his mother's breast and carrying over the sloping fields. In a short while he heard his father go down the back steps, slam the car door and drive away.

Arnold lay still as a fugitive, listening to the cows eating close by. If his parents never called him, he thought, he would stay up in the loft forever, out of the way. In the night he would sneak down for a drink of water from the faucet over the trough and for whatever food they left for him by the barn.

The rattle of his father's car as it turned down the lane recalled him to the present. He heard the voices of his Uncle Andy and Aunt Alice as they and his father went past the barn to the lake. He could feel the morning growing heavier with sun. Someone, probably Nora, had let the chickens out of their coops and they were cackling in the yard.

After a while, a car, followed by another car, turned down the road off the highway. The cars drew to a stop and he heard the voices of strange men. The men also went past the barn and down to the lake. The sheriff's men and the undertakers, whom his father must have phoned from Uncle Andy's house, had arrived from Corinth. Then he heard everybody come back and heard the cars turn around and leave.

"Arnold!" It was his father calling from the yard.

He climbed down the ladder and went out into the sun, picking wisps of hay from his overalls.

Corinth, nine miles away, was the county seat. Arnold sat in the front seat of the old Ford between his father, who was driving, and Uncle Andy. No one spoke. Uncle Andy was his mother's brother, and he had been fond of Eugie because Eugie had resembled him. Andy had taken Eugie hunting and had given him a knife and a lot of things, and now Andy, his eyes narrowed, sat tall and stiff beside Arnold.

Arnold's father parked the car before the courthouse. It was a two-story brick building with a lamp on each side of the bottom step. They went up the wide stone steps, Arnold and his father going first, and entered the darkly paneled hallway. The shirtsleeved man in the sheriff's office said that the sheriff was at Carlson's Parlor examining the boy who was shot.

Andy went off to get the sheriff while Arnold and his father waited on a bench in the corridor. Arnold felt his father watching him, and he lifted his eyes with painful casualness to the announcement, on the opposite wall, of the Corinth County Annual Rodeo, and then to the clock with its loudly clucking pendulum. After he had come down from the loft his father and Uncle Andy had stood in the yard with him and asked him to tell them everything, and he had explained to them how the gun had caught on the wire. But when they had asked him why he hadn't run back to the house to tell his parents, he had had no answer—all he could say was that he had gone down into the garden to pick the peas. His father had stared at him in a pale, puzzled way, and it was then he had felt his father and the others set their cold, turbulent silence against him. Arnold shifted on the bench, his only feeling a small one of compunction imposed by his father's eyes.

At a quarter past nine, Andy and the sheriff came in. They all went into the sheriff's private office, and Arnold was sent forward to sit in the chair by the sheriff's desk. His father and Andy sat down on the bench against the wall.

The sheriff slumped down into his swivel chair and swung toward Arnold. He was an old man with white hair like wheat stubble. His restless green eyes made him seem not to be in his office but to be hurrying and bobbing around somewhere else.

"What did you say your name was?" the sheriff asked.

"Arnold," he replied, but he could not remember telling the sheriff his name before.

"What were you doing with a .22, Arnold?"

"It's mine," he said.

"Okay. What were you going to shoot?"

"Some ducks," he replied.

"Out of season?"

He nodded.

"That's bad," said the sheriff. "Were you and your brother good friends?"

What did he mean—good friends? Eugie was his brother. That was different from a friend. A best friend was your own age, but Eugie was almost a man. Eugie had had a way of looking at him, slyly and mockingly and yet confidentially, that had summed up how they both felt about being brothers. Arnold had wanted to be with Eugie more than with anybody else, but he couldn't say they had been good friends.

"Did they ever quarrel?" the sheriff asked his father.

"Not that I know," his father replied. "It seemed to me that Arnold cared a lot for Eugie."

"Did you?" the sheriff asked Arnold.

If it seemed so to his father, then it was so. Arnold nodded.

"Were you mad at him this morning?"

"No."

"How did you happen to shoot him?"

"We was crawlin' through the fence."

"Yes?"

"An' the gun got caught on the wire."

"Seems the hammer must of caught," his father put in.

"All right, that's what happened," said the sheriff. "But what I want you to tell me is this. Why didn't you go back to the house and tell your father right away? Why did you go and pick peas for an hour?"

Arnold gazed over his shoulder at his father, expecting his father to have an answer for this also. But his father's eyes, larger and even lighter blue than usual, were fixed upon him curiously. Arnold picked at a callus in his right palm. It seemed odd now that he had not run back to the house and wakened his father, but he could not remember why he had not. They were all waiting for him to answer.

"I come down to pick peas," he said.

"Didn't you think," asked the sheriff, stepping carefully from word to word, "that it was more important for you to go tell your parents what happened?"

"The sun was gonna come up," Arnold said.

"What's that got to do with it?"

"It's better to pick peas while they're cold."

The sheriff swung away from him and laid both hands flat on his desk. "Well, all I can say is," he said across to Arnold's father and Uncle Andy, "he's either a moron or he's so reasonable that he's way ahead of us." He gave a challenging snort. "It's come to my notice that the most reasonable guys are mean ones. They don't feel nothing."

For a moment the three men sat still. Then the sheriff lifted his hand like a man taking an oath. "Take him home," he said.

"You don't want him?" Andy asked.

"Not now," replied the sheriff. "Maybe in a few years."

Arnold's father stood up. He held his hat against his chest. "The gun ain't his no more," he said wanly.

Arnold went first through the hallway, hearing behind him the heels of his father and Uncle Andy striking the floorboards. He went down the steps ahead of them and climbed into the back seat of the car. Andy paused as he was getting into the front seat and gazed back at Arnold, and Arnold saw that his uncle's eyes had absorbed the knowingness from the sheriff's eyes. Andy and his father and the sheriff had discovered what made him go down into the garden. It was because he was cruel, the sheriff had said, and didn't care about his brother. Arnold lowered his eyelids meekly against his uncle's stare.

The rest of the day he did his tasks around the farm, keeping apart from the family. At evening, when he saw his father stomp tiredly into the house, Arnold did not put down his hammer and leave the chicken coop he was repairing. He was afraid that they did not want him to eat supper with them. But in a few minutes another fear that they would go to the trouble of calling him and that he would be made conspicuous by his tardiness made him follow his father into the house. As he went through the kitchen he saw the jars of peas standing in rows on the workbench, a reproach to him.

No one spoke at supper, and his mother, who sat next to him, leaned her head in her hand all through the meal, curving her fingers over her eyes so as not to see him. They were finishing their small, silent supper when the visitors began to arrive, knocking hard on the back door. The men were coming from their farms now that it was growing dark and they could not work anymore.

Old Man Matthews, gray and stocky, came first, with his two sons, Orion, the elder, and Clint, who was Eugie's age. As the callers entered the parlor, Arnold sat down in a rocking chair. Even as he had been undecided before supper whether to remain outside or take his place at the table, he now thought that he should go upstairs, and yet he stayed. If he stayed, he thought, as he always stayed and listened when visitors came, they would see that he was only Arnold and not the person the sheriff thought he was. He sat with his arms crossed and his hands tucked into his armpits and did not lift his eyes.

The Matthews men had hardly settled down around the table, after Arnold's mother and Nora cleared away the dishes, when another car rattled down the road and someone else rapped on the back door. This time it was Sullivan, a spare and sandy man, so nimble of gesture and expression that Arnold had never been able to catch more than a few of his meanings. Sullivan, in dusty jeans, sat down in another rocker, shot out his skinny legs and began to talk in his fast way, recalling everything that Eugene had ever said to him. The other men interrupted to tell of occasions they remembered, and after a time Clint's young voice, hoarse like Eugene's, broke in to tell about the time Eugene had beat him in a wrestling match.

Out in the kitchen the voices of Orion's wife and of Mrs. Sullivan mingled with Nora's voice but not, Arnold noticed, his mother's. Then dry little Mr. Cram came, leaving large Mrs. Cram in the kitchen, and there was no chair left for Mr. Cram to sit in. No one asked Arnold to get up and he was unable to rise. He knew that the story had got around to them during the day about how he had gone and picked peas after he had shot his brother, and he knew that although they were talking only about Eugie they were thinking about him, and if he got up, if he moved even his foot, they would all be alerted. Then Uncle Andy arrived and leaned his tall, lanky body against the doorjamb, and there were two men standing.

Presently Arnold was aware that the talk had stopped. He knew without looking up that the men were watching him.

"Not a tear in his eye," said Andy, and Arnold knew that his uncle had gestured the men to attention.

"He don't give a hoot, is that how it goes?" asked Sullivan.

"He's a reasonable fellow," Andy explained. "That's what the sheriff said. It's us who ain't reasonable. If we'd've shot our brother, we'd've come runnin' back to the house, cryin' like a baby. Well, we'd've been unreasonable. What would of been the use of actin' like that? If your brother is shot dead, he's shot dead. What's the use of gettin' emotional about it? The thing to do is go down to the garden and pick peas. Am I right?"

The men around the room shifted their heavy, satisfying weight of unreasonableness.

Matthews' son Orion said, "If I'd of done what he done, Pa would've hung my pelt by the side of that big coyote's in the barn."

Arnold sat in the rocker until the last man filed out. While his family was out in the kitchen bidding the callers good night and the cars were driving away down the dirt lane to the highway, he picked up one of the kerosene lamps and slipped quickly up the stairs. In his room he undressed by lamplight, although he and Eugie had always undressed in the dark, and not until he was lying in his bed did he blow out the flame. He felt nothing, not any grief. There was only the same immense silence and crawling inside of him, the way the house and fields must feel under a merciless sun.

He awoke suddenly. The sound that had waked him was the step of his father as he got up from the rocker and went down the back steps, and he knew that his father was out in the yard, closing the doors of the chicken houses, and he knew that his mother was awake in their bed.

Throwing off the covers, he rose swiftly and went down the stairs and across the dark parlor to his parents' room. He rapped on the door.

"Mother?"

From the closed room her voice rose to him, a seeking and retreating voice. "Yes?"

"Mother?" he asked insistently. He had expected her to realize that he wanted to go down on his knees by her bed and tell her that Eugie was dead. She did not know it yet, nobody knew it, and yet she was sitting up in bed, waiting to be told. He had expected her to tell him to come in and allow him to dig his head into her blankets and tell her about the terror he had felt when he had knelt beside his brother. He had come to clasp her in his arms and pommel her breasts with his head, grieving with her for Eugene. He put his hand on the knob.

"Go back to bed, Arnold," she called sharply.

But he waited.

"Go back! Is night when you get afraid?"

At first he did not understand. Then, silently, he left the door and for a stricken moment stood by the rocker. Outside everything was still. The fences, the shocks of wheat seen through the window before him were so still it was as if they moved and breathed in the daytime and had fallen silent with the lateness of the hour. It was a silence that seemed to observe his father, a figure moving alone around the yard, his lantern casting a circle of light by his feet. In a few minutes his father would enter the dark house, the lantern still lighting his way.

Arnold was aware suddenly that he was naked. He had thrown off his blankets and come down the stairs to tell his mother how he felt about Eugie, but she had refused to listen to him and his nakedness had become unpardonable. At once he went back up the stairs, fleeing from his father's lantern.

At breakfast he kept his eyelids lowered to deny the night. Nora, sitting at his left, did not pass the pitcher of milk to him and he did not ask for it. He would never again, he vowed, ask them for anything, and he ate his fried eggs and potatoes only because everybody ate meals—the cattle ate, and the dogs and cats. It was natural for everybody to eat.

"Nora, you gonna keep that pitcher for yourself?" his father asked.

Nora lowered her head unsurely.

"Pass it on to Arnold," his father said.

Nora put her hands in her lap.

His father picked up the metal pitcher and set it down at Arnold's plate.

Arnold, pretending to be deaf to the discord, did not glance up, but relief rained over his shoulders at the thought that his parents recognized him again. They must have lain awake after his father had come in from the yard: had they realized together why he had come down the stairs and knocked at their door?

"Bessie's missin' this morning," his father called out to his mother, who had gone into the kitchen. "She went up the mountain last night and had her calf, most likely. Somebody's got to go up and find her 'fore the coyotes get the calf."

That had been Eugie's job, Arnold thought. Eugie would climb the cattle trails in search of a newborn calf and come down the mountain carrying the calf across his back, with the cow running behind him, mooing with alarm.

Arnold ate a few more forkfuls of his breakfast, put his hands on the edge of the table and pushed back his chair. If he went for the calf he'd be away from the farm all morning. He could switch the cow down the mountain slowly, and the calf would run along at its mother's side.

When he passed through the kitchen, his mother was setting a kettle of water on the stove. "Where you going?" she asked awkwardly.

"Up to get the calf," he replied, averting his face.

"Arnold?"

At the door he paused reluctantly, his back to her, knowing that she was seeking him out, as his father was doing.

"Was you knocking at my door last night?"

He looked over his shoulder at her, his eyes narrow.

"What'd you want?" she asked humbly.

"I didn't want nothing," he said flatly.

Then he went out the door and down the back steps, frightened by his answer.

Anna Lisa's Nose

*I*t was a family of three sons and four daughters, every one of whom had a great arched nose. Since both the mother and father had a nose of that kind and before their marriage were often mistaken for brother and sister, there was hardly room for variation among the children. The family had other features in common. They had richly dark hair, fair skin highly suffused with rose, and large, dark eyes with heavy lids. They were tall and strong, and the women were voluptuous. These characteristics were, however, overshadowed by their great bony noses whose arch began to jut out directly between the thick brows without waiting, without discipline from any natural accord of features.

The family, except for one child, accepted this nose without complaint and some were proud of it, the father and mother especially, as they would be of a son who had become a general. But the next-to-the-youngest daughter contended with it as with an arrogant parasite. At the age of eighteen, a few days after her birthday, she underwent surgery for its removal, or the removal of half of it. The surgeon's fee was taken care of by her father who, although not a prosperous man, a vine grower with a small vineyard and winery, was so affected by her threats to run away and never come back that he had come to feel a personal blame for not only his children's noses but his own, as if in his mother's womb he had asked the Creator for just that kind of nose. The night that he gave in was the most alarming night the family had ever known. When their sister threw herself down before their father, tearing at her long hair and beating her fists on the floor, the younger children jumped from their beds and, holding one another, cried, and the older ones sprang up from their homework. Her mother fell down beside her child, holding the writhing body to her bosom, wailing *Anna Leesa, Anna Leesa*, while the father, exhausted from nights and months of defending the shape of his family's nose, stood above them, unbuckling his belt, at last defeated and on his way to bed.

The night before she left home, Anna Lisa stood for an hour before the mirror above the basin, transfixed by the nose that was so beautiful it was like a gift direct from heaven. No surgeon, no fee figured in the transformation. It seemed to her that her future was like tremendous angel wings urging her body to rise.

With the money she had earned at a poultry farm, candling eggs every day after school, she bought a bus ticket to New York. She wore a tan, belted raincoat that before the transformation had been no more than a raincoat on a girl with a large nose. It was now a raincoat on a girl with a beautiful figure whose face, glanced at in the depot by curious men coming from behind her, did not fail them. On that bus ride she received two proposals of marriage: one from a Texan, a radio singer in a cowboy hat, and the other from a Missourian, a bulldozer operator, and for the first time in her life was kissed by a man. In that dark bus roaring across the country, as the clustered lights of towns and the sole lights far afield were left behind a hundred times over, she put her lips to a cigarette that, in the same moment, had been on a stranger's lips, and then felt the stranger's mouth itself on hers, and this was her initiation into the world of the normal, the unobsessed, the indefective. When the Texan got off, the Missourian got on.

She found a job modeling coats in a department store. She was a bit too large to model dresses and, although she was pleased to model anything because to model meant that she was an ideal, and, although the big fur ruffs framed her face like a reward for her years of shame and suffering, she felt that to lose a few pounds was a challenge. She felt that she must answer any challenge now because of a sense of betrayal that underlay her exhilaration. To do her exercises and to diet was not of minor consequence, for from that more tasks would follow, more challenges and more successes that would prove to those at home that the alteration of her nose was not a frivolous act, was not a derogation of them but a rite that had conditioned her to take life by the horns. When her hips were less she felt perfect enough to apply for a job with the famous couturiere Natasha.

In time she was invited to Natasha's parties. The woman was rather overbearing, crackling with energy and with commands that she thought were the most subtle of hints, as she often said of herself that her one virtue was diplomacy. Anna Lisa was grateful for the woman's friendship and did not in the least mind the woman's large, curved nose. She felt that Natasha's obliviousness to her nose was to be commended, for that unconcern made all other noses a matter of no significance. It made the alteration of Anna Lisa's nose so minor an act that she felt she ought to forget about it and not be troubled by it and always believe that she had been born with the present one. The significance of Natasha's nose was recalled for her one night after a party, when a young man she had met there, an attorney, was fondling her in his Lincoln. In the first interval, while they smoked cigarettes, he began to criticize their hostess.

"She presides," he said. "She's got a presiding nose. That's how she got where she is. The most casual conversation, not to say trivial, she's got to preside over it. And that's why she never got married and never will, she'd preside over the lovemaking. With a nose like that she can't do anything but preside."

The young man, aware that Anna Lisa was no longer burgeoning against him, embraced her again at once. She wanted to dispute his theory but she had no words to begin; neither had she a leg to stand on, for hadn't she herself fallen for that theory, convinced that people had mistaken her nose for the shape of her entire being, and mistaking it herself? Yet, after all, didn't she feel that her true self was the girl in this man's arms, in the arms of this tall and well-to-do young man who was satisfied with nothing less than the best in everything, and not the girl who had been forced by nature to present a false front? At this point she lost patience with the couturiere. If Natasha allowed her nose to misguide, then she must suffer the consequences. Anna Lisa's flesh began again to swell, and at that moment the young man underwent the premonition that the astounding girl in his arms was to be his wife.

In the month preceding the marriage, Anna Lisa could not bear Natasha. It was as if the woman had become a member of her family and might disgrace her, and since Anna Lisa did not tell her family of the marriage until after the ceremony, fearing that someone might show up a day or two before, she felt that Natasha ought not to know about it, either. Anybody else, anywhere, on a bus or in a restaurant or in an elevator, who resembled her family was avoided in her mounting fear of her family and its power to ruin her life. Natasha, who had brought Anna Lisa and Richard together, was avoided as if she had attempted to keep them apart.

Anna Lisa left the establishment after her marriage. She became a model for fashion photographers and because of her large eyes and square face and abundant hair and because she was angular and rounded at the angles, and could, at will, assume a coercive stare, and because she appeared to possess the moody material of experience such as that of a mistress of a man in high places, she was among their favorites. After several years among the anonymously famous, those women whose faces and bodies are famous and whose names are unknown, she began to weary of her career. She had seen herself so often in the magazines, she had seen herself in so many poses, lying and leaning and curled up into a ball, and against so many foreign palms and rocks and urchins, deserts and seas, ancestral stairs and arches, that she was quite convinced of her fame. She was quite convinced that the alteration of her nose had been entirely justified by the fame that followed, that, indeed, it had been a kind of public service. She was now nearing thirty and felt the need to retire into her marriage, to give of herself to her husband who had become a partner in a law firm whose counsel was sought by great corporations and the federal government. They left the apartment in the city for a remodeled farmhouse and garden in the country.

Richard had often mused on the images of four children resembling himself and Anna Lisa in four combinations, but because he was proud of her career and preferred not to disrupt it at its peak, he had never brought up the subject except in jest. Among his friends there were many who, at his age, were already fathers of three and four children, and one, whose wife had died after bearing two, had married a woman with three of her own. Now that Anna Lisa had quit her career, he wanted very much to be caught up by the waves of the generations, to be swept off his feet by that cognizance of his own mortality and the endurance of the race. She said that she was not yet in the mood to devote herself to a child. She had given so many years to her career and felt that she deserved a period of rest in which, of course, she intended to study all the things she had neglected. She took up the piano again—at the age of twelve and again at fifteen she had had some lessons, and she began the study of botany in order to become a wizard of a gardener, and she did become that and grew the most beautiful garden in the county. She also developed a genius for exotic meals, Japanese and Samoan and North Chinese and Balinese, and so her time was taken up with music and botany and gardening and the preparation of rare suppers, and all these talents enhanced her in the eyes of her husband and dissuaded him from insisting on a child. She hinted that she was afraid of childbirth, but this was not her real fear. She was afraid that the child, boy or girl, would bear a great, arched nose—strangely, because both she and her husband had small noses. Then he would suspect that she was unfaithful to him or, worse, suspect that she was not the woman he had chosen to be the mother of his children.

It was while she was in the midst of these several gratifying pursuits that she received a letter from her brother in the army. He wrote that he was coming up to New York for a few days, on leave from his base in the South. The prospect of her brother's visit was unbalancing. One minute she resolved to write to him, telling him she would be out of town; the next minute, conscience-stricken about her previous decision, she made up her mind to meet him at a designated place in the city; the minute after that, she vowed to bring him home, and the vow brought on an awful contraction in her stomach that forced her to walk around hunched over. She changed her mind and sat at her desk, imploring him to forgive her for having to depart for Europe the day before his arrival, but unable to lift the pen and write it down. She walked through the house and garden for an entire day, wringing her hands, feeling a five-pound loss, unable to eat or to sit.

She met him at a restaurant that no one she knew patronized. He was her youngest brother, now nineteen, and with his great, arched nose in a face saddened by army life, he was someone she was glad she was not taking home. He was tall and thin and shy, slow-moving and awkward, conscious of his dull uniform and of her beauty that seemed unrelated to him. She told him that her husband was sick with the flu. Since he had not expected to be invited to her home, he took this information for a warning that she could not remain with him long. Under harassment by the aborted time, he lost whatever voice and color he had, and ate with his eyes always down. Anna Lisa, desiring silence so that the meal would be over sooner and yet anticipating that once she was home again she would collapse and curse herself for a traitor and a coward, plied him with sisterly questions about mother, father, sisters, brothers. Then, to her surprise, she heard herself confessing an unhappy marriage. She said that her husband was running around with other women. She lied so that he could tell their family that the deed to make her different from them had not brought her happiness. Sullenly, he insisted on paying his own check. On the sidewalk they parted, shaking hands. At the last minute she kissed him on the cheek, and as she felt his poor, sunken chest against her she reexperienced the agony of her adolescence. He lacked the vigor and breadth of the other men in her family and she felt responsible for his lagging condition. Had she stirred up in him a shame about himself, back on that night when he was a child watching her beat the floor?

From that time on she complained to her husband that he was ignorant of her inner life, and yet felt that if he knew it he would be as intolerant of it as he would have been of her sad and large-nosed brother. And she began to suspect and investigate others' dissatisfactions. They were very friendly with a couple so smugly similar she sometimes, in her thoughts, almost confused one with the other. They were both painters, neither having more recognition than the other nor more talent, and they were both not much over five feet tall, the wife reaching that height, however, only in very high heels; they were both of delicate frame, both with moon faces, both with cultured drawls that expressed the same opinions. Anna Lisa, at the edge of her round bathing pool in the garden, questioned the wife just before the couple left after a Sunday visit. The husband was still inside the house with Richard.

"Do you feel that your husband really loves you?" Anna Lisa asked. "I mean," she said, "do you feel that he is forced to love you because you are just his size? I mean, do you think that he wonders at times what kind of woman he would have spent his life with if he were, say, six feet tall? Do you think he resents you because he was forced to love you because of his height?"

"You're out of your mind," her friend said. "What I think he thinks is that there are tall people and medium-sized people and short people and all the nor-nor'east and sou'-sou'west in-between people and that he happens to fall in the short group along with a woman who seems to have been made just for him."

"You don't feel he's dissatisfied then?"

"With what?"

"Well, with you. With himself."

"Well, one night he said to me, 'Thank God for small women,' but I didn't take it as synonymous with small favors. I felt that it was praise unto me. But God, maybe I was wrong."

"Nooo, no," Anna Lisa cried. "I think that he's the kind of man who, if he'd fallen in love with a woman six feet tall, would have wooed her and married her."

"You make him sound like a courageous midget," said the wife who by this time had swiftly pinned up some loose strands of hair, thrust her yarn and needles into her bag, dug her feet into her high-heeled sandals, and stood up.

Anna Lisa was secretly glad when this couple did not come by anymore and word came back to her, through a friend, that they thought Anna Lisa unbearable. They had always disturbed her; she had suffered for them for the very reason that they appeared to be unconscious of any need to suffer for themselves. They had reminded her of the unconcern of her brothers and sisters who accepted their noses with no despair and went about the business of living.

One day she received a telegram that her mother was dying. When she was packing, after having made reservations on an evening plane to the

Coast, another telegram informed her that her mother was dead. She ran to her closest neighbor and threw herself into the woman's arms, weeping with grief and with guilt for not returning to see her mother in the almost ten years since she had left home. The memory of her mother as she had been when Anna Lisa was a child, the memory of her drudgery and of her pleasures, of her cascading Italian, and of her consoling wail that she had hoped would take the place of Anna Lisa's operation—these memories put a wild sound into her weeping. When her husband came home, Anna Lisa hid herself in his arms from a decision about the funeral. She told him that there was no point in her attending it since she had not gone back to see her mother alive; it was a sanctimonious practice, the return of the child to the body of the parent. And what comfort could she bring her father and her brothers and her sisters, since she was like a stranger? She wept and wandered and, fatigued by her day of grief and guilt, fell onto her bed.

She felt compelled now to deny her husband the love she had denied her family; she felt compelled to criticize him as she had criticized her family with her years of keeping her distance. Baffled by this cruel change, he made love to her by force. He tumbled her down, his years of bag-punching and rope-skipping at the athletic club put to an ultimate use; yet, once down, her sudden lassitude spurned him as much as her fighting. She took revenge on him for his ignorance of her secret, she took her revenge on him for surely turning away from her if he had met her with her other nose, for refusing her as his bride, for not even entertaining a thought of her as his bride, and for refusing her family as his family-in-law. And when their marriage became intolerable and he developed an ulcer, on that night he was first stricken with a terrible pain in the pit of his stomach, a pain so fierce that he ran his car into a fence and had to be driven home in somebody else's car, sweating and incoherent, on that night she became more solicitous, more tender than she had ever been before.

She saw to the strict observance of his diet, of his hours of rest, of his abstention from liquor, saw to it all with a concentration born of remorse and abiding love. And when he was calm again and had put on twenty pounds from his diet of milk and starch and his disinclination to exercise, and their discord was a thing of the past, she told him that she was going to invite her eldest sister, who was a widow, to stay with them for a time. As a result of his own suffering, he might, she thought, be able to comprehend, at her sister's arrival, what she, Anna Lisa, was suffering.

Anna Lisa did not invite her sister outright, however. She wrote that she hoped the time might come when her sister could see her way clear to visit, and even that inert invitation kept her in a state of agitation until the reply. The sister declined, and she was both relieved and miserable that her courage had come to nothing. The sister wrote that she did not, for the present, wish to leave her home, because her daughter was expecting a baby and, besides, a job was promised her by their eldest brother who ran a small variety store and whose wife, who had assisted him for years, was failing in health. *She is very heavy now*, the sister wrote. *It's a sad sight, she is so heavy. The doctor says it's a glandular disease, and it's better that it is a disease than a willful act because she has an excuse. But, believe me, he got more woman than he bargained for.*

It was not long after the letter that Anna Lisa began to put on weight. Complaining that she found it a nuisance to prepare two kinds of meals, she ate the cream and potatoes that his diet called for and swelled out until her clothes were obscenely tight and began to split at the seams. She bought loose garments where before she had preferred those garments that fit like a glove; she wore muumuus, kimonos, Roman togas, and gave up high heels because they wavered under her weight. Her husband suggested that what was good for his health was not necessarily good for hers, but she smiled a surfeited smile. The once famous angular face was blurred by the Rubens flesh. Her long dark hair was not glossy anymore, since she seldom felt the energy to go to a hairdresser, and she wore it dragged up to the top of her head. Her husband gave up suggesting. Since *he* was not in his former condition, he felt that it was unfair of him to demand that she be as attractive as before.

In that time of her fleshy indolence, as she lay one day on her chaise longue in her weedy and overgrown garden, a woman rode up on a bicycle to her gate.

"Oh, just a bit of water," the woman called through with a reedy voice and an English accent. "It's such a beastly hot day I've drunk all the water in my thermos jug, drunk it all up."

Even from where she lay, and in spite of the obscuring mesh of the gate, Anna Lisa saw that the woman was burdened with a nose so large, so curved, she resembled a supplicant bird. Her age, which was rather advanced, her size, which was small, the fact that her short, skinny legs were bare below the knees and encased in black Bermuda shorts above, and that a blazing blue handkerchief was tied on her head and hung in a triangle at the back, all contributed to the effect of that beaklike nose.

"If you please," the woman's imperious voice rose over the garden. "Can you spare a bit of water for my thermos jug?"

It seemed to Anna Lisa that the woman was a member of an accursed race to which she, Anna Lisa, also belonged but whose membership she had been able to conceal with artifice and with the energy of the best years of her life, and, her large legs quivering with penitential longing, she rose to admit the woman.

"Oh, my dear, and herbs!" the woman cried, breaking off tiny leaves to rub between her fingers and raise to her nostrils that were like the flying buttresses of a cathedral. Water was brought by Anna Lisa in a capacious pitcher. She forgot a glass, forgot also that the woman had her own thermos cup, and ran back into the kitchen, and since Anna Lisa had gone to the trouble of running twice to the kitchen, the supplicant felt called upon to be congenial beyond the degree expected of someone given water from only one run. She sat down in an elaborate wicker chair and said that she was a housekeeper for a family that just a fortnight ago had returned to England; he was with the United Nations, she said, but had got a liver affliction and given up the diplomatic service. She had some nice offers, but she was taking a bit of a vacation. She loved to bicycle, she said, and if Anna Lisa had a bicycle or could borrow one she would show her some delightful roads. Anna Lisa offered her the position of housekeeper and the woman accepted. She had never felt the need of a housekeeper, but a stubborn coveting of this woman rose in her breast.

One afternoon, a few days after the woman came to live with them, Anna Lisa, returning on the train from the city, thought she saw reflected in the glass next to her face, as the train passed through shade, a great, arched nose that appeared to be on her own reflected profile. She clapped her hand to her nose and was assured that its size had not increased.

"God bless you," said the voice of a confident man who knew his far-flung influence. "Go on and sneeze, don't be shy. Don't hold back what is part of nature."

She turned her head and saw that the reflected nose was his. A large man with white plump skin that gave off an antiseptic perfume, he had a bald head fuzzed over with gold and a small beard of darker gold. When he told her that he was a dentist, she told him that she found her own dentist rather indifferent, taking her for granted as the years went by, and he nodded reluctantly, knowingly, a man pained to admit the malpractice of others in his profession. Not only did she promise to make an appointment with his nurse, she also promised that she and her husband would come by the following Sunday to see the dentist's collection of music boxes.

Not long after the encounter on the train with Dr. Braun, Anna Lisa and Richard attended the opening of a gallery exhibit by a young artist by the name of Hagopian, also from California. There was a crowd around him, and as her husband, taking her hand, drew her through the crowd to meet the artist, she again underwent that panicky yet not unpleasant sensation of retribution. The artist's nose was so large that the dark hair that rose in a high wave, arching from ear to ear like a lion's mane, seemed to frame the nose rather than the face. They purchased a painting, and Anna Lisa, in what appeared to be a mood of near-infatuation, asked the artist to visit them.

On the drive home her husband expressed some jealousy. "I bet he has a difficult time of it, using his brushes," he said. "His nose gets in the way."

"That's why he's an Abstract Expressionist," she said. "He stands off from his canvas and thrashes it on. And he gets more on it than those artists with nothing in their way."

It was unexplainable, the number of persons she met with large noses. She had never run into so many before. A harpsichordist moved in a few doors north, a buxom woman with flaxen and gray hair that hung in one huge braid down her broad back, and a nose like one half of a castle door. Anna Lisa called on her with bulbs. Shortly after, a friend who was an interior decorator brought over a woman he had taken into partnership, a young Frenchwoman with a nose so large that, observed from the front, it divided her very thin smile in two. These persons, lately met, were more of the material of friends than any persons she had ever met, and they were frequent guests in her home. A frenzied, obsequious desire to please them caused her to lose most of the weight she had gained, but not quite aware of the loss she still went about in muumuus and kimonos that were too loose and too large but also, because of that, more evocative of the body to be found somewhere in the folds and airy spaces, and in them resembled a servant who wears the castoffs of an obese and indiligent mistress.

One evening she gave a party for all of them and observed to herself, in the midst of them, that it was like a party for members of the same order or lodge for the purpose of interesting a few others in the rites and regimen that would grow them noses as large. She felt that she was hallucinating, that she was among people whose souls perched on their faces. She was ecstatic and drank too much, jabbering and sprawling and almost falling, singing, and hanging on the arms of her guests. The artist and the dentist attempted to kiss her, misinterpreting her behavior as erotic, but she could not bear to have the exalted meaning of their noses lost, and tore herself away from their embraces.

In the clutter and stale smoke after everyone had departed, her husband commented on the similarity among their guests. "They're all of a sameness," he said.

"Yes, they've all got souls," she cried.

"That's not what I meant," he said.

"Why don't you sit there and notice their souls?" she cried.

"I think they are extremely talented people, all of them," he said placatingly, "but it just so happens they've all got large—"

"They've all got enormously large souls," she cried, striking herself above her breasts, throwing her head back. "Oh, my God, I might have had as large a soul as any of them."

"Anna Lisa," he begged, following her over ashtrays strewn on the floor. "Anna Lisa, you have a soul as good as any of them. Just because they play the harpsichord or paint. That's not the soul, Anna Lisa. A talent isn't the soul."

"I know what the soul is," she cried. "You don't have to tell me what the soul is."

He went into his room, too weary to debate her soul with her.

It was not many weeks after the party that Anna Lisa ran off to Europe with Dr. Braun. After that night—indeed, before the night was over, Anna Lisa began to yearn for the embrace she had repulsed. She preferred the dentist to the artist because the artist had a meditative hand always hovering over his nose, whereas the dentist was not in the least discomfited by his nose. Her desire for the gold-bearded dentist began to consume her. It seemed to her that it was a desire that had lain dormant all her life and that her desire for her husband, back in the beginning, had been only a fraction of the desire that now ran rampant through her body. She had acted unrealistically the several times that night she had repulsed the dentist's embrace for the sake of her obsession with his soul. There was no way to revere his soul other than to throw herself into his arms.

She left a long letter on her bed, begging her husband to forgive her and thanking him for the nine years of love and largess. She had not been, she wrote, an easy person to live with, this she realized. Then she kissed her housekeeper on both cheeks, and the women wept together. The dentist left his affairs in order, having taken the time to find a bright young dentist to replace him and to print up announcements of his leave. These were not mailed until the night before he left, and his wife and son, on the mailing list, did not learn of his departure any sooner than his patients.

Seven months later, Dr. Braun returned alone. It was obvious that he had been through an ordeal. For six months, he told his friends, they had enjoyed themselves, traveling from London to Paris to Rome. She had been devoted to him, almost idolatrous, anticipating his every want, no matter how small, and responding to his desire with equal desire. They had moved on to Greece and Turkey and Iran, and it was in Teheran that she changed toward him. She became infatuated, he said, with the proprietor of a café. In one day she developed an inordinate craving for coffee.

"The man was not what you would call irresistible," he said, "but for her he was. I have never seen a woman so infatuated. It was like watching her come down with a fatal fever. But the man," he repeated, rubbing his troubled white hands together as he sat bent forward, his head down, "the man was not what you would call attractive. That man was a public freak, let us say. He was known as the man with the largest nose in the city. The British colony called him Muhammad because he was stuck with his mountain. They proposed to set him up as a ruler in case of civil strife. Muhammad returns, you know. It was their daily joke at his tables. He had, I understand, a wife, although it was hard to believe. He had a wife and six children, but that didn't bother Anna Lisa, not at all. She became his mistress." He lifted his eyes to his friends and the incredulity in them was not less than on that day when she had confessed her love for the other man.

Some friends who visited her in Teheran a year later found her still the mistress of the café owner. On their return they reported that she lay around all day in a room that he rented for her, reeking of sweet oil and jangling with cheap jewelry. They did not try to persuade her to return with them, they did not even bring up the subject, because her subjection to the man forbade it, because she was, they said, like a convert whose subjection makes it a profanation to question a belief with even one, small, timid question.

Works of the
Imagination

*T*he silent train ascended through forest and alongside a torrent so cold and so swift the water was white, and small white birds flew up like spray. On a bridge undergoing repairs the train came to a halt. Just outside Thomas Lang's window, a workman in a black knit cap was hammering at a railing, and the silence all around isolated each ring of the hammer.

Lang arrived in Grindelwald in the evening, coming from Bern where, contrary to his intention to call on a friend from the States and tell him about the insoluble task his memoirs had become, he had stayed only half a day and called on no one. In the early night he wandered along a path on the outskirts of the town. The day was a national holiday, and fireworks opened in languid sprays all around in the dusk, and the boom of fireworks echoed against the mountains. Someone approached him on the path, a figure twice as tall as himself. Closer, he saw it was a little girl, half as tall as himself, carrying a long stick covered with tallow, the torch at its tip casting around her a high, black figure of shadows. Up on the dark mountains small lights burned here and there, far, far apart—fires perched on the night itself. In the morning, a snowy mountain stood just outside his hotel window, brought closer by the sun almost to within reach of his hand.

On a small, quiet train he went higher, up to Kleine Scheidegg, up to an old hotel where twelve years ago he had stayed a few days in winter, and not alone. The mountains had impressed him then as a phenomenon on display, but now he was shocked by their immensity, hypnotized by their beauty and crystal silence. Cowbells and voices rang in the silence with an entrancingly pure pitch, and the density of the stone was silence in another guise.

The elderly, elegant manager registered him at the desk in the small lobby. A very tall, strong man, also elderly, in a dark green apron, whom Lang had observed carrying up four suitcases at a time, carried up his two, while another assistant, also in a green apron, a slight, dark man, surely Spanish, graciously shy, stepped in a lively way to the foot of the wide, curving staircase and gestured for him to go up. Lang climbed the stairs with his hand on the rail. He had not often assisted himself that way and had no need to now. He was an erect, lean, and healthy sixty, and why, then, was his hand on the banister?

The silence in the room was like an invasion, a possession by the great silent mountains. The cloth on the walls, a print of pastoral scenes with amorous couples, flute players, and lambs, roused a memory of another room, somewhere else in this hotel, where he had lain in an embrace with a woman who, at the time, was very dear. All that he remembered of the previous visit were the three persons he had been traveling with—the woman, a close friend, and the friend's wife—all now no longer in touch with him and perhaps not with one another. They had come to watch a movie being made of a novel of his. In the novel there had been only a brief mention of the Alps, but the movie director and the scriptwriter had worked out a counterfeit scene from that remark, and he had watched, amused and apart.

Once in the night he was wakened by his heart. His heart always wakened him in time for him to witness his own dying, and he waited now with his hand over his chest. When the fear subsided he took his notebook from the bedside table and fumbled to uncap his pen. Through the translucent curtains the sky and the white mountains gave him enough light to write by, but his hand was given no reason to write. Was this another place he would leave, his notebook empty? Traveling all spring and into the summer, he had found no place where he could begin his memoirs. If one place had been so full of the sound of the ocean—not just the waves, whose monotonous beat often went unheard, but the threat in the depths—another place was too full of the sounds of the city—insane noises. And in quiet places he heard, in memory, the voices of his healers back in the States, men who had never truly known just what it was he had lost, and gave the loss such facile names—confidence, faith, whatever—and the names of several persons who had been dear to him and were lost to him. These healers had promised him his completed memoirs, and other novels in the future, if only he would begin, because, they said, work itself wrought miracles and brought the spirit back from the grave. But there was a loss beyond their probing, a loss they were unwilling to accept as the finality he knew it was, a loss, a failing, that might even be commonplace and yet was a sacrilege. It was indifference, like a drugged sleep, to everyone else on earth. Ah, how could that change have come about in himself when his very reason for writing had been the belief that all life was miraculous?

He got up and drew aside the mistlike curtains. The train station was faintly lit, the awning rippling a little in the night wind. Out on the dark hills a few hazy lights burned through the night, miles apart. And beyond and all around, the luminous mountains. When he was inside the hotel their unseen presence warned him of his breath's impending abeyance, but now, gazing out at them, he felt his chest deepen to take in their cold breath across the distance, a vast breath as necessary to him as his own.

The day brought hikers up from the cities, way below. They came up in the small, silent trains, and wore big boots, thick socks, and knapsacks, as if bound for a climb of several days. But they roamed over the grassy hills for an hour or so and converged at the tables below the hotel's lower windows. They sat under colored umbrellas and under the windows' reflections of the mountains, and ate what appeared to be savory food. He kept a distance from them. There was room enough.

The only guests in the spacious parlor were far off, a family group playing cards at a table covered with green cloth. On the parquetry floors lay rich, red Persian rugs, and the many couches and chairs of antique beauty took up only small space in the large room. A long and narrow glassed-in sunporch with an abundance of wicker chairs adjoined the parlor, and he paced along its length, remembering the hotel in winter, the parlor's black-and-white marble fireplace ablaze, the pleasurable jostling and agitation of the many guests, and the hieroglyphs of distant, dark figures against the snow. He settled himself at a large table in a corner of the parlor, but all he could do was trace the glow and grain of the wood around his empty notebook.

On his way down the hall, restless, wondering if he would move on the next day, he paused before the first of several framed photographs along the wall, an early one of four climbers assembled in the photographer's studio against a backdrop of a painted mountain, all in hats and ties and heavy boots, with pots, picks, a goat. Few attempted the scaling of mountains in those years; now climbers were swarming up every mountain on earth. Farther along, he stopped before a photograph of *Der Eiger*, the mountain looming up over this hotel and over the town, miles below, a sheer, vertical face of stone. White lines were painted on the photograph, marking the ascents to the top, and at the base were the names of the fallen, preceded by white crosses. He passed along before the faces of the triumphant ones, a row of them, all young, and spent a longer time before a couple from Germany, a man and a woman, she a strongly smiling blonde and he a curly-haired handsome fellow, the kind who would take a woman along.

Then he went out, keeping apart from the many hikers who walked in a line toward Eiger as if on a pilgrimage. He strode over the lush grass, over the rise and fall of the hills, and on the crest of a hill he halted to take a look at the great stone's face. Two figures were slowly, slowly, climbing. His vision lost them in an instant and it took him some time to locate them again, so small were they and at the mercy of the atmosphere, appearing and disappearing. He sat down on the grass to watch them, his hand above his eyes to prevent the sun from playing tricks on him. The roar of an avalanche shocked him, convincing him that a mountain was collapsing, and then he saw the source of the thunder—a small fall of snow, far, far away. Somewhere he had read that the Alps had moved one hundred miles from their original location in Italy, and he wondered if the move had been centuries long, or cataclysmic, in a time when there were no human beings around to be obliterated. When his eyes began to ache from the searching, from the finding and losing of the specks that were his climbers, he returned to his room and lay down, his hand over his stone-struck eyes.

Toward twilight, when no one sat under the mountains' reflections, when they had all gone down on the trains, he went out again, strolling to higher ground over patches of tiny wildflowers that were like luminous rugs on the grass. Up near the entrance to the train tunnel that cut through stone to the top of the Jungfrau, he came to a large, heavy-wire pen where several restless dogs roved. The dogs resembled wolves, tawny with black markings, and their wild intelligent Mongol faces reminded him of the faces of nineteenth-century Russian writers. It was a comparison that amused him, and he felt light-headed over it. They paused to look into his face and into his eyes, slipped by along the fence, then returned, curious about him as he was about them. Soon in the darkening air he felt he was gazing at Gogol, at Tolstoy, at Chekhov, their faces intent on his own.

Stumbling a time or two, he made his way back down to the hotel that stood in a nimbus of its own lights. Before he went in he took a last look at the great stone. No fire burned anywhere on its enormous expanse. The climbers had made a bivouac for the night on a ledge and were already asleep. Late in the night he was wakened by a deep wondering about the couple on the ledge. The fact of their lying on a ledge somewhere on that great stone stirred in him a concern for all persons he had ever loved. Then he slept again, and the couple was lying somewhere on the cold vastness of the night, on no ledge.

In the morning he went out under an overcast sky, before any hikers appeared. The stone was monstrous. Each sight of it failed to diminish, by repetition, the shock of it. So steep was the north side, the mountain must have been split down the very center, and the other half was a hundred miles away. The climbers were not yet halfway up the wall. Often, as before, he lost sight of them, found one again and not the other, and then found the other after losing the first. After a time he covered his eyes to rest them. If they fell, would the silence and the distance deny to him the tragicness of their end? He lowered his hand, searched again, and found one dark figure on a snowy ledge. The figure fell the instant he found it. It fell so fast he was unable to trace its fall and unable to find it on a lower ledge or at the base. Nowhere, now, was the other climber. Then both had fallen, and their mortal terror struck at his heart. With his hand on his chest he went back over the hills to the hotel.

No one was at the desk in the lobby, neither the manager nor one or the other of his assistants in their green aprons. One of them would confirm the tragedy. Somewhere, back in an office, there must be a radio voice informing everyone of the climbers' fate. Outside, the murmur of the crowd under the umbrellas and the fitful, labored music of an accordion were like the sounds the deaf make, that are unheard by them. In the parlor he found the shy assistant passing through, the one he was convinced had been a child refugee from the Spanish Civil War.

"*El hombre y la mujer en la montaña, ellos se cayeron?*"

The man smiled sadly, graciously, implying with his smile that if he did not understand Spanish at least he understood the importance of the question for the one who asked it.

With faltering German he tried to repeat the question, but a strong resistance, following disappointment, whisked away his small vocabulary. He went back to the lobby.

The manager, wearing a fine suit the same gray as his hair, was now standing at the desk, glancing through some papers. A fire wavered in the small fireplace.

"The couple on Eiger, they fell?"

The manager's brow, high, smooth for a man his age, underwent a brief overcast. "May I ask who?"

"The couple on Eiger."

"Ah, yes, the photographs in the corridor? Only those who succeeded. Only those."

"The couple up there now," he said.

"There is no one climbing now."

"Then they fell?"

"No one is climbing and no one is falling."

Lang went up the stairs, hand on the rail, a weakness in his being from the lives lost, no matter if the climbers were only specks, motes, undulations of the atmosphere. Up in his room he sat down at the desk, opened his notebook, and wrote the first word on the first of the faint lines that he likened now to infinitely fine, blue veins.

The Mistress

*I*t was not long after his arrival before he was introduced to her, but in that time she watched him from her vantage point that gave her a view of the long room filled with people, and, out the window, a view of the garden. She watched him because she knew at once, gazing down through the diamond panes, that he was the son of the man who had been her lover ten years ago, the son who had been six then. She knew, because the similarity was so striking she felt that she was gazing down upon the lover as he must have been at sixteen and at a moment when he had lifted his face to attempt an impassive scanning of the windows and found, in one, the face of a strange woman transfixed by him. She watched him enter the room, be kissed by the hostess, and thread his way between groups and couples, looking for no one in particular but only yearning, she suspected, to be halted, to be embraced, to be enclosed by some group and by the entire party. For several minutes he stood only a yard away from her, half-in and half-out of a group, holding his goblet of sherry and gazing down as if waiting for the wine to be joggled from his glass to the rug.

He was tall, he was almost a man, he was on the verge of composure—
she saw it alternate with discomfort, and his presence among adults,
most of whom were strangers to him, reminded her of the legend of
Theseus entering as a stranger the kingdom he was to rule someday.

She watched him because he was completely absorbing, combining as
he did the familiar figure of the father with the enticing strangeness of
the boy himself. She was thirty-six, the number of her husbands was
three—the present one had been unable to attend the afternoon party—
and the number of her lovers who had meant something to her was firmly
fixed in her memory at one and that one was the father of the boy whom
she was now spying on. The elderly man beside her on the bench was so
enamored of her, his old black eyes glancing out untiringly from far inside the folds of eyelids at her crossed legs and bare, braceleted arms, that
he was unaware of and therefore unhurt by her own glancing and gazing
at someone else.

The boy was following the hostess as she went her rounds. Every joke,
every anecdote being more amusing to her than to anybody else, she was
constantly bending her knees to laugh, bending her body in the tight
green dress, and for a time she used the boy as a partner in this dance of
hers, grasping his arm and bending toward him until her forehead
touched the pit of his stomach. But she was almost as small as an elf and
whatever postures she adopted were not exaggerated, as they would be
with a larger person, but simply made her presence known. Although he
chatted eagerly enough with those she introduced him to, he always left
them after a time to find the hostess again, as if nobody but she could give
him a reason for being there, and when, at last, the hostess brought him
over to her in her window, she knew as they approached that the hostess
regarded her as perhaps the only person who could restrain the boy from
his trailing.

So here was the boy, at last, the resemblance to his father defined less
by closeness than by distance; now he was himself altogether, there was
nothing that was a replica of his father, there were only sharp clues, a
continual reminding. The elderly man to her right, rather than appear to
be pushed off into oblivion by the two younger persons, rose with a
sprightly tugging at tie and coat and offered to bring her another gin and
tonic. She refused the offer charmingly, relieved and also reluctant to see

him go, for any man's attentiveness was appreciated. She had always felt the need to thank the admirer for admiring.

"She's a good friend of my mother," he said, when they spoke of the hostess and her vivacity.

"Is your mother here?" she asked brightly, implying that if the son was so delightful a person to meet then the mother must also be met before the party was over.

He said that his mother was staying with her sister in another city, and she wondered if the woman was being cared for by the sister, remembering that at one time during her affair with the boy's father, the wife had left, after a wild scene with him, and gone to her sister's, taking the child, and had been ill there for several weeks.

"Your father? Is he here?" she asked, knowing that he was in London and that he had transferred himself there four years ago, right after the divorce.

"He lives in London." The boy fumbled out a packet of matches from his coat pocket and lit her cigarette with a steady flame that compensated for his clumsiness. "I spent last summer over there."

"How is he?" she asked. "He was once a friend of mine." That innocuous information, when told to the son, was like a revelation of the truth. When recalled to the son, the memory of the father was as fresh and pervasive to her as if the affair had begun or ended only the day before.

"Great, great," the son said. "He's married again, and they've got a baby now, a little girl." She felt, listening, that the son and herself were both attached to him by love, by resentment, by all the responses of the ones left in the past of somebody of prominence and promise and with a life of his own, and who had no time or inclination for memories of past loves. "I wouldn't like living there all the time," he said. "London, that is," laughing in case she might think he meant living in his father's house.

"How does he look now?" she asked.

"Look?"

"Fatter, skinnier, gray or bald?"

"Oh, thinner, I'd say."

"Oh, yes, thinner," she cried, laughing. "He's the fibrous kind. They get tough like dried fruit." They let themselves go with laughing. Other guests glanced over at them, surprised by and disapproving of this sudden intrusion of laughter into the several conversations. "Gray yet?" she asked, arching her brows.

"No, no, not at all," he said. "Got fewer gray hairs than I do." A splash of sherry on her leg as he, clumsy with clowning, transferred the glass to riffle his hair with his right hand.

"Nothing," she assured him. "It's nothing." But the clumsiness reminded them of that insufficiency in the self, the manqué element that is felt by persons left in somebody else's past, persons who were not in step and who were dismayed by their falling behind. She saw that he was wondering about her—why she should laugh so eagerly over the present description of an old friend and why she could so easily compel him to join with her.

She rose, reaching down for his hand, all done in a moment as if he were doing the convincing and she was spontaneously amenable. "Come on, let's walk in the garden," she said over her shoulder as he followed her through the crowd, their hands linked. She turned her profile to him as they stood delayed by a congestion of guests near the door and spoke into his ear as he complyingly bent his head down. "When the air gets thick with smoke and gossip, I can't breathe," she whispered hoarsely, and, seeing him frown solicitously, baffled, as if she had named a rare disease, she patted his cheek to convey to him that her complaint wasn't serious. They each enjoyed the other's concern and, laughing about it, pushed out onto the wide arc of the brick steps.

She released his hand the moment they were in the open and took his elbow, instead, and swung along beside him with a movement in her hips more pronounced than she had tried for in a long time, yet wondering why her responses to the boy must be so extravagant. They crossed the bricks she had watched him cross and stepped out into the garden where other guests were walking the brick paths or sitting around the white, fancy ironwork tables. The flowers were so large and perfect that the garden seemed a greenhouse, and this illusion was intensified by the humid air.

"It reminds me of Mazatlán, this weather," she said. "The weeks before the rains came. Hot, hot, everybody out along the beaches, the esplanade, till way past midnight, children and everybody. I remember the night the storm came, the first storm. The little trees by the window were bent over horizontal and the lightning continuous, sheets of lightning, and the rain and the wind, and the coolness coming into the windows, but the air still warm. I remember I went out into it, wrapped my raincoat over me and went out, but someone looking out a window told me to get back in, it was dangerous—the lightning, and the rain all over the ground in a flood." She glanced away. "The sand there is pink and gold, and weird birds—I guess they're vultures of some sort—hover over the beach. At night you can see the lights of La Paz across the water, or think you can. Your father was there at the time. He was there, too. In Mazatlán."

"Did you meet him there?" he asked.

"We knew each other before," she said, and was impatient to reveal to him a woman from out of his father's life, a woman he had not known existed, impatient to compel him to see her as he would imagine his father had seen her and to experience for a time, for the rest of the day, what she had meant to his father. Impatient to re-create the father and herself, the lovers. With her head bowed over a yellow leaf she had picked up, she strolled down the path a step ahead of him to contend with her urge to reveal to him that which ought to be left in the father's past and in her own.

"I remember he went to Mexico when I was six," he said. "He wrote me a letter. I was just learning to write and I answered him. He kept my letter. My mother has it. God, the spelling!"

"He went there with me," she said. "Or I went with him. We were lovers."

She had told him in order to experience again, as she was doing now as he followed her, the delight of being both desired and desirous as she had known it then. She had told him in order to experience again that greater awareness of herself, of the shifting and floating of the weightless silk around her thighs, of the threads of her hair that, glimpsed from the corner of her eye, were like flying spider silk in the sun, seen and not seen. She had told him in order to experience again that woman she had been years ago, followed by the man, the father. When he came alongside her she glanced at him to see her effect upon him, and saw the face of a sick child.

They stood in the shade of trees; and all things, the fragrance of the flowers, the tang of the limes from the drinks on a table close by, the voices in conversation among the trees and flowers, the heat of the day, some dust in the air from somewhere on the other side of the high, wrought-iron fence, everything served to make his face that of a boy taken sick at a picnic. "I remember you," he said, pressing at the leaves on the path with his heel. "I don't mean that I met you. I just mean that I remember you."

"How?" she asked.

"The time, I mean," he said. "I remember the time."

"The time?" She felt the loss of herself, as if she no longer existed even in anyone's memory, her features, her voice, all forgotten. Only the time remained as a frame empty of its picture of a woman.

"My mother used to cry," he explained. "She seemed to be crying all the time. And they would quarrel when he came home. The mascara would run down her cheeks and make black tears."

"But they weren't getting along even before he met me."

"Yes, I suppose," he said. "But she cried anyway about you."

He lifted his eyes in the silence he had enforced, and they were a child's accusing eyes, the eyes of a boy troubled by his mother's troubles, seeing his mother's face streaked by the mascara, hearing the quarreling through a wall, through a door left open.

"You shouldn't have told me," he said.

"Or committed the crime ten years ago?"

"No, no, I know more about people now," he said, defending his store of wisdom. "I just said you shouldn't have said it," trying to tell her that he was ashamed for reacting as a child, thrusting his mother between them, and that she should not have forced him back into the past, into the child loyal to the mother, when he was enjoying her company, the company of a strange woman who was giving him her time and gracefulness and wit, gifts that implied his maturity.

The shame he felt for reacting as a child and the love aroused for his mother struggled together, denying him any further ease with her. They walked side by side past guests who fell silent as they went silently by, much like lovers who have had their concluding quarrel. They made a circle of the garden, and at the table nearest the porch she stopped to chat with a friend. The boy went on before she could introduce him, and, glancing after him, she saw him striding down the driveway and out the wide-open gate.

The woman she was chatting with drew out from behind her a round, yellow cushion and tossed it into the empty chair. She sat down and continued the chatting, smoking and smiling, and seeing the face of his mother weeping black, bitter tears. She sat with her bare arms on the table, observing how the circle of trees and the soft, pointillistic light through the leaves all gave the group around the table the intimacy of a group in a painting, but seeing, all the time, the face of the weeping woman. There was unhappiness and tears for that woman long before she, the mistress, appeared in their lives, there was nothing that could have been done even if this feeling for the other woman had been experienced at that time, but her indifference, then, struck her now as a failing. She felt that she was a hundred years old, at last discovering that the person in her memory who affected her the most was not the one she had loved the most but the one she had understood the least.

She turned partly away and, reaching over the back of her chair, picked a leaf from a small tree blossoming with purple flowers, and with this activity concealed her face from the woman with whom she'd been talking.

Lonesome Road

*U*p on the sidewalk, glancing down through the high wire fence at the playground and the mothers on the benches, he recognized her by the way she bowed her head over her knitting as she used to bow it over her radical magazines—engrossed and eager to do somebody some good with what was in the print. He went down the concrete ramp and across the tanbark and spoke to her over the children in the sandbox.

She lifted her basket from the bench to the ground, hastily, to forestall, he knew, any embarrassment there might be for them in the curious stares and glances of the other women because he was a black man approaching a white woman, and he went around the sandbox and sat down where the basket had been.

"You haven't changed much," he said.

"Don't tell me that!" she laughed.

"You got kids you're watching?" he asked, searching among the ones in the sand for one to resemble her. A little girl with light hair was watching them. She turned away with solemn shyness, when her mother introduced her, and resumed her digging.

"I have a boy, too," she said, looking out over the playground to the baseball formation. "He's older. He's eight."

It was as if she had even closer allies now, allies she herself had created to reject him with, some other man's children. "That's a little army," he said. "I got a little army, too. I got three in mine, two girls and a boy. The other day the boy climbed up to the medicine cabinet and swallowed the iron tablets and had to go to the hospital to get pumped out. They're out of their minds," he said, laughing with her.

As the laughing waned she pushed back her bangs, a gesture he remembered that hid her face for a second. Her hair had darkened, and her eyes, glancing at him from under her hand with a flash of shyness, seemed less blue, faded to the color of a dim sky. He knew that she saw him as better-looking than he'd been twelve years ago. Then he'd had a skinny, agitated look; now, at least, he was a little heavier, a lot calmer, his expensive suit the reward and requisite of a publicity man for a big insurance company. If one of them was at a disadvantage it was she. She was nobody to be possessed by, anymore, to be saved by, to beg from. Up on the sidewalk he had seen that she was less than she had been and it was this lessening that had enabled him to approach her.

"That's what they'll do, scare the wits out of you," she said, and sighed, laughing. "I guess every joy brings a burden along with it. You don't realize that so much until you've got kids."

"That's true, that's true," he said, disparaging with a smile her ready wisdom. In the past she had given out her left-wing maxims but this had the sound of religion or domesticity. "You can reverse it, too," he said, mocking her homily, its simpleness. "Like, every burden brings its joy."

"That's so," she agreed, taking him seriously. "A burden can make you more humane, more compassionate"—her voice fading out as it used to do when she had tried to help him with her aspirin kind of radical remedy for a disease that had got him by the throat.

"I can't hear you," he said, bending his head toward her.

"I was just agreeing with you," she said.

"If they don't kill you."

"Who?" she asked. Her irritation was with herself, not him. He knew the sound.

"The burdens, the burdens. Weren't you telling me about burdens?" he said, keeping up his smile to make a joke of their conversation, which was going awry, sooner than in the past, as if they were making up for lost time. "You never used to talk that way," he said. "When you were always deploring burdens there wasn't any any compensation that came along with them."

"But I still deplore them," she said.

"That's good," he said drolly. "That's good. And are you still on the right track? About how to get rid of burdens? Though the way I heard it, that track collapsed."

She was not cornered, he saw. "What we learned from that," she said, "is there are more answers than one."

"Ah, yes, ah, yes," he said, nodding, engaged, clasping his crossed knee. "And what are you doing with all the answers?"

She glanced at him to see his purpose. "They're taking the struggle into their own hands now," she said, and glanced at him again. "I still use the same old cliché words, don't I?"

"It *is* a struggle," he said.

"I mean, they're on their own," she explained, flushing.

She's all melted down to a spoonful of owlshit, he thought. He had refused her politics in that year he had known her, he had argued with her for hours, but now he found himself contemptuous of her for getting melted down in the heat of lost battles. The men she had introduced him to, those men who had cornered him with their barrage of knowledge until he felt like a criminal in his ignorance—were they all melted down? Though he had opposed them, he felt now that they had deserted him.

"Yeh, they're on their own," he agreed. "They were always on their own," reminding himself, with that retaliation, of their last meeting. She had called it quits and he had gone to hell, and he had begged her to come back, one time more. She had come up with a hamburger in a paper bag, trying to make it seem that all he required was food in his stomach so no more could be asked of her. He had been drinking for three days and he was sick, vomit was on his shirt and sour whiskey on his breath. He had wanted to reveal himself to her in all his obnoxious misery, and he had wanted her to love him in spite of all and because of all. He had taken her face in his hands and covered it with kisses from the mouth that had cursed her, telling himself it was what she had come for. She had stayed with him from noon to midnight, but it was the end.

A boy was coming across the tanbark, gazing at them, a kid with a wondering, bored look. He stood up and shook hands with the boy, who found a sandwich in the basket and walked away, eating.

"Do you want a sandwich?" she asked the little girl, who was watching, and the girl hung her head. "Come on," said the mother, and he heard again that sweetness in her voice that he remembered from their beginning, when he had telephoned her every evening and talked with her for hours, always with his radio turned up loud with a symphony so that she could hear in that background music the possibilities between them, the young social worker with her unmistaken politics and the young reporter with his unmistakable intelligence.

"She shy?" he asked. "Mine is shy, too. The littlest girl. Always hanging out behind her mama."

"They grow out of it," she said.

"They do, they do," he said, laughing indulgently.

She looked around for her knitting and found it beside her.

"You got thin," he said.

"Oh, maybe," she shrugged.

"You well?" he asked her kindly. Her hands were working the needles, her head bowed again. In among the darkening hairs were gray ones; no polish on her nails; socks instead of nylons; and old tennis shoes. He looked at her closely and thought: Was it just the way some women age fast? Or was it that her substance was gone, her certainty gone. That certainty that in the past had infuriated him and he had attacked by attacking her politics. That certainty, that control over her own life, over all her choices of acceptance and rejection, that certainty she herself would have denied but that he had been as sure about as he'd been about her heart beating in her breast.

"Aside from the usual winter colds," she said, "I haven't been sick a day. And you?"

"Not sick a minute," he said.

From the sandbox rose a chorus of wailing and screaming. One child stood pouring sand over another's head, and a third tossed sand over both contestants. She got up to go for her child, who had covered her face with her hands and was crying, and something about the way she moved that was no longer the way she had moved up the stairs ahead of him on the way to his apartment, with his hands on her hips to feel their movement, something about the change brought on the memory that he had held off since the moment he sat down beside her on the bench. He remembered the time just before the end, when, lying in his bed, she had covered herself with the blankets because she had a question to ask and she wanted to disappear before she asked it. They had got honest with each other again, maybe because he had begged her again to marry him. I have to ask you, she had said, *because how can we know each other if I don't ask you?* and she had asked him if he loved her because she was white. Simpering up his face to imitate her, he had hurled newspapers and clothes around the room until she got out of bed and got dressed, frightened by his tormenting mimicry of her question and by his answer—that if there had to be truth to cement the damn thing together, then the truth was that he hated her, she was too goddamn much trouble. He watched her now, taking the child by the hand, leading her away from the melee and with the hem of her skirt wiping away wet sand from the crying mouth, and knew now, watching her, that more was in that question she had asked him that time, more than the desire to be rid of him, more than the desire to come at last to the core of their love and find no core.

"Never a dull moment," she said, sitting down on the bench, laughing, her short hair falling across her cheek as she bent to the basket to find something to appease the child, who sat on the other side of her.

"Oh, God, never," he agreed.

For a few more minutes he sat with her, leaning forward to say a few words to the child and leaning back to laugh with the mother. When he stood up, she lifted her hand to shade her face from the sun, smiling up at him. She was relieved, he knew, to see him go. He walked briskly, with the step of good health, up the concrete ramp, and on the sidewalk again, as he leaned against the fence to pick a scratchy piece of tanbark off his sock, he saw that she was lifting the girl's hand and waving it at him, but he pretended not to see them. He could not bring himself to wave back at them, because his pity for her, the pity that he had failed to experience in the time of his love, forbade him small and amiable signals.

Myra

On the weedy floor of the valley lie the mud-brown matchboxes, each a row of ten rooms under one flat roof, and a narrow wooden porch runs the length of it, each man's porch his neighbor's also. Four boxes face each other to form a square, the earth of it hard as rock in summer, rutty with holes in the rain, and the many boxes and their squares are a maze that covers the valley. A few small trees, straggling lines of them hardly as high as the low dwellings, prettify the roads that intersect the project. Sometimes a loud, topheavy flickering and haggling of sparrows make a tree's presence known, or they make themselves known in the spring by their sun-green foliage, but for most of the year they are lost in the barren scene, under them stripped cars rusting or new ones, red and pink and blue-jay blue, reflecting the sun in their chrome.

The hills rise around three sides of the valley and thick upon them are more dwellings, but up here the houses are in pairs, family houses, standing back to back, and crowding in upon the highest of them are groves of oak and eucalyptus and madrona. Up here, the tenants can see the islands and the bay, can see, across a narrow inlet, brown hills casting brown reflections and the white egrets standing on their matchstick legs in the shallows; can see, farther out, the high cliffs of Belvedere with the raw, flesh-colored frames of the new houses hanging out over the water; can see the traffic on the highway that runs past the project—the huge trucks with their names read half a mile away and the cars swerving around the trucks on the long climb up to the bridge.

On Sunday, the men who dig the earth for the foundations of the houses all over the county, pour the concrete, carry the lumber on their shoulders, light the early morning fires for the carpenters to warm their hands by, on Sunday, some of them, some of the younger ones, lounge in their cars way up on the rim of the project. They sit in their cars and drink from beer cans and bottles, and their high-low laughter, their richly loud voices sound among the trees behind them, along with the fall of the cans on the carpet of wrinkled pods and acorns. They sit up here and survey all.

Their women are left to themselves. They do their household tasks as they do on weekdays; they go to church in the morning, and in the afternoon they visit next door, an hour or so over a beer, with the door open onto the common porch, a rock for a doorstop, to let out the heat from the room and the smell of mustard greens and the kerosene that feeds the stove, and then they go back and lie down on their beds and nap, and the sweat breaks out in rings around their eyes. In the hot weather there is no current of air, and in the cold, the high, capricious heat is piped along above the ceiling, all along the rooms. This Sunday abandonment happened to Myra Hall, young as she was, comely as she was, slender and tall, with her head high and her eyes always down, her skin the color of the madrona tree when the bark peels away, and as smooth.

It began at the end of the first year of their marriage. Before that, she and Lionel did things together on Sunday. They drove up to visit his brother's family on the outskirts of Petaluma, spending the day there, and when they walked around the yard, holding hands, she would scuffle up red chicken feathers with the toes of her high-heeled sandals. She was a city-bred girl, born in San Francisco and never away from there in her nineteen years. The country delighted her, and sometimes, because she like to see her hands clutching his shirt, she exaggerated her response to a garter snake, a tomato worm, a spider with a body like a cherry. On other Sundays they went fishing in Sausalito, out on the old ferry slip, picnicking on fried chicken and pie. All around them the seagulls sat on pilings or walked close on the planks to see what was to be done with the bait and the fish. The seawater thudded and smacked around the old timbers, and far across the water the white fog blew in, its feathery edges melting in the sun and the shining towers of the city floating above it; and once in a while he would duck his head and kiss her nipple, take sweater and nipple into his mouth, and her eyes would narrow down and all she could see was a long glitter, like a glittering wave. Or they stayed in their room all Sunday, the door still locked from the night and the green blinds down and the lace curtains closed, and while people passed along the wooden porch and cars pulled in and out of the lot and dogs tumbled and growled together against the door and a mixed-up cat meowed at the crack and the heavy, dusty Sunday weighed down upon all the flat roofs, they stayed in there to love. With the covers thrown down at the foot of the bed, they slept. They took turns fixing something to eat, and when she stood in her dark nakedness by the stove he would say, "Come here, come back, forget that." All those Sundays belonged to the first year; then he began to go out without her.

Along about eleven o'clock in the morning, as she was washing dishes in the narrow kitchen that was filled with the smell of bacon and shaving soap, he would open the door and go out into the coming noon, and she never knew where he was going. He didn't know himself, he said, "So how can I tell *you*, woman?" She swore at him when he left and when he returned, and if she was out to a movie or visiting a girlfriend and returned and found him playing solitaire or already in bed, she swore at him then. He would tell her where he had been, with this fellow or that one, as if it were the most natural thing in the world for him to be with his men friends all day Sunday.

When she got pregnant, unable to express to him the secret pleasures of the experience and, in a way, not wanting to, she fell silent, was sullenly, spiritedly silent, hoping that the pleasureless part of it, the leaning over the toilet bowl and the shuddering return to bed, would rouse his love. But he seemed to think that her bearing a child was the most natural thing in the world and undeserving of his attention. In the early months she almost miscarried. Opal came in from two doors down the porch and did her chores for her; she said, "You cry, you fidget so much, no wonder you gonna lose that baby. You as itchy as a worm in hot ashes," and left her alone. She lay in the dimmed room with nothing upon its partition walls but a sky-blue placard with gilt letters, *God Bless Our Home*, left by tenants before them. A salmon-pink upholstered chair, a coffee table, a kitchen table, and the bed on which she lay, a bed with its dark green spread—a room both crowded and bare. The windows were closed against the strong winds that came after hot weather, the blind clicking in the stream of wind that came in through a crack. She lay alone in the room between two other rooms, the one on the west side burnt out, its tattered green blinds hanging at the paneless windows—months ago a kerosene stove had exploded, and the black, damp wood was still like pepper in the nostrils—and the other, an old couple's room, the man lying all day on a sofa by the door, his long, handsome body in soft and clean, yellowy long underwear, tended by his woman with her Old South kerchief on her head that was bent over the Bible she read to him or the bowl of food she fed him. She heard the cindery silence on the one side and the celled-in voices on the other, and remembered a sleepwalking night that Lionel had told her about, laughing, a night that had happened to him when he was a boy on his father's farm near Baton Rouge. He had killed a cricket, and that night the cricket was on him; he had walked in his sleep and seen rabbits swarming up out of the well and woke up out there bawling for his mother. But nothing was on his conscience now for stepping on a woman.

When the cramps weighed like an iron inside her, she went out to the green telephone booth standing like a sentry box by the road and phoned the clinic in the city. "Go back to bed," her doctor commanded, "and stay there," and she hung up without asking him about the other method of saving babies she had heard about—they gave the woman a hypo or something—and found her way back, a clothesline making a welt across her face. A colored baby was dirt to them, those smoothy doctors. They didn't care whether a colored baby got born or not. When she went again to the clinic, as she did each month, and told the doctor that she had almost lost the baby, he said to her, "Calm down or we'll tie you down to a bed here and keep you down until delivery," and for a while, there in the examination room, in the reception room as she went out past the rows of waiting women, and part of the way home on the bus, she believed that they could do that to her, keep her prisoner because she could not calm herself.

One evening, as she stood by the stove, stirring up potatoes in the frying pan, her hand with the spatula in it was stopped by his slowing down as he took off his jacket; she sensed from his slowness that he was *seeing* her. "Maybe you better refuse them jobs," he said. "You don't want to be losing it. What you about now?"

She was struck by his concern as by a blow. She spread her hand over her rounding belly, closed her eyes, threw back her head and began to wail with the desire to be close to him again. She stepped to him and clasped his body around, and he, after a moment of surprise, put his jacket on the table and began to stroke her back, but it took a long time before she felt his hands upon her. While he showered, she sat on the toilet lid, and when he stepped from the stall, drying himself with his army towel, she caressed him to prevent his returning again to ignorance of her.

Confined by her behavior, he stayed home that evening. With a small comment about her condition he had triggered an avalanche of affection and he was pinned beneath it. He carried himself cautiously, stiffly, his eyes glancing away from hers. At eight o'clock a friend of his rapped at the door, and he invited him in, a fellow with a loud body and face but no voice. Myra sat at the table with them while they drank their beer, her eyelids stretched far down over her shifting green eyes that rounded out the lids in the way her pregnancy rounded out her breasts and belly. Only Lionel talked, rubbing and crossing his legs as he told a funny story. The visit was short, but somewhere in the midst of it Lionel slipped out from under her mood. He went out on the porch to say good-bye to his friend, and Myra, still at the table, heard their voices rising released into the night. Just at the moment when she thought he would enter the room again, she heard his voice farther out in the parking lot. For an hour he sat in his friend's car, and when he returned she knew by his face, which was remembering banter, remembering gossip, remembering the clues given him to future joys, that she was again only in the margin of his sight. She sat with her forearms out upon the table, catlike, watching him sit himself down on the big chair's edge and riffle the cards for solitaire on the coffee table. She knew in her heart that he had no other woman, but she also knew that he might have one soon. His return to the company of men stirred up in him the need of pursuit again, and the woman would be somebody else's wife, someone whose husband was in the army or away in Alaska working in the canneries, because having himself a married woman was the next step above having himself a girl. And she knew the way he'd treat that woman, because she'd seen it done by other men: *You can cling to me all you want, woman, hold me around with your arms and your thighs, but I ain't yours, I ain't nobody's*, a way that would drive that silly woman crazy, whoever she was. She crawled into bed with her dress on.

Opal rapped at the door a few minutes after Lionel had left for work. A woman in Ross was asking Myra to come to work that day, Opal said, leading the way back to her room, her blue satin mules knocking against the porchboards, her behind moving like a nest of snakes in the tight, shiny nightgown. "Why'n she call you last night 'stead of this mornin?" Opal complained, spitefully speaking forward instead of over her shoulder.

Myra sat sleepily at the foot of the bed, the phone in her lap. The caller was a woman she liked, an elderly, strong-voiced woman, an ex-nurse who lived in a two-story house within a garden. She always felt friendly toward this woman, and she responded now without resentment to the masculine voice explaining that guests were coming that evening to stay for several days, that she had just learned late last night. Please, couldn't Myra come today?—a little ironing, a little cleaning up? "Yes," she said, yes, she'd come, she'd be there by nine o'clock, and heard the woman's laugh, a harsh and broken laugh, the kind a person puts on to make you think she was at your mercy and you granted her her life. But when she hung up she remembered the weariness that came after her last job for another woman, a couple of weeks ago; she had stood all afternoon on the concrete floor of a basement, ironing fine sheets, frilly blouses, little girls' pinafores, linen napkins, while a tall gray poodle wandered in and out, out into the flowers and sun and up the high porch steps, his nails clicking on the floor above her head, a dog possessing the run of the house and the air. *What do you care if I die, you bastard?* she said to Lionel. *What do you care if I come back and die?*

Opal was in under the covers again. "What you say yes for?"

"I like that woman."

"You like her better'n your own baby?"

She went back along the porch on her bare feet, feeling apart from everyone, feeling jagged in her mind, hating the woman she had agreed to work for, that woman telephoning at half past seven in the morning, sure about claiming a servant woman's day.

On the way back from the job, almost the moment she climbed down from the bus at the depot shack, the pangs began. She ran across the yards, the sooner to lie down, ducking under empty clotheslines, grappling and slapping her way through hanging laundry. By the time she got to her door, she was already tearing at the buttons of her blouse. She lay down in her slip and drew the covers up over her mouth.

Lionel fixed the ice bag for her the minute he got home. After he had showered, he cooked supper and brought her a plate of rice and leftover stew, and she leaned on her elbow to eat it, her head in her hand. The unshaded light above the table where he sat, facing her, deprived his narrow, bony face of its contours, flattening it into a newspaper face. "You strain yourself?" he asked her. "What you do to yourself?"

"I did my chores," she told him, sarcastic.

No words from him, just the tink of his fork on the plate and the stuffed-nose way he breathed when he ate. Her arm began to quake with weariness, and at that moment she wondered if even her half-up position was risky. She leaned over the side of the bed to put the plate on the floor and lay back, and her disgust with the few forkfuls she had eaten and with his happy drudgery way of eating and with the nothingness between them in this hour when the child was losing its poor, watery-handed hold on life rose up in a long wrench of a cry.

"Jesus," he whispered. "What you want of me?"

She stared up at the stains of rain on the ceiling, the pictures of bears and monkeys they had picked out long ago as they lay there. How could a man change like that? His entire body aware of her, even the soles of his feet against her feet, and then be that person no more? And why was it she could not tell anybody of what it did to her, though it sat day and night in her mind? Even if her mother came alive again, came back on a nightmare visit and knocked at the door, she could not tell *her*, though she came wearing her black faille dress and gloves and hat, came to be *told*.

"You want me to get Opal?" he asked.

"Don't bother yourself," she said and, turning her face to the wall, experienced a great longing love for the abused child within her, the child that was only becoming and that was treated so cruelly by its mother even so early, so soon. She dozed, wrapped in the quilts and in the heat that was forced into the room and into all the rooms down the box and all the boxes in the valley, until heat and quilts and pain became one, an unbearable, strangling quilt that brought her awake, and she called to him. She heard a chair pushed back and saw him stand, and knew by the slouch in his body, by the quietness in the yards, that early evening had passed and it was night. "Go get somebody," she told him, and felt no love anymore for the child or for anybody.

Opal came, and the old woman with the pale yellow scarf tight over her skull and a grin of sorrowing exertion whose center was a tooth's gold cap, perforated with a four-leaf clover, a cap gleaming like the hope of prosperity. They took it from her and hid it away, a silent thing not a child, that must have been her anger against him, the pain of her anger against him. They washed her bent legs and her feet, and the rest of her, and she felt that the lashing-out had quit her tongue forever. By the time a stranger doctor came, a long time after Lionel had phoned him, she was falling asleep under the women's hands.

The Houses
of the City

On some days he longed to be with his mother before the hour of her return to their rooms, and in the afternoon he would seek her out at whatever house she was cleaning that day, even though the place was halfway across the city, up in the heights where the big houses stood apart like rich merchants' wives watching their husbands' ships entering the bay below. In his small body was the quality of the pointer dog. He walked slightly stooped, pushing forward, his feet going down in a plodding way.

It was late in his tenth year when he began this practice. He would be in the midst of a scuffle after school, along a sidewalk somewhere, and suddenly he would think of her and at that moment offer nothing further to the struggle. This silent urgency was more effective in breaking his opponent's grip than was his fierce, animal strength. Always in the morning she told him where she would be that day, so that if anything happened to him at school his teacher could call her right away. He felt that it was impossible for anything to harm him; but anything could harm her.

She was alarmed the first time she opened a door to him. He was not sick, he told her. But he had no other reason to give. Of his fear of her dying he could not tell, because to give words to this fear was like pronouncing sentence upon her. If he kept it to himself, the fear might prove groundless. After the first time they said nothing on his arrival. He made no demands, and sat in the chair she pointed to, his hands folded obviously away from the lure of knickknacks and magazines. He listened to the sounds of her cleaning in other rooms, and was not restless.

Certain women were fascinated by him, as if, in his silent clinging to one chair, he were a large moth, its intentions unknown. Once, as he sat in a glass-enclosed sunporch, a large-leafed plant, growing from a blue glazed bowl on the carpet, fingered his cheek, touched his elbow each time he fidgeted, but he did not move to another chair, hypnotized by the plant and its curiosity as if it were the lady of the house. Then one afternoon he was sitting in the hallway of an upstairs apartment, facing in a dutiful way the opposite wall and taking a small liberty in examining minutely the oval piece of wood that hung on the wall, a yellow horse painted on it, the long, white tail of the horse touching the green grass sprouting up. Aside from the sounds of his mother at her tasks, he heard another person astir in the bedroom beyond the oval picture. He heard the sluggish movement of a person turning under blankets, then the sound of slippers scraped along the floor. He heard a man talking to himself with the voice that is acquired while the body is lying down: a voice pocketed deep in the throat, granular, caressing, complaining.

From the half-open bedroom door came a young man, not much older than a high school boy. His hair was red and stood up in curls, as if startled in advance, and he paused there in the doorway, staring in exaggerated surprise at the boy in the hallway chair. He was tying the tasseled belt of his bathrobe, which was a jewel-green silk, and one end of the belt he held in surprise across the palm of his right hand.

"Fran!" he called. "Who is this you let in?" His voice was cajoling and demanding; he listened to his own voice like a violin pupil listens to the music he makes. "Do you want to see me?" he asked, dropping his head in a pointing way. "If you have any business with me, speak up! If it's a debt I owe, let me congratulate you on getting past the door. Most of my creditors sit on the steps outside. Well, how much do I owe you? Whatever it is, I can't pay it."

Now he placed his hands on the arms of the chair, leaning over the boy, and the boy turned his face away, embarrassed, from the corners of his eyes meeting the young man's eyes.

"I can't pay you for this reason," explained the young man. "Do you see this house, how clean it is? Well, you should have seen it before that woman took a mop and vacuum to it." His close face was sleepily plump, and his hair, so near, was something to be puzzled out, its curls were so many and entwined. "If anyone is going to be paid," he said, "it's her, and you'll have to wait your turn. She works like a dog and stands for a lot of abuse from her employers, and she's constantly worrying all the time about that son of hers. She's got to keep him decently clothed, you know, and fed." Their eyes met again, forced by the young man's eyes to a mutual comprehension of her plight. "But I'll tell you," he said, laying his hand on the boy's shoulder. "Come into the kitchen with me and settle for a cup of chocolate."

Under the spell the boy slid off the chair so abruptly that his head hit the young man in the chest. With the nape of his neck in his host's hand, the boy was marched down the hallway. In the kitchen his mother was seated on a high stool, polishing silverware at the sink, a scarf of many faded colors wrapped around her head. She glanced over her shoulder at them, an absentness in her eyes as if she watched a dog or a cat, a household pet, saunter into the kitchen. Afraid suddenly that his presence jeopardized her job and that she was not going to recognize him, he stumbled as the young man pressed him down into a chair. For a moment he did not know who he should be, her son or the bill collector.

From the refrigerator, the host drew out a bottle of milk and poured some into a pan. Then he stirred in several teaspoons of cocoa and several of sugar, in this process spilling some of both on the waxed linoleum, and his leather slippers made a sticky, rasping sound as, uncaring, unhearing, he walked about.

"He don't need no chocolate," she said.

Up went the young man's spoon in a gesture of disbelief and dismay. The young man was startled by this rudeness. "Is that the way to talk to a guest of mine?"

The boy laughed out loud because he was sure now of who he was, and he shifted in his chair, granted a freedom of movement in the chairs of this house.

"For that," said the young man to her, "you can't have any. She can't, can she?" he asked, but he asked it of her, bringing his face close to hers, delicately close, the two profiles, presented to the boy in the chair, reminding him of the approach and ascent of butterflies, touching and yet not touching. At once he was left out of the game. He had thought the game was for him and he learned that it was played only to accentuate some secret between his mother and the young man. And the boy was caught in the midst of his laughter, his elbows lifted eccentrically behind him like wings going up.

They had hot chocolate together, the young man and he, the host sitting with his legs apart, his robe falling away from his bare thighs, not at all embarrassed that a woman could see so much of his body. The young man drank in a hungry, nervous way, bobbing his head down impatiently to meet the cup on its way up. It was when he was lifting his head, swallowing elaborately in his haste to continue what he was saying, that he spoke the boy's name: "Matt," he said, "you've got catchall ears. Listen to this," and went on with his story. But the boy glanced up at his mother, unbelievingly. She had told his name to the young man, but of the young man the boy had been told not a thing.

When the host said, "Well, come along," Matt followed him up the hallway and into the bedroom. The curtains were closed, and the young man switched on the lamp by the bed, got down on his knee, and rummaged through a pile of magazines that lay under the bed. This room hadn't been cleaned yet. It smelled of cigarette smoke, of night perspiration, and upon the lamp's table were strewn a number of little things: theater tickets, manicure scissors, a red glass ashtray, a man's handkerchief, a Lifesaver candy, a dime and four pennies. Was the young man an actor? he wondered, for he had heard that actors slept all day. There was something dramatic in the young man's bowed back, covered with the slick green robe, and in the leg, stretched out behind the bent knee, with its white knot of calf and its quivering heel. Rising, the young man placed in the boy's hand a thick magazine, a photograph of a Dalmatian dog on its cover, and gently prodded him to turn around; and the boy, lifting his head so that he could find his way out through the dimness beyond the lamp, saw his mother's black coat thrown over the back of a chair, and on the seat of the chair lay her small red hat.

Again he sat in the hallway, turning the pages of the sports magazine, while in the bedroom the young man poked about, getting dressed. The magazine had pictures of men in hip boots, fishing, of dogs carrying ducks from reedy water, of horses; and the smell of the paper was clean, strong as lacquer, the pages satin smooth and weighted in his hands. He turned up the palm of his right hand to see if it were dirty and would soil the white luster. Usually, he thought, she left her coat and hat in the kitchen. Once, in another house, when it was time for them to go, she had brought her coat from the back porch, where a late afternoon rain had flicked it through the screen; it was too shabby, she had said, to hang in the hall closet, because, if a guest came, he would not want to hang his coat next to hers. But in this house her coat was lying on a chair in a bedroom. His right hand was again on the magazine, but he still could not say whether his hands were clean or grimy. Lifting his hand again, he decided that it was not clean enough, and he closed the magazine, placing it on the floor beside his chair.

Closely, he listened to the sound of her in the kitchen, his hands clasped in his lap. By such devout observance of her presence he was proving to her that he was a more loving son than the young man could ever be, no matter how hard the other tried.

They would ride home together in the evening, boarding a trolley or a cable car, depending upon which neighborhood she was working in, and something in the waning day and in sitting beside her, watching the tall, narrow houses slip by like boards in one long fence, caused him to become tired of premonition. With the onset of evening's soft glamour, she would become for him quite alive and everlasting. On their journey home that evening, he sat beside her in the trolley, clasping between his knees her shopping bag, and each time she laid her hand on his knee, the love and shame of the betrayed wrinkled across his face. If he was unduly frightened by the way her hands were turning translucent, by the way her veins were rising along her forearms, if she was, after all, not going to die, there was, he thought, another way she could be lost. When they climbed down from the trolley and walked along the street to their apartment house, he swung the shopping bag in his left hand so that the bag separated her and himself. But when the bag, light as it was, scraped against her ankle, his heart contracted with remorse as if he had deliberately hit her.

When she unlocked the door, he slipped in before her and lay directly down on the couch. Since their kitchen had no window, she switched on its ceiling light, and gradually as the street grew darker, as the sun, shining eastward down the street, withdrew its flame from the lamp at the corner, leaving a dark gray smudge in the globe, the panes of the bow window in which he lay became black mirrors and he saw in the one that was near to his face the reflection of the kitchen doorway and his mother by the stove. The picture was miniature, unreal, and when she spoke to him he answered her by speaking to the reflection, but this disturbed him and he turned his face to the room.

She came from the kitchen carrying plates, but instead of placing them on the table she continued to hold them in her hands while she faced him, pressing her hip against the edge of the table. Her face and the front of her were obscured by the darkness of the room, but the outline of her thin body and some outer strands of her short hair were lit by the light from the kitchen behind her. She laughed a bit, in a wry way that did not change the set of her head.

"What do you want to follow me for?"

He put his hands over his ears.

When she had set the table, she came and stood above him. Into this room whose cold was not yet dispelled by the warm air from the kitchen, she brought in her body the heat from the stove and on her skin the steam.

"Well?" And, hearing no answer, "Come, sit down and eat."

Obediently he sat up, but as he got to his feet she put her hands against his chest, pushing him down again; before he knew it, she was lying beside him and they were holding each other so closely that to breathe he had to turn his face upward.

"What do you want to follow me for?"

With his arms around her, he found himself listening to her body and heard her listening to his, and it was comical, almost, like two persons staring at each other through the same keyhole. In that moment he changed his reason for following her. It was not the possibility of her dying that troubled him, but something else he had picked up just an hour ago. The young man was pretending to be her son, and she did not object. This disloyalty of hers became so loud in their bodies that she had to let go of him and sit up.

"How did he know my name?"

"I told him," she said. "Can't I talk about my own son?"

"But you never told me you told him my name."

"Do I have to tell you about everybody I tell about my son?"

Was it something he had exaggerated all along, he wondered, their alliance against the persons she worked for? Although she came home bringing stories about them, describing them and their visitors jabbingly, vindictively, had he believed mistakenly that with these stories she bound herself and him together?

"Come now," she said. "Get up and eat."

But he made no effort to rise. She was standing away from him, as if weary of her guilt, but he knew she was uncertain over which side she was on, his or the young man's with the crudely bared legs.

Nocturne

So the old woman got herself a yellow apple today. Val, entering quietly by the front door, saw Eulalia sprawled in the rocker, the visitor who came every day, her pink felt hat over her gray curls lest the family think she was making herself at home. Her skinny legs stretched out, her eyes closed, she rocked forward and back, atwitter with a thousand comments on the delight of eating an apple given to her as a gift.

Beyond the rocking figure in the living room, Mrs. Rand, Val's mother-in-law, was squatting down before the hot water tank in the kitchen, turning up the flame, grasping the back of a chair so she could rise again; she was too big to rise without help.

Val slipped down the hallway to her bedroom; there she leaned over her baby, sleeping in a laundry basket on the bed, and kicked off her high-heeled shoes.

"Val?" called Mrs. Rand. "Did I hear her come home?" she asked Eulalia.

"I'm here!" called Val.

"We're going to Monterey!"

"For fish dinner!" cried Eulalia, who wasn't going at all.

"John and me and Mr. Bellucci," Mrs. Rand shouted on. "Bellucci's brother got a fish boat down there, got a nice little house, and we're all going to visit him, Bellucci and John and me. If we leave before Bessie gets home from work, you tell her where we took her son, and tell her we'll be back tomorrow, Saturday." Her voice changed to a cooing: "John's going to take a bath, ain't you, John?" And Val heard the boy flying around the living room, snuggling up against walls. "You go to Eulalia," Mrs. Rand coaxed him. "Here, Eulalia, is his picture book, it'll calm him. What kind of animals you got there, Eulalia?"

Val heard the old woman sing out the names of the animals, heard John repeating the song, and suddenly Mrs. Rand was behind Val, a soft body bungling against her.

"She'll probably stay on after we leave so she can beg something more to eat." Mrs. Rand's whispering voice was like something frying in a pan. "But don't you give her anything, please, honey."

Val nodded, unbuttoning her jacket. Up to now she had paid little or no attention to Mrs. Rand's cautioning, but now she realized she had walked backwards to a point of least resistance. It wasn't, she reflected, a matter of her mother-in-law's selfishness wearing down her, Val's, generosity. In the first place, she wasn't generous with Eulalia, she was simply uncomfortable in the presence of a hunger that buzzed like a huge bee. If she gave the old woman a slice of cheese, a bunch of grapes, an orange, it was only to stop, for a few minutes, that constant sound. And, in the second place, Mrs. Rand wasn't selfish, she was simply afraid that Eulalia, given more, might begin to take with her own hands rather than receive, and already the grown-ups and children crowding the apartment—her daughter Bessie and grandson John, son Ralph (whenever he came home) and son's wife, Val, and their two children, the baby and four-year-old Greg—all opened their mouths for food like baby birds whose gaping beaks make the nest appear smaller.

"You always slip her something," Mrs. Rand complained. "She never had it so good before you came. I bet she's put on five pounds in the month you been here. The food around here is yours as much as mine, you help pay for it. But it's the principle of the thing, honey. She'll be crawling into your bed. . . ."

All right, Val said to herself, nodding. Today I'll slap Eulalia's wrist. Beggars soon learn not to pity each other. It didn't matter that one came posturing for food and the other, herself, hung around for a different kind of sustenance, for the sour wine of familial sympathy, poured almost as generously by Mrs. Rand as Val's own mother would have poured it. They were both beggars, Eulalia and she, and it was time to elbow Eulalia aside.

"Besides, she gets her old age check. It ain't much, but they don't let them starve," Mrs. Rand went on. "She just likes to eat with us. I can see how she feels, not having a family or anybody, but that's kind of selfish of her, ain't it?"

"All right, all right," Val chanted, nodding and nodding. "Not anymore." An answer that sent Mrs. Rand back to the kitchen on conspiratorial feet.

Val lifted the baby high, smudging his white gown with the day's office ink on her fingers. If we leave here, she said to him, if we leave your father, who never comes home anyway, if we leave Anna Rand's embrace, who will take care of you while I work? Will the woman who materializes from the classified ad, *Board and Room with working mother and children*, drop cigarette ashes into your bawling mouth when I'm away? She felt no inclination to kiss the baby's face, hanging above hers. It would be a Judas kiss, a kiss of false promise, for she was a weak sort of person, lacking the courage to end the marriage and to go out into the city with her children. Returning the smiling, uncritical baby to his basket, she went on bare feet to the kitchen to prepare the formula.

Mrs. Rand was sitting by the kitchen table, peeling John's clothes off. In his underclothes he leaned against her knee, his shoulders twitching. "Naked John, naked John," crooned Mrs. Rand. "Shall we go and take a bath, little naked John?" With both hands she stroked his pale head, trying to impart to it, as one imparts liniment to the ailing chest, the concept of reality that every nine-year-old ought to have and that this poor one lacked. Lumberingly, she arose, nudged him along into the bathroom, and shut herself in with him and the steam and the rushing water.

Eulalia moved herself into the chair vacated by Mrs. Rand and set her elbows modishly, languidly upon the red oilcloth. "Monterey, dear, has nothing to compare with a fish dinner you used to get down on the wharf, right here in San Francisco, oh, twenty years ago. You didn't have to go all of fifty miles to that Portuguese town just to get a fish cooked right. One night I remember we had scallops, fried scallops, each one like a man's gold watch. . . ." But senility whisked her meal away, like a proprietor who has just learned from behind someone's hand that this patron was unable to pay, and she sat blinking with her moment's loss of memory, an old woman whose clothes were so seldom changed and faded to so neutral a color that they seemed to be a part of her by nature.

Ah, God, will I look like that? asked Val. An old woman, she thought, is more piteous than an old man because she is less pitied, for there was something like a betrayal about a woman's growing old, she seems to be betraying her own nature. You didn't quite know what she was when she got old. . . . Val poured the formula into the row of bottles on the sink, set the empty pan on the stove, then picked up a loaf of bread that sat so tantalizingly under Eulalia's nose and slipped the loaf into the tin breadbox on the refrigerator. In the moment her back was turned to Eulalia, Val saw herself with the old woman's eyes, saw something shrewish in her girl's body, in her straggly, bleached hair.

Bellucci knocked with dignity and dispatch, and entered at Val's bidding, wearing a trim suit and a Panama hat, carrying an overnight case of simulated alligator. He was, this heavy, rich-eyed old man, who carried his chest as carefully as if it were a leaking wine barrel, a friend of hers the moment he met her, bringing small gifts of candy to her because she was a hard worker, but repaying himself by teasing her. Val poured coffee for him and for Eulalia while he waited at the kitchen table, his eyes restless for Mrs. Rand, his Annie Aniseed.

"Did you ever eat fish roe?" cried Eulalia, drunk on the afternoon's second cup of coffee, granted her because of Bellucci. He spread his hand over his heart with the pain her foolish question gave him.

Anna Rand was ready to go, her short, gray hair combed with water, her nurse's shoes white as chalk. She carried John's tweed coat in one hand and a twine shopping bag, stuffed with oranges, her purse, and a box of crackers in the other hand. John at her side wore a tan gabardine suit, cut and sewn for him by his grandmother from a discarded suit of Bessie's. He was a little spider caught in a jar, unable to conceive of the jar's destination. Bellucci rose, picked up her round, red overnight bag, picked up his own.

"There's corn chowder on the stove for everybody, and potatoes, and there's chops in the icebox," Mrs. Rand said. "And if that son of mine comes home tonight, there's a couple chops extra for him," she called from the doorway.

Bellucci, halfway down the long, outdoor flight of stairs, shouted up: "Hey you, Val? Whatsa matter with you your husband don't stay home? You don't kiss him enough, maybe?"

They descended the stairs stompingly, and it seemed to Val, waving from the doorway, that their bodies were already fatigued by the journey. It was the step of return and they were setting out with it.

Eulalia cried good-bye from where she sat by her cup, airily swinging her crossed-over leg. This is what you'll come to, Val thought, sitting down across from Eulalia to drink a cup of coffee and pursue her dread. Only you'll have no fluttering gestures to cover your senility, as this woman has. You'll be the bulky kind and you'll wear men's shoes on your swollen feet, the leather slit to accommodate the pain. Your legs will be flumpy with veins, little curling carrot-tops of whiskers will sprout from your chin, and your white hair will be cut straight across your neck to oblige the executioner.

"After Harry Rand died of a heart attack, the family almost starved," Eulalia began without preliminaries, for Val's sitting across the table from her in an empty house called for great revelations. "She couldn't make any money with her sewing, so my husband and me, we took in Ralph, we took in Ralph when he was a little fellow and made him our son. My husband had a position in the post office, worked right through the Depression, and you should've seen that boy eat. That first dinner he scared us, he ate so much. He stayed with us for six months, put on a little flesh. But he's still got a mean, hungry look in his eyes. No matter how much he eats, he's never going to be able to get rid of that look. It's there until he dies. What did you see in him, honey? What you hang around him for?"

See in him? It wasn't anymore what she saw in him, Val mused, it was just that she couldn't see the future. The first year they were sufficient unto themselves and there was no need to see a future, and, during the worsening years when Ralph couldn't get up before noon (*the goddamn day rises with its back to me,* he used to say, *and I don't have the strength to make it turn around*) and she had worked, and Greg had crawled around the one-room apartment in wet diapers heavy as a stone, she was able, somehow, to imagine a rosy future. But then she got pregnant again, and when the baby was two months old, Ralph quit his clerking job and disappeared, and she had moved Greg and the baby and herself to Mrs. Rand's. After she'd been a couple of days at her mother-in-law's, Ralph showed up again, and when he lay down beside her that night they both had cried, they had cried from love and weariness of spirit. But while they kissed each other's eyes, she felt the certain loss of the future. It was as if someone told her in words, bending over the bed, and she had felt as bereft as when they had told her about her mother.

"Paupers, paupers," Eulalia said. "His clothes stank. My husband and I had to buy him new clothes so I could wash the old ones. And that tall daughter of hers, that Bessie with the big head and the long legs, built strong enough to give birth to twelve children, what does she have but an idiot? A boy with a cup of water where his brain should be. Maybe it isn't Bessie's fault, maybe it isn't in the blood like you think. Maybe it's her husband's fault, but she should've known better than to marry a steward on a ship, the way they carry on with all the women on board. Don't ever come around to see what he brought on himself, does he?"

Val sat huddling her cigarette, her bare heels caught on the rung of the chair. Eulalia, she knew, was telling her these things to shame the Rand family for drawing Val at last into the conspiracy against an old woman; she was exonerating Val for snatching the bread away, telling her that she was a hapless victim, like Oliver Twist in Fagin's gang. But Val declined the pardon. What she had done was done by herself. Eulalia had become, all in a tired moment at the end of the day, an intolerable image, the end result of Val herself. Val, too, would grow old, and who would care that in her youth her face had been dimpled and her fingertips pointed, and who would care that she had read a thing or two and carried bits of wisdom like a bouquet of tiny flowers other minds had given her because they loved her. Whatever flowers Eulalia had carried were lost now, and the possession she prized the most was the ingratiating manner that got her a yellow apple, and there was no one who cared enough for her to speculate about who she had been in her youth.

Val dropped her cigarette into her coffee cup, unknotted herself and went into the bedroom for the baby, calling to Eulalia that she was going to the nursery school to bring Greg home. Eulalia, forbidden by Mrs. Rand to remain alone in the apartment, ran around the living room, searching for her purse, and followed Val down the stairs, her flat heels clacking. At the corner by the gray stucco high school in whose basement the public nursery school was housed, Eulalia parted from her, scooting down the street, hugging her elbows, her step still imitating Val's, the busy, determined step of a young mother setting out to find her child.

Giant red apples were pasted above the blackboard, blanching by contrast the faces of the children who sat at the long, low table, awaiting their mothers. Greg sat knee-by-knee with a girl older than he, who was reading to him from a picture book. When he saw his mother, he knocked his chair backwards and ran to clutch her legs. Val pinched his face, and he laughed up at her in a silly, gasping way from the folds of her corduroy skirt. By the door hung a large cardboard sheet with rows of paper pockets on it, and she paused to see if there was a note in Greg's pocket. The folded paper stuck up like the tip of a trim white handkerchief, startling her. It was the first note since she had enrolled him a month ago, the day after they moved in with Mrs. Rand. Had he stolen something? Or did he sit with mouth agape, wanting spectacles? Val released his hand and reached for the note, aware that the young teacher in a blue denim smock was only a few yards away, talking with another mother. *Seems to like his music class very much*, said the upright handwriting. *Listens to the records and tells us whenever he hears a violin. Does someone in your family play the violin?*

They climbed the concrete stairs, and the wind of evening met them on the street, blew her skirt between her thighs, blew Greg's straw hair into a peak. *So he listens to music, this bit of a creature!* she thought. Was he born with it, this taste, like some human beings are born with vestigial fish gills, something that didn't belong in the atmosphere they were born into? Was it left over from the years of her dreaming, before she had ever met Ralph? To his small hand in hers, to his hand with the thin thread of its own will, she said, *Kid, you'll only make it tough for yourself. Don't listen*

anymore to the sounds of the violin, or the flute, or any of the other instruments
that lead you up and away from the ground that ought to be under your feet.
The wind was strapping her forehead with a lock of hair, and, desiring to
be neat in the eyes of her son, she reached up and wound it back among
the others.

Up in the kitchen Greg hopped around her as she took the loaf from
the box and spread butter on a slice. The baby began to complain from
the couch in the living room where she had laid him down, and Greg,
afraid that she would leave her task undone, stepped between her feet
and stretched up his arms stiffly as high as they would go.

She gave him his bread, and the mealy laughter down in his satisfied
throat did not dispel the man he was to become. And if, she wondered,
she came holding Greg's hand, could she enter Eulalia's room without
flinching and ask her to come to supper? She had entered it once before,
when Eulalia was sick and Mrs. Rand had asked her to take over a jar of
chicken soup. An old woman is so public in her aging that her room becomes her only refuge, more intimate than the room of a girl waiting for
her lover. But if, this time, Val came holding her son's hand, she would
have no fear of the old woman and of her possessions, of the curved
amber comb and the webbed china cup on the dresser, and of the thin bed
with the putty-colored crocheted spread. It was a matter of braving the
lions' den, holding the hand of Daniel.

"You want to come with me to Eulalia's?" she asked him.

"No," he said. He did not like Eulalia.

"You'll come along anyway," she told him.

Greg bent his knees and did a shuffling dance into the living room,
eating his bread, a small figure in a blue sweater and with no inkling at all
that it was he who led.

Like a
Motherless
Child

*T*he old woman crossing the street had a blue scarf drawn over her head and tied under her chin, and the string of lights at the market entrance so enlivened the color that the men drinking their beer in the row of cars at the curb transformed her for a few alert moments into a girl. When a car's headlights came fast down the hill, she darted to an island in the road and told her age in the shadowy scoop in her skirt made by the space between her scuttling thighs, a cradling bare of comfort.

Jennie Griggs wasn't one to wait for a car to pass, she always ran when she saw one coming, not in panic but because her own intentions came first. The ground was caked in this area around the market. A week ago a heavy storm had filled it with water; the muddy water ran down from the hills all around and filled it like a bowl, and cars bogged down and branches floated on it. After seven days of hot sun, the layer of mud over the asphalt curled up into patches of dry crust like the bark of a tree, and hop-skipping across it in her gray tennis shoes, Jennie thought: It's nice for children to jump on and crackle, but for old people it's only confusing.

In she went among the eucalyptus trees towering behind the market, a midnight area in the green light of early evening, with a clearing in its heart for the padlocked red kerosene shack where tenants filled their jars and gallon cans, and came out, after a high, gaspy step over a ditch, onto the road that led her up to the houses among the hills. The April evening had settled down only half an hour ago, waiting until everybody had eaten supper by daylight, and waiting, even, for some women to remember their washing and gather it in, but not waiting, it never did, for children to come in from the roads and the grassy slopes. She heard them around her, taking leave of one another by climbing the porches of home and running down again, by wrestling with arms that wouldn't let go, and the fennel they had trampled in the day's roaming was fragrant on the cooling air.

She paused in the grass by the turn of the road, by the porch of the house that was the nursery school by day and used at night by whatever group wanted it, to listen to the stamping of feet and the women singing. The flat-roofed, redwood house was like all the others, but over the lower half of its windows red paper was glued, and the light from within transformed the panes into the ruby red of stained glass. The women rode along upon the pulsation, upon the stamping and clapping beat, like faraway women carried along a river, waving their arms, and she thought if she had lived among black people when she was young and had heard this beat of this neverending river, she would surely have given in to it and got religion, gone to prayer meeting six times a week, hung a colored picture of Jesus above her bed, and crocheted *Jesus Saves* for a front-door curtain. It was too late now, but she might have learned some humility then, she mused, stumbling back onto the road. Now she liked to manipulate things herself too much, she had a little bit of Jehovah in herself, a bit of His cunning and His domination, and she didn't want to give it up.

Her legs were toughened from climbing the hills for twelve years, calling on her friends, but she took more time than she had taken in the early years because now her breath was traitorous. The more infirm she became, the less tolerant of infirmity, and whenever she lay sick or was hobbled by arthritis, she accused the parts of her body of betrayal, and right along with her spirit's alienation from her body she feared betrayal by her friends, a scorning of her words, a gesture of ridicule at her departure. Once in a while she glimpsed this trend in herself and was afraid of it, but it was out of hand like the brittling of her bones. God must have been awfully old and shaky when He created Man, she thought, because in the Bible He was always accusing people, always coming up behind them.

Up among the houses by the highest road she sought for the shadow of the apricot tree that was thrown upon N. T. Gatewood's door by the porch light of the house facing his. She had ways of finding the houses of everybody she called on, for it was easy to knock at the wrong door. All the house were alike, and a dim bulb here and there didn't reveal the faded white numbers painted on the walls.

N. T. Gatewood rose from his green plastic lounge chair—she saw him through the window to the right of the door—and in his elderly surprise knocked askew the rosy lampshade. N. T. never called out for anyone to enter, he preferred the formality of opening the door himself, and he took so long this time, pushing his slippers across the room, trying to get his stockinged feet into them as he walked, that his daughter came out into the hallway to help him answer the knock, drawing her white satin robe around her.

N. T. was not a petty hypocrite; if he was not pleased to see you he did not smile and greet you, he gazed at you with glum curiosity. Jennie Griggs always countered this reception by becoming offensively forward, like a small, nervous dog that does not distinguish between the learned and the unlearned when it barks at people. In the doorway she bristled up at him, "You seen the notice they got posted over by Keever's office?"

He nodded, opening his mouth to say something.

"Let me tell you what it says," she went on.

"I read it, I tell you," he broke in, greatly irritated, and flapped his hand toward the sofa.

"You read it?" she asked the girl, and the girl shook her head. They had never met, and this was the spontaneous, irreverent way Jennie liked to meet a person. Only a few days ago the girl had moved over from the city to live with her father. He was ailing, and he wanted the comfort of calling to his daughter in the night.

N. T. folded up inside his chair, saying that this was Jennie Griggs and this was his daughter Vida, and old Jennie, already crossing her legs on the couch, nodded at the girl, who nodded back in an efficiently lovely way and disappeared down the hallway.

"My daughter is a social worker," N. T. said. "All my children are doing well," he went on, since his visitor did not agreeably remind him of it. "Darcey, he's my oldest boy, he's a lawyer in Chicago, got some big clients. Clyde, he's a newspaperman in Los Angeles." He chuckled mechanically, as if she were clucking her tongue with envy. "I used to be in the newspaper game myself, got the job for him. Vida, she interviews people over at the University Hospital. She helps those that need help and she weeds out the dishonest ones."

His shirt was too large for him, the collar rose higher as he sank lower. A wine wool shirt of expensive cut, it had probably been sent as a hand-me-down by the Chicago son, and the color of it put a coppery fever in the old man's dark skin, as from an agitation of parental pride. His narrow slippers were of fine leather, glowing with wax, a recent gift, perhaps for Easter, and the chair, that, too, was a gift from some time back. That's why you've gone to seed in your old age, she said to him silently—your children turned out well and things aren't as bad as you thought they were when you were young. If my children sent me a big slick chair I wouldn't be using the edge of your sofa.

She untied the blue scarf. "Well, you seen the sign," she said, spreading her hands over her thin tangled hair to feel for hanging hairpins.

A click of contempt in his nostrils. "What's the matter with you that you didn't expect it all along?" he asked her, carefully enunciating as for a lip reader. "We've known for years that someday we'd be told to remove ourselves and all our earthly possessions from this place. Do you wish to remain here forever?" He waved a long, limp hand toward the kitchen. "The houses will soon be falling down around us. The time we had the storm, the rain filled up a roasting pan we put in the corner under the drip, filled it up in half an hour. We called Keever, and he sent a man over to fix it. But there's other things wrong, too. Afflictions seldom come one at a time. It's the same way with a person. My heart is not my only trouble."

She smoothed her skirt over her knees to keep her eyes away from the inward musing of his face, for she knew that in his manhood he would never have complained about anything physical. Somewhere along the line, she thought, we begin to give in to the things we detest.

"You think that's bad?" she countered. "The rain came in so bad down in the flats where we are, we had to move Henrietta's bed, and then we couldn't sleep all night for the rain pounding in the buckets. She don't see well, you know, and everything sounded double bad to her, and she says, 'Sounds like Noah's rain must've sounded in the pots and pans of them wicked people.' But you think it's going to make us happy to get kicked out altogether? It'll rain just as bad inside some other place we go. You think I ain't lived in those basements over in San Francisco? Dark in the middle of summer like you're walking around in your grave. Say, I lived over there. And the walls like a big map of the United States, all made by water seeping in. And I lived over on Larkspur Creek in this county, when my daughter and her husband had a houseboat over there. Shook and rocked in a storm, and everything green mold, even your nightgown when you got up in the morning. If you're poor you're wet wherever you go."

The lag of defeat in his eyes, N. T. gazed at her large hands flying now to the scarf in her lap to shake it and smooth it, now to her sweater pocket to stuff the scarf away.

"But in nice weather," she went on without delay, "there's things here you can't find anywhere else. Look out your own windows, you can see the green hills all around, and the oaks. I can see them when I hang out the laundry, I got to go out in the yard, but you can see them standing on a rug."

N. T. picked his newspaper off the floor and folded it up. "You look at history," he said, "and you'll see people have got to move along, move around. Some people move three miles and some twenty, and some people plant apple seeds in the wilderness, they set up their tents on alien soil."

Nodding vigorously, she cried, "That's right, that's right. That's what I mean when I say the government got no right to kick us off this land, because most of us we come from somewhere else, we come here to build Liberty ships, and they was good enough to put up houses for us right above the shipyards because they wanted us here. And some of our kids, the first thing they ever saw was the green hills around. That's right," she said, still nodding hard.

Now with fitful fingers he unfolded the newspaper, spreading it across his lap and bending forward to see if he could do anything about the edge that extended beyond his knees. "What're you coming to me for?" he asked.

"You got pull," she said. "Take a man like Keever, he hops for you. Whenever somebody needs a faucet or a pane of glass or the oil stove don't work, and they can't get Keever to do anything, don't they come up and see you?" And don't you always, she thought, explain like a lawyer that it's not Keever's fault that the government don't come through with decent appropriations anymore for the upkeep, before you put your hat on and go see him? And if he's got no excuse, you figure one out for him. You hop for Keever, that's why he hops to get your roof fixed. You're his apology man. "And that congressman—what's his name, McMahon?— he'd hop for you, too. He's a friend of yours, ain't he? You was handing out his picture to elect him, you was in charge of getting him votes in this project. Write him a letter for the people who live here and ask him what he can do to see the people don't get kicked off the land. So if there's a law that says the government is going to tear down the houses by June next year and sell the land, you can tell him that houses may've been built for temporary but people never was built that way, they was built to last a lifetime and what's the government going to do about the folks that got no place to go? Where *you* going?" she challenged him, and before he could answer, "Henrietta's niece, she says to me—she's got three kids— 'Where'm I gonna go? Over in the Fillmore in the city that's the only place we're allowed, and they're tearing that down because it's slums and they got a hard enough time settling the families that's evicted.' That's what she said to me." She was sitting stiffly as if on a leather chair in the office of the congressman, afraid that to relax was to compromise.

N. T., as she harassed him, pretended to peer down the columns of the newspaper. "By the time it takes to get a new law passed," he informed her, "we'll all be cleared out anyway, long before."

"You ought to write that letter, anyway," she said.

He slapped the open newspaper with the side of his hand, wedging the paper down between his knees. "What I'm saying is this," he cried, his voice rising over hers like a larger bird. "When they pass a law it's got a lot of reasoning behind it, and nobody there in the nation's capital is going to be in any hurry to do away with a law that got put on the books after all the hearings and that sort of thing. I'm not saying there aren't some laws that should never have got passed, and I'm not saying there aren't some wicked men who get themselves elected to public office, but someday they've got to answer for their sins, and if the people don't punish them, God will. What I'm saying is, you're not going to move mountains with any letter. There are only a few of these projects left, and Congress isn't going to change any law just to take care of one or two. The people who were made to go from those other projects, they'd be sore." After speaking, he struggled to uncrease the newspaper, swatting at it and spreading it out.

Jennie wiped her dry, limber nose with the blue scarf. "It don't matter and it never did matter how many victims go before it's your turn or your children's turn. If you got any heart in you, you still try to save them from whatever they been condemned to. You don't say let 'em go because you don't want to hurt the feelings of them that are dead already."

The scarf, left by Joyce on her last visit, was rippled with the odor of cologne, and she wished that she had not worn it, for if N. T.'s daughter had got the scent of it, the girl would remember the scarf as verification of the story her father was sure to tell her, of Jennie's daughter. She rose, shook out the scarf flauntingly as if it were a square of sky, biblically blue, tied it under her chin again, and turned the doorknob, her agility denying the despair caused by her ramming attack upon an ailing old man who could do nothing more than write a letter in longhand. They were flattering each other with abuse and that was all they could do.

Out on the porch, she saw, beyond old N. T. in the doorway, his daughter coming down the hallway. The girl was in a slim black coat over a flowered dress, silver earrings tingled with light, and she was plunging her hand into a large leather purse, searching for keys to the smart gray car parked alongside the house.

Padding her way along the dirt road with two small dogs sneezing and snarling at her bare ankles, Jennie found the porch with the pots of plants along the rail that marked the shortcut down the hill. It was a risky descent, the steps hewn into the earth by children's leapings and women climbing up and down to visit. She ought to have kept along the road, she chided herself as her foot felt out the depth of a step, but the girl would have stopped the car to ask if she wanted a lift to the flats, and she didn't want to sit beside the girl, folding her hands in a posture of gratefulness. The girl had the quality of a finished product; she was—Jennie was sure of it—dominatingly slow in explaining things to the ignoramuses and failures who came to her for help, the way most of the social workers were who had questioned her through the years. The girl aroused in her a sympathy akin to that she felt for small and lovely, thin-legged birds, but in this retreat from Gatewood's presence, Jennie felt the need to damn them both.

From up here she could see the city, glittering hard as glass in the night with all the soft colors of sun and air and mist, and the pink streamers of light that the city sent out into the black waters of the bay almost touched the shore at the foot of the hills where the dark remains of the shipyard lay. The only light down there shone above the auto wrecking yard that occupied an acre of the deserted place. Sometime soon, she said, they won't allow no pensioner old lady to see around from up here. The sight of the city will belong to those who can afford it, and no little black faces will wonder at windowsills at night about the blinking red lights on the tips of the towers of the bridges. Gutturally she said, "Get away, get away" to the dogs that had left her heels way back on the road above.

She passed close to houses, hearing the aerated voices from the radios and TV sets, her descent relayed by the barking of dogs and the rattling of the gates that confined them to the narrow porches. Along in the grass by the lower road she bent over, her hand on her knee to brace herself, to pick up a child's tinny trinket glinting, a birdcage no larger than the cushion of her thumb that was rubbing dirt from it. Oh, say, wouldn't Orville like this! she crowed. Or Joyce or Hamden or Justin, placing her children in her room in the flats, all waiting cozily in a circle on the floor, telling stories in low voices and laughing high at the end of them. And their faces were long ovals, their sandy hair scrubby where her scissors had cut, and their eyes in the lamplight like the black cabochon eyes of little animals in the forest. How many trinkets had she brought to them, and shells, and bird feathers, beach pebbles and gold-veined rocks? Although she had picked them up matter-of-factly, as though compelled by her tidy nature to clean up after molting birds and geological shiftings, she had given them to her children with an air of mystery. Some benevolent spirit had dropped them in her path, conveying to her, with these many small gifts, the news that her children were to be favored by fate, were to be beautiful and great, humane and beloved. She had no child at home now, but she cocked her head at the trinket.

Say now, look at that, Justin! she cried. Inside the cage was a tiny green parrot on a perch. More than the rest of her children, Justin had perceived the prophecy in the things she brought home, the richness of existence that the things foretold, and he had died the youngest. In the Philippines, bombed to the bottom of the sea. The names of the islands were cruel words, untranslatable except in the sorrow of the bereaved. She squinted at the trinket turning in her fingers and knew that she had climbed to Old Man Gatewood for a selfish reason, no matter how she had barked at him about saving his own people. For she had come in her old age into a fertile valley and she had no provisions for the wilderness. She was an old woman afraid of another room, another street, another cashier in another market, afraid now, almost, of the people of her own skin, finding comfort among the ostracized. She was an old woman, seventy-one, stopping to pick up a trinket in the belief that it was a token for her to take home to her children. But Justin was at the bottom of the sea; and Orville worked in the Texas oil fields and wrote to her once a year, and his children had never seen her; and Hamden—nobody had heard from him in twelve years—and, sometimes, when she got her pension check and went into the city with her paper shopping bag to look around in the basements of the stores, she'd go into a cafeteria, after, and be afraid that she'd see him among the unshaven men hanging their poor wino heads over their bowls of navy bean soup; and Joyce—it wasn't her husband who had been with them at the Creek, and she might as well have been born to another mother, there was no spirit in her for her own rights, only the rights of the men who wanted her. They were lost to her, her children, every one of them, and she was as timorous in the night as a motherless child.

She pocketed the tiny birdcage in her sweater and kept it with two fingers from jumping out. But it was only a trinket from a penny gum machine, and she ought to have left it in the grass for the child who lost it to find it or another child to find it and claim it. What shameful thing was she doing, stealing from children?

The Science
of Life

*A*t nine o'clock the wife came home alone. The babysitter was startled by the reckless sound of the tires and the scattering of gravel. She was a homely girl with such a consciousness of herself that she felt under scrutiny even when alone. She felt that people saw her as someone not to be trusted because there was so much that was wanting about her, so much that was unpardonable, as if she herself had chosen how she was to look and chosen badly. Whenever she was hired to take care of children at night, she remained in one chair, reading her schoolbooks while they slept. So now, hearing the car and the woman's high heels on the porch, the girl sat still long enough for the woman to see that she had not been surprised in some tacitly forbidden part of the house. When the woman threw off her coat, the girl got up and reached for her own coat on the back of the chair.

"Did they wake up?" the woman asked.

"No," the girl said, pulling on her coat.

"Is there a boy waiting for you?" the woman asked, her voice climbing.

"No," the girl said, tossing her scarf around her throat.

"Then what's your hurry?"

The woman walked away, swinging her hips so that the skirt of her red strapless dress flared out. "Come on and have a little cognac. You can't say no to that. You can't go out there without a little cognac. It's cold, cold enough to snow. You ever seen snow?" she asked, confrontingly. "So many kids out here, they've never seen snow. It never ceases to surprise me. Where I come from it snows up to your eyebrows."

She jerked at an earring to remove it, then clapped her hand over her ear, weaving up and down in pain. "The brandy's there," she cried.

The girl slid open the doors of the dark, polished cabinet. She could not identify the cognac bottle among the three rows of bottles. "There!" the woman said, coming up behind her just long enough to point out the bottle. Then she flung herself down on the sofa and lay with one arm across her eyes. The girl found glasses and poured the cognac near the woman's hand that hung out over the coffee table. The hand was plump, the fingers long, and the nails were the same red as the dress.

"You can't drink it standing up," the woman said, her arm still across her face.

The girl sat down in the same chair, holding her glass in both hands. The woman sat up and leaned forward to lift her glass. "You picked the right glasses," she said.

The girl was confused by the remark. If she accepted it as praise, would she be a fool because it was intended as derision? She could not even begin to speculate why a woman in a dress so beautiful, a woman with her dark hair in angelic curls, her slender legs in black nylons and her feet in delicate sandals with high heels, why a woman so perfect for the party would come home early and sit with a girl who was almost a stranger.

"You want me to call a taxi for you?" the woman asked.

"It's only a few blocks," the girl said. "It's early."

"Besides, you're a big girl," the woman said. "How tall are you?"

The girl was tallest in her class. Her legs were long and strong, but though they were awkward indoors, they ran fast and never tired.

"What're you going to do when you graduate?" the woman asked, not waiting for an answer to her other question. "What is your ambition?" she asked with mock solemnity.

The girl stared at her bare knees. "I think I'll be a biology teacher, or something in biology."

"Oh, biology!" The woman sat up. "You're just the person I want to ask. What is the difference between a man and a woman?" She gave a short, sharp laugh.

The girl wondered if she was being told that she would have a difficult time coming to any knowledge of a man outside a textbook. She stared over her glass at her knees, wanting to escape this assault, which must also be a plea to attend the woman's unhappiness.

"So you're going to be a biologist," the woman said. "Isn't that what you'd call a fundamental thing? I mean, here you are studying about plants and animals, life on earth. I remember something about it, things like assimilation and excretion, and what is the name of that—what is it called, phenomenon—where the plant turns toward the sun? That's always seemed remarkable to me. You can turn the plant upside down, and it makes a U-turn and starts to grow upward again, or sideways, wherever the sun is. Do you think it's remarkable or are you used to it?"

The girl had never been asked a question like that. If she were to say, Yes, it was remarkable, would the woman think she was a simpleton?

"Oh, well, don't answer," the woman said. "You professional people, you don't let us laymen in on your deep secrets. You think that when I say, 'Oh, isn't that remarkable?' that I'm only asking a silly question. Only you people way down under the sea or way up there in the stratosphere know how really remarkable it is. Isn't that right? No, never mind," she said, waving her hand. "Don't tell me. I'd never feel your kind of remarkable even if you spent the whole night explaining it to me."

Outside, a car came to a stop on the gravel and a car door slammed. The woman bent her head toward her knees and waited in that contrite position.

The husband came into the room, averting his eyes from his wife. "I didn't know you were still here," he said to the girl. "I would have had the taxi wait. I'll take you home now."

The woman got up and with the same agitated swing in her hips began to walk around the room. "She's not just any old babysitter," she said. "I asked her to stay with me. She's got something fundamental. I knew it when I first saw her. You really ought to sit and listen to her."

The girl caught the man's glance at her and found in it a puzzlement, an attempt to comprehend the joke. The wife, apparently relieved that he had followed her home but afraid of his anger, went on walking around, twisting her rings, slapping at cushions. "You can't say that about anybody at that party," she said, her voice trembling. "Nobody there was what you could call fundamental. They were all trivial. What's it called when a plant turns toward the sun? I felt myself turning homeward because I knew she was here."

The overcoat made his anger more perilous—he could turn around and never come back. "You call them trivial," he shouted, "because you can't stand my interest in them."

"All of them are, and you and me," she cried. "And whatever it was you were saying to her for so long while everybody was looking at me to see how I was taking it, that was the most trivial of everything ever said on earth. I wanted to come home because I knew there's a girl here who's got nothing to be trivial about." The woman covered her face. "She thinks I'm making fun of her, but I wish I were her so I could forget all the trivia she doesn't know about. When she suffers it won't be like this, something you know isn't suffering but there's no other name to call it."

One of the children began to call and the woman ran down the hallway. The girl picked up her textbooks. The woman's prophecy about her was the worst of the night's ridicule. It was impossible to imagine how her suffering was to be in any way enviable. If there was suffering here, between this man and the woman, it was a kind reserved for those fortunate enough to know the pleasures, also. She drew her scarf up over her head, pulling it in against her cheeks to conceal her face from their mistaken sight of her.

"Come on, I'll drive you home," the man said, hurrying to open the door. Before he put his hand on the knob he took three dollar bills from his wallet and handed them to her. She pushed them into her coat pocket. "I hope you'll be warm enough," he said, smiling at her to make up for everything his wife had said, but her eyes avoided his smile that was more attentive to the charm of the apology than to her.

Felis Catus

*W*hen they awoke their first Sunday morning in their very own house
and slippered across their sea-grass rugs to eat their breakfast on orange
pottery, with the soft blue bay and the dark green trees and the houses
farther down the hill all blurring together beyond the bamboo screen like
an Impressionist painting; when now, after four years of apartments, they
were settled at last, they talked together about finding a cat to live with
them.

Mayda, chatting with the girls under her supervision at the telephone
company, let it be known that she and her husband were in the market for
a cat. After all, it was one of those homey, prosaic subjects that she was
always looking for to maintain common ground with the girls, ground
fast slipping away; for they were resentful, she knew, that her interest in
the arts had procured for her, tall and ungainly as she was, a tall and cultured husband, and they suspected that he had sat down and planned
with her, like a military strategy, a cultural life together that ruled out
companionship with the girls. But when one of the switchboard opera-

tors showed up in the morning with a gray-striped kitten in a shoebox, Mayda regretted having touched upon the subject. Unable to refuse it, she grew quite attached to it in the first week, for it did have a great deal of whirligig energy that one would never have anticipated from the *paleness* of it. Afraid, however, that their friends would think them indiscriminate, they drove up one weekend to a Siamese cattery near Guerneville and returned home with two seal points, adolescent brothers. Charles, watching the lean, beige brothers slide under the furniture and step high and bouncy upon the piles of cushions, said, with satisfaction, that they were losing no time in making themselves at home. But Mayda was a bit intimidated by the formality of their purebred bodies and went into the kitchen to get down on her knees and try to coax the gray one out from behind the stove.

Browsing in the rare books store a few blocks from the London Men's Shop where he clerked, Charles came upon many a reference to cats in books that, topically, were in no way concerned with them, and he began to buy books that he would not otherwise have cared for—a Victorian-era travel book on Italy because of some wonderful passages about the cats of the Forum Romanum, and a biography of a famous English surgeon because of the photograph it contained of that bearded gentleman with a huge tabby cat upon his lap. For the first time he was made aware of the predilection for cat companionship on the part of many renowned persons who had made their contribution to society in every field from entomology to religion, and the resemblance he bore to those persons in that respect increased his dissatisfaction with his job and reinforced the tantalizing idea, always in the back of his mind, of trying his hand as a novelist or an art critic. In Chinatown one afternoon he spied, in a window crowded with kimonos and carven teak boxes, a hanging glass shelf holding an assortment of tiny, painted ivory cats that overcame his antipathy for bric-a-brac, and he bought one—a yellow-striped tomcat on its haunches. And at the Museum of Modern Art one evening they bought two Foujita prints of young cats, and Charles matted them on black silk.

When they had been living in their new home for six weeks, Mayda found time to reply to her sister, Martha, in Sacramento. She told how happy they were to be breathing what Charles called "green air," tending their garden and their cats, and told what a relief it was to drive out of San

Francisco every evening, what a pleasure to drive back across the bridge to their charming hill town of Sausalito and contemplate across the bay the city where they worked all day; and she commented wryly that Charles's mother, in leaving him a sum of money large enough to make a down payment on a home, had finally contributed something to his comfort. Martha replied promptly, as usual, glad to hear they'd found a house "all cut out for them," and in uncomplaining comparison told them about the disrepair into which her own house had fallen. She'd taken a lot of time off from her work, she said, because she hadn't been feeling well for the past few months, and the money she had set aside for repainting and reroofing was used up. *Oh, well,* she wrote, *it doesn't look any worse than its neighbors, and that goes for me, too.* One of the items in her letter was about a college girl who had taken a room for a while in Martha's house. The girl had followed a state assemblyman to the capital, Martha wrote, but just before the assembly recessed the fellow must have broken everything off, because the girl cried all night long, so loudly that the children kept waking up and whimpering. *She was a strange girl,* Martha wrote. *The next morning she said she was going to Mexico and that we could have her cat. Then she packed her clothes and drove off in her foreign car. Peter tells me it's a Jaguar. You can have the cat if you want it. It's a handsome sir. She told me once what kind it was, something rare, but I can't remember. The kids always forget to feed the poor thing. Usually, I wouldn't mind seeing to it myself, but my chores seem to be piling up on me lately. Did I tell you I was down to 109 pounds?*

The following Sunday they drove up to Sacramento, leaving early in the morning and knocking at Martha's door at ten o'clock with tender, surprise smiles on their faces. Martha, in a faded housecoat, was eating breakfast alone, the children having run out to play. She pushed aside the dishes and served the visitors coffee, repeating what a nice surprise this was—How long was it now since they'd visited last? Three years? They said they had come because they were alarmed by her letter, and Mayda, pulling up a chair to the table, thought her sister's appearance gave them ample reason for a visit. And when Martha, her eyes rickracked by teary eyelashes, reached spontaneously across the table to pinch Mayda's cheek, to plump it out as one fondly does a baby's cheek, crying, "Maydine, you rascal!" utterly forgetting that her younger sister's every letter in the past four years had been signed by the new name Charles had chosen, even the displeasure Mayda felt over the discarded name was quashed by the pleasure the ailing woman took in saying it.

"Charlie," Martha said, when they had hardly lifted their heads from the first sip of coffee, "why don't you poke your head out the back door and call the kids? Just call loud, they're somewhere around."

He got up reluctantly. "Don't they come home for lunch?"

"But they've just had their breakfast," Martha said.

"Well, why can't we wait?" he asked querulously. "We're not leaving so soon." And he sat down again, frowning.

"Never mind!" Martha cried hastily. "If you'd rather just sit and talk that suits me fine. Once they come, we won't get a chance." Then with sincere concern she asked him, "And how is your asthma these days?"

He shrugged, surprised that he should be questioned about something that had not bothered him for almost four years, not since the early months of his marriage. But Mayda, perceiving that her sister was tracing his petulance to some lurking illness, cried with obliging cheer, "Oh, he's much better now. But we keep our fingers crossed."

The sisters took up again, as if their letters had been actual conversation between them, the news about themselves, and, stimulated by this sitting face to face with each other, they recalled their parents, recalled their friends, and soon Martha was recalling again that rainy day, six years ago, when her husband, a taxi driver, had lost his life in the streets not far from the capitol building. They had heard it all before, but, to Mayda, it was more tragic now than it had been even at the first telling, because of Martha's thinly striving voice. And so she was dismayed when she felt Charles's hand upon her knee, and, glancing at him, saw that he was sorry about his disagreeableness. His hand was reminding her that he was always upset to the point of surliness by the suffering of others, by their physical deterioration. It was because he wanted so badly to express his sympathy and yet sympathy seemed so inadequate. *Darling, you know how it is with me?* his hand said. She did not respond. All this under-the-table apologetics was an affront to Martha, who could see that he was not listening. But when, a few moments later, a cat brushed against Mayda's ankle and was gone, her own eyes lost their listening, she moved her feet searchingly.

The cat leaped onto Martha's lap and from there onto the table, where it stepped among the dishes in the manner of a prince slumming along narrow, winding streets. Martha feigned a sideways brush-off, rising from her chair and crying, "Did you ever?" But Mayda reached for it, lifting it from the table and setting it down on the floor, not attempting to take it into her lap, for it had the inviolable weight of someone else's property. It belonged to the girl in the Jaguar.

"What kind is it, Charles?" she asked eagerly.

"Peter knows," Martha said. "He remembers brand names and things like that."

The cat elongated itself toward a cracked white saucer under the high-legged stove, found the food there not to its liking, and sat down with its back to everyone, musing in the heat that still remained in the region of the stove. Never had they seen a cat with fur of rich brown, and the combination of topaz eyes and glossy brown coat and long, thin legs was the height of elegance.

"How old is Peter now?" Charles asked, lifting the percolator from the hot pad and shaking it.

"Here, here, I'll make some more!" Martha cried, reaching for it.

"No, no! I can do it!" Charles rose, glancing up at her cupboards. "Just tell me where you keep the coffee."

"Peter's nine now," Martha said, while Charles was filling the percolator, jostling the aluminum parts around and making himself at home. "And Norine's seven. Could I borrow a cigarette, I wonder?" she asked, leaning back and smiling a pale flirtation. "I'm not supposed to smoke, and so I've got none in the house. Peter caught me smoking once and he really had a tantrum. He's terribly worried about me, that boy. They're both as nice as pie, it almost makes me cry. They're so tidy! But you know the way kids tidy things up? Everything looks kind of odd, like there were little shrines all over the house." She leaned forward to accept a light from Mayda, holding the cigarette clumsily to her lips. "They're angels, but I'm not going to brag about it."

"Suppose we call them?" Charles suggested, setting the percolator on the flame.

"Wait'll I finish this cigarette," Martha begged, and Charles put his hands into his pockets and strolled about the kitchen, gazing at trinkets and potted cactus plants on the windowsill, and he leaned against the door frame, gazing out through the screen and remarking about the huge fig tree in the yard. Then he was purposefully gone, and they heard him calling. A few minutes later he held open the screen door, and under his arm, as under a bridge, the children entered, and he came in after them, smiling.

"God, they've grown!" he exclaimed. "They didn't even remember me, they couldn't imagine who'd be calling them. You should have seen their faces when they came through the hedge."

"It's Uncle Charles," Martha assured them. "Don't you remember Uncle Charles and Aunt Maydine? How can you forget so fast?" she cried. "He got afraid of a man's voice," Martha explained. "He thought something was wrong, he thought it was the doctor calling."

"I'm sorry, old man," Charles said, and Mayda shot an unbelieving glance at him, never having heard him use that term before. The triteness of it must surely, she thought, go against his grain. "I didn't mean to frighten you, but your mother was telling me all about you. About how tall you are and what an enormous memory you've got. She said you know what kind of cat the girl left."

"That cat? It's a Burmese," the boy said, not yet able to look Charles in the face. Beckoned by the sound of the children, the cat, having wandered up the hallway, now wandered in again and poked its muzzle at the food in the saucer, this time eating it reluctantly, its tongue smacking a delicate distaste. Ambivalently, its slender body seemed to be backing away from the saucer, for its front legs were in a low crouch while its hind legs were up straight and shifting weight, as if the cat were unwilling to admit to spectators that it was finally accepting this gray, crumbly food.

"Its name is Rangoon," the boy said, warming up. "She called it Baby all the time, and I asked her if that was his real name, and she said it was Rangoon. I thought that was a funny name. I'd never call a pet of mine a goon like that. I didn't say that, I just asked her why she wanted to call it Rangoon, and she said Rangoon was the name of a river in Burma and Burma was where the cat's ancestors came from. She said a guy who loved cats, he was in Burma when a war broke out, and he escaped with the cats with bullets flying all around him and brought them to the United States." He had slid from his mother's knee and was standing in a pose of jaunty authority, his ankles crossed and his hand on his hip.

"I should think she'd want to keep it," Charles asked, "with all the history it's got."

"She was spoiled," Martha said.

"She cried all night," Norine told the visitors.

"That's because she was spoiled," Martha explained to the child, who was leaning against her. "Norine feels sorry for her, but I say it did her good to lose that man. You couldn't contradict that girl one little bit."

All at once Peter and the cat were wrestling amicably in the hall doorway, and no one knew whether Peter had intercepted the cat's flight or whether the cat had seen Peter moving toward it. After a moment the cat hung down from Peter's hands, the long body tentatively resigned, the tail swishing.

"If you want that cat you take him," Martha said to Charles.

A grimace wrinkled up Peter's face. It wasn't a prelude to a weeping kind of frown but had a senility to it. He looked, Mayda thought, like an old man attempting to read fine print.

"But you never take care of it," his mother reminded him.

"Never mind," Charles said. "We've got our hands full of cats."

"But this is a rare one," Martha insisted above the sudden rattling of the percolator as it shot up jets of steam.

Charles fumbled the pot to a cold grill, all the comfortable agility gone from his movements. "Rare, smare," he said. "At night all cats are gray."

"Take it! I don't want it!" Peter had dropped the cat and turned his back on them, and was standing rigid, shouting up the hallway as if to someone at the other end.

Not at all dismayed by her brother's shouting, the girl said recitingly, "Once we had a cat that ate clam chowder. But this one can't keep nothing on its stomach. Peter told me he'd rather have a tabby cat because they can eat anything. He said he didn't think this one could even eat a mouse. He said he wasn't sure it was a real cat."

"Well then, it's good riddance, isn't it, Peter?" his mother asked, and chidingly, "People like you more when you're generous."

The jagged atmosphere was soon dispelled by Charles's blandishments and by the children's desire to be swayed by him. After a while the girl took his hand and led him into the backyard to see her vegetable garden. Peter followed them out, and towed Charles back through the kitchen to examine the boy's collection of rocks and gems, and, emerging from the children's bedroom, Charles informed Mayda that Peter had given him the name of a firm that sold Arizona rubies for twenty-five cents a packet. At lunch they sat crowded around the kitchen table, and Charles made jokes, the halting way he had of relating an anecdote or posing a riddle interfering to no degree with the children's appreciation of him, expressed in whoops and sputtering attempts to tell as funny a joke. In the midst of it, Mayda wondered with an unpleasant shock if he appeared naturally comic to the children. Sometimes children saw things and people disproportionately, and perhaps they misconstrued his tall, thin body and the sharp contrast of his black crew cut with his large, pale eyes. Even the pink shirt, so popular in the city with young career men, might appear to the youngsters to be comically inappropriate for a grown man, and part of a clown's costume. After a time, the children got overexcited, and Martha's weary voice darted in among their cries. She clasped Peter's wrist, and to force him to pay attention to her, shook his hand until it was limp and tractable.

At three o'clock they left, after an hour or so of parlor sitting with Martha. Under his arm Charles carried Rangoon, and as soon as they were alone in the car and the cat was leaping in leisurely curiosity from Mayda's lap to the back of the seat and down again, they were immediately silenced by their feeling of uneasy gain. The fact that they were taking Rangoon home with them made their whole visit suspect, even in the stronghold of their mated minds, and there was nothing they wanted to say to each other.

Within a few days, Mayda wrote to her sister, addressing the letter placatingly to Peter, too, and to Norine, and reported that Rangoon was getting along famously, that a friend of theirs who was a reporter for a daily paper and who had covered a cat show once had been over for supper, and he thought Rangoon was championship quality. But they weren't going to enter the cat in any competition, since they had no record of its ancestry. Can you imagine?—there was a studbook for cats wherein cats of known ancestry through four generations were listed, and another listing called the Foundation Record for cats of less than four generations of traceable ancestry? Wasn't that a kick? The reply came from Peter. It was written with pencil on lined tablet paper, and folded crookedly into the envelope, and he said that he was writing because his mother thought he ought to because Rangoon had been his cat; he told them about his and Norine's trip to a swimming pool and how they came home with their hair wet, and closed the letter on the same page he had begun it, hoping it found them in good health and signing it, *Your dear nephew, Peter.*

"Martha dictated it," Charles commented, and later, when the bomb had exploded, he remembered that casual observation of his and was able to say with sickly triumph, "What did I tell you?" Two weeks later, a letter from Martha came, the longest she had ever written to them, and following the news that her doctor had called in a bone specialist for consultation and that they had persuaded her to enter a clinic, *They think I'm such a rare duck, they don't want to lose hold of me*; following the information that the few silver serving spoons left to her by their mother, and the family photographs, were being sent to Maydine, for she didn't want precious things at the mercy of the tenants who'd be renting the house; following the prediction, *You wait, Maydine, I'll bet my new boudoir slippers I'll be waltzing out of there in no time*, she at last asked them, Charles and Maydine, to take her two children into their home until she was well and could fetch them.

As customary on their return from work, they had taken the mail from the box that stood at street level, and, climbing the long flight of brick steps, had opened first that which promised to be most interesting. On that evening their choice was a letter from a couple vacationing in Spain and from whom they had expected no letter at all, being, as they were, on the outer edge of that couple's circle, and they had paused halfway up the steps to read it. It was not until they were already in lounging clothes and sipping their wine that she opened her sister's letter. They ate their supper with no appetite, and Charles asked, picking at the casserole and green salad on his plate, "Do we have to decide tonight?"

"Don't be silly," she said, feeling an impending annoyance with him. "She's not leaving for three weeks yet. We've all that time."

She recalled to herself with a kind of pain, with a feeling of lameness, how plain the children were. If they were beautiful, they'd be a little easier to have around; the admiration of visitors would compensate for the trouble of caring for them, and their beauty would reflect, in a way, upon herself, for they were her sister's children. But they were as plain as the rest of the family, as she herself had been, and now that she had taken the edge off a bit with the way she bound up her dark hair, with the wearing of Mexican silver necklaces that sometimes seemed as heavy and eliciting of favor as a religious ornament between her breasts, did she want to be constantly reminded by the children of her own essential plainness? Idling her fork around her plate, she was overcome by an irrational anger against Charles, and drew her feet in farther under her chair. What was the matter with being plain? What was the matter with being lanky and plain, as long as your heart was in the right place? Why must he be so particular about how she appeared to other people?

"This place isn't big enough," he was saying.

"There's an extra bedroom," she said, not to be persuasive but simply to state a fact.

"That's not an extra bedroom," he bristled. "It's got a north light, and it's going to be my studio. There's no *bed* in it, is there?"

She made no reply, scourging herself for her rural mentality that called a room a bedroom just because it was empty. But at once she felt allied with Martha, with her own dear sister, her own dear, honest and uncomprehending sister who continued to call her by her real name, and she stood up, choking on her misery.

He followed her into the front room and stroked her bowed head and made her get up a minute from the chair so he could sit down and take her onto his lap, and he comforted her and said he was sorry and if she wanted the children to come and live with them, it was all right with him. They were nice kids and old enough to take care of themselves after school. But she didn't *know*, she said. She had a closeness with him, she told him, that she had never had with anyone, with her mother or father or even with Martha, and she didn't want it destroyed by any relatives of hers imposing on them, by the children who would probably shatter this affinity by denying it nourishment like time and seclusion and the indulgence of little idiosyncrasies. She didn't *know*.

Only once did they bring themselves to mention the problem, when one evening Charles, bending over to set down upon the floor the large blue platter spread with canned mackerel, asked Mayda, "Where'll they go if they don't come here?" and gently with his foot pushed aside the cats who were rising up on their hind legs or running against one another just beneath the descending plate.

"Go? They'll go to some neighbor, I guess," she said. "If there are any that generous."

"Will they wonder if we don't take the kids?"

"Who?"

"The neighbors, the neighbors," he said.

"They're *not* your neighbors," she replied acridly.

That night he came down with an asthma attack the like of which he had not experienced since his childhood. He sat bolt upright in bed, his chest hollowed out by his long, hoarse breaths that drew her up beside him. She switched on the lamp above their bed and saw that the four cats, bedded down over the expanse of comforter, had already been watching him in the darkness, their heads high and alerted. So frightened were the animals by the sounds he was making that when she slipped from under the covers and ran to fetch his nebulizer, they fled the room. She sat beside him on the bed, fervently kissing his shoulder, and when at last he had some relief and lay back, she asked him, "What could have done it, darling?"

"My life's slipping by," he replied with hoarse sarcasm. "It worries me."

"It might be the cats," she speculated.

"The cats?" Tossing her cooling hand off his brow. "Why not pollen, or eggs, or anything? That little lost cat we smuggled up to our apartment that time—it slept on my neck all night, it liked to sleep there, and did I get an attack?"

Already shaken by his spell, she could only stare down at him timidly, her long hair falling around her arms like a shawl protecting her from his cruelty. He softened, stroking her arm and explaining to her that he was sick of his job, literally sick of it, that he didn't have it in him to be a salesman, no matter how well he was doing at it. He tried hard to be capable, he said, just because he hated it so. She agreed that it was time for him to quit the London Shop. If he wanted, she said, to take a few months off and look around for something more congenial, or even do a critical article, why they'd get along for a time with just her salary. They'd meet the house payments and the car payments all right, they just wouldn't be able to bank anything or buy clothes or things like recordings.

The next evening he told her that he could not bring himself that day to give his notice of resignation. Maybe he wouldn't have another attack for a long time, he told her. Maybe the one last night had been a fluky thing. But a few hours later, when he had barely laid his head on the pillow, he came down with an attack the nebulizer was not equal to, and she called in the local doctor, who gave Charles a shot and left some pills and told him to drop by for a checkup when he got the chance. In the morning he was too weak to rise, and he agreed to her proposal that she would phone his shop as soon as she got to work and inform the manager that Charles was suffering from asthma and suggest that, since she didn't know how long he'd be away from work, they'd better interview some other man for the job.

When she came home that evening she sprawled in the canvas butterfly chair. No words spoken, he brought her a whiskey and water as if she had ordered it, and sat down on some pillows on the floor, his long bones at odds with one another. Whenever, before, he had revealed a momentary fear of her, her vantage had put her into a panic, but now she took a cloudy pleasure in seeing him uncomfortable. He was leading her by the nose into a conspiracy against the children, and he *ought* to be uncomfortable about it. He *ought* to be feeling guilty. She slid farther down into her chair, stretching her legs out like a slattern into a position he had chided her about in the past and cured her of.

Not long after supper he retired to the bedroom as if he had been banished there. Until it grew dark she busied herself in the garden, troweling here and there, and three of the cats kept her company. Enlivened by the cool of the evening, they were scuffling together, or calling throatily, or darting at insects she could not see in the dusk. She had no view of the bay from this rear garden, but the absence only increased her appreciation of the place, for she knew the bay was there, waiting, while she occupied herself within this garden that was filled with absolving fragrances and enclosed by plum and madrona trees. Charles had closed the bedroom windows against the garden with as much finality as if a decree had been read to him, denying him the pleasures of the evening. The bamboo screens and tan silk curtains were both in use, and through this double film she saw only the glow of the lamp above the bed and that was all. She thought of him propped up by a mountain of colored pillows from the living room and suffering pangs of guilt, and her resentment of his maneuvering against Peter and Norine was dispersed by her gratitude to him for the composite gift he had given her—for marriage and this home and this garden. She troweled under the bedroom windows, thinking of her childhood and what she had learned of his. They hadn't been happy, either. No happier than Peter or Norine. Charles in military school, seeing his mother once a year and his father never, and herself going to work at fourteen, passing for eighteen because she was so tall and overgrown, and crying at night for all the things so bountifully possessed by the small-size girls. Now, for the first time, they were on compatible terms with life. They had each other and they had this house that, although it was built to the specifications of the previous owner, seemed built for themselves, and in its interior decoration expressed Charles's talents that had been so frustrated by his years spent in stuffy, small apartments. After an evening at a concert, they could return here and find a certain leisure in which to remember and assimilate. They had no more time than they had before, but they had room and graciousness in this little house that gave the impression of being time. And did they not deserve this?

She stood in the doorway of the bedroom, clasping the lapels of her sweater across each other as if she had caught a chill in the garden, and said to him, "I'll write Martha tonight. I'll say we're sorry, but we can't possibly take the children because we're having some trouble . . . you've got your asthma again, and this time it's so bad you've had to quit your job. I'll explain it as a kind of nervous breakdown, and say that we'll just be able to make ends meet for a while."

He said, "Oh, God, Mayda, I feel like a dog," and laid his book on the comforter and could not look at her, and then, in a moment, broke, bowing his head and rubbing his hand over his face, saying to her, "Come here, come here."

She went down on her knees by the bed, and they embraced, and he stroked her hair back to kiss her brow, while she assured him that it was not his fault he was laid low by his desire to do more than just sell clothes for the rest of his life. It was not his fault at all that they couldn't take the children. They wept together in relief, for now they were again in accord, and they wept for Martha and the kids and the whole tragic situation in that little family.

In the days that followed he set himself a regimen of reading and researching for the article on Paul Klee he had in mind, and this activity, and Mayda's enthusiasm about his project, had a calming effect upon his nights and he slept well. But on the fifth night he was again victimized by his asthma; not so severe a spell, but distressing enough. In the last gray hour before she got up, she suggested that he really ought to go down and see the doctor for some allergy tests, and, feeling that their accord was certain enough now that he would not think she was belatedly accusing him, she again brought up the possibility that the cats might be causing his spells. Lying upon his back, his hand spread appeasingly upon his chest, he considered this at length, and they agreed to experiment. They would prohibit the cats from entering the bedroom, and twice a week she would brush the cats thoroughly and throw away the brushings in a paper bag, precautions that would rid the air of the irritant, to an extent. And to further convince her of his amenability all along, he began to muse upon who, among their friends, would be most glad to receive the cats, if the experiment did not work and they might be forced to give the cats away. The Siamese brothers could go to that young couple who had bought the house on upper Broadway in the city and who said they were going to get around some day to buying a Siamese; they were just acquaintances, but at least he knew them well enough to see that they would be appreciative. The gray cat Grisette could go to the child next door, and Rangoon? Well, Rangoon could go to Lizbeth, that elderly photographer who kept the most exquisite cats. It was six months now since the evening they'd been introduced to her at her exhibit in the museum and had gone up to her studio afterward. She hadn't been by to visit them, and they'd phone her once more and say they had a surprise for her.

So when, a few days later, Charles strolled down the hill to the doctor's office and the doctor told him to get rid of the cats that had been underfoot that night of his house call, Charles was able to say that Mayda and he were already experimenting. And when he told Mayda about it that evening, repeating what the doctor had said—that the asthma was only a symptom and that what he really had was an extravagant fondness for cats, a disease, said the doctor, called Felis Catus—Charles laughed pleasurably in the manner of one recalling a compliment.

They needn't have fretted where to place Rangoon, for one Sunday afternoon, a few weeks after the experimenting was begun, while Charles was cutting away the grass from between the brick steps, a white Jaguar drew up in the street below and through the trees he saw a girl bend from under the low, sleek top and stretch her leg to the road. Turning to his cutting again, he heard a girl's heels on the bricks below him, and gazing around to her and prepared to tell her where this neighbor or that lived, he saw her paused below, her face lifted. "I'm looking for Charles Corbett," she told him, "or his wife. "

At once he recalled the Jaguar of the girl who had roomed in Martha's house, and he smiled a sweet quirk of a smile, replying, "You flatter us. It's Rangoon you're looking for."

They laughed together, and he put his clippers aside and led the way up to the house, not in any hurry, moving with an erect ease in his long body to convey to her that they had her kind of visitor every day. Under the fuchsia bushes by the front door, one of the Siamese brothers was sitting drowsily. The girl bent to stroke it, but it sprang away from her and bellied out of sight, setting the little red flowers aquiver. "One has to introduce oneself, of course," the girl said.

Charles chuckled ruminatively, opened the door and called Mayda. Fortunately, she had just freshened herself after a day in the garden and was in a crisp yellow frock and Japanese sandals.

"Mayda, this is Rangoon's mistress," he said, and they all laughed because the cat was given more importance than the girl.

Charles went in search of Rangoon, returned in a minute, when Mayda was asking the girl what drink she preferred, with the cat riding backwards in his arms, paws upon his shoulder, muzzle delicately examining his ear. He placed the cat in the girl's lap, and Rangoon stood for a moment startled, balancing on spindly legs. The girl cupped the cat's narrow face, cooed its name, and asked if it had missed her.

"They thought I'd forsaken it, can you believe it?" she cried to Mayda. "When I left I was so upset, I was mad at everybody, even Rangoon, and

I said I didn't know when I'd be back." She had, Mayda thought, the languidly clutching manner of the University Beauty, and she wondered if the girl left the cat with a certain design, a studied carelessness. "Believe me," she said, "I couldn't have gone back any sooner because I couldn't bear it. The town, I mean. Emotionally, you know. But yesterday I drove up, and there were absolute strangers in the house. The woman said there was no cat around like I described. She told me her landlady was in a hospital, and the kids were staying with friends down the street. She pointed the house out to me, and I went over and knocked on the door, and there were about six kids swarming to answer it, and I thought, Oh, my God, they've skinned it! And I recognized the boy and shook him and screamed at him, What have you done with my cat? Well, he told me you'd taken it, but he didn't know your address, so I had to put in a call to the hospital and get his mother on the line, and she told me where you live."

"And how is she?" Mayda asked, alarmed, and happening at that moment to be seating herself with drink in hand, she hoped that the activity of her body—the flouncing skirt, the crossing of legs—obscured her voice so that the girl would neither hear nor answer.

"She didn't say, she just said to give you her love and that she hoped Charles was better. She said she was awfully sorry to hear about Charles's breakdown. . . ." The girl looked him over, and Mayda hastened to explain that it wasn't a breakdown, really. "It's only that the cats bring on his asthma," Mayda said. "He went through several awful spells of it and had to take a vacation from his work. We're so attached to the creatures that we really can't bring ourselves to part with them. You can't do it at the drop of a hat, you know," she said. "So we're in the midst of experimenting now, we're forbidding them to come into the bedroom, and I brush their fur ritually. If that doesn't work we'll simply have to give them away."

"Oh, for God's sake, Mayda," Charles protested, as if she were praising him, for the girl was gazing at him with glittering sympathy.

"But how selfless of you!" the girl cried at him. "Rangoon couldn't have asked for nicer folks to live with. He won't want to come home with me now. But things were so upset," she explained, and, bowing her head and stroking the cat alongside her hip, she was pouring out the story of the assemblyman and herself: that she had followed him to the capital and met him in an East Indian restaurant she'd discovered for them, and that he had his opposition to her all jotted down on a card, like notes for a speech, and that she had prevailed against him. She was discreet enough to withhold his name and the part of the state she was from, but that was her only discretion in the rambling story.

With misgivings, Rangoon went along with the girl, cradled in her arms. Going down the brick steps, she felt her way with the pointy toes of her high-heeled pumps, for she had to bend her head to soothe him so he wouldn't bolt, and Mayda and Charles, following after her, were poised to catch him if he ran back up the steps. In the car Rangoon inhaled the odor of the red leather upholstery, and, standing on his hind legs, rediscovered the familiarity of the top of the seat. Leaping up there and stretching out, the cat gazed with mollified yellow eyes at Mayda and Charles who had bent their heads under the top to gaze at him.

"Thanks again, awfully," the girl said, and her white cotton dress slipped back from her young knee as she put her foot to the clutch. They waited in the middle of the road until the car reached the turn that went downhill, where the girl slowed and waved to them. They stood waving back appealingly until the car was hidden by the trees.

The Light
at Birth

*T*he immensity of light—the glare from the winter sky and the reflected glare from the ocean—shocked her asleep at noon, at two o'clock, at any hour of the day. She had always resisted sleep in the day except when she was sick and when, after loving, she had fallen asleep with a lover; but this sleep was an edict as from a healer more powerful than her own self, the self that had lost for a time the sense of how to heal itself in its own way.

The house where she lay, upstairs, on a rug, on a couch, on the bed, was a brown-shingled, two-story house trusted to pilings sunk deep into the sand. At high tide the water came sweeping in under the house, exposing more length of the upright logs, and the constant sound of the waves worked along with the light to make her sleep. The small noises, the low voices from downstairs where the owner of the house lived—a

German woman, with her ninety-six-year-old mother—did not disturb her sleep; only the sharp sounds woke her, the barking of the three little dogs whenever a visitor stepped onto the porch or they fussed among themselves over a preferred place.

The ocean had been her first sight of the vastness of the earth when she was a child in a beach town down near the border, and she had come to the ocean again, to this town north of San Francisco, to find again that vastness, now when she was in dire need of release from constrictions on the mind, which was such easy prey to all things that kept it small and afraid. The sleep was like basking in light, and after three days of it she came awake.

Out on her small, high porch, she threw bits of bread into the air, and the seagulls came swooping in. Close, hovering, their spread wings and tails pure white and translucent in the light, they were unfamiliar, name-less creatures. When there was no more bread and they returned to the sand, they became again familiar.

The old mother, wrapped in a large, richly blue woolen shawl, sat on a sofa in the front room, and her blue, long-lidded eyes appeared un-seeing. A storm, rising up over the horizon at noon, was sweeping tatters of fog before it, and the room was dark one moment and bright again the next. The old woman seemed unaware of this play of light and shadow over her. She spoke only in German and only to her daughter. Once, when the dogs were dozing, she spoke a few words to the room, and Ma-rie, on the other old sofa, facing the mother, a low table between them, called to the daughter who was in the little kitchen, "Is she speaking to me?"

"She spoke to Paulie. He's her favorite."

The darts of light disappeared again from the glasses and bottles in the room, and the colors in the stained glass window facing the ocean, colors that only a minute before were cast on the old woman's face, went dark. The old mother's face was from antiquity, and though her body was small and she could be half-carried to the sofa, her being was formidable with the past. And when Leni, the tall, robust, sixty-year-old daughter, sat down beside her mother—the daughter's smooth white hair drawn back from the brow, the mother's gray hair drawn back from the brow, both women's eyes the blue of an ideal sky—the visitor felt the same confusion in her heart, the same confrontation as on that night in Cologne, last summer. The night she and her lover came into their first city in Europe. They had boarded a bus at the airport in Luxembourg because the bus was sleek and empty and they were exhilarated and uncaring about which direction they took, and the bus went along a placid highway through forests to Cologne. Then, in the restaurant of the railway depot at midnight—so few patrons, so many empty tables, and a sad, pale, limping waiter in a shabby black jacket with a black satin stripe down the sleeves—she had felt past terrors lurking, as if what had happened in that country was happening still or was about to happen always. *You see our waiter,* he had said, his face steamed up by the food on his plate, *our limping waiter? He mistook strangers for the enemy, just like you're doing now.* But she was listening not to him but to her heart, to hear if it was willing to come along with her into that country.

Leni saw that the shawl was slipping and tucked it around her mother again. The mother wore quilted, padded long underwear of soft wool, fawn color. "They belonged to my brother, he hasn't worn them since his university days," Leni said, her voice a young girl's. "When he came to visit us he looked at them with longing in his eyes." The brother, a retired physician, older than Leni, had returned to Europe and was living now in Switzerland, and his bones were feeling the cold, she said, no matter how much he danced with young women.

"Where did you go in Germany? Did you go to Heidelberg?" Leni asked. "We were born there, my brother and me. Up above the river is the Philosophers' Path, and there you walk and look down at the river and the old bridge, and below you on the slopes are the hill gardens. We lived up there. Up there are almond trees, they're the first to bloom. And wild peach trees, the wild ones have bigger blossoms than the cultivated ones. The seed falls into the earth and it grows. And old cherry trees, the one in our yard was two stories high. So many in bloom, people streamed up there to walk under them."

The storm was on them, the house went dark in the heavy rain. She ran back up the stairs and into her rooms and watched the waves flinging ashore timbers and branches that had been rushed down the rivers weeks ago, in a storm all along the coast. South across the water she could see the silver shine of the city under rain, only the tip of it where the channel opened into the sea. And back in the classroom in the city, the rain pouring down the windows and voices barely heard, was any student wondering what had become of her, the lost professor? So many gentle sermons she had delivered on the necessity to clear one's mind of its landmines, of its traps for strangers who come near, those deathtraps that destroy the self as well as the stranger. *Let in some light*, she had told them. *Let in some light*, she pleaded with herself, alone.

She was kept awake all night by the rain striking the windows and the waves pounding all along the beach, up against every house's flimsy barricade of rocks and dunes, and by the wild brilliance of the buoy lights tossed into the air by the black waters, and by the white shimmer that was the city, a net of lights afloat. Downstairs it must be dark, the only light that of the white waves reflected on the windowpanes. They were asleep, she was sure, familiar with storms on the edge of the ocean after twelve years in this rugged old house that had been their beach house in the years before, when they had lived in the city with Leni's brother. The old mother in her tiny bedroom on the safer side of the house, the daughter in her slightly larger room, and the three little dogs in their chosen places.

When it was light, the sky was revealed as clear. A flock of blackbirds pecked along the wet sand and flew up to the wires, preening themselves in a row. At noon she knocked again at the screen door. The dogs barked, Leni called out, and she went in.

The old woman was not on the sofa. The white dog with matted fur lay there; another dog was stirring somewhere, and the third was out on the sand, nosing the debris. Marie sat down in her usual place, and Leni came out from the mother's room, sat down on the other sofa, and took up her knitting.

"When I was a girl," Marie began, and the listener must tell by the tremble in her voice that she had gone over this in the night, "we had a garden, too. My mother had orange trees and lemon trees and lots of rosebushes. One was as tall as the trees and its boughs hung down to the ground like a tent covered with roses. They were Jewish, my father and mother, refugees from Germany. They went to Cuba first and my father worked in a cigar factory where they hand-rolled the tobacco leaves, and then they came to California."

It left her with an anguish in her breast, this confession, this chronicle told in one minute, this begging for release from somebody else's false image of you and of those dear to you.

No change in the woman's face, no pause of the knitting needles over the white sweater. "The earth is like a refugee camp," the woman said. "So many are refugees. They don't save their lives, maybe, but they save their souls. My mother and me, we were on the last voyage of the *Bremen*. My brother was already over here. They were suspicious of my mother. We had birth records, church records, city hall records, but it didn't matter. When she was an infant she wasn't well, and her parents took her to her grandmother in the country, and when she came back to her parents, the neighbors thought she was not their child. That strange child, who was she and where did she come from? Isn't it terrible, how neighbors remember about a strange child, after years go by? On that last voyage there were one hundred, maybe one hundred and fifty passengers, and the ship could hold two thousand. Young men weren't allowed to leave Germany, so that was one reason it was empty. The few Jewish people never came to meals, they ate in their cabins. They were told to stay in there, I guess. So many empty tables in the dining salon, when always there were three serving times, and in the lounge—is it called?—many huge empty easy chairs. An English minister who was a passenger gave sermons, and I went to hear every one. He felt sorrow for the world. We all felt sorrow for the world on that empty big ship."

She went along over the wide strip of wet sand and broken shells as far as the lagoon, a long way. Higher up on the sand lay a number of shore birds, dead from the storm. The sea was dazzling, and the air so clear the little islands, miles away, were visible. She came back while the sun was forming into an oblong blazing jewel at the horizon.

The old mother still lay in her room, the next day at noon. Marie had never looked into that room, but from her usual place on the sofa she could see that it was darker than the other rooms and hardly more than an alcove.

"She dreams of garden parties," Leni said. "I think it's one that keeps going on because the light is so beautiful, she says. She told me they had a banquet and I could have the leftovers. Last night I asked her, Shall I turn off the light? She said, If it's all right with them. She calls them *Herrschaften*, nobility. They're strangers. She asks me who this one is and who that one is, and I tell her I never met them. This morning she told me she saw the Kaiser in splendid clothes. No, it was the Lord, on second thought. Come and take a little look at her. She told me you were her girl friend in Freiburg, where she was born, and I didn't tell her you only got as far as Cologne."

The little mother lay turned toward the wall, and the blankets over her were the color of her gray hair and pale skin. She took up no more space in the bed than a child. That was how her own mother had looked, though never as old as this one. No breath visible, the breath making not the slightest move under the covers. She had to back away from the sight, step back and cover her face to hide her grimace of sorrow over the old mother, over the memory of her own mother, dying.

She was wakened in the night by the strangers at the old mother's garden party. Visions of light and of luminous strangers in that light, that was what the dying saw. She knew who they were, those strangers. They were the first of all the many strangers in your life, the ones there when you come out of the dark womb into the amazing light of earth, and never to be seen again in just that way until your last hours. She got up and walked about, barefoot, careful to make no sound that would intrude on that gathering of strangers in the little room, below.